# JENNIFER ESTEP

# THE Spider

## AN ELEMENTAL ASSASSIN BOOK

POCKET BOOKS

New York   London   Toronto   Sydney   New Delhi

Pocket Books
A Division of Simon & Schuster, Inc.
1230 Avenue of the Americas
New York, NY 10020

This book is a work of fiction. Any references to historical events, real people, or real places are used fictitiously. Other names, characters, places, and events are products of the author's imagination, and any resemblance to actual events or places or persons, living or dead, is entirely coincidental.

Copyright © 2014 by Jennifer Estep

All rights reserved, including the right to reproduce this book or portions thereof in any form whatsoever. For information address Pocket Books Subsidiary Rights Department, 1230 Avenue of the Americas, New York, NY 10020

First Pocket Books paperback edition January 2014

POCKET and colophon are registered trademarks of Simon & Schuster, Inc.

For information about special discounts for bulk purchases, please contact Simon & Schuster Special Sales at 1-866-506-1949 or business@simonandschuster.com.

The Simon & Schuster Speakers Bureau can bring authors to your live event. For more information or to book an event, contact the Simon & Schuster Speakers Bureau at 1-866-248-3049 or visit our website at www.simonspeakers.com.

Manufactured in the United States of America

10  9  8  7  6  5  4  3  2  1

ISBN 978-1-4516-8901-3
ISBN 978-1-4516-8906-8 (ebook)

*To my mom, my grandma, and Andre—
for your love, patience, and everything else that
you've given to me over the years.*

*To my papaw—you will be missed.*

*To all of the fans of Gin and the gang out there—
this one's for you.*

# ACKNOWLEDGMENTS

Once again, my heartfelt thanks go out to all the folks who help turn my words into a book.

Thanks go to my agent, Annelise Robey, and editors, Adam Wilson and Lauren McKenna, for all their helpful advice, support, and encouragement. Thanks also to Julia Fincher.

Thanks to Tony Mauro for designing another terrific cover, and thanks to Louise Burke, Lisa Litwack, and everyone else at Pocket Books and Simon & Schuster for their work on the cover, the book, and the series.

And finally, a big thanks to all the readers. Knowing that folks read and enjoy my books is truly humbling, and I'm glad that you are all enjoying Gin and her adventures.

I appreciate you all more than you will ever know.

Happy reading!

# ✳ 1 ✳

The day the box came started out like any other.

I opened up the Pork Pit, the barbecue restaurant that I ran in downtown Ashland, right on schedule. Turned on the appliances, tied a blue work apron on over my clothes, and flipped the sign on the front door over to *Open*. Then I spent the rest of the morning and on into the afternoon cooking up burgers, baked beans, and the thick, hearty barbecue sandwiches that my gin joint was so famous for. In between filling orders, I chatted with the waitstaff, wiped down tables, and made sure that my customers had everything they needed to enjoy their hot, greasy meals.

All the while, though, I kept waiting for someone to try to kill me.

Not for the first time today, my gaze swept over the storefront, which featured an assortment of tables and chairs, along with blue and pink vinyl booths. Matching, faded, peeling pig tracks on the floor led to the men's and women's bathrooms, respectively. A long counter with padded stools ran along the back wall of the restaurant.

Since it was after six, the dinner rush was on, and almost every seat was taken. The waitstaff bustled back and forth, taking orders, fetching food, and topping off drinks, and the *clink-clank* of dishes filled the restaurant, along with the steady *scrape-scrape-scrape* of forks, knives, and spoons on plates and bowls. Murmurs of more than a dozen different conversations added to the pleasant mix of sounds, while the rich, hearty smells of cumin, black pepper, and other spices tickled my nose.

Everything was as it should be, but I still looked at first one diner, then another. A few folks swallowed and quickly glanced away when they realized that I was watching them, not daring to meet my gaze for more than a second. But most were happily focused on their food and their companions and paid me no more attention than they should have. They were just here for the Southern treats the restaurant served up—not to try to murder me and cash in on my reputation as the Spider, Ashland's most notorious assassin.

"Gin?" A deep male voice cut into my latest examination of the storefront and its occupants.

I looked over at the man perched on the stool closest to the cash register. Despite his slightly crooked nose and a scar that cut across his chin, he was ruggedly handsome, with intense violet eyes and black hair shot through with blue highlights. His navy business suit and white shirt highlighted the coiled strength in his chest and shoulders, and I wasn't the only woman who paused to give him an admiring glance.

"Is everything okay?" Owen Grayson, my lover, asked.

My eyes cut left and right one more time before I answered him. "Seems to be. For the moment."

Owen nodded and went back to his meal, while I grabbed a rag and started wiping down the counter.

Actually, so far, the afternoon had passed in a perfectly normal fashion, with the glaring exception that no one had tried to murder me—yet.

Thinking that I might actually get through the workday unscathed for a change, I let myself relax, at least until the bell over the front door chimed. I glanced over at the entrance, expecting to see some new customers ready, willing, and eager to get their barbecue on.

Only this wasn't a customer—it was a short, thin man wearing a delivery uniform of black boots and matching coveralls.

The guy glanced around the storefront for a minute before his eyes locked on me, and he headed in my direction. I tensed, eyeing the long white box in his hand, and dropped my right arm down behind the counter out of sight. A second later, a knife slid into my hand, one of five weapons that I had hidden on me. This wasn't the first time someone had dressed up like a deliveryman to try to get close to me at the restaurant. The last guy was still in the cooler out back, awaiting the skills of Sophia Deveraux, the head cook at the Pork Pit, who also moonlighted as my own personal body disposer.

But the guy stepped right up to the cash register, as though this was a simple delivery.

"I've got a package here for Gin Blanco," he said in a bored voice. "Is that you?"

"Yeah."

"Here. Sign this."

He shoved an electronic scanner at me. I slid my knife into a slot below the cash register, where it would still be out of sight, and took the device from him. The man waited while I used the attached pen to scrawl something that sort of looked like my signature onto the screen. The second I was done, the guy snatched the scanner away from me and shoved the white box into my hands at the same time.

He tipped his head at me. "Have a nice day."

He started to walk away, but I reached out and latched onto his arm. The guy stopped, looked at me over his shoulder, and frowned, as if I'd violated some sort of secret delivery-guy protocol by touching him. Maybe I had.

"Yeah?" he asked. "You need something else?"

I carefully set the box down on the counter. The seat next to Owen was empty, so I was able to slide it several precious inches away from us. "What's in the box?"

The guy shrugged. "I don't know, and I don't care. I just deliver 'em. I don't look inside."

He started to pull away, but I tightened my grip on his arm. "You should really tell me what's in the box."

He rolled his eyes. "And why should I do that?"

"So I can be sure that there's nothing . . . nasty inside."

Confusion filled his face. "Nasty? Why would you think that?"

"Oh, I don't know," I drawled. "Why don't you check the name on the delivery order again?"

He glanced down at his scanner and hit a button on the device. "Yeah, it says deliver to Gin Blanco, care of the Pork Pit restaurant, downtown Ashland. So what? Is that supposed to mean something to me—"

Comprehension dawned in his eyes as he finally recognized my name and realized who and what I really was. Gin Blanco. Restaurant owner. And, most important, the assassin the Spider.

He swallowed, his Adam's apple bobbing up and down in his throat. "Look, I don't want any trouble, lady. I'm just a delivery guy. I don't know what's in the box, and that info's not on my scanner. I swear."

I kept my grip on his arm, staring into his eyes, but I didn't see anything but a burning desire to get away from me as fast as he could. Smart man. Still, I let him sweat a few more seconds before I released his arm. "Okay. You can go now."

The guy whipped around. He had started to take a step forward when I called out to him again.

"Wait. One more thing."

He froze. He teetered on his feet, and I could almost see the wheels spinning in his mind as he debated making a break for the door. But he must have realized how foolish that would make him look, because he finally turned and faced me again. I crooked my finger at him. The guy swallowed again, but he eased back over to me, although he made sure to stay out of arm's reach and keep the cash register between us. Very smart man.

By this point, my words and actions had attracted the attention of a few of the customers, who stared at me with wide eyes, as if I were going to whip out a knife and slice open the delivery guy right in front of them. Please. I preferred to be a little more discreet about such things, if only to keep up appearances.

I stared at the delivery guy for a few more seconds before reaching down and grabbing something just below the cash register. He swallowed a third time, and beads of sweat had formed on his forehead, despite the restaurant's air-conditioning. I raised my hand, and he tensed up more.

I reached up and tucked a hundred-dollar bill into the pocket on the front of his coveralls.

"Have a nice day," I said in a sweet voice.

The guy stared at me, his mouth gaping open, as if he couldn't believe that I was sending him on his way without so much as a scratch on him. But he quickly got with the program. He nodded at me, his head snapping up and down, as he backed toward the door.

"Y'all come back now," I called out. "Sometime when you have a chance to sit down and eat. The food here is terrific, in case you hadn't heard."

The delivery guy didn't respond, but he kept his eyes on me until his ass hit the doorknob. Then he gulped down a breath, threw the door open, and dashed outside as fast as he could without actually running.

Owen raised an eyebrow at me. "I think you about gave that poor guy a heart attack."

A grin curved my lips. "Serves him right for not being able to tell me what was in the package."

His gaze flicked to the white box sitting off to the side. "You going to open that?"

"Later," I murmured. "When we're alone. If there is

something nasty inside, there's no use letting everyone see it."

"And if it's not something nasty?"

I snorted. "Then I'll be pleasantly surprised. I'm not holding my breath about it, though."

Owen finished his cheeseburger and onion rings and had a piece of cherry pie with vanilla bean ice cream for dessert, while I spent the next hour working. Slicing up more potatoes for the last of the day's French fries. Checking on the pot of Fletcher's secret barbecue sauce that was bubbling away on one of the back burners. Refilling drinks and ringing up orders.

I also took the package into the back and placed it in one of the freezers. I didn't know what surprises the box might contain, but I didn't want my staff or customers to get injured by whatever might be lurking inside.

Finally, around seven o'clock, the last of the customers paid up and left, and I decided to close the restaurant early for the night. I sent Sophia and the waitstaff home, turned off all the appliances, and flipped the sign over to *Closed* before locking the front door.

Now all that was left to do was open the box.

I carefully pulled it out of the freezer, took it into the storefront, and put it down on the counter in the same spot as before. I made Owen move to the other side of the restaurant, well out of range of any elemental Fire or other magic that might erupt from it. Then I bent down and peered at the package.

A shipping order was taped to the top, with my name and the Pork Pit's address. But there was nothing on the slip of paper to tell me who might have sent the box or where it had come from. All of that information had been left blank, which only made me more suspicious about what might be inside.

And the box itself didn't offer any more clues. It was simply a sturdy white box, long, rectangular, and about nine inches wide. No marks, runes, or symbols decorated the surface, not even so much as a manufacturer's stamp to tell me who had made the box. I hesitated, then put my ear down close to the top and listened, in case someone had decided to put a bomb with an old-fashioned clock *tick-tick-tick*ing away inside. Stranger things had happened in my line of work.

But no sounds escaped from the container. No smells either, and I didn't sense any elemental magic emanating from it.

"Anything?" Owen asked from his position by the front door.

I shook my head. "Nothing so far."

The lid of the box had been taped down, so I palmed one of my knives and sliced through the material, careful not to jiggle the package any more than necessary. Then I waited, counting off the seconds in my head. *Ten . . . twenty . . . thirty . . . forty-five . . . sixty . . .*

After two minutes had passed, I was reasonably sure that nothing would happen until I actually *opened* the box.

"Here goes nothing," I called out to Owen.

I slowly drew the top off the box and reached for my Stone magic, using it to harden my skin, head, hair, eyes, and any other part of me that might get caught in a blast from a bomb or any rune trap that might be hidden inside. A sunburst rune that would make elemental Fire explode in my face, a saw symbol that would send sharp, daggerlike needles of Ice shooting out at me, maybe even some sort of Air elemental cloud design that would suck all of the oxygen away from me and suffocate me on the spot.

But none of those things happened, and all I saw was a thick layer of white tissue paper wrapped around whatever was inside.

I carefully pushed one side of the paper out of the way, then the other, still holding on to my Stone power to protect myself from any possible problems. But to my surprise, the box held something innocuous after all: flowers.

Roses, to be exact—black roses.

I let go of my magic, my skin reverting back to its normal soft texture, and frowned, wondering who would send me roses. I picked up one of the flowers, mindful of the sharp, curved thorns sticking out from the stem, and turned the blossom around and around, as if it held some sort of clue that would tell me who had sent it and why.

And it did.

Because this wasn't your typical rose. The stem was a milky white instead of the usual green, while the thorns were the same pale shade. But really, it was the petals that caught my attention, because they weren't black so much as they were a deep, dark, vivid blue, a color that I'd only seen one place before.

"All clear," I said.

Owen stepped over to the counter and looked into the box. "Roses? Somebody sent you roses?"

"It looks that way," I murmured.

A white card was lying on top of the flowers, and I picked it up. Only two words were scrawled across the front in black ink and tight, cursive handwriting: *Happy anniversary.*

That was it. That was all the card said, and no other marks, runes, or symbols decorated the stationery.

I rubbed my fingers over the card. Not what I had expected it to say. Some sort of death threat would have been far more appropriate. Then again, I hadn't thought that I'd get a package like this today either. But most troublesome was the fact that the two simple words gave me no clue to the writer's tone, state of mind, or true meaning. The card, the message, the roses could have been anything from a simple greeting to the most biting sort of sarcasm. If I was betting, though, I'd put my money on sarcasm. Or perhaps a warning. Maybe even a promise of payback, retribution, revenge.

"Happy anniversary?" Owen asked, peering at the card. "Anniversary of what?"

I glanced to the left at the calendar that I'd tacked up on the wall near the cash register. August twenty-fifth. It had happened ten years ago to the day. Funny, but right now, it seemed like ten minutes ago, given how hard my heart was hammering in my chest. I breathed in, trying to calm myself, but the sweet, sickening stench of the flowers rose up to fill my mouth and slither down my throat like perfumed poison. For a moment, I was back there, back with the roses, back in the shadows, beaten and bloody and wondering how I was going to survive what was coming next—

"Gin? Are you okay?" Owen asked. "You look like you're somewhere far away right now."

"I am," I said in a distracted voice, still seeing things that he couldn't, memories of another time, another place.

Another man.

Owen reached over and put his hand on top of mine. "Do you want to tell me about it?" he asked in a soft voice.

His touch broke the spell that the roses had cast on me, and I pulled myself out of my memories and stared at him. Owen looked back at me, his violet eyes warm with care, concern, and worry. It always surprised me to see those feelings reflected in his face, especially since we'd almost called it quits for good a few months ago. But we were back together and stronger than ever now. More important, he deserved to know about this. He deserved to know why I am the way I am—and who had helped make me this way.

I gestured for him to take his seat on the stool again, while I laid the dark blue rose back down in the box with the others. I kept the card in my hand, though, my thumb tracing over the words again and again. Then I sat down on my own stool, leaned my elbows on the counter, and looked at Owen.

"Get comfortable," I said. "Because it's a long story. Funny enough, it all begins with a girl—a stupid, arrogant girl who thought that she could do no wrong . . ."

# ✢ 2 ✢

## TEN YEARS AGO

My target never even saw me coming.

He had apparently forgotten the fact that I was just as cunning and even more ruthless than he was. He thought he was so smart, so clever, so very *safe*, perched on top of the rocks in his little sniper's nest, that he didn't remember one of the most important rules: watch your own back first.

He'd picked an excellent spot for his ambush, the highest point in this part of the old Ashland Rock Quarry, which let him see for a quarter-mile in every direction. The stack of rocks curved up, up, and up, before spreading out into a large shelf, almost like the trunk of a tree sprouting up and out into one long, thick, sturdy branch. A couple of small pine trees and rhododendron bushes had somehow managed to embed themselves in the top of the rocky shelf, giving him even more cover. He'd camouflaged himself well too, his gray T-shirt and khaki pants blending into the muted colors of the rocks and foliage. If I hadn't already known he was out here hunting me, I might never have spotted him.

But I had—and now he was going to pay for his mistake.

His position indicated that he'd focused his attention on the quarry entrance, where a tall iron gate stood, one that was missing more than a few of its bars, as though they were teeth that had been knocked out of its metal mouth. Even though I was a hundred feet away from the gate, I could still hear the rusty sign attached to the remaining bars *creak-creak-creak*ing back and forth in the gusty breeze. Every once in a while, I caught a glimpse of the faded words painted on the sign: *Enter at your own risk*.

Rather appropriate, since the man on the stone shelf had been sent here to get the best of me. But I was going to outsmart him instead. My source had told me that the sniper would be lurking somewhere in the quarry, so instead of strolling in through the front gate like he'd expected, I'd hiked into the area via a little-used access road, the same one that Bria and I used to race down when we were kids and heading to the quarry to play.

My heart tightened at the thought of my dead baby sister, with her big blue eyes, rosy cheeks, and a head full of bouncing golden curls. But I ruthlessly forced the memory from my mind, along with the anger, sorrow, and helplessness that always came with it.

I wasn't helpless anymore, and I was here to beat my enemy, not moon about the past and things that couldn't be changed.

It had taken me the better part of half an hour to find the sniper's perch, but I'd eased from rock to rock and one side of the quarry to the other until I'd located him. Now all that was left to do was to get close enough to strike. If he'd been down here, I could have gotten on with things already, but he'd decided to make things difficult.

He always did.

A bit of annoyance flitted through me as I stared up at the ridge. The sniper stayed where he was in the shadows cast out by the trees, the black barrel of his gun barely peeping over the lip of the rock. I was huddled underneath a small stone outcropping off to his right, so he couldn't see me unless he turned and specifically looked in this direction.

He *wouldn't* see me—until it was too late.

But there was one more thing I needed to do before I approached him, so I placed my hand on the stone formation next to me and reached out with my magic.

All around me, the rocks whispered of their history, of everything that had happened to them, of all the things that people had done on, in, and around them over the years. As a Stone elemental, not only could I hear those emotional vibrations, but I could also interpret them.

The quarry rocks muttered with anger about how they'd been blasted, broken, and bored into, forced to give up the precious gems, ores, and minerals that they had contained until now there was nothing left of them but these empty, crumbling shells. But there were softer, gentler murmurs too, ones that spoke of the rocks' relief that the summer sun had started to descend behind the western mountains, taking all of its stifling heat along with it.

I reached out, sinking even deeper into the stone and listening for any signs of worry, distress, or danger.

But I didn't hear any evil intentions rippling through the sunbaked rocks, only their desire to be left alone and their cranky grumbles about the weather that constantly eroded them bit by tiny bit. Few folks came here anymore, except for bums looking for a quiet place to make camp or people with small pickaxes digging for whatever leftover gems or chunks of ore they could find in the jagged formations.

Satisfied that the sniper was alone, I dropped my hand from the rocks.

His position on top of the ridge might have given him a great view of the entrance, but he couldn't see what was directly below him, so he didn't notice me dart from one stone outcropping to the next until I'd worked my way around to the back side of his location.

I shielded my eyes against the sun's glare and stared up at the stones. The ridge rose about a hundred feet, much of it sheer and slick with age, but a few rocks jutted out here and there to offer handholds and climbing perches. More annoyance spurted through me; I wanted to take out my enemy and be done with things, but my mentor firmly believed in the old saying that good things came to those who waited. Actually, I thought that good things came to those who took action.

So I stepped over to the ridge and placed my hand on the rocks, once again listening to them, but they still only murmured of the hot sun and the damage that had been done to them. I curled my fingers around the rocks, feeling the sharp edges digging into my palms, and hoisted myself off the ground a few inches, making sure that they would hold my weight and not crumble to dust.

Of course, I could have used my magic to help me climb—my Ice magic.

In addition to my Stone power, I was one of the rare elementals who was gifted in another one of the four main areas—Ice, in my case—although that magic was far weaker than my Stone power. Still, I could have made a couple of small Ice knives to dig into the rocks and help me work my way up the ridge.

But I decided not to. The sniper didn't have any magic, so he wouldn't sense me actively using my power like another elemental might have. But he'd made it to the top without using magic. So would I. Besides, I didn't like using my magic any more than necessary. I didn't want it to become a crutch that I couldn't function without.

I couldn't afford for that to happen—not as the Spider.

I would have liked to have hoisted myself up the rocks as quickly as possible, but that would be far too noisy, and I was too determined to win to risk my victory like that. So I slowly, carefully, quietly scaled the ridge, moving from one patch of rocks to the next and working my way higher and higher up the steep slope. It was after eight in the evening, and while the sun might not be directly overhead anymore, heat still shimmered up out of the quarry, rising in sultry, sticky waves. It was almost August, which was often the hottest month in Ashland, but the heat seemed particularly blistering this year. The rocks were pleasantly warm under my hands, while bits of white and rose quartz glittered like pale, milky diamonds between my grasping fingers. Perhaps when I had taken care of the sniper, I'd get my own pickax, come back out here one day, and see if I could find any gemstones for myself.

I reached the top of the ridge and hung there for a moment, like a spider dangling from the top of its own stony web. Then, still being as quiet as possible, I slowly hoisted myself up so that I could peer over the lip of rock and see what the sniper was doing and whether he'd heard my approach and aimed his rifle in my direction, ready to put three bullets through my right eye the second he saw me.

The sniper was here, all right, but he hadn't realized that I was too.

Another rule he'd forgotten: arrogance will get you, every single time.

He was turned away from me, lying flat on his stomach, his rifle pointed out toward the gate at the front of the quarry, in the same position as when I'd first seen him. In fact, it looked like he hadn't moved an inch the whole time I'd been climbing. He had his right eye close to the scope mounted on the weapon, and his entire body was a study in stillness as he waited for me to step into his sights. Good for him for being so diligent. Too bad it wasn't going to save him.

"Where are you?" he whispered, the breeze blowing his words back to me. "Where are you hiding?"

I grinned. He'd find that out in another minute, two tops.

Still being as quiet as possible, I hooked one leg over the edge of the ridge, then the other, before coming up into a low crouch. The sniper might have his rifle, but I had something even better: my five silverstone knives.

One up either sleeve, one tucked into the small of my back, and two hidden in the sides of my boots.

Still crouching low, I palmed one of the knives up my sleeve and headed toward the sniper. I didn't try to be quiet anymore, not now, when I knew that I had already won.

Too late, he heard my boots scrape against the stones. He rolled over, trying to raise his rifle to get a shot off at me, but I was quicker. I kicked the weapon out of his hands, sending it skittering across the rocks. He reached for the second gun tucked into the holster on his black leather belt, but I threw myself on top of him and pressed my knife up against his throat, telling him exactly what would happen if he decided to struggle.

Action always triumphs—and so do I.

"Say it." I sneered in his face. "C'mon. *Say it*."

My opponent arched his head away from me, as if I would be dumb enough to drop the knife from his throat just because he wanted me to. My foster brother's green eyes blazed with anger in his handsome face, although his walnut-colored hair had remained perfectly, artfully in place, despite our scuffle.

"Fine," Finnegan Lane muttered. "You win, Gin. *Again*. There, are you happy now?"

I grinned. "Ecstatic."

I rolled off him, bounced up onto my feet, and tucked my knife back up my sleeve. Then I leaned over and held out my hand to him. Finn stared at the silvery mark branded into my palm, a small circle surrounded by eight thin rays. A spider rune—the symbol for patience and my assassin name.

Finn gave me another sour look, but he reached up, took my hand, and let me pull him to his feet. He might be my foster brother, but he didn't like to lose when we played our war games. Then again, neither did I.

"So where do you think the old man is?" Finn asked, staring down into the quarry.

I froze. "You haven't seen him? Then that means—"

A red dot appeared on Finn's chest. Before I could react, before I could move, before I could try to duck, the dot zoomed over to land on my chest, right over my heart.

*Dammit.* My annoyance returned, stronger than ever, along with more than a little anger. At him for being such a sneaky bastard but mostly at myself for falling for such a simple trick.

"That means I've just killed you both," a low, deep voice called out.

Finn might have taken the primo spot at the front of the ridge beneath the pines, but a few scraggly rhododendron bushes clung to the far left side, along with a tangle of blackberry briars. The bushes and thorny branches whipped back and forth as a man stood up and eased out of the dense thicket of leaves and limbs.

He wore a short-sleeved blue work shirt, along with matching pants, while brown boots covered his feet. His hair was more silver than walnut now, with a slight wave in the front, while faint lines fanned out from his eyes and grooved around his mouth, showing all of the living he'd done in his sixty-some years. Still, his eyes were the same glassy green as Finn's and just as sharp and bright as his son's. A rifle with a laser sight attached to it was propped up on his right shoulder—the weapon he'd used to mock-kill us with.

Fletcher Lane. Finn's dad. My mentor. The assassin the Tin Man.

"You should have made sure that you were the only one clever enough to think of using this ridge as a sniper's perch," Fletcher drawled, eyeing his son. "I'd already been up here for twenty minutes before you showed up."

"I know, I know," Finn grumbled. "There are no original ideas anymore, especially when it comes to the assassination business."

Fletcher nodded before he fixed his gaze on me. "And you should have made sure that he was alone before you approached him. That someone wasn't lying in wait to kill you both."

His voice was far sterner with me than it had been with Finn, since Fletcher was training me to be an assassin, training me to be the Spider, like he had ever since he'd taken me in off the streets when I was thirteen.

I gave him a curt nod. I managed to hide my wince, if not the embarrassed flush that stained my cheeks. Even though I was twenty now, Fletcher still had the ability to make me feel like that lost little girl, the one who had no clue how to defend herself. Seven years of training, and he'd gotten the best of me—again—not by being tougher or stronger or having more magic but simply by being *smarter*.

Fletcher was always telling me to take things slow, to think, to wait and plot and plan, but I'd seen an opportunity to beat Finn, so I'd seized it without doing any of those things. My action had gotten me exactly one thing: eliminated. Fletcher was right. I should have known better.

I *had* to know better, or I'd get dead for real one day.

Fletcher stared at me another moment before nodding again, satisfied that I'd learned my lesson, at least for today. "All right. I think that's enough for tonight."

"Finally," Finn muttered, leaning down to grab his rifle from where it had landed. "We've been out here for three hours already. I thought the day was never going to end."

"Aw, you wouldn't be saying that if you had managed to kill me a single time," I drawled. "Just because I've killed you five times since we've been here is no reason to pout."

Finn narrowed his eyes at my crowing. Before we'd played sniper-versus-assassin, we'd done a few rounds of hand-to-hand combat, all of which I'd easily won. All of which I'd loved, since that was one arena where quick, decisive action always came in handy, instead of the wait-and-see approach that Fletcher preferred.

"Whatever," Finn muttered again. "I've gotta go. I've got work to do."

"More boring reports to read for your summer job?"

He sniffed. "The reports are *not* boring, and it's *not* some lame summer job. It's an *internship* with one of the most prestigious banks in Ashland. If I play my cards right, this could lead to a full-time position."

I rolled my eyes at his snotty, superior tone. Finn had recently turned twenty-three and was finishing up his MBA with his internship and some sort of accounting program that he was taking online through a university in Bigtime, New York. With his new job and fancy suits, Finn thought that he was it on a stick—and then some.

"Whatever. I'd rather be cooking in the Pork Pit than sitting in some stuffy old bank day after day."

Finn sniffed again, but he didn't respond to my taunt this time.

Fletcher didn't comment on our sniping. He'd long ago given up trying to referee the two of us.

"Come on," the old man said. "I want to go home and get some supper."

The three of us climbed down the ridge using some rope that Fletcher had brought along, piled into his beat-up white van, and headed back to the city. Thirty minutes later, Fletcher dropped Finn off at his apartment building downtown.

"You coming by the restaurant for lunch tomorrow?" Fletcher asked through his open window.

Finn hesitated. "I'll try, but it depends on work. I'll call and let you know, okay?"

Fletcher nodded and smiled, but not before I saw the flicker of hurt that pinched his face. Finn hadn't been around much this summer, spending more time at that stupid bank than he had with his dad. Anger sizzled in my chest that he could be so thoughtless toward Fletcher. Finn should be grateful that he still had a dad, especially one like Fletcher. But I kept my mouth shut. There was no use arguing with Finn. He was even more stubborn than I was.

Finn waved at his dad, then headed into his building. He didn't wave at me or tell me good-bye, though. He was still pissed that I'd beaten him so many times tonight. I grinned. Too bad.

Fletcher threw the van into gear, pulled away from the curb, and drove through downtown, going by the Pork Pit. Since it was after nine now, the restaurant was closed, although the neon pig sign over the front door burned with bright, multicolored lights. The sight never failed to cheer me up.

"You know, I noticed that there are a couple of apartments for rent in that building across from the Pit," I said, trying to make my voice light and casual as I pointed out the window. "See the sign right there? I thought I might call about one and see how much the rent is."

Fletcher *harrumph*ed in the back of his throat, but that was his only reaction. Finn had his own apartment, and I was itching to move out of Fletcher's house too. I loved the old man, really, I did, but I was an assassin. I was the Spider. Fletcher had been sending me on solo jobs for a while now, and I felt like I should have my own place, my own space, and not what I'd carved out for myself in his cluttered house.

"So?" I asked, impatience creeping into my voice. "What do you think? About the apartment?"

Fletcher stared out the windshield, instead of looking at me. "We'll see."

I wanted to pester him about it and get him to say yes right then, but I forced myself to wait, even though I ended up grinding my teeth the whole time.

But that was all he said.

If Finn and I were stubborn, then Fletcher was doubly so, and I knew that nothing short of being quartered by wild horses would make him say another word before he was ready to.

It was difficult, but I made myself unclench my jaw, although I couldn't keep from tapping my fingers against the open window frame in frustration. As I watched the passing scenery, I wondered how much longer it would be before the old man realized that I was all grown up.

## ✵ 3 ✵

Twenty minutes later, Fletcher stopped the van in front of his house, which perched on top of one of the many ridges that ran through and around Ashland as part of the Appalachian Mountains.

I hopped out of the vehicle and headed toward the front porch, ready to wash away all of the grime, dust, and sweat from our war games. But Fletcher stayed by the van, as was his usual routine, scanning the dark woods that lay to one side of the house before his gaze moved across the yard and over to the rocky cliff that marked the edge of the property.

I didn't know why he bothered. Fletcher was extremely careful as the Tin Man, using all sorts of cutouts, aliases, and back doors to book jobs and then being even more careful to leave no evidence behind at the scenes of his crimes, much less any clues to who he really was. There was no way that anyone could trace what he did—what *we* did now—back to us, but every time we came home, he still stopped, looked, and listened like he expected an attack at any second.

I sighed and waited by the front door, my arms crossed over my chest and my right foot tapping a staccato pattern against the weathered wooden porch. I was all for being cautious, but this bordered on the ridiculously paranoid.

After about three minutes, Fletcher was *finally* satisfied that no one was lying in wait to try to kill us, and he left the van and headed toward the house. He inserted his key in the lock, turning the knob to open the door, but the wood wouldn't budge.

"Stupid door," he muttered. "The wood always sticks in this humidity. I should go ahead and get that black granite one installed like I've been thinking about."

I rolled my eyes. The house was already a hulking monstrosity. Several folks had owned it over the years, and each of them had added on a room or two. All in different styles, colors, and materials, including white clapboard, brown brick, and gray stone. And Fletcher had only added to the oddness by installing a bright, shiny tin roof and coal-black shutters a few months ago. I always wondered why he didn't remodel the entire structure and give it some sort of cohesive style, but he seemed to like the strange angles and mismatched pieces of wood and stone. I supposed that a black granite door would fit right in with the eclectic feel of the rest of the house.

Fletcher put his shoulder into the wood, and the door finally wrenched open with a violent *screech*.

We stepped inside the house, which had as many odd corners and incongruous styles as the outside did, and went our separate ways. I headed upstairs, took a shower, and threw on a thin blue cotton robe over a white T-shirt and some short pink pajama bottoms patterned with garish green limes. Then I went back downstairs to the kitchen to get something to eat.

I rustled around in the refrigerator, grabbing cold cuts, cheese, and more, before taking everything over to the counter, where a fresh loaf of Sophia's sourdough bread was waiting. I hummed under my breath as I built my meal. Thin slices of smoked turkey and honey ham; thick slabs of sharp cheddar cheese; sweet, crispy romaine lettuce; a couple of rings of red onion; sliced fresh tomatoes sprinkled with salt and pepper; all of it topped off with a hearty layer of mayonnaise, a dollop of mustard, and another piece of bread. Three minutes later, I had the perfect sandwich.

Too hungry to get a plate, I stood at the counter and sank my teeth into the layers of goodness. The tomatoes were like a bright burst of summer in my mouth, brought out by the creamy mayonnaise. The meats were the ideal blend of smoky and sweet, while the lettuce and onions gave every bite a healthy bit of crunch. I quickly finished that sandwich and made myself another one.

Fletcher entered the kitchen, still dressed in his blue work clothes, although he'd taken the time to wash his hands and face. He wandered over to the counter.

"That looks good." His stomach rumbled in time with his words.

I gave Fletcher the second sandwich and fixed a third one. He put it on a napkin, poured himself a glass of sweet iced sun tea that I'd made this morning, and carried everything into the den. I thought he might turn on the TV, but the area remained quiet. I stayed in the kitchen, finished my sandwich, and opened the fridge again, wondering what I could whip up for dessert. I had some chocolate chip cookies that I'd baked yesterday. Maybe I'd use them and a pint of fudge ice cream to make some quick and easy ice cream sandwiches—

"Gin," Fletcher called out. "Come here, please."

I sighed at the interruption, but I closed the refrigerator and trooped into the den, where he was sitting on the worn plaid sofa. "Yeah?"

He hesitated, then picked up a manila folder from the scarred wooden coffee table and waved it at me.

I perked up, forgetting all about dessert. "What's that?"

"A job—maybe."

I sat down on the sofa next to him. "Why is it just a *maybe*?"

He shrugged.

Fletcher wasn't an elemental, so the stones never whispered to him of any potential dangers like they did to me. But more than once, he'd turned down a job because something didn't feel right to him. And more than once, he'd found out after the fact that he'd been right to refuse it. That the assignment had been some sort of trap or double-cross or that the client was only going to pay half the money and then try to take him out after the job was done. I might have my magic, but Fletcher had his instincts.

He hesitated a moment longer, then handed me the file. "I was going to wait on this. At least until I could check out a few more things, like exactly who the client is and why they want this person dead. But apparently, the client wants to remain as anonymous as I do, because I haven't been able to find out anything about them so far."

"How did they make contact?" I asked.

"I answered a rather cryptic newspaper classified ad asking for information about pork prices, followed up by some more pointed conversations through one of my anonymous e-mail accounts."

Newspaper ads, untraceable e-mails, and throwaway cell phones were some of Fletcher's standard ways of booking jobs, while the mention of pork prices was one of his codes. Other codes included more tongue-in-cheek references to *Wizard of Oz* memorabilia, given that the Tin Man was Fletcher's assassin alias. That way, all he had to do was scan the newspaper every morning to see if someone might want the services of an assassin and then follow up on the info he spied there. Even then, he remained anonymous, and he still screened potential clients as much as possible, in case of setups and traps.

"There was nothing unusual about how the client contacted me, but something still feels a little off." He shrugged. "But the down payment is already sitting in the bank, and everything else seems legit, so I figured that we might as well talk about it."

"Who's the target?"

"Cesar Vaughn. A Stone elemental."

I frowned. "Why do I know that name?"

"He owns Vaughn Construction," Fletcher replied. "It's become a big firm in Ashland in recent years. You've probably seen the name on signs at construction sites around the city. Vaughn and his company have put up a lot of the new office buildings downtown."

I opened the folder. The first item inside was a photo of Cesar Vaughn, taken at some groundbreaking event. He was wearing a business suit, holding a shovel full of dirt, and grinning at the camera. He looked to be younger than Fletcher, maybe fifty or so, with a shock of peppery hair, tan skin, and dark brown eyes. He was beaming in the photo, giving him a proud, pleasant appearance, but I knew how deceiving looks could be.

More photos showed Vaughn at various construction sites. It looked like he was more than a corporate figurehead, given the fact that several of the pictures featured him loading bags onto trucks, driving nails into boards, and even pouring concrete. He seemed happy sweating alongside his crew, and his smiles were even wider in these photos, as if he actually enjoyed the hard, physical labor of building something from the ground up.

One close-up shot showed the logo for Vaughn Construction. The words were simple enough, written in a plain font, although what looked like two thorns curved together to form the V in Vaughn. That must be his business rune. Curious. I would have expected a stack of bricks or something similar for a Stone elemental. I wondered what the thorns represented to Vaughn.

"So what's he done?"

It was the same question I always asked. Oh, I knew that what we were doing wasn't right. We were assassins, after all, trained, ruthless killers for hire to anyone who had enough money to meet our asking prices. But the people we took out were usually worse than we were.

Someone didn't pay hundreds of thousands or even millions of dollars to off their kid's piano teacher or the barista who made them a lousy cup of coffee. Well, not usually. You had to do *something* to someone, royally piss them off, be a dangerous threat, or stand in the way of whatever they wanted. That's when we got called in.

Besides, Fletcher had his own set of rules as an assassin, ones that he'd taught me to live by: no kids, no pets, no torture. So you didn't get on the Tin Man's radar by being innocent.

Sometimes I thought that we did everyone a favor by taking out the folks that we did. It didn't make us the good guys by any stretch of the imagination, but we weren't the most evil folks around either. Not by a long shot. Not in Ashland.

Fletcher shrugged again. "It could be any number of things. Maybe Vaughn didn't spread enough bribe money around to the right people, and they're angry about it. Maybe he took a job that a competitor wanted. Maybe he's building on someone's land who wants his project to disappear."

As with most other businesses in Ashland, there were certain rules when it came to the construction industry. Certain people you had to pay off for everything from building plans to zoning permits to construction materials. Such things helped to keep . . . accidents from happening—to you and yours.

"But I'm guessing that the assignment has something to do with that incident up in Northtown a couple of months ago," Fletcher continued. "The one at that new shopping center."

"I remember that. Some enormous third-story stone terrace collapsed at a restaurant on opening night. It was all over the news."

"Five people died, and a dozen more were injured," Fletcher said. "They're still investigating the cause. But guess who built the restaurant and the rest of the shopping center?"

"Cesar Vaughn."

He nodded.

"So what? You think someone blames him for the accident?"

"It's possible," Fletcher said. "Especially if Vaughn used substandard building materials or cut corners. That's what the rumor is, anyway. That he skimped on supplies, labor, and more, and that's why the terrace collapsed. Supposedly, the families of the victims are getting ready to sue him over it, bankrupt him over it."

I waved the folder at him. "Yeah, but if someone wants Vaughn dead now, then it sounds like they don't want to wait around for a lawsuit or any money they might get. They just want his blood."

Fletcher nodded. "Or maybe they realize that a lawsuit will probably drag on for years, if it doesn't get thrown out of court somewhere along the way. Look at who his lawyer is."

I flipped past the photos and scanned through some court documents that Fletcher had included in the file. "Jonah McAllister? But I thought he was Mab Monroe's personal lawyer. That he worked for her and her alone."

"He is, and he does," Fletcher replied. "But Mab happens to own a significant stake in Vaughn's company. So she has a vested interest in making sure that any trouble Vaughn is in disappears. It wouldn't surprise me if she's already gotten Elliot Slater to go pay visits to some of the victims' families to make them reconsider filing their lawsuits."

Slater was the giant who served as the head of Mab's security detail and oversaw her bodyguards. At least, that's what he was on paper. But everyone in the underworld knew that Slater was her top enforcer, who carried out all of her ruthless commands. No visit from Slater was ever pleasant, and most ended with blood and broken bones—at the bare minimum.

"You think Mab wants Vaughn dead? With him gone, that might make it a little harder for the victims' families to sue."

Fletcher shrugged a third time. "Maybe. But Vaughn's company is a cash cow for Mab. He's probably worth more to her alive and running things smoothly than he is dead and buried." He hesitated again. "But there's something else."

"What?"

"According to our mysterious client, Vaughn has been under some serious stress for months now, and he's been taking that stress out on his daughter, Charlotte. Hitting her, slapping her, screaming at her."

"Where's her mom?" I asked. "Why isn't she protecting Charlotte?"

"Samantha Vaughn died in a car crash several years ago," Fletcher answered. "I checked it out with some of my sources. Vaughn has had an Air elemental healer over to his mansion to see to his daughter four times in the last six months, three times for broken bones and once for a concussion. Supposedly, she fell down some stairs, fell off her bike, et cetera, et cetera."

I snorted. "Yeah. Right."

I kept going through the file until I found a photo of Charlotte Vaughn. She was a pretty girl, with the same brown eyes that her father had and glossy black hair that had been pulled back into two messy pigtails. She was staring at the camera, but her lips were barely curved up, and her gaze seemed dark and troubled, too dark and troubled for someone so young.

"How old is she?" I asked.

"Thirteen."

Thirteen. The same age I'd been when a Fire elemental had stormed into my house and murdered my mother, Eira, and my older sister, Annabella. Before torturing me. Before I'd used my magic to collapse the stones of our mansion, accidentally killing my younger sister, Bria, in the process.

My fingers curled inward, my nails digging into my left palm and the spider rune scar there, that small circle surrounded by eight thin rays. Once upon a time, the rune had been a silverstone pendant, which I'd worn until the Fire elemental had superheated the rune with her magic, searing it into my palms like a cattle brand.

For a moment, the stench of charred flesh filled my nose, and I was back in the smoky, ruined remains of my family's home, trying to swallow down my screams, my palms still burning, burning, burning from the silverstone that had been so cruelly, so brutally, melted into my skin—

"Gin?" Fletcher asked. "What are you thinking about?"

"Nothing."

I forced the memories back into the past where they belonged and concentrated on the file in my hand, letting the smooth, slick feel of the photos and papers ground me in the here and now. I flipped through some more pictures of Charlotte, until I came to one of her standing with a guy who looked to be in his mid-twenties. He had the same black hair, tan skin, and brown eyes and was quite handsome, like a younger, leaner, more polished version of his father. The sly grin that he was giving the camera told me that he knew exactly how gorgeous he was. I saw the same smug smile on Finn's face every day.

"Who's he?" I asked, showing Fletcher the photo.

"Sebastian Vaughn, Charlotte's older brother. He's twenty-three and one of the vice presidents in his father's construction company. Cesar made him the number two man in the firm a few months ago."

"Any indication that he knows what caused the terrace to collapse? Or the abuse that their father is inflicting on Charlotte?"

Fletcher shook his head. "Not that I've been able to find. Some of his father's business dealings may be questionable, but Sebastian seems to have kept his nose clean so far. Supposedly, he dotes on Charlotte and is always bringing her presents. If he knew about the abuse, he would probably try to stop it. At least, that's what my sources think."

"So what's the problem? Vaughn obviously isn't squeaky clean, not if he's in business with Mab Monroe, and he likes to slap his daughter around. What are we waiting for?"

Fletcher shook his head. "I'm not sure. On the surface, everything seems legit and straightforward. But I've been looking into everyone who died that night at the restaurant and all of their friends and family members, and I can't find anyone with enough cash to pay for a hit, at least not until some of the insurance settlements kick in. But half of the money has already been paid out, and I can't trace it back to anyone. Of course, someone could have some hidden funds squirreled away that I haven't found out about yet. It wouldn't be the first time."

"But?"

"But I've got this feeling that there's something a little bit . . . off about this job. Something I'm missing about the whole situation, although I can't quite put my finger on what it might be."

"Did you ask Jo-Jo about it?"

Jolene "Jo-Jo" Deveraux was the dwarven Air elemental who healed Fletcher and me whenever we got injured during a job. And similar to my Stone power, Jo-Jo's Air magic whispered to her—of all the things that might come to pass. The stones muttered about the actions that people had already taken in a given spot, the crimes they had already committed, but the wind brought with it whispers of all the ways people might act in the future. Usually, if Fletcher had misgivings about a job, he ran things by Jo-Jo to see what she thought and if she might notice something that he'd missed. Sometimes she was able to tell him whether his worry was warranted.

Fletcher picked at a loose thread on one of the couch

cushions. "I did ask Jo-Jo, but she said that she couldn't get a clear sense of things from the information I gave her."

That wasn't unusual. Jo-Jo didn't get supersharp glimpses of the future on cue. Like me, she had to listen to and interpret all the whispers that she heard. People's thoughts and feelings were constantly changing, shifting even more than the wind, and things often simply got lost in translation. Sometimes Fletcher and I just had to trust in ourselves, that we were smart, sly, and strong enough to do the job and get away with it.

I stared at that photo of Charlotte Vaughn again, the one where she seemed so sad and wary. I didn't have any reservations, hesitations, or misgivings about this job, not a single one, not when a young girl's life was in danger. Maybe next time, her father wouldn't be content with giving her bruises and broken bones. Maybe next time, his rage would be greater than it had ever been before. Maybe next time, he wouldn't stop hitting her until she was dead.

"Let's do it," I said, making up my mind and closing the file on Cesar Vaughn. "The sooner, the better, as far as I'm concerned."

Fletcher wanted to wait until he had more info about the client, but I pushed him, loudly and repeatedly pointing out that Vaughn was a ticking time bomb as far as Charlotte was concerned, and he finally, reluctantly, agreed and said that he'd work on some of the details.

I would have been more than happy to grab my knives, drive over to Vaughn's mansion, sneak inside, and do the deed tonight, but Fletcher wanted to do some scouting first and to be overly cautious about things, the way he *always* was. Even though I chafed at the thought of Charlotte being terrorized and in danger a second longer than necessary, I gave in to his wishes. As much as I hated to admit it, going in blind was never a good idea. Fletcher had told me that over and over, and he'd proven it earlier tonight when he'd mock-killed Finn and me.

But I told Fletcher flat-out that if he got any more reports of Charlotte being injured, I would go straight from recon to the action portion of the job. He nodded, knowing that I meant what I said.

Fletcher stayed in the den to review the file again. He gave me the copy he'd made, which I took up to my room and set aside before crawling into bed.

One moment, I was in the soft blackness of sleep, dreaming of nothing in particular. The next, I was tied down to a chair, my spider rune duct-taped in between my palms, the superhot silverstone melting, melting, melting into my skin. And all the while, I could hear the Fire elemental who was torturing me laughing in her low, throaty, silky voice, laughing about how much she was hurting me and how very much she was enjoying it.

But no matter how I struggled against the ropes that held me down, no matter how hard I tried to rip off the cloth that blindfolded me, no matter how long and loud I screamed, the torture, pain, and laughter didn't stop.

*Nothing* made it stop.

I don't know how long I was trapped there in that dream world, in my own horrible memories, before I managed to jerk myself awake. All I could think about was the pain. Then, suddenly, I was sitting bolt upright in bed, my heart pounding, my breath coming in short, ragged gasps, my palms burning as if I were still holding on to my own hot spider rune.

Before I realized what I was doing, my hand darted under my pillow and gripped the knife that I always kept there, even though I was as safe as I could be in Fletcher's house. But the cool, solid, substantial feel of the metal cut through the phantom burning sensation and helped me snap back to reality. Slowly, I made myself uncurl my hand from the weapon, even though my fingers cramped from where I'd been clutching the hilt so tightly. It took me longer still to slow my racing heart, catch my breath, and wipe the sweat from my forehead.

I used to have nightmares all the time when I was younger. More than once, I'd woken up screaming in the middle of the night, which had made Fletcher and Finn come running into my room to see what was wrong. But eventually, they'd stopped coming when they realized that I was going to yell whether they were there or not. I couldn't blame them for that, though. Hard to soothe someone when she wouldn't even tell you what her nightmares were about. And I never said a word about them, the torture, or my dead family to Fletcher or Finn. The nightmares, the memories, the heartache and loss and pain were my own burdens to bear, not theirs.

I couldn't go back to sleep, not yet, so I snapped on the light, figuring that I'd review the information on Cesar Vaughn again.

Business dealings, friends, restaurants that he liked to frequent, his finances, the charities he gave money to, the women he dated. Fletcher was nothing if not thorough, and the file gave me a pretty good picture of Vaughn's life.

Cesar Vaughn presented himself as a respectable, responsible businessman, and that's exactly what he was on paper—and in real life too. Vaughn had tens of millions in the bank, but he was still careful with his finances, not overextending himself with too many new construction projects at once, not spending wildly on cars, jets, or boats, not trading up for a bigger and better mansion or a newer and hotter trophy wife every other year. He paid his workers good wages and gave them all the health insurance and other benefits they were due. He was known for doing quality work and bringing projects in on time and on budget. From all accounts, he was a stern boss who expected the best from his workers, but he was a fair one too.

Yeah, some of Vaughn's business dealings were a little shady, just like Fletcher had said, especially the exorbitant amount he paid out in "consulting fees"—bribe money, in other words. But that was nothing new in Ashland. It would have been stranger if Vaughn's hands weren't dirty at all. Still, he wasn't the worst guy Fletcher had ever sent me after. Other than the terrace collapse and potential lawsuits, there seemed to be no real reason anyone would want Vaughn dead badly enough to reach out to Fletcher to make it happen. So I could see why the old man had a hinky feeling about the job.

But I didn't—not when I looked at the photo of Charlotte.

I plucked the picture out of the file and stared at her. Something was going on with her. She had the same dark, wounded, haunted look that I'd had after my family was murdered, the same look that I could see in the mirror to this day.

Oh, yes, Vaughn might seem like a respectable businessman, but he was abusing his daughter. I was sure of it. And that alone was reason enough for me to kill him.

It was one thing to hurt another adult, whether it was a friend, a lover, a business partner, or even a family member. That's what people did to one another, whether they meant to or not. That was just *life*. But it was especially that way in Ashland, where everyone with money, power, magic, and prestige was almost always trying to fuck over everyone else with money, power, magic, and prestige.

But beating up a thirteen-year-old girl? That was *unacceptable*. Hurting *any* kid for *any* reason was unacceptable, but what really pissed me off were the folks like Vaughn. The ones with enough of that money, power, magic, and prestige to get away with it. The ones who could afford to hire an Air elemental healer to cover up the bruises and broken bones that they'd given their children. The ones who thought nothing of hitting their sons and daughters again and again, because they enjoyed the sick thrill and the illusion of power it gave them. Those were the sort of people who made my blood boil, the ones I was all too happy to target as an assassin.

Cesar Vaughn wasn't going to hurt his daughter ever again, not if I could help it.

"I'm going to save you from him," I whispered.

In the photo, Charlotte kept staring at me with her big brown eyes, that worried look frozen on her face, as if she didn't believe that I'd keep my word. That I'd save her from the nightmare she was enduring. I knew what it was like to be tortured, to be helpless to stop the pain and fear and terror. When Fletcher had taken me in, when he'd started training me, I'd made myself a promise that no one would ever do that to me again, that I'd never feel that way again, that I would never be *weak* again.

That was one of the driving reasons that I'd become an assassin. Sure, part of me wanted to be a total, confident, cold-as-ice badass who could take care of herself, the sort of person people whispered about in hushed tones as she walked by. Even though no one would probably ever realize that I was an assassin, that I was the Spider, it was enough that *I* knew it deep down inside. But even more important than that, I wanted to be strong so I could protect the people I cared about. Fletcher, Jo-Jo, even Finn and Sophia. I wasn't letting anyone take them away from me, not like my mom and sister had been.

And here was another girl who was in pain, who was being hurt like I had been hurt once upon a time. I hadn't been able to save Bria, but I could help Charlotte—I *would* help her. I wasn't weak, helpless, or afraid anymore, and I was going to enjoy showing Cesar Vaughn exactly how strong I was, right before I laid his throat open with my knife.

"Soon," I whispered to Charlotte's picture again. "You'll be free from him soon."

My promise affirmed, I slid her photo back into the file, put it aside, turned out the light, and went back to sleep.

## ❊ 4 ❊

Two nights later, I found myself in a rustic dining room.

A long rectangular table made out of polished wood took up a large portion of the area, so big that it required three separate chandeliers to light the various sections. But instead of the usual brass or crystal, these chandeliers were made out of deer, elk, and other antlers that had been strung together. Giant wagon wheels covered the walls, along with what I could only describe as cowboy duds—shiny silver spurs, coiled lassos, and even a pair of old-timey revolvers crisscrossed over each other. A stuffed bison head that was almost as big as I was hung over the fireplace in the back wall. The bison's dark eyes were fixed in a perpetual angry squint, as if the creature wanted to leap down and gore everyone in sight with the short, curved horns that it still had left on its head.

The dining room and all of its western furnishings were the property of Tobias Dawson, and the dwarf had apparently dressed to match the decor, sporting a droopy handlebar mustache, a turquoise lariat tie, and black snakeskin boots, along with a black business suit. A black ten-gallon hat perched on top of his head, although it couldn't contain his sandy mane of hair, which fell to his shoulders. Dawson threw back his head and laughed at something a gorgeous vampire was murmuring to him.

Dawson was some big coal mine owner, with operations located throughout the Appalachian Mountains. Speculation among the other diners was that Dawson was thinking about expanding into the Rockies or even up into Canada. I'd have to tell Fletcher what I'd overheard. The old man lived for juicy bits of gossip like that.

Somehow Fletcher had gotten wind that Dawson had invited thirty of his closest friends and business associates to his home for a dinner party. Now here I was, smack dab in the middle of a crowd of women wearing expensive evening gowns and men sporting designer suits that cost just as much, although all of their finery seemed a bit at odds with the country cowboy collection adorning the walls—

"Hey, sweetheart, you going to stand there and gawk, or you going to offer me something to drink?" a low voice growled.

A large shadow fell over me, blotting out the light from the antler chandelier overhead and snapping me out of my snide observations. Because I wasn't here as one of Dawson's well-to-do guests. Instead of a satin gown and cascades of diamonds, I wore a black button-up shirt, a white tuxedo vest, and a matching white bow tie over a pair of black pants and boots. Cinderella, I was not.

No, tonight I was the help.

Actually, I was the help most nights. Fletcher often hired himself out for events like this, since it was a great way to surreptitiously scope out potential targets. See how many guards a businessman employed, whom he talked to, whom he snubbed, whom he was sleeping with. You never knew what information could be useful and help you get close enough to put your target down for good. I'd been coming along with the old man on catering jobs like these for years now, mostly working as a waiter, although I also helped him in the kitchen every now and then.

"Well, sweetheart?" the voice growled again, the tone a little sharper and more demanding than before. "What's it going to be?"

I glanced up . . . and up . . . and up, until my gaze landed on the face of the giant in front of me. Everything about him was pale, from his skin to his hazel eyes to his wispy thatch of blond hair. His features were so light—almost albino, really—that he might have faded into the background if not for the sheer, solid size of him, seven towering feet of thick muscles anchored by a rock-solid chest. No, Elliot Slater was not someone you overlooked, not if you wanted to live through whatever encounter you had with him.

"Champagne, sir?" I asked, careful to keep my voice soft and neutral but still respectful.

I might be an assassin, but Fletcher had taught me that discretion was the better part of valor, and Elliot Slater could snap my neck with one hand if he wanted to. And he just might, since I was masquerading as an anonymous waiter. No doubt, Dawson and his guests would howl with laughter at such a casual, brutal display of the giant's strength. They'd have to, because Slater could easily turn his wrath on them.

Slater grabbed a glass of champagne off the silver tray that I was now carefully, politely holding out to him. "That's more like it," he snapped.

He downed that glass of champagne and three more in quick succession. All the while, he stared at me, his cold gaze tracking up and down my body, from my pony-tail to my breasts to my legs and back again. Apparently, he wasn't too impressed with what he saw, because he snorted, grabbed a final glass of champagne, and shooed me away with a wave of his hand. The dismissive motion made the diamond in his pinkie ring spark and flash underneath the lights.

I gripped my tray a little tighter, but I made myself smile and politely, blandly, nod my head at him before turning away. It took more effort still to make my walk slow and controlled, as though I weren't concerned about the fact that a vicious giant was staring at my ass, assessing it as coldly as he had the rest of me. Animals like Slater were attracted to fear more than anything else.

But he wasn't the only one watching me—Fletcher was too.

He stood with four other chefs along the front wall of the dining room. Apparently, Dawson had thought that it would be fun to let his guests watch their food being prepared, although they were all far too busy bullshit-ting and boozing it up even to glance at the chefs as they whacked their way through mounds of vegetables, con-cocted creamy sauces, and flambéed various delicacies.

Dinner wasn't due to start for another forty-five minutes, so the guests milled around, laughing, talking, sizing up their rivals, and plotting against everyone in sight.

Including Cesar Vaughn.

He was over in a corner, chatting with an older woman who was wearing several ropes of pearls that Jo-Jo would have admired. Vaughn was an even more imposing and impressive figure in person. Fit, trim, strong, handsome. But there was a . . . roughness to him, one that his expensive suit couldn't quite hide. I could easily imagine him swinging a hammer, wielding a shovel, or lugging around bags of supplies, just like he had in the photos that Fletcher had shown me. And it seemed like Vaughn would have preferred to be doing any one of those things right now, judging from his many glances at his watch and the way his hand kept creeping up to his blue tie and yanking on the fabric, as though he found the knot there uncomfortably tight.

Well, that made two of us who were ill at ease, since I would have much preferred to have been killing him right now. If I thought I could have gotten away with it, I would have lured Vaughn to some dark corner and strangled him with his own tie. No muss, no fuss, no blood on my clothes. I'd even gone so far as to propose the idea to Fletcher on the ride over here, but he'd shot me down the way I knew he would. Even I would admit that it wasn't the smartest plan, but taking Vaughn out as quickly as I could had its appeal.

Our target had been on Dawson's guest list because he'd done some work on buildings at the dwarf's coal mines, and also on his mansion, and he was the reason that Fletcher and I were here. Fletcher wanted to check out Vaughn's security—or lack thereof—in person before we moved on to the next phase of the job.

Unlike some of the other movers and shakers, Vaughn hadn't brought any bodyguards along with him. In fact, according to what Fletcher had been able to uncover, except for a few guards at his estate and a couple more who served as drivers, Vaughn didn't employ any other giants specifically to protect him.

Then again, he didn't need to, given his Stone magic.

Still dispensing glasses of champagne, I maneuvered through the crowd and over to Vaughn's corner of the room until I was close enough to feel the magic emanating off him. Stone elementals were fairly rare, but Vaughn had the more common elemental trait of constantly giving off invisible waves of magic, even when he wasn't using his power. In his case, a sense of solidness continually rippled off his body, as though his muscles and bones were encased in cement, instead of just skin, and your hand would shatter if you tried to punch him in the jaw.

Besides Vaughn's abuse of Charlotte, his magic was the other most troubling thing about him and the one that could be the most dangerous when I finally went in for the kill. Vaughn wasn't the strongest elemental I'd ever encountered, but it felt like he had a decent amount of power, more than enough to make anyone think twice about messing with him. I'd have to put him down quickly when we had our inevitable confrontation—

Vaughn's phone chirped. He pulled the device out of his jacket, stared at the screen, and frowned. Then he tucked the phone away, excused himself from the woman he'd been talking to, and strode out of the room. I wondered what could be so important that would make Vaughn leave the party. Well, I was going to find out.

I glanced over at Fletcher, who was whipping together a raspberry sauce to top the molten dark chocolate soufflés that he'd prepared earlier. I tipped my head at Vaughn's retreating figure, and Fletcher gave me a tiny nod, telling me to go ahead. He knew as well as I did that any information we could gather about Vaughn might be useful in plotting his death.

I moved through the crowd, passing out glass after glass of champagne. Elliot Slater had already diminished most of my supply, so it didn't take long. When my tray was empty, I headed toward the open double doors, as though I were going to the kitchen to replenish my stock of bubbly. I might do that . . . eventually. But right now, I was much more interested in what Vaughn was up to.

I glanced around to make sure that no one was watching me, then slipped out of the dining room and followed my target.

Cesar Vaughn strode through the halls of Tobias Dawson's mansion like it was his own. His strides were long and purposeful, indicating that he knew exactly where he was going. I wondered whom he might be meeting. A business associate to negotiate a hush-hush deal? A rival he wanted to warn away from a potential project? A secret lover? It could be anyone.

Vaughn rounded a corner and disappeared from sight. I hurried after him—

"Hey! Where do you think you're going?"

I whipped around at the sound of the voice behind me.

A woman dressed in the same tuxedo clothes that I wore strode down the hallway toward me. She clutched a clipboard in one hand, while a headset arced across her head like a plastic crown, unsuccessfully trying to flatten her frizzy black curls. Meredith Ruiz, the event planner for tonight's dinner and many others that I'd worked. She stopped in front of me and straightened up to her full height, which was a few inches short of five feet, since she was a dwarf.

"Where do you think you're going?" Meredith snapped.

I gave her my best, most innocent, and most clueless smile and held up my empty tray like a shield in front of me. Too bad the metal wouldn't actually protect me from her wrath. "I was headed to the kitchen to get some more champagne. Thirsty crowd tonight."

Her brown eyes narrowed, sizing me up, but I kept right on smiling at her, as if I were doing absolutely no wrong instead of being up to absolutely no good.

"Well, the kitchen's the other way," Meredith said. "Come on. I'll take you there."

I glanced over my shoulder, but Vaughn was long gone. I bit back a curse. Of course he was. But that was just luck for you. A capricious mistress at best, one who would give you a break every now and then but mostly just screwed you over time and time again. My bad luck was one of the most frustrating things about being an assassin. Because no matter how many times I reviewed someone's file, no matter how much I planned, no matter how careful I was, something inevitably came up that interrupted my schemes. Like a nosy event planner appearing at exactly the wrong moment.

"Come on," Meredith said, gesturing with her hand. "This way. Let's go."

"What's the rush?" I asked, still playing dumb and innocent.

She snorted. "You had the right idea to go get more champagne. Believe me when I tell you that you do not want these folks to be thirsty—or sober."

She clamped her hand on my arm and started dragging me down the hallway. An easy thing for her to do, given her dwarven strength. My hands tightened around my tray, and I considered bashing her over the head with it. But the flimsy metal wouldn't put so much as a dent in her thick skull. Besides, she wasn't my target, and collateral damage was something that Fletcher had taught me to avoid at all costs.

"Something wrong?" Meredith barked.

There was nothing I could do. Not without arousing even more of her suspicions, so I shook my head and let her march me down the hall in the opposite direction from Vaughn.

Meredith led me to the far side of the mansion where the kitchen was. That was bad enough, but she also watched while one of the wine stewards poured several fresh glasses of champagne and arranged them on my tray.

"You take that straight back to the dining room," she barked when the steward had finished. "And don't even *think* about stealing a glass for yourself. You're here to work. Not booze it up."

"Yes, ma'am," I drawled, grabbing the tray and hurrying away from her.

The whole thing only took five minutes, but that was enough time for me to completely lose track of Vaughn. I made it back to the spot where I'd last seen him and looked up and down the hallway, which was empty. I bit back another curse. Where had he gone?

I reined in my anger and thought about the floor plans for Dawson's mansion that Fletcher and I had reviewed earlier today. Vaughn had been moving down this hallway toward the west wing. If he was hooking up with a lover, there were plenty of bedrooms, sitting areas, and other secluded corners where a pair of paramours could meet and get down and dirty with each other. But Vaughn didn't strike me as the kind of guy to wander off and engage in a quickie, especially not at a business dinner. He was too solid, too sensible for that sort of thing. So whom could he be meeting, and where would they go? It had to be something important, something serious, for him to slip out of Dawson's soiree.

*The library,* I thought. That was the only other room in this part of the mansion where folks might have a quiet discussion that they wanted to go unnoticed by everyone else.

So I headed in that direction, careful to keep out of sight of the giants roaming the hallways. Like Vaughn, Tobias Dawson didn't have all that many guards, but I didn't want one to spot me and wonder what I was doing so far away from the dining room—or, worse, call for backup.

I made it to the library without any problems, although I was faced with one the second I got there: the double doors were closed.

I slowly, carefully, quietly tried the brass knobs, which were shaped like bison heads, but both doors were locked from the inside. Faint murmurs sounded on the other side of the heavy wood, and I was willing to bet that at least one of the folks in there was Vaughn. I wanted to see what he was up to, but I couldn't just barge in. Even if the doors hadn't been locked, my ditzy-waitress act wouldn't fly here, and that would be a one-way ticket to getting dead.

Yep, my bad luck was out in full force, and she was being a real bitch tonight.

I stood there, fuming for a few seconds, before I forced myself to dampen my frustration. I thought about the mansion's floor plans again. But I didn't remember there being any other entrance to the library, although there were several windows set into the back of the room—

A smile curved my lips. Windows. Of course.

Still carrying my tray of champagne, I hurried away from the doors and into the hallway that ran parallel to the library. A large window was at the end of the corridor. Perfect.

I put my tray down on the floor behind a table that was shaped like an oversize barrel, hoping that no one would notice it sitting there in the shadows. Then I opened the window and stuck my head outside.

The dining room and the library were both on the third floor, but for once, I was in luck, because a ledge ran beneath the window and continued on the entire length of the mansion. I calculated the distance from this window over to the next set, the ones in the library.

It looked to be about fifty feet over to those windows

and fifty feet down to the ground below. A troubling distance. If I slipped and fell, I might not have enough time to reach for my Stone magic to harden my skin before I hit the ground. If that happened, I'd break at least a few bones, if not my neck outright. And moaning and groaning from the pain would be a quick way to get noticed—and probably executed—by Dawson's guards.

Fletcher probably would have told me to close the window, scurry back to the dining room, and blend in with the rest of the servers. That this was a risky idea at best and a fatal one at worst. But it was worth the danger to see whom Vaughn was talking to. Besides, at least this way, I'd feel like I was actually *doing* something to help Charlotte, instead of just standing around, twiddling my thumbs, and watching Vaughn.

So I hoisted myself up and out the window.

Holding on to the sill, I scraped my boots down the stone until my toes touched the ledge, which was about three feet below the window. I moved to my left a few inches and then to my right, carefully testing my balance. The ledge was thin, no more than two inches wide and more of a pretty decoration than anything else, but it was sturdy enough to hold my weight. So I flattened my body against the wall, let go of the sill, and started tiptoeing toward my destination.

It was hard hugging the side of the mansion, especially since my fingers had nothing to grip but pitted stone. But I decided not to use my Stone magic to help me hold on. Vaughn might sense it, even through the thick walls, and I didn't want to give him any clue that I was watching him.

Inch by inch, foot by foot, I sidled closer to the library

windows, crawling my fingers over the stone and scooting my toes along the ledge. It was after eight now. A thunderstorm was blowing in from the west, and the hot summer wind whipped and howled around me, as jagged streaks of lightning danced across the darkening sky. I had a sudden image of a white fork bolting down from the thick, blue-gray clouds and frying me on the spot, leaving nothing behind but the black, smoking outline of my body on the wall, like a cartoon character.

I grimaced. Maybe this hadn't been quite as brilliant a plan as I'd thought. But I was more than halfway there, so I edged onward.

Finally, I made it over to the library windows. Once again, I was surprised with a bit of good luck in that the windows had been cracked open, probably to let some cool air from the approaching storm blow into the room. I hooked my arms over one of the black shutters so I would have a better grip and to take some of the pressure off my legs. When I felt steady enough, I peered around the edge of the shutter and in through the windows.

The library had the same rustic feel as the rest of the mansion, with lots of barrels, bison heads, and antlers decorating everything from the tables to the chairs to the light fixtures overhead. If I hadn't known better, I would have thought that Dawson was a cowboy instead of a miner. As expected, shelves filled with expensive-looking leather-bound books lined two of the walls, but my attention was drawn to the center of the room, where Vaughn was standing in front of an ornate wood-and-brass desk.

I hadn't expected Vaughn to be alone, but I was mildly surprised to see his son, Sebastian, standing by his side.

Sebastian's name was on the guest list, but I hadn't spotted him in the dining room. Perhaps he'd come straight here instead of stopping off for a drink.

Either way, the Vaughns looked like they were facing a firing squad. Both were stretched up to their full six-foot heights, their bodies stiff and tight with tension, their wary eyes fixed on someone sitting in the dark green leather chair behind the desk.

Tobias Dawson lounged on a sofa off to one side of the room, along with Elliot Slater. They must have left the dining room when I'd taken my forced detour to the kitchen. Both men looked far more relaxed than the Vaughns did.

"You can imagine my concern," a low, smoky feminine voice drifted out the cracked windows to me.

Vaughn dry-washed his hands a few times before he realized what he was doing. His hands stilled, and he clasped his fingers together to keep himself from repeating the nervous, worried motion. Sebastian's dark eyes flitted to his father, but that was his only reaction.

"I do understand your concern," Vaughn said, his voice stronger than I thought it would be, given his obvious apprehension. "But as I've told you repeatedly, I have no idea what happened. I've been over everything a dozen times—the materials, the work history, even the crew that did the job—and I can't find anything wrong. Not one single *thing*. I don't know why that terrace collapsed."

My eyes narrowed. They were talking about the accident at the restaurant, the one that had killed and injured so many people. The most likely reason that someone wanted Vaughn dead.

"Does it really matter why?" the woman asked.

Vaughn gave her a helpless look.

"Of course not," she answered her own question. "All that does matter is that it *did* happen. And now we need to find someone to blame for it."

For a moment, Vaughn's gaze cut to his son, but no one else seemed to notice. If Vaughn was capable of abusing his own daughter, I had no doubt that he would throw Sebastian to the wolves in front of him in order to save his own skin.

So he was a coward too. Another thing that made me want to kill him.

A rustle of silk sounded, and the woman in the chair gracefully rose to her feet. She wore a deep emerald-green gown that clung to her curves in all the right places, and a bit of gold glinted around her neck.

Vaughn and Sebastian both swallowed, as if they were afraid that the woman was going to snap her fingers and kill them on the spot. I wondered whom they could be more scared of than Slater, but I got my answer a moment later. The woman turned toward the windows, and I finally got a good look at her face.

Her coppery hair was smoothed back into a sleek bun, the bright color a stark contrast to the absolute blackness of her eyes. Her skin was pale and luminous, dotted here and there with faint freckles above the generous swell of her décolletage. But my gaze locked onto the necklace that ringed her throat: several dozen wavy golden rays with a large ruby set in the middle of the design. I recognized it—and her—immediately.

A sunburst, the symbol for fire, the personal rune of Mab Monroe.

# 5

Mab paused, almost as if she were posing to let everyone in the room get a good look at her in all her glory. Then she did the worst thing possible.

She walked toward the windows.

Mab moved closer and closer to the glass, her green gown rippling out like water around her, the fabric swirling away and then settling back against her body, every fold and drape perfectly in place once more. She walked slowly, carefully, deliberately, as though every step were a great debate of some sort—probably about whether Cesar and Sebastian lived or died.

And me too if she spotted me.

I froze, scarcely daring to breathe, but Mab kept coming and coming, heading right toward the windows—and me. Five more feet, and she'd see me hanging on to the shutter. It was no longer a matter of *if* she noticed me but *when*. Four feet . . . three . . . two . . . one . . .

Mab stopped.

She clasped her hands behind her back and peered straight out through the glass, her black eyes scanning the ominous clouds and the lightning that was still crackling in the distance.

I stayed exactly where I was, hanging on to the shutter, my toes perched on the ledge below the windows, not moving so much as a single muscle, not wanting to do anything that might catch her eye. I wouldn't have even breathed if I could have managed it.

Because if Mab noticed me, if she realized that I was eavesdropping, she would raise her hands and incinerate me with her Fire magic. Everyone knew that Mab was the most powerful person in Ashland. Some even said that she was the strongest elemental born in the last five hundred years. I might have scoffed at the rumors before but not now—because I could feel *exactly* how powerful she really was.

My magic was self-contained, in that another elemental couldn't sense that I had any power at all unless I was actively using it in some way, like making an Ice knife or shattering a bit of rock. But others, like Vaughn, continually emanated magic, like heat shimmering up from the pavement on a summer day, even when they weren't doing anything more strenuous than blinking.

And Mab did too.

The hot, pulsing feel of her power blasted right through the glass and stone that separated us, as though I had stuck my face into a furnace. Dozens of tiny, invisible needles stabbed into my skin, each one leaving behind a burning pinch of pain, and the sensation only intensified the longer she stared out the windows. My breath came in shallow pants, and sweat dripped down my face, streaming into my eyes. I bit my lip against the hot, phantom pain and focused on maintaining my grip on the shutter and the ledge, which was doubly hard now when all I wanted to do was let go, if only to get away from the horrid feel of her magic washing over me again and again.

Mab kept gazing out through the glass, as though she were contemplating all the secrets of the universe. All she had to do was turn her head to the left a few scant inches, and she would see me. I bit my lip again, but I stayed where I was, knowing that even the slightest movement might make her dark gaze shift to mine—and mean my death.

A minute passed, then two, then three, and still, Mab kept staring out the damn windows. My fingers twitched, my legs trembled, and my muscles ached from holding the same position for so long, but I stayed put. I didn't have any other choice.

At first, I wondered what Mab could possibly find so fascinating about the approaching storm, but then I realized that it was all just a ploy to make Vaughn and Sebastian sweat. It was working too, judging from the fine sheen of perspiration on Vaughn's forehead. I wondered if he could feel her Fire magic the same way that I could, and realized how easily she could scorch him to death with it.

Finally, Mab turned away from the glass and walked back toward the two men, taking the hot, stabbing feel of her magic with her. I let out a soft sigh of relief and slowly eased my fingers and toes this way and that, shifting my weight and trying to ease the burning sensation in my muscles. That had been the longest five minutes of my life.

"So the inspectors haven't found anything yet?" she asked.

Vaughn's head whipped back and forth as he hurried to reassure her. "No, nothing. Nothing to indicate that the accident was anything other than that."

"Nothing that you can be held accountable for as the builder?" Mab asked, her smoky voice dipping even lower.

He kept shaking his head. "No, nothing. Nothing at all. I've told you before, and I'll tell you again, *I* don't even know what happened. I don't know what went wrong. If I did know, I would tell you. I would tell everyone."

Mab studied him, her black eyes taking in everything from his clenched jaw to his stiff posture to the fact that he was dry-washing his hands again. Sebastian, Dawson, and Slater stayed where they were, as frozen as I had been a moment ago. They knew as well as I did that Cesar Vaughn's fate was hanging by a thread, one that Mab could char to ash if she wanted to, right here, right now.

"Well, then," Mab said. "I'll ask Jonah to look into things to make sure that you stay blameless in all of this. But if things take a turn for the worse, I may have to go through with my original plan to sever all ties with Vaughn Construction. And you know what that would mean."

Vaughn couldn't hide the shudder that rippled through his body. "Of course. I understand."

Yeah, we all knew exactly what Mab meant—that Vaughn would be the one to suffer if anything else happened that displeased her in the slightest way.

Fletcher didn't need me to kill Vaughn. Neither did whoever had hired us. Mab would probably take care of Vaughn herself in a few more days, maybe weeks, if he was lucky.

"I'm glad we understand each other." Mab smiled at him, but the only warmth in her face was the Fire magic burning in her eyes, making them seem as dark and hot as two black, smoking coals. "For your sake, I hope that the building inspectors continue to find you . . . blameless."

Vaughn paled, his tan skin taking on a sickly, sallow tint, but he slowly squared his shoulders and gave her a respectful nod.

Her warning delivered, Mab swept past Vaughn, unlocked the doors, threw them open, and strolled out of the library, with Dawson and Slater getting to their feet and trailing along behind her.

Vaughn and Sebastian stared at the open doors. Then Vaughn stumbled forward, clutched the back of a nearby chair, and sagged against it. He plucked a white silk handkerchief from the breast pocket of his suit jacket and dabbed the sweat off his forehead. But he was made of sterner stuff than I thought, because he tucked the bit of damp silk away and straightened back up.

"Well, that went about as well as could be expected," he grumbled. "I suppose I should be grateful that she didn't use her Fire magic on me to really make her point."

"Well, there is that small favor," Sebastian drawled.

Vaughn eyed his son, as if he was surprised by his snarky tone, but he didn't respond. Instead, he paced back and forth before striding past the desk and walking over to the windows, coming even closer to the glass than Mab had.

I grimaced and gripped the shutter and ledge more tightly, trying to press myself even closer against the wall so that he wouldn't look to his left and see me hanging right next to him. What was it with everyone coming over to stare moodily out through the glass tonight? You'd think that they'd never seen the great outdoors before.

Sebastian strode over and put his hand on his father's shoulder.

"It needs to stop, Papa," Sebastian said, his voice kinder than it had been before. "You need to stop blaming yourself for what happened at that restaurant. You did nothing wrong. When the inspectors release their report and say so, everyone else will realize it too. It was just an accident, just a freak occurrence, nothing more. There's no one to blame, nothing you could have done to stop it, and nothing you can do to make it right now."

His impassioned words showed his loyalty to his father, even if Vaughn didn't deserve it. I wondered if Sebastian knew what his father was doing to Charlotte, how Cesar was hurting her whenever the mood struck him. I wondered what he would think of his beloved papa then.

Vaughn shrugged off his son's hand. "We'll see what the inspectors find. Until then, I'm not discounting any possibility. Perhaps a bad batch of materials got mixed in with what I had ordered, after all. It could still be my fault, whether I know it or not. All of those people, their families . . . their loss, their pain, their suffering . . . it could still be because of me."

The sad, wounded, defeated tone in Vaughn's voice

made me frown. He seemed genuinely upset by all the deaths and injuries that had resulted from the terrace collapse. Not how I would have expected him to feel, but maybe the guilt had finally overwhelmed his greed, if he had, in fact, cut corners on the job. But it didn't much matter. My assignment was to kill him, not speculate about who wanted him dead.

Vaughn turned away from the windows. "Anyway, I must return to the dinner. I wouldn't want the others to think that something is wrong."

"Oh, no," Sebastian drawled again. "We wouldn't want that."

Cesar gave his son another odd look, then strode out of the library. Sebastian followed him, although he was walking much more slowly.

Since there was nothing else to do or see here, I let go of the shutter, gripped the stone with my fingers again, and headed back in the direction from which I'd originally come.

The climb back was much quicker, and I made it across the wall and in through the open window without any problems. Dust and dirt from the stone had smeared across my white tuxedo vest and black pants, and I wiped it off the best I could, hoping that no one would notice the faint stains or the tiny tears in the white silk from where bits of rock had scraped against the thin material. I also untucked my shirt and used the ends to wipe the sweat off my face before stuffing the fabric back down into my pants again.

When I was more or less presentable, I headed toward the end of the hallway. I'd gone ten feet before I realized that I'd forgotten the most important thing: the tray of champagne that I was supposed to have been circulating through the dining room twenty minutes ago.

I grumbled, turned around, and grabbed the tray from where I'd set it down on the floor. I hoisted it into position in the crook of my elbow and scurried down the hallway toward the main corridor. I was about to round the corner when someone stepped into view in front of me.

Sebastian Vaughn.

# ☀ 6 ☀

Sebastian stopped, as surprised to see me as I was to see him. He must have dawdled in the library longer than I'd thought.

We stared at each other for several seconds before I finally managed to do the appropriate thing and extend the serving tray out to him.

"Champagne, sir?"

Sebastian blinked, as if my offering him a drink was somehow surprising, but he grabbed a glass of bubbly. Well, actually, it wasn't quite as bubbly now as when it had been poured in the kitchen, but I was hoping that he wouldn't notice—or wonder what I was doing here.

"Thank you," he murmured.

I nodded and stepped to one side, ready to make my exit.

He spoke again. "Tell me, what are you doing in this part of the mansion? I thought that everyone was supposed to be in the dining room already."

My hands tightened around the tray. No such luck. Of course not.

I couldn't tell him the truth, so I did my best ditzy, embarrassed grimace. "I, ah, got a little turned around going from the kitchen to the dining room. All of these hallways look the same, especially with all of the lassos, guns, and creepy animal heads."

I gestured at the head of a longhorn cattle that hung on the wall and let out an exaggerated mock shiver, as though the sight scared me to death. Actually, I felt sorry for the poor critter. What a sad, sad fate, going from wandering with your herd to being stuffed and mounted in some rich man's house.

Sebastian frowned, as if he didn't believe my story, so I upped the wattage on my smile, nodded again, and started to ease past him. "Anyway, I really need to be getting back. Wouldn't want to get fired just for getting lost. So please excuse me, sir . . ."

A grin flitted across his face. "Don't call me *sir*. I can't be that much older than you."

I wasn't sure what to say, and I especially wasn't sure what to make of the frank, assessing way he was staring at me, almost like he was . . . intrigued by me. But that couldn't be right. I'd "worked" dozens of dinners and had run into more guys like Sebastian Vaughn than I cared to remember. The only things most of them were interested in was how much liquor I could serve them, how fast, and if I was willing to let them fuck me in some dark corner to help pass the time.

The answer to that last question was always a loud, resounding *no*. Most of the guys shrugged and moved on to the next waitress, but there were a few who didn't want to take no for an answer. But they soon realized that the shattered edge of a champagne glass made for an excellent weapon and that maybe they shouldn't fuck with the help after all—because the help might just fuck back with them.

But Sebastian kept staring at me, his interest growing instead of waning, so I tried to figure out what sort of game he was playing. I'd thought before that he resembled a younger version of his father, with his black hair, tan skin, and brown eyes. That was true, but the pictures in Fletcher's file didn't do Sebastian justice. No mere photo could adequately capture the absolute perfection of his features, his straight nose, the slight curve of his lips, the square set of his jaw, the faint flecks of amber in his deep, dark mahogany gaze. Not to mention the way his suit draped over his lean figure, hinting at all of the smooth, supple muscles that lay underneath the fabric.

I breathed in, catching a whiff of his cologne, a spicy, heady scent with a soft, sweet note that made me think of roses. Somehow, though, the floral combination only made him seem more masculine. Oh, yes, I'd thought Sebastian Vaughn handsome enough in the photos, and again when I'd spotted him in the library, but in person, face-to-face, he was simply . . . *dazzling*.

Especially given the way he was looking at me, with such intent interest, as though I were the most important person in all of Ashland. As an assassin, I was used to blending into the shadows, disappearing into the darkness, no one ever seeing me until it was far too late—for him. It was a bit disconcerting to be the focus of so much attention, especially when that attention came in such an attractive package. But it was also kind of flattering. Fun, even.

Still, I had a job to do—as a waitress and otherwise— and I couldn't afford to be away from the dining room any longer. I didn't want to get yelled at for slacking off by Meredith, the event planner, but I also didn't want Fletcher to worry about me. And he would worry. He *always* worried, about *everything*.

So I gave Sebastian a bright smile and started down the hallway a third time. But he stopped me again, this time going so far as to step directly into my path. I pulled up short, the glasses on my tray rattling ominously, but I managed to keep from spilling any of the champagne, which would have been a worse offense than disappearing from the dining room.

"What's your name?" Sebastian asked, his tone sounding genuinely curious.

I should have been annoyed with him, but his voice was as perfect as the rest of him, low and strong, with a bit of a deep bass that rumbled through each and every one of his words. The sort of voice that you could sit and listen to for hours.

I thought about it, but I didn't see the harm in telling him. I'd probably never see him again after tonight. Besides, I doubted that Sebastian lacked for female attention. He wasn't the sort of guy who would remember a waitress, not even a lost one like me. I was a momentary distraction, a faint curiosity, something to alleviate his boredom for a few minutes before he returned to the dinner. Nothing more. Funny, though, how that cold reality made a faint twinge of longing stir in my heart, longing to step out of the shadows, longing to be something *more*.

"Gin," I finally said. "My name is Gin."

"Jen?"

"No, Gin."

He frowned. "Gen?"

I shook my head. I had this same problem every time I told someone my name. Everyone always thought my name was something other than what it was. Frustrated, I shifted on my feet. The motion made a few bubbles fizz up in the champagne on my tray. A thought struck me.

"Gin," I finally said, nodding my head at the glasses. "My name is Gin, like the liquor." I hesitated. "Well, not *this* liquor, exactly, but you get the idea."

His face cleared. "Oh, that makes sense."

Well, if I'd known it was that easy, I would have started introducing myself like this to people years ago.

"So, Gin," Sebastian said, his voice taking on a light, teasing note, "what's a pretty girl like you doing working as a waitress? You should be drinking champagne instead."

He raised his glass and toasted me, giving me a sly wink before his lips drew back into a small, knowing, devastating smile. Seriously, he practically oozed sex appeal, the way Mab Monroe had Fire magic, although being this close to Sebastian was far more enjoyable. Not even Finn was that charming, cute—or confident.

For a moment, I was dazzled speechless by him, but then I shook away the fairy-tale idea, the appealing mirage that he could somehow be attracted to me.

"Look, you're cute and all, but I don't date guys I meet at work."

His smile widened, the expression causing a bit of heat to simmer in my veins. "Cute? Just cute? Is that all? I was hoping for handsome, at the very least."

Despite my exasperation, I couldn't help but return his smile. "Okay, okay, you're handsome, sophisticated, gorgeous, even. Happy now?"

He quirked an eyebrow. "Gorgeous?" He thought about it. "Yeah, that sounds about right."

My smile sharpened. "Egotistical too."

With most guys, that would have ended the flirting right then and there, but not with Sebastian. The suave smile never slipped from his face, despite my pointed insult. Instead, he toasted me with his glass again. He didn't back down from me, which made me like him more.

"Beautiful and witty," he murmured. "I approve. But my earlier question stands. What are you doing working as a waitress?"

I shrugged. "It's what I do. Here, there, everywhere."

"Oh. You have a day job too?"

"Yeah, at a restaurant downtown."

It was one thing to give him my first name, but that was as much info as I was willing to share. Fletcher always said that the best lies were mostly truth, and being a poor, working-stiff waitress fit in perfectly with the persona I'd developed for tonight. Besides, I could always have the bad luck of running into him at another party. On the off chance that Sebastian did remember me, all he would recall was some vague, slightly flirty conversation we'd had about my being a waitress. Nothing personal and certainly nothing important.

Nothing that would give him any clue to what I was planning to do to his father.

"Maybe I can come by your restaurant sometime," he said. "Take you out after your shift is over."

I snorted.

"What?"

I gave him a flat look. "Guys like you don't go out with girls like me. At least, not for very long."

"How long is not very?"

I snorted again. "Just long enough for you to get what you want, before moving on to the next girl. You might slum it for a few weeks out in the suburbs or even down in Southtown, if you're feeling especially dangerous, but guys like you always go back to your rich Northtown honeys sooner or later. Besides, you wouldn't want to risk pissing off Daddy and having him cut off access to your trust fund. No girl's worth that, right?" By the time I finished, my voice was dripping with venom, disdain, and sarcasm.

His eyes glittered. "Well, maybe I'm an exception."

I shrugged. "Maybe. But it doesn't much matter."

Sebastian stepped even closer to me, his voice dropping to a low, husky murmur. "Doesn't it? Wouldn't you like to find out? Because I certainly want to know more about you, Gin."

I should have given him another derisive snort. Should have made some harsh, biting comment about his lame lines. Should have shoved past him and headed back to the dining room without another word. But something in his intense gaze made me hold my tongue, something in his handsome face made me take another look at him, and something in his tall, strong stance made me want to put my tray down, run my hands over his shoulders, and see if his muscles were as firm as they looked.

Sebastian must have sensed my hesitation, because he reached out, gently tugging on the end of my dark brown ponytail. "You know," he said in that same husky tone, "I bet you would look even more amazing with your hair down."

"Certainly. But that's something you'll never find out."

Sebastian grinned and clutched his hands over his heart in mock exaggeration, as though I'd mortally wounded him with my words. If only he knew how easily I could do that with one of the knives tucked up my sleeves, he wouldn't be giving me such smoldering looks. No, he would have been sweating, screaming, and running away from me as fast as he could.

Of course, I wasn't exactly being smart right now either. I should have meekly excused myself from this conversation long ago, not stood here trading mocking insults and flirty banter with the son of the man I was planning to kill. Fletcher had taught me better than that. He would have been horrified by how many of his rules I'd broken in the last five minutes: Don't be memorable. Don't do anything to attract attention to yourself. Don't engage potential enemies or targets in any way.

But for some reason, tonight, I just didn't care about the old man's rules.

Maybe it was how handsome Sebastian looked with the light glinting off his black hair. Maybe it was the way he focused all of his attention on me. Or maybe it was the simple fact that I enjoyed being with someone who actually gave as good as he got. But I liked talking to him—far more than I should have.

Other waiters and waitresses enjoyed quick dalliances with guests at these dinners all the time. Tonight, for the first time, I wanted my own seven minutes of heaven, and it took me longer than it should have to quash this wild, reckless feeling that Sebastian stirred in me.

He gave my ponytail another gentle tug. "I don't know, Gin," he murmured again, his dark gaze locking with my light one. "I can be *very* persuasive when I put my mind to it."

And I could be *very* deadly, although I didn't tell him that. Instead, I tightened my grip on my tray.

"I'm sure you can be . . . on some other girl. Now, I really have to get back to work. Please excuse me."

This time, I finally did move past him, careful not to spill the champagne. I strode down the corridor as fast as I could without rattling the delicate glasses. All the while, though, I was aware of Sebastian standing behind me, and it almost seemed like I could feel his eyes on me, tracking the soft swing of my hips. More heat simmered through my veins at the thought of him watching me.

"You're going to change your mind about me, Gin," he called out. "I'll come by your restaurant and take you out one night. Count on it."

I reached the end of the corridor. The smart thing would have been to keep right on walking, but I stopped and turned around to face him.

"I never count on anything. Especially not promises from cute rich guys."

He grinned. "Not just cute. Gorgeous, remember?"

Oh, yes. Sebastian Vaughn was far too handsome and far too egotistical for his own good. Still, I found myself grinning back at him before I shook my head and hurried around the corner.

I made it back to the dining room without running into anyone else, including Meredith, the event planner. The cocktail portion of the evening had come to a close while I'd been talking to Sebastian, and I had to hustle over to where the chefs were set up so I could get in line with the other servers.

Sebastian came strolling into the room a minute later. His gaze zoomed over to me, and he flashed me another cocky grin. A few of the other waitresses gave me sour looks, no doubt thinking that I'd been off fucking one of the guests instead of doing my job and jealous that it had been someone as handsome as Sebastian. I ignored their petty stares and disapproving sniffs. Let them think what they wanted to. It didn't matter to me in the slightest.

But there was one person's opinion that I did care about—Fletcher's—and the hard set of his wrinkled features told me that he wasn't too happy with me. He stabbed his index finger at me, then jerked it to the right. I sighed, knowing that I was probably going to get a lecture, but I followed him over to the far end of the serving line, out of earshot of the other chefs and waiters.

"Where have you been?" he asked, plucking the champagne flutes off my tray and replacing them with baskets of hot buttered bread. "I was getting worried."

"Recon," I murmured. "Vaughn snuck off to have a secret meeting with Mab Monroe in the library."

I glanced around, but I didn't see Mab in the dining room, although Dawson and Slater had both returned and taken seats at the head of the table. I wondered if the Fire elemental had left as soon as she'd delivered her threats to Vaughn. While Fletcher piled baskets of bread onto my tray, I quickly and quietly told him everything that Mab had said to Vaughn and all the shaky promises that he'd made to her in return. Fletcher would want to know, and I hoped that the intel would cut off any potential lecture before it ever got started.

"Do you think that Mab is behind the hit on Vaughn after all?" I asked when I'd finished.

Fletcher put a final basket of bread on my tray. "I'm not sure. I wouldn't put it past her, but she usually prefers to do that sort of dirty work herself. She likes the message that it sends to all of her enemies about how powerful she is. Besides, if she really wanted Vaughn dead, she could have used her magic, killed him in the library, and gotten Slater and Dawson to dispose of his charred remains. I'll see if I can find out any more information about who wants Vaughn dead. Now, scoot. You can tell me the rest of it on the drive home."

"The rest of what?"

He arched his eyebrows. "Like why Sebastian Vaughn is eyeing you like you're part of the dinner menu."

I should have known that I couldn't get anything past Fletcher. He could be annoyingly perceptive at times. I also knew better than to glance over my shoulder, but I did it anyway. Sebastian was staring at me. He raised his wineglass to me in salute before giving me another sly wink. Heat flooded my cheeks, and I had a difficult time looking Fletcher in the eye.

"It's nothing," I mumbled. "I ran into him in the hallway outside the library when I was heading back this way. He flirted with me, so I flirted back so he wouldn't think too much about what I was doing there. That's all."

Fletcher didn't say anything, but disapproval radiated off him like the heat from the bread. He didn't tell me that I should have known better, that he had taught me better, because we both knew that he had. One of the keys to being an assassin was being as invisible as possible. Not only when you did the actual hit on your target but also in all the moments leading up to that final, fatal one.

More than one assassin had been caught because he'd made himself too visible in the target's world. Like being the recently hired mechanic who'd worked on the target's car hours before the brakes had catastrophically failed and the car had plunged off the side of a mountain road. Or being the new pool boy when the target had slipped, hit his head, and drowned in the shallow end. Or even being seen out on a date with the target the night he mysteriously got mugged and beaten to death walking home from dinner.

Killing someone was easy—getting away with it was what was truly challenging.

"I'm sorry," I said. "I thought that it wouldn't hurt to talk to him. He probably would have thought it odder if I had completely brushed him off."

I didn't add that Sebastian had seemed to enjoy our conversation as much as I had or the promise that he'd made to track me down for a date. Fletcher would have pulled me off the job immediately if he'd known about any of that. But I was going to be the one to kill Vaughn, not him. I *wanted* to be the one to do the hit, for Charlotte's sake.

"All right," Fletcher replied. "You did the best you could. I know his type. A pretty boy who thinks that he's entitled to whatever he wants. Just ignore him. He'll move on to someone else soon enough."

I nodded, picked up the tray of bread, and hurried over to the table with it. I moved behind the row of guests, stopping every few feet to deposit baskets in the appropriate spots. All too soon, though, I reached Sebastian's seat. Instead of ignoring me like all the other diners had, he turned in his chair and took the basket from me, his fingers brushing against mine for the briefest instant.

Once again, that strange, unwanted heat flooded my face, before the flush spread down my neck, but it was nothing compared with the warmth racing through the rest of my body. Sebastian noticed my embarrassment, and his lips curved up into a smile. I hurried on with the rest of the bread, but all the while, I was aware of his gaze on me, and I couldn't help but glance in his direction. He was still staring at me, that same small, satisfied smile on his face, his eyes dark with some sort of secret triumph.

I swallowed and continued with my serving duties, but I couldn't help but think that ignoring Sebastian Vaughn was easier said than done.

## * 7 *

The rest of the night passed by in a blur—except for the heated looks that Sebastian kept giving me.

His gaze stayed on me most of the evening, long enough that his father noticed and started frowning, as though he didn't like the thought of his son making googly eyes at a lowly waitress. I wondered if Vaughn would have changed his mind if he knew exactly who and what I was.

Probably not.

But I kept my head down and blended in with the other waiters, serving soup, salad, and the main course, which was some sort of seared bear steak that Dawson had flown in special from Alaska. Naturally. I wondered if he'd gone out there and killed the bears himself so he could add their heads to his collection.

Finally, three hours later, I cleared away the remains of the dessert course, the chocolate soufflés that Fletcher had made earlier, along with fresh summer berries topped with a light, airy vanilla bean pudding and garnished with thin, crispy shortbread cookies. The party was over, and Dawson stood by the open doors, shaking hands with his guests as they headed out to their limos, which were waiting in the front drive to whisk them back to their own mansions.

Sebastian hesitated, like he wanted to come over and flirt with me one final time, but his father clapped his hand on his son's shoulder and led him out of the room. Good. That was good, despite the strange sense of disappointment that filled me. I didn't know why I felt that way. Sebastian Vaughn wasn't the first pretty boy ever to chat me up, but he'd definitely made more of an impression than most.

Fletcher and I helped the rest of the staff clean up, and it was after one in the morning when we got into his van and left Dawson's estate. We drove in silence for about ten minutes before the old man spoke.

"I shouldn't have to say this," Fletcher began, a small note of reproach in his voice. "But you need to stay away from Sebastian Vaughn."

I sighed. "Like I told you before, we talked outside the library. That's all."

"That didn't look like all it was in the dining room. The two of you were staring at each other all through dinner."

I sank a little lower in my seat and crossed my arms over my chest. "It's nothing," I repeated. "He was having a little fun. Amusing himself with the help. You know how it goes."

"And what were *you* doing?"

I rolled my eyes. "So maybe I was having a little fun too. A cute guy wanted to talk to me. Sue me for enjoying the attention. But that's all it was. He won't even remember what I look like tomorrow."

"Maybe," Fletcher murmured. "Maybe not. Either way, things are starting to get complicated. I don't like how exposed you were tonight. Vaughn noticed you too, or at least he noticed his son staring at you. I think it's time to pull the plug on the job, return the up-front money, and tell the client to find someone else."

I straightened up. "No! You can't do that."

"Why not?"

Charlotte's sorrowful face filled my mind.

"Because . . . because . . . it would be unprofessional," I finished in a weak voice. "You told the client that you would do the job—that *I* would do the job. You can't back out now. Besides, we're trying to build up my reputation as an assassin, remember? I'm finally starting to make a quiet name for myself, and my asking price is slowly rising. Passing on this job will set us back months."

"Is this about protecting your burgeoning reputation as the Spider or something else?"

"What else would it be about?"

"Charlotte Vaughn."

Damn. No, that one word wasn't enough to adequately express my surprise and frustration. Damn . . . and . . . and . . . double damn. I should have known that I couldn't hide anything from Fletcher, especially not my own murky motivations. Still, that didn't keep me from trying.

"Of course not," I insisted. "I don't make jobs be about people, and I don't let anyone's situation influence me in any way, shape, or form. Book the assignment, do the research, complete the hit, take the money, and walk away. That's what assassins do. That's what *you've* taught me to do as the Spider. Nothing else matters."

"Not even a girl being abused?" Fletcher asked again in a soft, knowing voice. "Being hurt like you were hurt, Gin?"

Every muscle in my body tightened with tension, until I felt like a taut bow string about to snap from the strain. The memories roared up in my mind, trying to crack my calm façade from the inside out. Memories of heat and smoke and fire and death and, most of all, the unending, unrelenting, unbearable agony in my hands. The spider rune scars embedded in my palms itched and burned with the phantom pain, the way they so often did when I thought about that horrible night and the torture that I'd endured. But I didn't give in to the searing sensation and start rubbing the marks. Instead, I made myself slowly flatten my palms against my legs and kept my features schooled into a perfect mask of blank indifference.

Fletcher had never really asked what had happened to my family or how I'd ended up living on the streets with silverstone branded into my hands, although I suspected that he'd found out on his own. The violent, gruesome deaths of the Snow family had been big news at the time, and it wouldn't have been too hard for him to connect the thin, ragged homeless girl digging through the Dumpsters behind the Pork Pit with Genevieve Snow, the middle daughter who'd supposedly perished in the fiery collapse of the family mansion, along with her mother and two sisters.

But he'd never asked, and I'd never told him. Fletcher respected my privacy that way, just as I respected his. The old man had his secrets, and I had mine, and we both had enough care, concern, and love for each other not to try to uncover them. Or at least to pretend that we weren't secretly prying and to keep all the facts that we did discover to ourselves.

"Gin?" Fletcher asked. "Is this about Cesar Vaughn? Or you and Charlotte?"

I turned so he could see how cold and hard my gray eyes were. "It's about doing the job, getting paid, and walking away. Nothing else. Now, are we going to talk about how I can best get close to Vaughn, or do you want to discuss my *feelings* some more?"

Fletcher stared at me, watching the play of light and shadow on my face. Given the late hour, there was darkness more than anything else. There always was.

"All right," he said, the earlier reproach in his voice melting into tired resignation. "Tell me everything you learned from watching Vaughn tonight."

Fletcher quizzed me about Vaughn the rest of the ride home, but he seemed satisfied with my answers. Yeah, maybe I'd been a bit more charmed by Sebastian than I should have, but I'd been there to do recon on my target, and I'd followed through with that.

I *always* did what was needed.

He pulled into the driveway, and we stepped into the house and went our separate ways. Fletcher ambled back to the den to watch some TV and unwind before going to bed, while I headed upstairs and took a long, hot shower.

As I brushed out my wet hair, I couldn't help but lean closer to the bathroom mirror and peer at my own reflection, trying to see myself through Sebastian's eyes. Oh, I was pretty enough, with my dark brown hair, pale skin, and gray eyes, but I was certainly no great beauty. Not like my mother, Eira, and Annabella had been, with their golden hair, rosy skin, and cornflower-blue eyes. And Bria would have been even more beautiful than both of them, if she'd gotten the chance to grow up.

My body was lean, fit, and strong, thanks to all the years training with Fletcher and then my time on the job as the Spider. My breasts weren't large, but they were decent enough, and I had a few soft curves here and there. All put together, it was a nice package, but I didn't know that it was enough to hook someone like Sebastian Vaughn and get him to look past my seeming lack of money, magic, and social standing—at least, not for very long.

But the way he'd smiled, laughed, and flirted with me . . . no man had looked at me like that . . . well, ever, really. Oh, I got enough attention from the guys at Ashland Community College, where I took some classes, but all they were interested in was banging me in between beers and ballgames. And the professors, well, they just wanted to feel young again by sleeping with a coed. Neither option exactly screamed romance. But more important, no one had really seemed interested in *me*, and absolutely none of them had sparked my own interest like Sebastian had.

But Fletcher was right. It was stupid to daydream about having any sort of relationship with Sebastian. Someone had hired me to kill his father. Not exactly the sort of thing that you looked for in a potential girlfriend.

Girlfriend? I snorted. What was I thinking? I'd never had that sort of relationship with any guy. I'd accused Sebastian of being a love-'em-and-leave-'em type, but the truth was that I was that way too. I had to be, as the Spider. And not just because I didn't want to end up dead or in jail for my many crimes. Because what kind of guy would ever really be okay with his girlfriend being a cold-hearted assassin?

Still, as I left the bathroom, put on my pajamas, and slid into bed, I couldn't help but think back to the warm interest in Sebastian's eyes, his teasing grins, and all the sly, saucy winks he'd given me during dinner. For once, I let myself remember. Not only that, but I reveled in the memories, replaying them over and over again in my mind.

Even though nothing would ever come of it, even though nothing *could* ever come of it, it was still nice to be noticed, to be admired, to be *wanted*, if only for an evening.

I went to sleep with a smile on my lips.

## 8

Over the next few days, I plotted the best way to kill Cesar Vaughn.

Where to do the job, how to get close to him, how to actually kill him and then slip away after the fact. I reviewed all of the information that Fletcher had given me, then went out and collected my own, discreetly following Vaughn as he went about his days, seeing what his routines were, how much security he had, and what his vices were, if he even had any. I wanted to go to his home the night after the dinner party and kill him, but Fletcher put his foot down, talking about "procedure" and "caution." Whatever. I gave in, if only because I knew that he would cancel the hit entirely if I didn't, and I wanted to protect Charlotte from her father.

But Vaughn was indeed the upstanding, hardworking, hands-on businessman that he appeared to be. After a quick visit to his office in the morning, he spent most of the day driving around Ashland, going from one construction site to the next and checking on his crews and their progress, before grabbing a quick lunch somewhere on the road.

This was the third day that I was following him, and I didn't think anything of it when he parked his car on one of the downtown streets, got out, and started ambling along the sidewalk. It was lunchtime, so he was probably on the prowl for some sort of vittles before going to the next job site. But as he walked by restaurant after restaurant, passing up everything from Mexican to Italian to Thai food, my unease slowly cranked up notch by notch by notch. Because Vaughn was rapidly running out of dining options in this part of town, unless he was in the mood for one thing in particular.

Barbecue.

Sure enough, he headed straight for the Pork Pit, opened the door, and stepped inside.

I was so surprised that I stopped cold in the middle of the sidewalk and would have stayed that way if someone hadn't bumped my shoulder, snapping me out of my shock. I hurried out of the flow of traffic on the sidewalk, but I stayed outside the restaurant, pretending to be talking on my cell phone, when I was really peering in through the storefront windows, wondering if I'd somehow been made, if Vaughn had figured out that I was following him, who I was, where I worked, and that I had plans to kill him as soon as I could.

My heart pounded, and a bit of nervous sweat gathered at the nape of my neck as I watched him walk to the back of the restaurant and take a seat at the counter, three stools down from where Fletcher was sitting behind the cash register.

Vaughn leaned over toward Fletcher, as though he were going to talk to him.

I tensed up a little more. This was bad, so very, very bad. . . .

He stretched his hand out toward Fletcher as though he were trying to get the old man's attention.

I sucked in a worried breath, wondering what I could do to get us out of this situation. . . .

Vaughn grabbed a menu that someone had left on the counter and leaned back, away from Fletcher.

I collapsed against the window in relief.

Fletcher must have seen Vaughn reach for the menu, because he looked up from his battered copy of *Where the Red Fern Grows*, which he'd had for as long as I could remember and which he read at least once a year. Fletcher started to go back to his story but did a double take when he recognized Vaughn. His gaze lingered on the other man a moment before cutting over to the windows. Fletcher spotted me lurking outside and raised his eyebrows in a silent question. I winced and then shrugged. As far as I could tell, Vaughn had a hankering for barbecue—nothing else. Otherwise, he would have confronted Fletcher already. Or called the cops. Or both.

Still, my nerves were frayed, and I tapped my fingers on the brick wall, like a junkie in need of a fix, as I watched Sophia whip up my target's barbecue pork sandwich, potato salad, onion rings, and lemonade. If I knew that he would come back for lunch one day soon, I could always slip something into his food, then let nature take its course. Poison wasn't my favorite method of execution. In fact, I thought it was rather sneaky, low-down, and cowardly, but you went with what worked. But there wasn't any pattern to Vaughn's lunch habits that I could see, so I couldn't count on him returning to the restaurant.

Besides, poison was too good a death for someone who enjoyed hurting his own daughter.

Either way, I was infinitely relieved when Vaughn finished his meal and left the Pork Pit without incident. I knew that I'd dodged a bullet, which was rather ironic, since I was the assassin here, not him.

After that, Vaughn spent the afternoon touring more job sites before heading back to his office. He never left work before eight at night, and he was always back by nine the next morning to start again. And it was rinse and repeat, with the same general routine every day that I watched him.

So I formulated my approach, secured my supplies, and made sure that my knives were good and sharp. I also reviewed my plan with Fletcher, who offered some suggestions, the biggest of which was that we postpone the job, at least until he figured out exactly who the client was.

"Seriously, what are we waiting for?" I asked him when he told me that one night at home.

I'd spent the day wasting time and watching Vaughn *again*, instead of moving in and finishing things. So I was in a bit of a mood.

"I'm trying to be smart about things," Fletcher replied, his voice far more even than mine was. "You should too, Gin."

I threw my hands up and stalked from one side of the den to the other. "I've been watching the man for days now. Trust me. Everything's fine, and everything will be even better once I do the job. I know what I'm doing. Can't you just trust me?"

Fletcher pressed his lips together, as though he wanted to say something but was holding back his words.

Well, I supposed that answered my question about trust. Hurt shot through me, along with more than a little anger, and I slapped my hands on my hips.

"Forget about the money and who the client is for a second. Do you want to see Charlotte's obituary in the newspaper?" I snapped. "Because I sure don't. But that could happen any day. As long as Vaughn is alive, she's in danger. So let's do this so she is at least safe. Okay?"

Yeah, it was a low blow, throwing Charlotte in his face like that, and I'd basically admitted that she was the reason that I wanted to do the job, but I didn't care. Fletcher might not trust me, but I *would* protect Charlotte, with or without his blessing.

Fletcher sighed, but he finally gave one sharp nod of his head.

I nodded back, already planning the hit for tomorrow.

It was three in the afternoon the next day, and I was working my usual shift at the Pork Pit as though I weren't planning on murdering someone that night. That was another thing Fletcher had taught me. Stick to your regular routines as much and for as long as possible, especially if you knew that you were going to be up to no good later on. Hard for the cops to connect the waitress who'd casually gone about her work with a cold-blooded assassin. A good cover took years to build, and I had too much invested in Gin Blanco to do anything stupid enough to attract more attention to her than absolutely necessary.

I had finished clearing away the dirty dishes and was wiping down the counter from my latest customers when the bell over the front door chimed. I plastered a smile on my face and looked up, ready to greet the newcomers. But my smile froze, then plummeted off my lips like an icicle cracking off a roof, as I realized exactly who had walked through the door.

Sebastian.

He was even more gorgeous than I remembered, even though he was dressed down in a pair of expensive jeans, boots, and a short-sleeved black polo shirt that brought out the beautiful tan color of his skin. The shirt was tucked into his jeans, showing off his lean waist and trim, muscled figure.

He turned and held out his hand, as though he were about to pull someone inside with him. A date, most likely. My heart sank even quicker than my smile had at the thought that he had brought another girl here, especially after he'd teased me about taking me out.

A girl did step inside the restaurant with him, but it wasn't the sweet blond thing I expected—it was Charlotte.

She was even prettier in person than in the photos in Fletcher's file. Long black hair pulled up into pigtails, tan skin, and big, beautiful brown eyes. At thirteen, she was adorable. In a few more years, she'd be a real heartbreaker.

Still, Charlotte's gaze was dark and wary as she looked

around the restaurant, as if she expected something bad to happen amid the clusters of booths, tables, and chairs. Even more than that, I sensed an aching sadness in her, as if she'd already seen so many terrible things in her young life that she'd never, ever be able to get over them. As if she'd already suffered so many horrible hurts that nothing could ever soothe them.

I knew those feelings all too well.

Sebastian glanced around the restaurant, as though he was looking for someone. Could it be possible . . . could he be here . . . could he actually have kept his promise to come find me? My heart spiraled up at the thought, even as I tried to quiet the sudden, fierce longing that I felt for it to be true.

But sure enough, Sebastian's eyes locked with mine, and a wide smile split his face. He gave me a cheery wave before tugging Charlotte in my direction.

"Who's that schmuck?" a voice grumbled. "And why is he waving at you?"

I glanced at Finn, who was sitting on the stool closest to the cash register. He'd finally come to the Pork Pit for lunch, like he'd promised Fletcher, although the old man had decided to take the afternoon off and go fishing, since business had been so slow. Fletcher had left fifteen minutes ago. He'd asked Finn to go with him, but Finn had said no. The disappointment in the old man's face had made me want to smack the stupid out of Finn for taking his father for granted *again*.

"Is he here to see you?" Finn sniped again. "Is that your new boyfriend or something?"

"Shut up," I hissed. "He is *not* my boyfriend."

Finn gave me an assessing look, his green eyes bright and knowing. "Oh . . . but you'd like him to be, wouldn't you?"

All I could do was stand there and fume, giving Finn his answer.

"Well, well, well, things just got a *lot* more interesting around here," he drawled. "Think I'll stick around and see the splendor of young love."

I glared at him. "If you mess this up for me, you will *wish* that you had gone fishing with Fletcher. You should have gone anyway. All he wanted was to spend some time with you."

Finn's eyes narrowed. "Don't tell me what to do about the old man, Gin. Not when you're so hot and bothered to move out of his house and start your life of grand adventure."

I opened my mouth to snap at him again, but Sebastian stepped up to the counter, along with Charlotte. I ignored Finn and plastered a smile on my face, as though I didn't want to reach across the counter and strangle him with my bare hands.

"Surprised?" Sebastian grinned back at me. "I told you that I'd track you down, Gin."

Instead of letting him see my pleasure and surprise, I arched an eyebrow. "Yes, you did. And you actually followed through with it."

He gave a modest shrug. "It wasn't hard. I got the event planner for the dinner party to ask around. She heard from a waitress who heard from a cook who heard from another cook who said that you mentioned some barbecue place. I've heard my dad talk about how good the food is here, so I thought that I'd take a chance and see if this was you."

I had to keep myself from grimacing. I had made some offhand remark to one of the cooks that the Pork Pit was the best barbecue joint in Ashland, and Sebastian had connected the dots. Probably all he'd had to do to get Meredith to ferret out the information was smile at her the way he was smiling at me right now. Sloppy, Gin.

"Well, good for you," I drawled. "If I had a gold star, I'd stick one on your shirt."

He let out a low, throaty laugh that made my heart sputter and my anger evaporate. "And I see you're as sassy as ever."

His eyes met mine again, and I found myself admiring the bits of amber that shimmered in his dark brown gaze, the sparks and flashes of color so intense that they resembled flecks of pure, polished gold. Maybe it wasn't such a disaster that he'd tracked me down after all—

Finn snorted louder than a plow horse, breaking the spell. I dragged my attention away from Sebastian and focused on Charlotte, who was still holding on to her brother's hand and standing slightly behind him. That was a little odd for a teenage girl.

"Hi, sweetheart," I said. "My name's Gin. What's yours?"

Charlotte didn't answer, although she kept staring at me.

Sebastian slung his arm around her shoulder and hugged her to his side. "Don't mind Charlotte. My sister is just a little shy."

I gave the girl another smile. "Well, most folks are,

including me. Why don't y'all have a seat, and we'll get you some food?"

She studied me in that intense way that kids so often did, as if she could see all the secrets of my soul simply by staring into my eyes. After a moment, she slowly nodded.

My heart clenched, but I flashed her another smile. I couldn't change what had happened to Charlotte, how her own father had abused her, but I could make sure that she had a nice meal. Yeah, it wasn't much in the grand scheme of things—it wasn't anything, really—but it was all that I could do right now.

I'd take care of the more pressing problem of her father tonight.

Sebastian took a seat on one of the stools, while Charlotte hopped up onto the one next to Finn. Being the terrible flirt that he was, my foster brother fixed his attention on her. Finn didn't care how young or old, or cute or not, someone was, but if she was female, then he felt this obsessive need to charm her into liking him.

"How are you today, little lady?" he drawled.

Charlotte stared at him, something almost like fear sparking in her eyes.

"Don't mind him," I said, reaching across the counter to punch Finn on the shoulder. "He likes to tease all the pretty girls who come in."

Finn gave her a saucy wink. "And you're as pretty as that peach pie in the cake stand over there."

Charlotte looked at him for a few seconds longer before her face abruptly crinkled into a delighted smile. A delicate blush tinted her cheeks. She ducked her head and started fiddling with the end of one of her long black pigtails, but her gaze kept sliding back to him, and I knew that Finnegan Lane had struck again. I shook my head. Sometimes I thought that Finn could make friends with a surly grizzly just by telling the creature how shiny its coat was.

But Sebastian had a different reaction to Finn's light-hearted banter. He put his arm around Charlotte's shoulder, drawing her close to him again. She froze, her hand clamping around her own hair, and her smile vanished.

"Are you a friend of Gin's?" Sebastian asked, his voice tight with suspicion.

Finn grinned, but there was no warmth in the expression, just a lot of teeth. "Not a friend—her *brother*."

I rolled my eyes. Finn always introduced himself that way to any guys I brought around Fletcher's house or to the restaurant. I think he had some old-fashioned notion that giving guys the stink-eye would keep them from trying to get into my pants. Please. Finn wasn't that scary.

But I certainly was.

"Oh." Sebastian looked back and forth between the two of us, as if trying to see the familial resemblance. "Well, it's nice to meet you. I'm Sebastian Vaughn."

He held out his hand, which Finn shook a little too enthusiastically for my liking. Finn also held it longer than was necessary, squeezing Sebastian's hand for all he was worth. Finn noticed me glaring at him again. I drew my finger in a subtle slash across my throat, telling him exactly what I was going to do to him if he didn't cut out the overprotective bullshit act. Finn glared back at me, but he dropped Sebastian's hand.

"And I'm the one, the only Finnegan Lane." Finn

gave an overly elaborate flourish with his hand, indicating his own greatness, before propping his elbow up on the counter. "You wouldn't happen to be related to Cesar Vaughn, would you? The big construction mogul?"

Sebastian nodded. "I'm his son."

Finn gave me a pointed look, one that said that he knew all about my latest assignment. Fletcher must have told him.

Before Finn could make some snide, thinly veiled remark to that effect, I whipped my order pad out of one of the back pockets of my jeans. "So what can I get for y'all?"

Sebastian ordered a barbecue beef sandwich, baked beans, and some macaroni salad, along with a cheeseburger, fries, and a triple chocolate milkshake for Charlotte.

Both Sebastian's and Charlotte's eyes widened as I went over and handed the order ticket to Sophia Deveraux, likely because Sophia was dressed in her usual Goth clothes—black boots, black jeans, and a black T-shirt that featured a white rose dripping blood. Grinning silver skulls dangled from the black leather collar around her neck, while red streaks shimmered in her black hair. Sophia looked at the ticket and grunted as she stirred a pot of Fletcher's secret barbecue sauce that was simmering on one of the stoves. She didn't talk much.

Sebastian laughed and joked with me while I helped Sophia fix their food, but Charlotte didn't say a word. Instead, she kept tracing her index finger over the counter, painting a pattern that only she could see. I wondered what she was thinking about. I wondered if she enjoyed being here with Sebastian or if she was already worried about returning home and what might happen there, what her father might do to her.

Well, she shouldn't have worried. Because after tonight, Cesar Vaughn wasn't going to hurt her ever again.

"Is something wrong?" Sebastian asked, noticing the dark look on my face.

I shook my head. "Of course not. Unless you turn out to be a lousy tipper."

He laughed, and I joined in with his hearty chuckles.

Finn looked at Sebastian, then at me. His frown deepened. No doubt, Finn would run straight to Fletcher as soon as Sebastian and Charlotte left and tell the old man all about the two of them coming into the restaurant. But there was nothing that I could do about that, so I decided to focus on my two customers—and enjoy this unexpected time with Sebastian.

I still had to work, of course, seeing to the needs of the few remaining diners, but I was able to spend most of my time hanging out at the counter with Sebastian. He was as warm, witty, and charming as he had been at the party. Maybe even more so, since today he was just a guy eating in a restaurant, flirting with a cute waitress who enjoyed every second of his attention.

Finn finally got up to help Sophia with something in the back of the restaurant, while Charlotte slipped off her stool and headed toward the bathroom.

"Alone at last," Sebastian murmured. "I thought your brother was *never* going to leave. He doesn't seem to like me very much."

I snorted. "Finn doesn't like anyone who's cuter than he is."

"So I'm cuter than he is? Good to know."

Sebastian grinned, and I felt myself blushing, just like Charlotte had earlier.

"And now for the real reason that I came here." He leaned forward and captured my hand with his, even though I was wiping down the counter again. "Go out with me, Gin."

I'd been having so much fun with Sebastian that I almost said yes without even thinking about it. But at the last moment, I swallowed my easy agreement. Maybe I'd been around Fletcher too long, because I couldn't quite quash the little whisper of worry in the back of my mind, the one that insisted that Sebastian had some secret agenda, the way rich guys almost always did.

"Why would someone like you want to go out with someone like me? We don't exactly run in the same circles." I made my voice light and teasing, as if it didn't really matter whether we went out or not. Although I was startled by just how much it suddenly did matter—to *me*.

His mouth set into a stubborn line. "I don't care whether you have money, if that's what you're asking. I don't care about anything like that. Not money, not power, not people and how I can use them. Not like my father does."

His lips pinched together, and I wondered if he was talking about Charlotte, and if he knew what his father was doing to her. But his sour expression melted away, and Sebastian smiled at me again.

"You're the most interesting woman I've met in ages, Gin. So c'mon. Give a guy a break. Let me take you out to dinner, a movie, coffee, something, anything you like."

His eyes met mine, and I stared into the dark, liquid depths, still trying to discern his true motives. But all I saw in his earnest, pleading gaze was a desire to get close to me. Maybe he really did want to get to know me, or maybe he thought that I'd be an easy lay, so bowled over by his suave moves and smoldering good looks that I'd let him do me before dinner. Either way, I felt myself wavering, despite what a bad idea it was. But really, I liked the attention, and I wanted it to last for at least a little while longer.

"All right," I said, laughing a little at how good it felt to give in to him. "All right. You win."

"I always do." He grinned again. "How about tonight?"

I thought of my plans for his father, plans that just wouldn't wait. My laughter vanished, and I shook my head. "I can't tonight. How about Friday?"

That was three days from now and a more natural date night than the current Tuesday. More important, it would be after I'd killed his father, and I had no doubt that Sebastian would have other things to think about then and would forget all about me.

A pang twinged through my chest at the thought, even though I knew it was for the best. Still, it surprised me how much I cared about seeing Sebastian again, even though I probably never would after today.

Maybe if I'd met Sebastian before Fletcher had gotten the Vaughn job. Maybe if I'd met him months after. But, of course, my terrible luck had made us cross paths at precisely the wrong moment. Fletcher was right—nothing could ever come of this. No matter how much I might have wanted it to. My heart squeezed tight.

Sebastian's grin widened. "Friday would be great."

"I still have to work."

"I understand. Pick you up here around seven?"

I smiled at him, keeping up the charade until the bitter end, even though my expression was as brittle as my heart. "It's a date."


Finn returned from the back of the restaurant, Charlotte stepped out of the bathroom, and they both took their seats again. Sebastian kept giving me sly little winks, though, as if we were in on some secret joke together.

If only he knew how many secrets I had to keep—especially from him.

Sebastian and Charlotte finished their food, while Finn finally scraped up the remains of the peach pie he'd been eating when they'd first arrived. I told Sebastian that the meal was on the house, but he insisted on paying and giving me an obscenely generous tip. Charlotte seemed too full for desert, given that she hadn't eaten all of her cheeseburger, so I packed up some chocolate-chip cookies for her to take home, putting them in a white paper bag with the Pork Pit's pig logo printed on the side.

I pushed the bag across the counter to her. "Here you go, sweetheart. In case you want a snack later."

Charlotte stared at the bag of cookies, then at me. She glanced at Sebastian, who nodded. She reached out and dragged the bag off the counter, hugging it to her chest, almost as if the crinkly white paper were a shield that would protect her from all of the terrible things in her life, including her father.

No bag, no cookies, could do that—but I *would*.

"Thank you," Charlotte whispered. It was the first time she'd uttered a single word since coming into the restaurant.

Sebastian gave his sister an encouraging smile, then put his arm around her shoulder again. Charlotte stiffened at his touch, but she let him lead her out of the restaurant, down the sidewalk, and out of sight.

Finn watched them walk away before swiveling around on his stool and facing me again.

I sighed. "All right. I know you know about the Vaughn job. I could tell by your reaction to Sebastian. So let loose. Let me have it. Tell me what a huge, horrible, terrible mistake I'm making with him."

Finn gave me a thoughtful look, then shook his head. "I'm not going to tell Dad, if that's what you're worried about."

I blinked. "Why not? You're usually not so . . . generous."

What I really meant was that he was a complete tattletale. Finn was all too happy to rat me out to Fletcher whenever I did something wrong, usually gleefully cackling all the while.

Finn puckered his lips, giving me a sour look. But then he glanced out the storefront windows again before turning back to me, his green eyes dark and serious. "Look, I know you're really into this guy," he said. "He's rich, handsome, and charming enough to make even *me* jealous. If I were you, I'd probably be into him too. I kind of was, anyway."

"But?"

"But I don't know. There's something about him that I just don't like. It's like he's . . . trying too hard. Like he has some desperate need for you to like him."

I snorted. "This coming from the guy who spends longer on his hair in the morning than I do. If that's not desperate, I don't know what is."

Finn sniffed, but he reached up and touched his hair, making sure that every dark lock was still perfectly in place. "It's not my fault that you think pulling your hair back into a ponytail every single day of the year is a rocking style."

I glared at him.

Finn glared back at me, but after a moment, his face softened. "Jealousy and everything else aside, you know that he's never going to be good enough for you, right?"

I snorted again. "According to you, the only guy who was ever good enough for me was *you*."

"True." He grinned. "So very true."

A few summers ago, Finn and I had had more than a brother-sister relationship—much more.

Maybe it had been inevitable, being around each other for so long, living, fighting, and training together, slowly taking over Fletcher's assassination business together. Maybe it was the secretive nature of the life we led and the fact that we could only really trust each other and not any outsiders. Or maybe it had been all of those teenage hormones raging through our systems. Either way, we'd spent a long, hot summer together before both of us realized that we were better off as friends.

In some ways, Finn and I were too much alike to have any sort of lasting romantic relationship. Too hard, too cold, too ruthless, each of us always thinking about the angles we could play and how best to go about getting exactly what we wanted from the other. In other ways, we were too different. He was still warm, carefree, and fun, all emotions that had been burned out of me the night my family was murdered.

These days, we had more of a sibling rivalry, especially as it became more and more apparent that I was better suited for the up-close and dirty work of being an assassin than Finn was. Sometimes I didn't think that Finn cared anything at all about the flings I had with other guys as much as it bugged him how much closer I was to Fletcher in this one crucial regard.

"Actually," Finn said, sniffing, "I was *too* good for you. I've ruined you for all other men."

"Hardly. I've had longer, deeper, more meaningful relationships with cheeseburgers than I did with you."

"Yes, but at least I didn't go straight to your ass," he said in a smug, superior tone.

I rolled my eyes and made that threatening, slashing motion with my finger again, letting Finn know exactly what I wanted to do to him. At the far end of the counter, Sophia snickered at our antics.

Finn and I both glared at her, but the Goth dwarf was immune to our dirty looks, and she kept right on slicing tomatoes for the rest of the day's sandwiches. She could pick us both up by the scruffs of our necks and shake us like disobedient puppies, and we all knew it.

Finn sniffed again, just to let Sophia know how annoyed he was with her. Then his glare disappeared, and he gave me a serious look again.

"All kidding aside, just be careful around this guy, okay, Gin? A slick smile can hide a lot of sins." He paused. "Trust me. I know all about that."

"Of course you do. You've broken far more hearts than I've ever cut into."

Despite my kidding, Finn kept giving me that dead-serious stare. "And no matter what, you should never, ever tell someone all of your secrets."

I sighed. "Don't worry. I'm not going to be stupid enough to tell Sebastian anything about what I do as you-know-who. Especially not since it's going to involve his father."

He shook his head. "I'm not just talking about what we do, what you do. I'm talking about other things."

"What other things?"

Finn shook his head again. "I can't tell you that. Not really. It's different for everybody. But the funny thing is that you won't even know that they're secrets until after you've said them—and realized that it's too late to take them back."

I stared at him, mystified. I didn't know what could be more important than what I did as the Spider. That was the deepest, darkest, blackest secret in my heart. Well, that and what had happened to my family. But I wasn't telling anyone about that—not *ever*.

Finn kept staring at me, his face suddenly seeming as old and wise as Fletcher's, as if he knew something important that I didn't. So I made myself nod, as though I understood exactly what he was talking about, even though I didn't have a clue.

"Don't worry," I said. "I won't be telling Sebastian Vaughn any of my secrets. Trust me. After tonight, I will be the last thing on his mind."

## ☀ ¶ ☀

A couple of hours later, I found myself sitting in a van outside the entrance to Vaughn Construction.

It was after eight now, and the warm rays of the setting sun made the chain-link fence that surrounded the site gleam like molten silver. Security lights burned at fifty-foot intervals along the fence, casting small pools of weak white light against the encroaching darkness. Two giant guards manned the main entrance, sitting in their flimsy wooden shack and rifling through magazines to try to alleviate their boredom at working the night shift. Deeper in the compound, lights blazed in the windows in Vaughn's office. He was working late again, just like he had every day that I'd watched him.

"You sure you want to do this?" Fletcher asked for the third time since we'd left the house. "Vaughn has a lot on his mind right now, with the terrace collapse and the impending lawsuits. Not to mention his meeting with

Mab at Dawson's party. He's bound to be jumpy and on edge."

I thought of the wariness in Charlotte's eyes earlier today at the Pork Pit and the way she'd scanned the restaurant again and again, as if she expected someone to hurt her at any second.

"I'm sure."

"You got everything you need?" Fletcher asked.

After finishing my shift at the restaurant, I'd traded my jeans and blue apron for my other work clothes, the ones that only came in one color: black. Now I wore them from head to toe—a long-sleeved black T-shirt, black cargo pants, and black boots. A black vest lined with silverstone covered my chest. In addition to absorbing all forms of elemental magic, silverstone was great at stopping bullets, and the vest would help keep me safe from any blasts of magic or bursts of gunfire that Vaughn might send my way. Despite the sweltering heat, I'd also pulled my hair back and tucked my ponytail underneath a snug black toboggan. As a final measure, I'd smeared a bit of black greasepaint under my eyes to break up the paleness of my face and help me blend in with the gathering shadows.

"Gin?" Fletcher asked again. "It never hurts to do a final check to make sure."

He was big on being as prepared as possible, especially when it came to being certain that you hadn't forgotten any important supplies. Sometimes Fletcher would check and re-check his weapons two, or three, or even more times before he was satisfied that he was ready to go, and he'd taught me to do the same thing.

So I shifted in my seat, doing one last mental inventory of my knives. Two up my sleeves, one tucked against the small of my back, and two in the sides of my boots, just like usual. I wasn't carrying a gun. I didn't need one. Not tonight.

Not for this job.

"Yeah, I've got everything."

Fletcher nodded and stared through the windshield at the compound again. Vaughn Construction took up its own fenced-in block in the downtown loop, although it was situated closer to Northtown than to Southtown. Several businesses lined the street across from the compound. Fletcher had parked the van in a restaurant lot with a dozen other cars, and no one had given it or us a second look. He was good at picking just the right spot to blend in with his surroundings.

"Sophia told me that boy came into the restaurant today," Fletcher said. "Sebastian."

I tensed. I'd been so concerned about Finn ratting me out that I'd never considered that Sophia might do it instead.

"Yeah. So what? It doesn't matter."

"Sophia said that the two of you looked awful cozy together."

"Not that cozy," I said. "Considering that he brought his baby sister along with him."

"Don't be a smartass. That's Finn's thing."

I shrugged.

Fletcher shook his head. "There's still something that I don't like about this job. And it's not just the boy's interest in you."

I bristled. He said "interest" like it was the worst thing *ever* that Sebastian liked me.

"Don't worry about that," I said, my voice harsh. "After I kill his father, Sebastian will forget all about me. He'll have too many other things to deal with. He won't even remember some random waitress he was supposed to go out with. Even if he does, I doubt that he'll come knocking on my door anytime soon. So see? You have nothing to worry about. Problem solved."

The words were as true as they'd been when I'd said them to Finn earlier. And once again, they shot an arrow of hurt straight into my heart. Fletcher stared at me, his green eyes bright and searching.

I returned his gaze with a cold, flat, impassive one of my own. No matter how I felt about Sebastian, this was no time for any sort of soft sentiment.

After several seconds, he nodded. "You're probably right."

He drew in a breath, like he was going to say something else. I waited, expecting him to ask me yet again if I really wanted to go through with this, but he didn't. Instead, his mouth turned down with a hint of sadness, although I had no idea why.

"Just be careful," Fletcher finally said.

I nodded. "Always."

I got out of the van. Fletcher stayed where he was behind the wheel, in case things didn't go as planned and I needed to make a quick getaway. But I didn't anticipate any problems—I was too motivated to fail.

I lowered my head, tucked my hands into my pockets,

and strolled down the street, heading away from the main gate of the compound. I kept my pace slow and easy, as though I were out for a late-night walk, instead of getting ready to murder a man for money. I thought about whistling to add to my cover but decided against it. Finn might have indulged in such theatrics but not me.

I made it to the end of the block and risked a quick glance around. Farther up the street, close to Fletcher's van, folks laughed, talked, and smoked underneath the red awning of a restaurant that stretched all the way out to the curb. The name *Underwood's* flowed across the awning fabric in an elaborate gold script. Some fancy new place that I'd heard Finn talk about, the kind of highfalutin joint where they charged you ten bucks for a glass of tap water. A few cars also drove by on the street, but no one so much as looked in my direction.

Good. That would make this easier.

When I was sure that no one was watching me, I crossed the intersection so that I was on the street that fronted the construction compound. I paused again at the corner, as though I were going to head on over to the next block, my gaze scanning over everything. Satisfied that I was still in the clear, I rounded the corner, stepped off the street, slid behind a tree, and wormed my way through a few patches of weeds until I reached the chain-link fence that surrounded Vaughn Construction.

I crouched down, looking left and right for any foot or vehicle traffic on the sidewalk or street and listening for any sounds in the compound. Any whispers of clothing rubbing together, the scuff of boots on the hard-packed ground, even the soft padding of a guard dog loping this way.

Nothing—I saw and heard nothing.

I unzipped one of the pockets on my vest, pulled out a small pair of wire cutters, and quickly snipped a straight line up the metal links. Despite all of the expensive equipment that lay beyond, Vaughn thought that the fence and all the lights strung around it were enough to keep people out, and he hadn't bothered to have the metal electrified. Fool. I was mildly surprised that members of some Southtown gang hadn't made their way over here, climbed the fence, and hot-wired some of Vaughn's pickup trucks, driving them right back out through the metal links.

I'd decided to make my run at Vaughn here, since there was even less security at the construction compound than there was at his estate. I didn't feel like ducking wandering giant guards just to get close enough to try to kill him. Besides, I didn't want Sebastian and especially Charlotte to find their father's body after the fact. I would spare them that trauma.

I hoped the cops would remove Vaughn's corpse from the compound before they notified Sebastian of his father's death, although I wasn't overly optimistic about it. The po-po were so crooked and lazy it wouldn't surprise me if they made Sebastian pay to have his father's body taken away in a timely manner. But that was a problem for tomorrow. I needed to focus on what I was doing here tonight.

When I finished snipping through the metal, I slid the wire cutters back into my vest and zipped that pocket up again. In addition to the rest of my black clothes, I was also wearing thin black leather gloves, so I wasn't worried about leaving behind any fingerprints or cutting myself on the fence as I carefully pulled the sliced edges away from one another.

I slipped through the opening to the other side and put the links back into place, making sure that I could remember the exact spot that I'd cut, in case I had to leave in a hurry. Then, still crouching low, I started making my way toward the office building in the heart of the compound.

Most of the space behind the fence was taken up with rows and rows of construction equipment. Bulldozers, backhoes, and other machines designed for tearing into the earth and then dump trucks to haul it away. Cement mixers for laying foundations, cranes to hoist beams into place high in the sky, and all the other equipment you would need to fill in all the spaces in between. A few metal outbuildings also squatted here and there, full of smaller tools, wiring, paint, drywall, and other supplies.

As I slid from one piece of equipment and one pool of darkness to the next, I listened to the stone around me.

Bricks, concrete, granite . . . all sorts of stone could be found throughout the compound, some of it out in the open, like the sturdy cinder blocks stacked on top of one another, while other, more expensive and delicate ones were safely behind lock and key, like the marble that I could hear murmuring inside one of the outbuildings.

Most of the whispers told of the shake, rattle, and roll of heavy machinery as the stones were continuously picked up and moved from one place to another before being shipped out to their ultimate destinations. But some of the more polished pieces, like the marble countertops, vainly sang of their own smooth, glossy beauty and how lovely they were going to look in whatever new house they would eventually be installed in. The more sensible, utilitarian stones grumbled in response, having no use for the marble's frippery. They were bricks, solid, stout, and sturdy, meant to protect, shield, and hold up against all of the rain, wind, sun, and snow they would be exposed to. That was more than enough for them.

Vanity, envy, exasperation . . . in many ways, stones were just like people, with all the pride, insecurities, and emotions to match.

But the longer I listened, the more I realized that there was a . . . darkness in the stones. No, not just darkness— evil, evil intent.

It rippled throughout the entire site, from the bricks and cinder blocks outside to the fine marble and gran- ite slabs housed indoors. A black, ominous, foreboding sense that someone here was capable of doing some very bad things at any moment—and had already commit- ted some gruesome sins at this very spot. One particular stack of bricks practically hummed with harsh, murder- ous whispers, indicating that one or more of them had been used to bash someone's head in and that the person hadn't gotten back up from the brutal attack.

My own mood darkened in response to the stones' cruel cries. I knew the cause of all the commotion: Cesar Vaughn. It was one more nail in the coffin of his guilt, as far as I was concerned. This was his compound, his busi- ness, his gin joint, so it only made sense that the stones would soak up his emotions and intentions, especially since he had the same power over them that I did. Stones tended to react even more to the elementals who could control them, sensing their primal connection to the elementals and reflecting back their actions more intensely.

But I shut the malicious murmurs out of my mind and kept heading toward the main office building, which was made out of lovely gray bricks. A few giants roamed through the site near the structure, shining their flashlights over the rows of equipment and the locks on the outbuildings, but their movements were slow, sloppy, and halfhearted. They weren't expecting any trouble. Good.

I crouched in the shadows behind a pickup truck and waited until the giants had moved on to the next part of their security sweep. Then I sprinted the last thirty feet over to the headquarters. If I'd been doing the hit during business hours, I would have sauntered up to the front door, pulled it open, and marched right on inside, like I belonged here. But since there was a giant guard posted at the desk inside the entrance and this wasn't exactly a business call, the direct approach was out.

Instead, I sidled all the way around the building until I reached a loading dock on the east side. The large metal door was shut and locked. Even if I'd had the strength to open it, it would have made far too much noise rattling upward. So I set my sights on a regular door in the wall a few feet away. I peered through the glass, but the hallway on the other side was empty, as I expected it to be. According to my calculations, Vaughn should be the only one still inside the building, besides the guard sitting at the front desk.

I took one more look around, this time reaching out and listening to the bricks' murmurs for any hints of danger, surprise, or unease. But the same whispers as before echoed back to me, perhaps a touch darker as I got closer to my victim and my own murderous goal.

Satisfied that the coast was clear, I reached out and tried the doorknob. Locked, but I could fix that. I pulled off one of my gloves and held my hand out, palm up. Then I reached for my Ice magic.

The power flowed through my veins, like a spring of cold crystal buried deep inside me. I could feel it the same way that I could hear the rasps of the gravel under my feet and the murmurs of the bricks that made up the building. But I couldn't access it as easily. Every time I reached for that frosty power, it slid away, like frozen raindrops falling through my hands. Or maybe it only seemed that way because my Ice magic was so much weaker than my Stone power.

So I concentrated, and a dim silver light flashed, flickered, and finally flared to life in the palm of my hand, centered on the spider rune scar there. It took me a minute, but I managed to bring enough magic to bear to form two small, slender shapes: Ice picks. Why carry around a set of lock picks when you could make your own?

I slid my glove back on and went to work on the lock with the Ice picks. Less than a minute later, the tumblers fell into place, and the door *snick*ed open. I dropped the picks onto the gravel, where they would soon melt away, given the warm, muggy night. Then I drew in a breath, stepped inside, and quietly closed and locked the door behind me.

I stood at the end of a long hallway that stretched for about fifty feet before splitting off left and right. I paused again, looking and listening, but I didn't hear any heavy footsteps from the guard stationed out front coming in this direction. No rustles of clothing, no *creak* of another door opening, and nothing else to indicate that someone had seen me approach and enter the building and was headed this way. That was another reason I'd decided to do the hit here: the lack of security cameras. Oh, a couple of cameras were trained on the compound entrance, out where the guards were sitting in their shack, but there was none at all inside the offices, which meant that there was no chance of anyone seeing or recording what I was here to do.

So I pushed away from the door and headed toward my ultimate destination: Cesar Vaughn's office.

According to everything I'd read and observed about him, Vaughn wasn't the sort of man who went in for a lot of frills, so the building was solid but bare. White paint covered the ceiling, and thick Persian carpets stretched across the floors, but that was it. No art decorated the walls, no sculptures sat in the corners, no potted plants perched in the windows. This building was about business and business only. I couldn't decide if I liked it or not.

I moved quickly and quietly through the hallways, gliding from one part of the structure to the next. I glanced into every room that I crept by, but all of the offices were dark. For a moment, I wondered what Sebastian was doing tonight, if he'd found another girl to spend the evening with since I'd turned him down, but I pushed away the pang of longing that rippled through me. Finn and Fletcher were right. I should forget all about Sebastian, because he was certainly going to do that to me. Besides, I needed to focus on the job at hand, not daydream like some silly, simpering girl who'd never been on a date before.

I crept up to the end of the hallway that I was skulking along and peered around the corner. Vaughn's office stood at the far end of the next corridor over. The door was closed, but he was in there. Light leaked out from under the door, highlighting the gold threads in the carpet in front of it, and I could hear the faint *tap-tap-tap* of his fingers on his keyboard. I felt safe enough to ease over to his office door.

Then I waited.

A minute passed, then another one, but those *tap-tap-tap*s kept up a soft, steady rhythm, as Vaughn typed out whatever report, e-mail, or other work he needed to finish. I drew in a breath and reached for the knob to see if the door was locked—

A phone in the office rang, making me freeze and momentarily interrupting Vaughn. A faint murmur sounded as he picked it up and spoke to whoever was on the other end of the line.

I bit my lip, hating the delay, but I couldn't exactly murder him while he was talking on the phone. So I drew in another breath, thought of Charlotte, and palmed one of my silverstone knives. The familiar weight of the weapon steadied me, centered me, and prepared me for what was to come next: the death of Cesar Vaughn.

I started to reach for the knob again, but the handle started turning on its own. Too late, I realized that I couldn't hear Vaughn talking or typing anymore. I bit back a vicious curse, because I'd made such a simple, rookie mistake. I'd been too cautious, too slow, and I'd waited too long to strike. Now he was leaving his office, for whatever reason.

And I had nowhere to go.

Oh, I could have rammed my knife into Vaughn's back the second he stepped through the doorway, but that wasn't my plan. No, I needed him to be in his office before I attacked, firmly out of earshot of the guard at the front desk on the far side of the building. If I tried to take him out here in the hallway, he might scream and bring the guard running. The chance of that happening was small, but I didn't want to risk it, not when I'd already screwed up my approach. No, I couldn't kill Vaughn now, not unless there was no other choice.

My eyes darted left and right, even though there was nothing to see. The hallway was too long for me to have any hope of sprinting down it and disappearing around the corner before Vaughn stepped out of his office. That left me with only one option.

The door opened outward, and I darted behind it and plastered myself to the wall there, hoping that Vaughn wouldn't shove the heavy wood open as wide as it would go and that he wouldn't stop to close the door behind him.

But Vaughn was in a hurry, and he merely pushed the door open and started moving down the corridor at a fast clip. I caught the wood right before it slammed into my face, then eased to one side so I could peek out from behind the edge of the door.

Vaughn never looked back. He thought that he was all alone, which made his sudden departure more puzzling.

It wasn't like he was strolling to another office to check in with one of his workers, and I didn't think that he was leaving the building for good. Otherwise, he would have taken the time to turn off his office lights and grab the briefcase that he always carried. I hesitated, wondering where he was heading and why he'd picked such an inconvenient time to go there. Maybe it had something to do with the call he'd received.

I had no choice but to follow him. For all I knew, Vaughn was, in fact, rushing home for the night, and I wasn't about to let him get anywhere near Charlotte again. Not after I'd seen that dark, haunted look in her eyes today at the Pork Pit. I wanted to kill Vaughn in his office in order to minimize the noise and maximize my getaway time, but if I had to improvise and take him out elsewhere, so be it.

Vaughn rounded the corner of the hallway and stepped out of sight. I pushed the door away from the wall, slipped out from behind it, and hurried after him.

# * 10 *

To my surprise, instead of heading toward the front of the building to speak with the guard, Vaughn made his way to the loading dock, stepping out of the same door that I'd Ice-picked open earlier. I was glad that I'd remembered to lock it behind me. Vaughn threw the lock, turned the knob, and went outside, disappearing from view again.

I bit back another curse, wondering where he was going and how many more ways I could mess up such an easy assignment. Vaughn should have been bleeding out on the floor of his office by now, not traipsing around like he didn't have a care in the world. Maybe Fletcher was right to keep looking over my shoulder. I hadn't exactly been the smooth, suave assassin so far tonight.

Determined to finish this, I hurried over to the door, which was cracked open a couple of inches from where Vaughn had forgotten to pull it shut behind him. I plastered my back against the wall, then crouched down and tipped my head forward so I could peer through the opening between the door and the frame.

Vaughn stood about ten feet away, pacing back and forth across the loading dock.

I frowned. He wasn't a smoker, so this wasn't some cigarette break. So what was he doing?

I got my answer two minutes later, when a car rounded the corner of the building. It was an older navy sedan, big, stout, square, and worn, the sort of car that criminals recognized the world over. A cop car if ever I'd seen one. One of the guards at the shack must have called Vaughn to let him know that he had a visitor.

The sedan rolled to a stop, and a man got out, carrying a thick, overstuffed manila folder. In contrast to Vaughn's business suit, the other man was dressed down in khakis, scuffed brown boots, and a loose white cotton shirt patterned with bright pink, garish roses. A straw hat perched on his head, hiding much of his dark brown hair, although he tipped the hat back on his forehead so he could get a better view of his surroundings. His pale eyes flicked over the compound, his gaze cool and assessing as it went from the construction equipment to the outbuildings to Vaughn standing on the loading dock. Oh, yeah. If he wasn't a cop, I'd eat one of my own knives—point first.

Great. Now my mistakes were starting to multiply exponentially. Because not only did Vaughn have a visitor, which meant that I couldn't kill him right now, but that visitor also happened to be a cop. Fletcher was going to love this. He wouldn't come right out and say "I told you so," but he'd definitely be thinking it.

Still, I held my position, trying to think things through and see how everything played out. Why *was* Vaughn meeting with a cop after hours? As far as Fletcher had been able to determine, Vaughn didn't have anything illegal cooking with the po-po, other than a few necessary bribes. But Fletcher had said that there was something about this job that felt slightly off. Maybe Vaughn having a cop on his payroll on the sly was it. Cops in Ashland didn't like their meal tickets being murdered. That was one of the few things that would prompt a thorough, comprehensive investigation into someone's death. In those cases, the cops were all too eager to find whoever had cut off their cash flow and punish them accordingly.

I studied the cop some more, but I didn't recognize him. Maybe Fletcher would know who he was when I described him. In addition to all of the criminals in town, the old man also kept tabs on the inner workings of the police department, including who was moving up, who was on his or her way down, and who was getting pushed aside in terms of power, prestige, and position.

The cop tromped up the steps to the loading dock. Vaughn stepped forward, and the two men shook hands.

"Nice shirt, Harry," Vaughn said.

Harry, the cop, grimaced. "A birthday present from my daughter. You know how much she likes roses."

Vaughn smiled. "I remember. How did she like the snow globe that Charlotte sent her for her birthday?"

"She loved it," Harry replied. "Especially since it was full of pink glitter. Naturally, pink is her favorite color right now. She's still talking about it. She's looking forward to the party and seeing Charlotte again."

Vaughn nodded. Among all the info that Fletcher had uncovered, he'd learned that Vaughn planned to throw a huge party in a few weeks in honor of his and Charlotte's birthday, which was on the same day. Friends, distant relatives, business associates. Vaughn had invited practically everyone he knew to his party, and he was going all out with the food and decorations, according to Fletcher.

Too bad Vaughn himself wasn't going to make it to the big celebration.

Vaughn nodded again. "Good. I'm sure Charlotte will be happy to see her."

The two men fell silent, although Vaughn couldn't quit looking at the folder in the cop's hand. I wondered what secrets it contained that were so important. Finally, Vaughn sighed and jerked his head at the folder.

"Tell me," he said. "Tell me what you found out."

Harry hesitated, and sympathy filled his face, momentarily softening his flat cop stare. "Maybe you should read through the file first. Then we can talk about things."

Vaughn kept staring at the folder. "So it's as bad as I feared, then."

"Worse, actually. All of your suspicions were correct."

"You're sure?"

Harry nodded. "I've been over all of it. Witness statements, building manifests, material logs, work orders. I even had a Stone elemental I know come in and take a look at the actual crime scene, including the rubble that was cleared away. He agreed with your assessment. You were right about what happened."

Crime scene? He must have been talking about the

terrace collapse at the restaurant. The one that had so many people screaming for Vaughn's blood and money. He must have gotten his cop buddy to look into the accident—only it sounded like Vaughn thought that it hadn't been an accident after all.

"Dammit." Vaughn pinched the bridge of his nose, as though he suddenly had a headache.

I frowned, wondering what suspicions the cop had confirmed and why the knowledge upset Vaughn so greatly. But it didn't much matter. All that did was making sure that Vaughn got dead. That was what I was here for; that was my assignment, my job. Nothing else. No matter how much curiosity that file raised in me.

Vaughn dropped his hand from his face and composed himself. Harry gave him the file. Vaughn sighed and slowly hefted the folder in his hand, as though it weighed as much as one of the cinder blocks out in the compound.

"Thank you for looking into this for me," Vaughn said, reaching out and shaking the other man's hand again. "You were the only one I could trust."

Harry gave him a thin smile. "What? You mean you put more stock in an old, washed-up cop from Blue Marsh than in Ashland's finest?"

Blue Marsh? I'd never heard of it, but the quirky name sounded like some sort of small town. I made a mental note to ask Fletcher where it was later.

Vaughn barked out a harsh, bitter laugh. "You know what the cops around here are like as well as I do."

Harry nodded his agreement, then looked at his friend again. "So what are you going to do?"

This time, Vaughn stared at the file in his hand as though it were a poisonous snake, one that was about to bite him. His lips curled with disgust. "What I have to. I have to make this right, no matter what it costs me."

Harry nodded again and clapped him on the shoulder. "Take care, Cesar. I'll see you at the party. If you need my help in the meantime, just let me know."

Vaughn nodded back, and the two men shook hands a final time. A bit of hope flared in my chest that maybe I could still go through with the job after all, hope that intensified when Harry got into his car, turned it around, and drove off toward the front gate. Vaughn watched his friend leave. Then he sighed, and his shoulders slumped, as though a load of bricks had been set on them. He turned toward the door—the one I was still hiding be-hind.

I quickly scooted away from the entrance, got to my feet, and ran down the hallway and around the corner. Heart racing, I slid through an open office door just as Vaughn appeared, and I stayed there until he vanished from view.

Vaughn went straight back to his office. He never even bothered to glance around to make sure that he was alone. But my streak of bad luck continued, because he left the door open behind him this time, which meant that he would see me coming before I could get close enough to take him out. I hissed out my frustration. Instead of just getting on with the business of killing him, I once again had to stop in the next hallway over, drop down into a crouch, and look around the corner, peering down the corridor and through the doorway.

Vaughn threw the file on top of his desk. He glared at it a moment before sitting down, pulling his chair up to the desk, opening the folder, and perusing all of the papers and photos inside. Whatever Harry had given him, it didn't make Vaughn happy. His frown deepened, and the lines on his face became more and more pronounced the longer he read through the information. By the time he closed the file, he looked sick and haggard, as though whatever was inside had thoroughly disgusted him.

Vaughn stared at the closed folder for the better part of a minute. Then he roused himself from his thoughts, grabbed the file, got up from the desk, and went over to the far right side of the office, out of my line of sight. A few seconds later, several soft *click-click-click*s sounded, along with the sharp *crack* of a lever being thrown open and then the loud *bang* of a door shutting. My eyes narrowed. He must have put the folder in his office safe, the one that was hidden behind a panel in the bottom of a bookcase, according to Fletcher's info.

Vaughn stepped back into view as he strode over to the far left side of his office. This time, I heard the *tink-tink-tink* of ice dropping into a glass, followed by bottles rattling together and a steady splash of liquid. Now he was pouring himself a drink, trying to drown the sorrow of whatever he'd learned.

I waited, thinking that Vaughn might take his drink back to his desk, but he stayed where he was, out of my line of sight. Well, if I couldn't see him, then that meant that he couldn't see me either.

And I was ready to end this.

I got to my feet and eased down the corridor, hugging

the wall. More bottles rattled, making me pause until I realized that Vaughn was fixing himself another drink. He must have decided to take his time with his second round, because I didn't hear anything else as I crept up to the open door, flattened myself against the wall outside the office, and peered inside, careful to stay as quiet and hidden as possible.

The office was a spacious area, taking up a corner chunk of the building, and it was the only room I'd seen so far that had a bit of luxury to it. More thick Persian rugs covered the floor, the bright reds and golds creating a pretty contrast against the gray stone, while all of the furniture was done in dark cherry wood, from the antique desk in the back of the room to the cushioned chairs that sat in front of it to the other small tables that perched here and there.

But the bookcase was the largest and most impressive thing in the office. It took up the entire right wall from floor to ceiling. But instead of being filled with books, the shelves were lined with small scale models. Tall, skinny skyscrapers with glittering silverstone points, long strip malls complete with toy cars sitting on tiny paved parking lots, a greenhouse with panes of glinting glass, even a miniature mausoleum surrounded by a carpet of fake grass and slender trees. All of the models were exquisite in their perfect detail, and all were crafted out of varying types of stone—granite for the skyscrapers, bricks for the strip mall, marble for the mausoleum.

I recognized a few of the buildings, mostly the downtown skyscrapers, since they had such distinctive shapes. The models must be scale versions of some of the buildings that Vaughn had built, restored, and worked on. His own way of memorializing his achievements. I wondered if he took the time to make the models himself. Probably, given his Stone magic.

My gaze dropped from the models to a square panel on the bottom of the bookcase, the one that hid Vaughn's safe. I wondered if I should get Vaughn to open the safe before I killed him, so I could grab the file of information and take it to Fletcher. But I decided not to. Vaughn would put up a struggle once he realized that I was going to kill him anyway, and a struggle meant more risk of noise and more chance of discovery. Besides, Charlotte's problems would vanish with her father dead, and that was all that I really cared about.

Vaughn turned away from the wet bar, a third drink in his hand. I drew back a bit, not wanting him to spot me lurking outside his office, but he didn't even glance in my direction. Instead, he stared at the spot where the safe was hidden in the bookcase, before sighing, ambling over to the windows behind the desk, and turning his back to the open door—and me.

I wanted to rush forward, but I forced myself to calm my heart and keep my breathing steady. I waited, thinking that Vaughn would soon get tired of the view of cinder blocks and concrete mixers, but he seemed content to sip his drink, stare out the windows, and brood.

I wouldn't get a better chance than this.

So I drew in a breath, clutched my knife tighter, and slipped into the office, making sure to close the door behind me. It shut with a soft *snick*. I winced, thinking that Vaughn would whirl around at the small sound, but he rattled the ice cubes in his glass and kept staring out the windows, lost in his own thoughts.

Heart still pounding, I locked the door, wincing again at the faint *click* that sounded, then headed toward Vaughn. The thick rugs drowned out my footsteps, but I still took care not to rustle my clothes any more than necessary. I made it from the door over to the chairs in front of his desk. I paused, but Vaughn still seemed oblivious to my presence, so I eased around the chairs and lined myself up with him, so that I had a straight shot at his back. Then I tiptoed forward again, still moving slowly, carefully, and quietly.

I was ten feet away from him, close enough that I could smell the harsh fumes of whatever whiskey he was drinking . . .

Seven feet . . . the overhead lights made the silver threads in his hair glint like the sharp points of the skyscrapers on the bookshelves . . .

Five . . . the facets of the crystal tumbler in his hand winked at me, one after another . . .

Three . . . now catching a hint of the day's sweat and sawdust that clung to his skin . . .

One . . . go!

I raised my knife to strike, but Vaughn must have finally heard the stones' sharp warnings about me, or perhaps he saw my reflection in the windows, or maybe I was just too damn slow again. Either way, he turned at the last possible second.

Vaughn took in my black clothes and the knife in my hand in an instant. His brain kicked into gear, and he dropped his drink and threw himself to one side, out of the way of my deadly strike. My knife skidded off the window with a loud, ear-splitting *screech*, as though it were diamond that I was trying to cut the glass with. I winced and lost my grip on the blade, which *thump*ed to the floor. I didn't want to waste time reaching for it, so I palmed another knife and whirled toward him.

He had scurried over to the far right side of his office and put his back against the bookcase. But he didn't make a break for the door. Instead, a grim, determined look filled his face, and he reached out and grabbed a stone model of a strip mall off the shelf. I tightened my grip on my knife and started forward. Vaughn reared back and threw the model at me, his aim surprisingly good. But that wasn't all he did. As the stone sailed through the air toward my head, I felt a hard wave of magic roll off Vaughn.

The model broke into a hundred pieces.

It was like a bomb had exploded in my face. Sharp shards of shrapnel zipped through the air, all of it purposefully propelled in my direction by Vaughn's magic. A neat trick, one that I'd have to remember for my own use later on. On instinct, I threw my hand up and reached for my own Stone magic, using it to harden my head, hair, skin, and eyes. The shrapnel pelted my body like nails, but the jagged pieces couldn't penetrate my skin, thanks to the protective shell of my magic.

Silence.

Then I dropped my hand, brushed the bits of shattered stone off my clothes, and looked at my target.

Vaughn's eyes widened to the point of almost bulging out of his face, as if I'd done something so surprising that he simply couldn't believe it. "Your magic . . . it's so strong . . ."

And that was all he got out before I went on the offensive again.

I took a step forward, but Vaughn was quicker than I was. He grabbed another model, this one a skyscraper, hurled it at me, and used his magic to make the stone explode in my face again. But I was still holding on to my own power, and the shrapnel hit my body and clattered off the same way it had before.

Back and forth we fought, with Vaughn moving from one side of the bookcase to the other, picking up every single model that he could get his hands on and tossing them all at me like grenades. I kept a grip on my own Stone magic and chased after him, but his miniature model bombs held me at bay.

Slowly, though, I started wearing him down. Vaughn was strong in his magic, but he was putting all of his power into his bomb blasts. It was much harder and far more draining to actively shatter thick chunks of solid stone over and over again, whereas I had the easier and far less magic-intensive task of keeping my skin just hard enough to withstand the assaults.

Vaughn threw another model at me, but this one only cracked into two pieces, instead of splintering into shrapnel like all the others. His breath came in ragged gasps, and sweat streamed down his face from the intense effort and the sheer amount of power he'd expended. I could feel the rest of his magic falling away, like the chips of stone dropping from my silverstone vest. Still, he made one final effort to take me down, this time with a particularly large model of a multistory mansion. But once again, he only managed to split the stone into two pieces, which plummeted to the floor before they even got close to me. Vaughn kept fighting, though, his hand reaching back toward the shelves for another model . . .

And coming up empty.

His eyes bulged again when he realized that he'd used up all his makeshift weapons, and his panicked gaze flicked to the door, as if he were finally thinking about running away. I needed to end the fight—*now*.

So I did.

While he hesitated, I leaped forward, raised my knife high, and drove it down into his chest.

Vaughn opened his mouth to scream, but I clamped my gloved hand over his lips, muffling the sound. He'd already made far too much noise setting off his model grenades, and it was a wonder that the guard hadn't come to check on him already—if he wasn't hurrying back here at this very second.

Vaughn's body went slack against mine, and I knew that the job was finally done.

I pulled the knife out and started to step away, but he reached up and grabbed my arm, his grip still surprisingly firm, given the blood gushing out of his chest.

"I don't know who sent you, but if this is about what happened at the restaurant . . ." he rasped. "Leave . . . my family . . . out of it. . . . Spare . . . them . . . please. . . ."

I leaned closer so he could see the coldness in my wintry gray eyes. "I *am* sparing them—from *you*. Did you think that you could slap around your kid and get away with it?"

Vaughn frowned, as though he didn't understand what I was talking about. Hard to think when your brain was shutting down along with the rest of your body. But after a moment, understanding flickered in his dark eyes, along with sadness.

"Charlotte," he rasped again, his voice even weaker than before, blood bubbling out of his lips. "Charlotte—"

Then the light faded from his eyes, his hand fell from my arm, and he dropped to the floor.

Dead.

# ❈ 11 ❈

I stood there and stared down at Cesar Vaughn's dead, crumpled figure.

Why had he thought of Charlotte at the end? He was the one who'd been hurting her. Or perhaps he thought that whoever had hired me had told me to kill his entire family. A common enough occurrence and a reasonable assumption in Ashland. Vaughn had seemed to think this was about payback for the terrace collapse. Maybe he reasoned that I'd been ordered to take out his loved ones, as eye-for-an-eye retribution for the dead and injured. But that hadn't been my assignment.

And for the first time, I wondered why it wasn't.

If someone really wanted to hurt Vaughn, to wound him, to make him *suffer* like they had suffered, then I should have been hired to kill Charlotte and Sebastian too. Not that I would ever hurt a kid, but if this was truly about payback, you'd think that my mysterious employer would have wanted to hit Vaughn where he would feel it the most. One would assume that would be by murdering his family. Plus, revenge would have been an obvious, logical move and motivation for someone who had been injured in the terrace collapse or who had lost a loved one because of it. But someone had simply wanted Vaughn dead instead.

Now, I didn't mind such short, sweet, and to-the-point assignments. In fact, I felt a great deal of dark satisfaction that I'd eliminated the threat to Charlotte and had gotten a bit of payback for the accident victims and their families. But, with the dirty deed done, for the first time doubts whispered in my mind, doubts about what this was all really about, who exactly had wanted Vaughn dead, and why.

I sighed, realizing that I was worrying too much, like Fletcher did. But it was far too late for any sorts of doubts and unanswered questions. The job was done, and Cesar Vaughn was bleeding out on the floor, his blood soaking into the rugs, the broken bits of his stone models already muttering about their master's murder.

Still, I couldn't quite quiet the worried whispers in my mind or shake off all of the warnings that Fletcher had drilled into my head over the years, so I stepped over Vaughn's body and crouched down in front of the bookcase. It only took me a moment to slide back the bottom wooden panel that hid his safe. It was a sturdy, old-fashioned device, a thick gray metal box with a simple spin lock. Enter the appropriate numbers, pull down the lever, and the safe would open. I didn't have the combination, but I still eyed the lock, wondering if I could somehow use my weak Ice magic to shatter it and open the safe that way—

A sharp knock sounded on the door. I whipped around on one knee, my bloody knife still clutched in my hand.

"Mr. Vaughn?" A muffled voice sounded through the wood. "Are you okay? I thought that I heard some sort of scuffle back here."

So the guard had finally come to investigate after all.

"Mr. Vaughn? Are you in there?"

Any second now, the guard would turn the knob to try to come inside and check on his boss. When he realized that the door was locked, he'd probably become even more worried, maybe even break down the wood with his massive shoulder.

Time for me to leave.

I got to my feet and hurried over to the windows at the back of the office, making sure to grab the knife that I'd dropped earlier during my fight with Vaughn.

"Mr. Vaughn?" the guard called out again. "Are you okay?"

The knob rattled as he tried to open the door.

I should be getting while the getting was good, but I hesitated, my gaze flicking back to the safe. Finn could have cracked it if he were here, probably before the guard busted into the office, but I wasn't as good with locks as he was, especially not with something a little more sophisticated like the safe. Besides, my escape was more important than any information that I might find.

So I opened one of the windows, slipped out of the construction magnate's office, and disappeared into the night.

\* \* \*

I made it through the compound, over to the opening I'd cut in the fence, and back down the block to where Fletcher was waiting in the van. I opened the passenger door and slid inside. He studied me, looking for injuries and taking in the blood that covered my vest, shirt, and gloves.

"Problems?"

I shook my head. "Vaughn used some of his Stone magic to try to fight me off, but I was able to get him in the end. I'm not even injured, so we don't have to go to Jo-Jo's tonight."

I told him everything that had happened, including Vaughn's mysterious visitor.

"Harry?" Fletcher asked, his green eyes sharpening with interest until they glinted like a cat's in the semi-darkness. "That was the cop's name? You're sure?"

"Yeah. Why?"

"No reason."

Fletcher's voice was as easy as ever, but he had hesitated a second too long before answering me. I studied him the same way that he'd looked at me when I'd first gotten into the van. I wondered what he knew about Harry that I didn't.

"This cop gave Vaughn a file?" Fletcher asked. "What kind of file?"

I shrugged. "I don't know. I didn't get a look at it or any of the information inside before Vaughn stuffed it into his safe."

"I'll have to see if I can get my hands on a copy of the police report, then," Fletcher murmured. "It might make some mention of the safe and what's inside it."

"But it doesn't much matter now, does it? The job is done, and Vaughn is dead. You thought this assignment would be a problem, but see? Everything is fine—just like I'd told you it would be."

Fletcher stared out through the windshield and drummed his fingers on the top of the steering wheel. Thinking. "Maybe. But I'd still like to know what was in that file that got Vaughn so hot and bothered, especially if it had something to do with the restaurant accident."

"The cop, Harry, mentioned a crime scene."

I deliberately used his name again to see if Fletcher would react, but he didn't so much as twitch an eyelash. Maybe I'd only imagined his earlier hesitation.

"He had to be talking about the restaurant."

"No doubt." Fletcher nodded, as if he'd made some sort of decision. "But you're right. The job is done—for tonight. Let's get you home so you can get cleaned up."

He turned the key in the ignition, and the van rumbled to life. Fletcher rolled out of the parking lot, turned right, and drove by the construction compound. The guards were no longer sitting inside their shack at the main gate, and it looked like all of the lights had been turned on inside the building. No doubt, the guards were searching every room, office, and hallway for their boss's killer. But I hadn't left anything behind for them to find—except Vaughn's body.

I grinned, and more of that dark satisfaction surged through me. Vaughn was dead, Charlotte was safe, and the job was finished. Who ordered the hit and why, that was all just background noise now, and it would soon fade away.

Fletcher leaned over and flipped on the police scanner attached to the van's dashboard. Another one of his safety precautions.

"We've got a call at Vaughn Construction," a voice crackled over the line. "Dead body."

Another voice crackled back. "Roger that. Just down the street from that location. On my way there now."

In the distance, a siren started to wail. A few seconds later, a pair of flashing blue and white lights popped into view about three blocks away, heading toward us. My hands curled around the armrests, and worried tension replaced my satisfaction—I was still covered with Vaughn's blood, and the cops could always set up a roadblock.

"Yep," Fletcher said in a calm voice, completely unconcerned by the commotion. "Definitely time for us to leave."

He stopped the van at the sign at the end of the block. The old man waited until the police car blasted by us, lights flashing and siren still wailing, then sedately made the turn toward home.

# ❊ 12 ❊

The death of Cesar Vaughn was big news in Ashland.

Bigger than I'd thought it would be, actually. Coverage consumed the newspapers and airwaves for the next few days, as story after story recapped all the grisly facts about the murder and then speculated about who had done it and why.

Of course, the most obvious thought was that one of the family members of the terrace collapse victims had decided to take matters into his own hands. The cops dutifully investigated each and every person who might have a grudge against Vaughn because of the tragedy, but they came up empty. Another reason that I'd decided to do the job on a Tuesday night: there was less chance of one of the victims' loved ones not having an alibi. People tended to wait until the weekend to get up to no good.

That was also why I'd done the job at Vaughn's office and had been so careful not to leave any evidence behind, so it would look exactly like the contracted hit that it was. I might be an assassin, but I didn't frame people for the crimes I committed. That was another part of Fletcher's code and one that I wholeheartedly agreed with. The people who'd lost their loved ones at that restaurant had already suffered enough. They didn't deserve to get blamed for Vaughn's murder too, even if one of them might have been behind the hit. Another reason that I'd used a knife on the job. That sort of stabbing attack was brutal, vicious, and, above all, up close and personal. Anyone could point a gun and pull the trigger from a distance, but not everyone could twist a knife into a man's heart, face-to-face, and watch the light leak out of his eyes.

Still, the cops investigated, and they got nowhere, like I knew they would. Fletcher had a couple of sources in the police department, so he was able to keep track of the investigation. But I wasn't worried. He had trained me too well, and no one had seen my attack on Vaughn.

The next day, I went about my regular routines as though nothing had happened. Waited tables at the Pork Pit, schlepped home to Fletcher's for a few hours, then schlepped back over to the community college for my usual classes.

Going to college was another part of my cover, since that's what most people my age did, and it was something that the old man had insisted on. Apparently, he thought that it would make me more well-rounded or something. You know, in case the whole assassin thing didn't work out.

But I didn't mind too much, especially when it came to the literature classes. Fletcher would read the same books that I was assigned, and then we'd talk about them during lulls at the restaurant. I loved our discussions, since it was another way that I could be close to him that Finn couldn't—or wouldn't.

Once my evening classes were done, I went back home for the night. And then I repeated the whole cycle again and again, just as I would until the next assignment came along.

The only thing I did that was out of the ordinary was read all of the articles about Sebastian Vaughn.

He appeared in story after story, both in the newspaper and on TV. And in every story, in every interview and sound bite, he was quite vocal about the piss-poor job he thought that the cops were doing in their so-far-unsuccessful attempt to find his father's killer—me. Sebastian even vowed to hire his own team of investigators to track down the culprit, but I wasn't worried. He'd never connect the waitress he'd flirted with once upon a time with the assassin who'd so coldly killed his father.

Still, I couldn't help but watch interview after interview with him on TV, and I read every single newspaper article that so much as mentioned his name. Sometimes two or three or even four times over, searching for any hint in his words about how he was doing, how he was feeling, now that his father was gone. I'd felt such an intense spark, such an immediate connection with Sebastian. I supposed that I wanted to keep feeling it, even though I'd never see him again.

One photo that ran over and over again in the newspapers was of Sebastian leaving his father's office the morning after the murder, a briefcase clutched in one hand.

His mouth was set in a hard line, his dark eyes fixed on something outside the frame. He had his free arm around Charlotte's shoulder, holding her close, as though he could somehow protect her from the hurt, shock, and bewilderment that the camera had captured in her young, heartbroken face.

I wasn't exactly sure what prompted me to cut out that photo and tuck it in between the pages of the latest book I was reading, *Murder for Christmas* by Agatha Christie, for my detective fiction class. But the book and the photo stayed on my nightstand. Every night, I would read another chapter or two, before using the photo as a bookmark. Sebastian's handsome, determined face was the last thing I saw before I shut the book.

Maybe it was crazy, but I wanted to reach out and help Sebastian, even though I didn't dare to—and even though I was the one who'd caused him so much pain in the first place. Oh, I didn't regret killing his father, not really, not when he'd been hurting his own daughter. But my heart still ached for the shock and suffering that I'd inflicted on Charlotte and Sebastian. So I kept tabs on him as best I could, hoping that his grief would slowly fade over time and knowing that he and especially Charlotte were better off without their father.

So life went on for me, Sebastian, Charlotte, and everyone else—except Cesar Vaughn.

Four days after the job, Saturday, I was alone in the Pork Pit and closing down the restaurant for the night when the bell over the front door chimed. I sighed, wishing that I'd thought to lock the door already, but I finished wiping down the counter, fixed a polite smile on my face, and turned around.

"Sorry, but we're already closed—"

A bolt of shock zinged through me. My lips parted, but no words came out, because the very last person I'd expected had just walked through the door.

Sebastian.

He wore a somber black suit—a funeral suit—over a white shirt and a shiny black tie, and his wing tips were as glossy as the floor that I'd just mopped. His black hair was slicked back, and lines of exhaustion were etched into his face, like faint cracks in a smooth marble bust, making him seem older than he really was. Still, despite my shock and unease about why he was here, I thought that he'd never looked more handsome—even though I was the cause of his grief. Maybe that was a little twisted of me.

"Hi," he said.

"Hi, yourself." I hesitated. "What are you doing here?"

Sebastian grinned, although his expression was more sad than happy. "I know I'm a little late, but I was wondering if we might have that date after all."

I stared at him, my mouth still hanging open, not sure what to do, what to say, and especially what to make of the sudden hope that surged through my heart. My attraction to him was crazy, stupid, and utterly foolish, especially given what I'd done to his father. But it was there all the same, and I didn't know how to deny it.

Or maybe I just didn't want to.

"I'm sorry," Sebastian said in a hoarse, ragged whisper. "For not calling or sending you a note. I know that I stood you up last night."

Last night, Friday, had been the night of our date. I might have been secretly disappointed, but I hadn't been surprised when he hadn't shown up. I was absolutely floored that he was here now.

I stood frozen in place, my attraction to him warring with all of my training, not to mention my own common sense. I could almost hear Fletcher's voice in my head, urgently whispering to me to get rid of Sebastian. Part of me wholeheartedly agreed with that plan. But there was another voice—my voice—that wondered what the harm of hearing him out would be.

Sebastian grinned again, although it seemed to be much more of an effort this time. "But I had a good excuse. You see, my father—"

"Is dead," I finished so he wouldn't have to. "I saw the news. I'm sorry for your loss, Sebastian."

And I truly was, even though I was responsible for it.

He nodded, accepting my condolences. Then he grinned again. "You know, I think that's the first time you've ever said my name."

I looked at him, not sure what to say. He walked over to where I stood in front of the counter, a wet rag still clutched in my hand. Sebastian stared at me, a hungry look flaring in his eyes. Anticipation and attraction surged through me at his nearness, silencing Fletcher's voice.

"I'm sorry," he repeated. "I should have called or sent a note, at the very least. But with everything that's been going on . . ." He shrugged, then winced, as if that simple motion caused him as much pain as his grief did.

I reached out and gently placed my hand on his arm. "I understand. Again, I'm so sorry. I know how hard it is to lose someone you love. Especially so violently and unexpectedly."

"You do?"

My lips opened, ready to tell him how my family had been murdered by a Fire elemental, ready to share my own private pain with him, ready to let him see that my broken heart wasn't as black as my deeds were.

But suddenly, Finn's voice echoed in my mind. *And no matter what, you should never, ever tell someone all of your secrets.*

I might be able to shut out Fletcher's voice and warnings, Finn's too, but I'd kept my family's death to myself for so long that it was second nature for me to hide it. I opened my mouth again, but no words came out, and I realized that I couldn't go through with my heartfelt confession. Not even for him. Maybe not for anyone ever.

"Gin?"

"What I meant was that it seems like violence is a way of life in Ashland," I finished lamely.

He shrugged again.

"Sit down, and let me fix you something to eat," I said, shifting the focus of the conversation back to him. "You can tell me everything that's been going on the last few days. If you want to, that is."

Sebastian let me guide him over to one of the stools close to the cash register. He put his elbows on the counter, then slumped down over it, as though all of the strength had suddenly seeped out of his bones.

"I feel like this has been the longest week of my life," he said. "The funeral was today. Charlotte cried through the whole thing. I've spent the last two hours at our mansion, dealing with the mourners. Finally, I just couldn't take it anymore. I had to get out of there, at least for a little while. So I left Charlotte with one of the giant drivers she likes, and I left. Does that make me a horrible person?"

"No," I said in a soft voice. "It just makes you human."

Sebastian drew in a breath and started talking. About the funeral, the words the minister had said, everyone who'd shown up at the service. While he talked, I turned a few of the appliances back on, rustled around in the refrigerators, and fixed him the best, most comforting meal that I knew how to make: a cheeseburger with all the fixings; hot, sizzling steak-cut fries; and a thick, rich, decadent triple chocolate milkshake.

Sebastian wound down about the time I finished cooking. I put all the food on a plate, then slid everything across the counter to him. He hesitated, then reached out and grabbed the burger, as if he was suddenly hungrier than he'd thought. He took a big bite of the layers of grilled beef, fresh veggies, and melted cheddar cheese. His eyes rolled up in his head in pleasure, and a sigh of contentment escaped his lips.

That's when I knew that I was doing the right thing. Maybe it was crazy, maybe it was foolish, maybe it was just plain *wrong*, talking to the son of the man I'd killed, but I couldn't send Sebastian away.

I just *couldn't*.

Finn and Fletcher would have been cold and calculating about things, would have seen this as an opportunity to subtly pump Sebastian for any information that he might have about the investigation into his father's death. Maybe I saw things that way too. But I also hoped that it was a chance to soothe his heartache, in whatever small way that I could.

I just hoped that Sebastian never found out what kind of man his father had truly been and how he'd hurt Charlotte again and again. That sort of cruel knowledge would cause him even more pain.

"How is Charlotte?" I asked, after Sebastian had eaten about half of his food.

He sighed and pushed his burger away, as though he'd lost his appetite. "As well as can be expected, I suppose. She's devastated by our father's death. She's been hiding in her room for most of the week. I've tried to be there for her as much as I can, but given all the funeral arrangements and the business deals that my father had going on . . ." His voice trailed off.

The helpless expression on his face made me reach across the counter and put my hand on top of his. "I'm sure she understands. It's hard when you lose someone . . . the way that you did. There are so many details to see to. She'll realize that you're doing the best that you can, for her and your father too, given the situation."

"I hope so."

I squeezed his hand. "Well, I know so."

He looked at me. "You're amazing, do you know that?"

"What do you mean?"

He gestured at his food. "I mean, the guy who stood you up shows up on your doorstep out of the blue, and you end up fixing him the best damn burger he's ever had. Are you sure that your name is Gin? Maybe it should be something else, something like . . . like . . . Genevieve." He snapped his fingers together. "There's a Saint Genevieve, you know."

My breath caught in my throat in surprise and wonderment. If only he knew that Genevieve was my real name. If only he knew who I really was, a girl who'd lost her family. If only he knew how much I could relate to his pain.

If only he knew that I'd killed his father.

That last thought squashed the yearning in my chest. "I'm no saint," I muttered. "More like a sinner."

Understatement of the century.

But Sebastian didn't seem to notice the dark murmur in my voice. He stood up, his hand still on mine. He hesitated, then drew his hand away and walked around the counter, coming to a stop beside the cash register so that we were standing face-to-face. He was several inches taller than I was, so I had to tip my head back to meet his gaze, my heart pounding in my chest in a way that it never had before. He stared back at me, his eyes smoldering like hot coals in his face, his features tight, and his body tense with need, want, guilt, grief, and desire.

Sebastian hesitated a moment longer, then pulled me into his arms and lowered his lips to mine.

The kiss was everything that I'd thought it would be, everything that I'd secretly dreamed it would be—soft, sweet, and utterly breathtaking. Sebastian Vaughn might be a rich guy who could have his pick of girls, but he was surprisingly gentle with me. His lips skimmed mine, his tongue slowly delving into my mouth before retreating. His fingers trailed down my arms before his hands settled on my waist, pulling me a little closer, but that was as far as he went.

His kiss and touch might have been sweet, but hot,

liquid desire thrummed through my body in response, more electric than any I'd ever felt before. Sebastian was hurting because of me, and I wanted to do whatever I could to ease that hurt, to take away that pain, if only for a few moments.

But more than that, I wanted *him*.

Oh, I'd tried to deny it, tried to ignore and forget about it, about *him*, but the truth was that I was desperately attracted to Sebastian. His wit, his charm, his smile, the easy way he teased me, but most important, the way he actually seemed to respond to *me*. For some reason, it seemed like Sebastian could see the real me, the real Gin Blanco, lurking beneath all the many masks that I presented to the world. I'd never had that sort of intense, immediate connection with someone before.

Finally, the kiss ended, although my heart continued to pound, its quick tempo matching the emotions surging through me. Desire. Attraction. Hope. Longing.

Sebastian dropped his hands from my waist. "I'm sorry," he said, running a hand through his hair and mussing the smooth locks, making him look even sexier. "I had no right to do that. It's just . . . the way you were looking at me . . . I couldn't help but kiss you."

"Don't worry about it. What girl wouldn't want to be kissed by a gorgeous guy?"

He smiled. "So I'm gorgeous again, huh?"

"After that kiss? Definitely."

We stared at each other. Sebastian's face clouded over, as if he was going to apologize again, but I cut him off by moving forward, standing on my tiptoes, and lightly pressing my lips to his again. He hesitated, then kissed me back.

I didn't want to, but this time, I broke it off. Because if I didn't, I knew that I was in danger of leading him into the back of the restaurant and making out with him until the sun came up, along with other, more intimate things—things that would rock me far more than a few lip-locks had.

I smoothed down his tie, hoping that he wouldn't notice my trembling fingers and all of the emotions that he stirred in me. Finally, I raised my eyes to his again.

"Come on, now," I said, making my voice light and teasing once more. "Your food's getting cold. Go sit down and finish the rest of your burger."

Sebastian grinned, then gave me a mock salute with his hand. "Yes, ma'am."

# * 13 *

Sebastian finished his food, seeming a little happier than before.

As he ate, I finished shutting down the restaurant, forcing myself to calm down and rein in my racing heart and raging hormones. I'd never considered myself the kind of person to be swept away by either pure emotion or physical attraction, much less give in to either one of them—unlike Finn and his constant, endless, shameless parade of girls—but I'd been in real danger of doing that with Sebastian. It was a bit troubling, how much he affected me. And how much I longed to just give in and enjoy everything he could offer me.

When he was done, I gathered up the dirty plates and stuck them into one of the sinks to wash in the morning. Sebastian insisted on paying me for the meal, and I tucked his money into a slot under the cash register.

Then we stood by the counter, not sure what to do.

"Thank you," Sebastian said. "For everything, but especially for listening." He ran his hand through his hair again. "With my dad and everything that's been going on, I've just felt . . . *numb* the last few days. Lost, alone, adrift. I wanted to feel, I *needed* to feel something tonight. Like somebody cared about me and what I was going through."

"And you came here? Why?"

He looked at me. "Because I had more fun talking with you at that dinner and then here again at the restaurant than I can remember having with anyone in a long time. I think it's your smile. When you look at me, it feels like . . . your smile just lights up something inside me."

My heart swelled with pleasure at his words—even as my stomach clenched with guilt.

"I know tonight wasn't what either one of us had in mind—" he began.

"It was perfect," I cut in. "Absolutely perfect."

Sebastian's eyes crinkled with warmth and gratitude. He nodded at me, then dropped his gaze from mine and cleared his throat, as if he was feeling all of the same emotions that I was.

Well, all of them except the guilt.

"Anyway," he continued, "I'd still like to take you out on that date. If you'll have me."

Once again, my mouth gaped open in surprise. He was hurting, he was grieving, and he was still considerate enough to think about a promise that he'd made to me, a girl he barely knew. More emotion surged through me, even softer, warmer, and more intense than what I'd felt when we'd kissed. Because that sort of thoughtfulness was rare, something to be admired and treasured.

There were so many reasons I should say no to him. So many reasons I should have shown him the door the second he'd arrived. So many reasons I shouldn't have kissed him. But none of them seemed to matter right now—nothing did but the hope shining in Sebastian's eyes.

"A date would be great," I said in a soft voice.

He sighed in relief, as if there had been some doubt about my answer. "Great. Pick you up here Monday night at seven? Just like we planned before?"

I nodded, too unsure of myself to say anything.

He reached out and squeezed my hand. "It's a date, then. But right now, I should be getting home. Charlotte's probably wondering what's happened to me."

"Of course."

He tightened his grip on my hand. "But there's one more thing I need to do before I go."

"Oh? What's that?"

"This."

Sebastian grinned and drew me into his arms for another kiss.

I didn't get home until late that night, and I couldn't keep the small, silly grin off my face or quiet my soft, nonsensical hums of happiness as I parked my car in the driveway, got out, and headed for the porch. After we'd kissed again, Sebastian had left the restaurant, promising to pick me up Monday evening for our date. I couldn't wait to see him again.

All I had to do in the meantime was sell Fletcher on the idea.

Seeing the house rising up out of the dark and knowing

the battle that waited for me inside finally dampened my good mood. The front door was stuck again because of the humidity, annoying me even more, and I had to put my shoulder into it to shove it open. The resulting *screech* made me wince. Maybe Fletcher should replace the door with that black granite one he wanted. It would be worth it not to blast my own eardrums every time I tried to get inside.

I locked the door behind me, dropped my keys into a crystal bowl on a table inside the foyer, and toed off my boots. Then I headed to the back of the house, where a couple of lights burned. Looked like Fletcher had waited up for me. I sighed. More often than not, he wouldn't go to bed until I was home, despite the fact that I was perfectly capable of taking care of myself—and killing anyone who was stupid enough to try to rob me when I was working late at the restaurant.

Sure enough, I found Fletcher sitting on the sofa in the den, with his blue work clothes still on and his white-socked feet stretched out on the battered coffee table in front of him. He was reading a book, although the TV was also on, tuned to some old western that he'd turned the volume down low on.

I plopped down onto one of the recliners. Fletcher kept right on reading his book. For the better part of a minute, the only sound was the steady *creak-creak-creak* of my chair, punctuated by an occasional *crack-crack-crack* of gunfire from the cowboys on TV. But for once, I didn't mind waiting for him to speak. It gave me time to shore up my own arguments.

"You're late," Fletcher finally said, and turned another page in his book. "I thought you'd be here an hour ago."

I drew in a breath, ready to spin my story. "Sebastian came into the restaurant right as I was closing up."

That was enough to make him look up from his book. "What did he want?"

"To say that he was sorry that he didn't keep our date last night."

I told Fletcher everything that Sebastian had said, from his talk of his father's funeral to trying to make sure that Charlotte was okay to his need to escape from all of the mourners who had gathered at the Vaughn mansion. The only thing I edited out was the fact that Sebastian and I had kissed. The old man *definitely* did not need to know about that. He'd claim that I was getting too emotionally involved with Sebastian. Maybe I was, but I could handle it.

I could handle anything as the Spider.

"He asked me out again," I finished up. "For Monday night."

Now came the tricky part. "I thought that I would go out with him, just to see if I can find out what he knows about the police investigation into his father's murder and to make sure there's nothing that can lead back to us. But I wanted to talk to you about it first."

A half-truth, at best. I would carefully nose around and see what information I could get out of Sebastian about the investigation, just to make sure that Fletcher and I were in the clear. But sometime between leaving the Pork Pit and walking into the den, I'd decided that I was seeing Sebastian again, with or without Fletcher's approval. I wanted to make sure that Sebastian was okay. I wanted to see him smile and laugh. But most of all, I wanted him to look at me again the way he had right before he'd kissed me tonight, like he was as desperately consumed by this bright flare of attraction between us as I was.

Still, I kept my face schooled into a calm, bland mask, as though it didn't matter to me whether I went out with Sebastian. Even though it very much did.

Instead of looking at me, Fletcher dropped his green gaze to his book. Thinking. I curled my hands into loose fists, pressing my fingers against the spider rune scars in my palms, to keep from fidgeting. The marks might be the symbol for patience, but having them branded into my hands didn't automatically give me that particular skill. Not even close.

Being patient was something that I still struggled with, whether it was as Gin Blanco, waiting on a customer to finally make up his mind about his order in the Pork Pit, or as the Spider, holding my position until my target was in exactly the right spot. It was probably the thing that Fletcher and I argued about the most. He said that patience was one of the most important skills for an assassin to have, and he was always telling me to slow down, wait, and let events unfold in my favor, to be absolutely sure of what I was doing before I went all in and committed myself wholeheartedly.

Well, I was sure now, so I dug my nails into the silverstone in my skin and held my tongue, waiting for him to say his piece.

After about three minutes, Fletcher finally nodded. "That might be a smart idea," he said. "You going out with Sebastian and seeing what he knows."

I blinked. That wasn't what I'd expected him to say—

not at all. I'd thought that he would warn me to keep my distance from Sebastian. Maybe Fletcher finally realized that I could keep my emotions in check. Maybe he was finally *fully* trusting me to see a job through to the end, despite the unexpected complications that had come up. Maybe the old man finally understood that I was all grown up and capable of making my own decisions. That I was my own person now and not just the lost little girl he'd trained in his own image.

"Especially since I still haven't been able to find out what was in that file that cop gave Vaughn," Fletcher finished his thought. "I got my hands on a copy of the evidence logs, but there's no mention of it being in the safe at Vaughn's office or of the police cataloging it as part of their investigation. In fact, there wasn't any mention of anything being in the safe. It's like the file just . . . disappeared."

Ah, so that's what he was up to. His sources hadn't been able to come up with the information he wanted, so he was willing to let me see if I could get it from Sebastian instead. Nothing bothered Fletcher more than loose ends and unanswered questions. I might not be as patient as he thought I should be, but he was more curious than a basket full of kittens exploring the world for the very first time. Still, I didn't mind him wanting me to track down the file, since I was going to use it as an excuse to see Sebastian again.

"But you found the cop, right?" I asked. "The one who gave Vaughn the file? Can't you just bribe him and ask him what he found?"

Fletcher shook his head. "Yeah, it wasn't too hard to locate him, since you got his first name and his hometown, but I'm afraid it's a little more complicated than that. The cop, Harry Coolidge, isn't from around here. He works down in a town called Blue Marsh, near Savannah. From what I know, Coolidge is a smart, honest, decent cop. He won't take any sort of bribe, and he'd start asking questions about how I even knew about the file. So that option is out."

Fletcher hesitated, as if he was choosing his next words carefully.

"Coolidge has a reputation for being thorough and tenacious, a good investigator who can find clues that others miss. If Vaughn hired him to look into the terrace collapse, maybe even someone who was involved in the construction, it's because that person was dirty—and clever enough to hide whatever he'd done."

"Okay," I said. "I'll find a way to see if Sebastian has any information about the file. Maybe the cops let him go ahead and empty out the safe since he was next of kin. He might have the file buried in a stack somewhere and not even know it."

"Maybe."

Fletcher's lips puckered, his nose scrunched up, and his eyes grew dark and distant, as if he was working through some sort of mental jigsaw puzzle and trying to make the pieces fit together in his head. But he shook off his thoughts and focused his attention on me again.

"All right. Feel Sebastian out during your date, and see if he knows anything about the file, where it is, or what Coolidge was looking into for Cesar. I'll keep digging with my own sources."

"You got it."

His green gaze locked with my gray one. "But be careful, Gin. There's something about this whole situation that's still not sitting right with me. This thing could still go sideways on us."

"Always."

Satisfied for now, Fletcher went back to his book. Our powwow complete, I got to my feet and headed toward the hallway, ready to go upstairs, take a shower, and slip into bed. I reached the doorway and stopped, wondering if I should tell him that I had more than a casual interest in Sebastian, that finding out what he knew about his father's file wasn't the only reason that I wanted to see him again.

But I decided not to. It was one date, and Sebastian could still turn out to be a toad, like all the other rich guys who hit on me at parties. And if he wasn't, if he was the person he'd been so far, the one who seemed so genuinely interested in me . . . well, I'd cross that bridge when I came to it.

"Gin? You need something else?" Fletcher's soft voice snapped me out of my thoughts.

I glanced over my shoulder at him and shook my head. "Nah. I just realized that I forgot to say good night. So . . . good night."

"Good night."

Fletcher focused on his book again. I stared at him, ignoring the guilty twinges in my chest. If he had looked up at that moment, I might have spilled my guts about my feelings for Sebastian and confessed everything to him.

But the old man turned a page, thoroughly engrossed in his story.

So I let out a soft, relieved sigh, left the den, and headed upstairs for the night.

# * 14 *

At precisely seven o'clock Monday evening, Sebastian Vaughn strolled into the Pork Pit, carrying a dozen roses. He grinned, crossed the storefront, and made a gallant bow before straightening back up and handing the flowers to me.

Instead of the typical red, these roses were a deep, dark color. At first, I thought they were black, but then, as I held them up to the light, I realized that the petals actually had a rich blue sheen. The stems were unusual too, milky white instead of the normal green. The thorns were the same pale color, although they seemed to be sharper and longer than usual. All put together, the flowers were beautiful, vibrant, and striking, just like Sebastian.

"Roses!" I exclaimed, playing the part of a girl who was thrilled by such things. It wasn't too much of a stretch. Secretly, I was delighted that he'd brought me flowers. No one ever had before.

"I know most folks like red roses, but I thought that I would bring you something really special. They're called Blue Velvet, and they're from my family's greenhouse," Sebastian said.

I buried my nose in the roses, breathing in deeply and inhaling their scent. They smelled much sweeter than I'd thought they would, given their dark blue color, as though someone had distilled the petals down to their purest, most intense essence. Truth be told, the scent was a bit overpowering, almost cloying, and I had to scrunch up my nose to keep from sneezing. Not exactly the aroma I would have picked if I'd been giving myself flowers, but I appreciated the gesture.

I was standing behind the counter, close to where Fletcher sat behind the cash register, reading. Beaming, I held the flowers out to him.

"Aren't they lovely?"

"Exquisite," he echoed back in a wry voice.

"Is this your . . . father?" Sebastian's eyebrows drew together as he looked back and forth between me and Fletcher, as if he was puzzled by the lack of familial resemblance.

"My cousin, actually," I said. "He . . . adopted me after my family died . . . in a car accident."

That was more or less the cover story that we'd developed long ago to explain my connection to Fletcher and Finn. Funny, but I'd never had a problem telling the lies before.

Sebastian nodded, his face clearing, and he stretched out his hand. "Nice to meet you, Mr. . . ."

"Lane," the old man said in a reluctant voice. "Fletcher Lane."

He took Sebastian's hand and shook it, even though I could tell that he didn't want to. Despite his desire to learn more about Vaughn's mystery file, Fletcher wasn't all that happy about me going out with Sebastian. Then again, he rarely liked any of the guys that I brought around the restaurant, not even the ones that we had no reason to be wary of. Fletcher's dislike of my dates was yet another way in which he was overprotective of me.

He stared at the younger man, his green eyes sharp and thoughtful. Sebastian smiled back at him, although his expression seemed a little uneasy around the edges. Then again, Fletcher's hard, laserlike stare was enough to make anyone nervous, even me.

Fletcher turned to me and held out his hand. "Let me put those in some water for you, Gin. You don't want to keep your young man waiting."

"Thanks," I said, handing the roses over to him. "Ouch!"

Fletcher took the flowers from me, and I pulled my hand back, wincing. I watched a bit of blood well up out of my right thumb, which I'd stabbed into one of the pale thorns.

Sebastian gave me a chagrined look. "Sorry. I should have warned you. They have bigger, sharper thorns than most roses. I think it has something to do with the color of the stems."

"It's okay," I said, grabbing a paper towel and wiping the scarlet drop off my thumb. "It's just a little blood. Nothing to worry about."

"If I could kiss it and make it better, I would," Sebastian said in a low voice that only I could hear.

His gaze locked onto my mouth, as if he was thinking about the soft kisses we'd shared the other night. I certainly was. Sebastian caught me staring at him. He grinned, then flashed me a quick, sly wink. I blushed and dropped my gaze from his.

While Fletcher grabbed an old jelly jar to use as a vase and filled it with water, I untied my work apron, pulled it over my head, and hung it on a hook on the back wall. Then I grabbed my purse, which contained two of my knives, from its slot under the cash register and stepped around the counter. Sebastian reached out and took my hand, careful of my injured thumb.

"So what are we doing tonight? Dinner and a movie?"

He shook his head. "Nothing so predictable as that. I thought you might like to see the greenhouse where your roses came from, along with the rest of my estate."

I glanced at Fletcher, who gave me a tiny nod as he kept arranging the flowers in the jelly jar. Getting invited to the Vaughn estate was too good an opportunity to pass up. Maybe Sebastian would give me a full tour, including a peek at his father's office. If I was extremely lucky, he might even leave me alone in there long enough for me to search for the mystery file.

But more than that, I wanted to see the estate for myself, inside and out. You could tell a lot about someone from his home and the furnishings, photos, and knick-knacks that adorned it, and I wanted to learn more about Sebastian. I wanted to know everything about him.

I flashed him another smile. "So what are we waiting for? Let's go."

Sebastian grinned and tugged me toward the door.

"Don't be too late," Fletcher called out.

I gave him a distracted wave of my hand, completely focused on following Sebastian out of the Pork Pit and into the hot summer night.

Sebastian had a sleek black town car waiting down the block.

"After you, madam," he said, opening the back door and bowing, as though he were a chauffeur.

I giggled and slid into the car. Sebastian shut the door, then went around and got into the other side. He gestured to the giant sitting in the driver's seat. The giant had forgone the usual black chauffeur's uniform in favor of a powder-blue suit that brought out the red color of his hair. Freckles were splattered across his nose and cheeks like brown blood drops, while his eyes were as pale as his suit.

"This is Porter," Sebastian said. "He's been the head of my father's security detail for years. He's agreed to stay on and work for me."

Oh, I knew all about Roy Porter, since Fletcher had included plenty of information about him in the initial file on Vaughn. Porter arranged the security at the estate, but more than that, he had acted as a sort of foreman for Vaughn, overseeing building-material deliveries, checking on crews, and generally making sure that everything ran smoothly at the job sites. He'd also been Vaughn's middleman, the one who actually doled out all the bribes necessary to keep his boss's construction projects chugging along.

From what Fletcher had been able to uncover, Porter went beyond dropping off bribes. Whenever there was a problem that Vaughn's money hadn't been able to fix, Porter had often taken care of it himself—with his fists. Like a couple of weeks before the terrace collapse, when Porter had found two Southtown punks spray-painting graffiti at one of the job sites and had beaten them both to death. A third guy who'd been waiting for his friends in the car had said that Porter had toyed with the punks, breaking their legs so they couldn't run away, then their arms so they couldn't fight back, before finally caving in their skulls with his fists.

Charges had been filed, but nothing ever came of them, because the last guy had been found dead a week later, beaten to death in an eerily similar manner. That time, Porter had been smart enough not to leave any witnesses behind.

I wondered if Sebastian knew what kind of vicious, violent, ruthless man Porter was. Probably not. He hadn't seemed to know about his father either. But seeing Porter cooled some of my enthusiasm for my date with Sebastian and reminded me that I still had work to do tonight.

Porter gave me a polite nod in the mirror. "Ma'am."

I nodded back at him. "Mr. Porter."

"Take us back to the mansion, Porter," Sebastian ordered.

Porter steered the car away from the curb. Sebastian kept up a steady stream of conversation all the way from the downtown loop up to Northtown, where his family's estate was located among Ashland's other mansions. In fact, the Vaughn estate was down the block from Mab Monroe's place. Well, perhaps that was a bit of an understatement. Given Mab's sprawling compound and the thick woods that surrounded it, Sebastian's home was a good two miles away, but he seemed to be the Fire elemental's closest neighbor.

Finally, after about thirty minutes of driving, Porter turned off the road. He reached down into the console between the front seats and picked up a small black clicker, which he used to open the gate that led into the estate. The giant steered the car through the opening and up a long driveway that curved to the top of a hill.

Even though I'd seen the Vaughn estate in the surveillance photographs that Fletcher had given me, I still peered out the window, as though I'd never seen the grounds or the house sitting in the middle of them before.

The mansion was impressive, even by Northtown standards. Six stories of stone towered into the air, old, solid, sturdy gray granite that had easily weathered the wear and tear of the years and would continue to do so for decades to come. The house had three separate wings, each sporting a variety of balconies and patios, while white trellises climbed from floor to floor, all with roses of different colors winding through them—red, white, pink, and even a pale green. The only shade that I didn't see was the dark blue of the flowers that Sebastian had given me earlier.

"Well," Sebastian said, grinning. "Home sweet home. What do you think of it?"

"It's gorgeous."

He squeezed my hand. "Just wait until you see the inside." He leaned even closer to me. "Especially my bedroom."

I knew that he was teasing me, but I couldn't help the blush that crept up my cheeks. Kissing Sebastian was one thing. So were raging hormones and getting caught up in the moment. But I wasn't going to be foolish enough to sleep with him—even though it was all that I could think about right now. His lips on mine, his warm skin flush with my own, his fingers slowly trailing down my body as he pulled me even closer . . .

I realized that Porter was staring at me in the rearview mirror, a flat, measured look on his freckled face as though I were an ant under a magnifying glass, one that he was thinking about burning with the lens. The soft smile slid from my lips, while the pleasant heat evaporated from my cheeks. A bucket of ice water couldn't have been more effective.

Porter kept looking at me, his own expression cold and level. What was his problem? Was he pissed that Vaughn was dead and he was working for his son now? Or did he not like playing chauffeur? I didn't know, but it made those whispered doubts rise up in my mind again.

"Come on," Sebastian said. "Let me show you around."

We got out of the car, which Porter then drove behind the house, probably to park it in the garage there. Sebastian threaded his fingers through mine and led me up the main steps and into the house.

The mansion was even more impressive on the inside than it was on the outside. High vaulted ceilings, crystal chandeliers, gleaming hardwood floors, marble staircases, exquisite antiques everywhere you looked. Everything was expensive, elegant, and polished to a high gloss, and the interior could have easily been featured in a magazine.

Still, something about the furnishings bothered me. Mainly because they didn't match up with the rather spartan decor I'd seen in Vaughn's office. In fact, the only thing that was similar was the thick Persian rugs that covered the floors.

"It's lovely," I said. "Everything is so fine."

Sebastian beamed. "Do you like it? The staff just finished putting everything together this morning. I've been doing a little redecorating since my father . . . passed away. He was never much for comfort, but after my mother died, he didn't want to add or change anything about the house. I think we've had the same curtains in every room for fifteen years now. But I wanted . . . a fresh start."

I nodded. I knew all about fresh starts, so I could understand his sentiment, despite the guilt that it stirred in my chest.

We strolled from room to room and floor to floor, passing all sorts of staff. Housekeepers dusting knickknacks in the living rooms, cooks slicing vegetables in the kitchen areas, even a guy dressed in a formal tuxedo in one of the dining rooms, like he was some stuffy English butler out of a movie ready to serve a table full of guests tea, scones, and insults. Funny, but Vaughn hadn't employed this many people. I supposed Sebastian had hired some extra folks to help with the funeral and all of the redecorating.

But they all bowed their heads when Sebastian passed, murmuring quiet, respectful hellos to "Mr. Vaughn." It took me a while to get used to the idea that Sebastian *was* Mr. Vaughn now—and that I was the one who'd made it happen.

Sebastian chatted throughout the tour, pointing out interesting paintings, drawing my attention to the way the crystal chandeliers glistened overhead, and even talking about some of the masonry work his father had done on the staircases. Apparently, Vaughn had built the mansion when Sebastian was a boy.

"I loved helping my father with his work," Sebastian said in a proud voice. "Even though all I could do back then was hand him his tools and watch him work his magic on the marble."

Until now, the stone of the mansion had been pretty subdued, much like the housekeeping staff, but whispers sprang to life at Sebastian's words, along with low, somber notes of sorrow. Stones couldn't cry—not like people did—but the murmurs told me that the marble and granite were grieving in their own way for Vaughn, the man who had spent so much time crafting and taking care of them.

"Your father was a Stone elemental, right?" I asked, even though I already knew the answer. "I remember hearing that on the news. Do you have the same sort of magic?"

Sebastian shook his head. "Unfortunately, no. I don't have any magic. Charlotte has a bit of his Stone power, but she's not as strong as he was."

The murmurs in the marble took on a darker, harsher cadence, almost as if they didn't like Sebastian's words. I frowned, wondering what was troubling them so much. Obviously, they were greatly upset by Vaughn's death, and the mourners and all of their feelings toward Vaughn were also sure to have left an impact. Perhaps the marble and granite were still trying to absorb all of those powerful emotions. Or could it be something else? I cocked my head to the side, listening to what the stones were trying to tell me—

"Is something wrong?" Sebastian asked. "You have a strange look on your face."

The dark murmurs vanished. I listened a second longer, but all I heard now were those low, somber notes of grief. "Everything's fine."

Sebastian smiled. "All right, then. Let's go upstairs . . ."

We continued with the tour, eventually winding up on the third floor.

"And now the library," Sebastian said, throwing the double doors wide open.

The library was the biggest room we'd been in so far. Actually, it was two rooms, divided into equal-sized sections by a granite fireplace that stood in the middle. A grate on either side of the fireplace let heat flow into both areas, while two archways, one at the front of the library and one at the back, led to the next room over. Floor-to-ceiling shelves lined with books covered the other walls in the left section, while a series of chairs and couches with thick cushions were scattered around the room.

"My father used this area as his office," Sebastian said, walking past the fireplace and into the right-hand section of the library. "It was his favorite room, not counting the greenhouse."

More bookcases, chairs, and couches took up this space, although I would have known it was Vaughn's office thanks to all the models. Stone models were lined up on the fireplace mantel, and even more perched on the bookshelves and end tables. A few even hung from the ceiling like clusters of wind chimes.

I eyed the scale buildings, remembering how Vaughn

had used his magic to shatter his miniature creations, before examining the rest of the room. A series of glass windows were set into the back wall, letting the evening sun spill over the large desk that stood in front of them—Vaughn's desk.

My gaze locked onto the antique wood, which was covered with a computer monitor, mouse, and keyboard, several small blocks of stone, and, most important, stacks and stacks of papers. I didn't spot the manila folder that Vaughn had put into his office safe, but this was the most likely place for it to be if Sebastian had emptied out the safe and brought the contents home.

"Well?" Sebastian asked, beaming with pride again. "What do you think?"

"I—"

A knock sounded on one of the open library doors, cutting me off, and Porter appeared. "Mr. Vaughn," he said. "A word, please."

Sebastian sighed. "Please excuse me."

"Sure."

Sebastian squeezed my hand, then moved over to see what Porter wanted. The two of them stepped into the left part of the library, out of my line of sight, and started murmuring. Their words were too low for me to make out easily, so I wandered around the office, pretending to be fascinated by the models. In truth, I *was* fascinated by them, but they weren't my focus right now—the desk was.

While Sebastian and Porter continued to speak in low tones, I made my way over to the desk, running my fingers over the smooth wood, as though I were admiring it, even as I scanned the surface. The computer monitor, mouse, and keyboard had been shoved to one side of the desk, along with the blocks of stone, as though someone had wanted them out of the way. Piles of papers squatted in the center, a high mound in the middle that tapered down like a snowdrift spreading across the rest of the wood. It looked like Sebastian had started going through his father's files already. It didn't surprise me. Just because a family member died didn't mean that the world stopped turning. There were still things to do, people to contact, funeral arrangements to make, bills to pay. In Sebastian's case, there was Vaughn Construction to run. Still, maybe the papers or something else tucked away in one of the desk drawers would tell me more about Vaughn's meeting with his cop buddy, Harry Coolidge.

I glanced over my shoulder, but Sebastian and Porter were still talking in the other section of the library, so they couldn't see me. I pulled the chair away from the desk so I could have better access to the drawers for my quick search—

A pink sneaker peeked out from underneath the edge of the wood.

I froze, wondering whose shoe it was, and then I remembered. I wondered if she realized what I'd been up to. I hoped not, but there was nothing I could do about it, so I rolled the chair out the rest of the way and bent down.

Charlotte Vaughn peered out at me from underneath the desk.

In addition to her pink sneakers, she was wearing pink shorts and a white T-shirt with a sparkly pink heart in the middle of it. Her long black hair was pulled back into a

French braid, showing off her pretty face. Apparently, I'd startled her as much as she had surprised me, because she stared up at me with wide, worried eyes.

I crouched down so that my face was level with hers. "Hi there, sweetheart. Do you remember me? I'm Sebastian's friend from the barbecue restaurant."

Charlotte stared at me and slowly nodded, her fingers curling around a book that was lying on the floor next to her. I tilted my head so I could see the title on the spine.

"*Redwall* by Brian Jacques." I nodded my head in approval. "That's one of my favorites."

She stared at me for several seconds. "Really?" Her voice was a low whisper.

"Really." I gave her a small smile. "I like to read too."

A hint of a smile tugged up her lips. But the spark of happiness fled just as quickly, and her face turned sad again as she dropped her gaze to the book and stroked her fingers over the cover.

"My papa gave it to me," she said. "Last week. We were reading it together."

Charlotte kept staring at her book, so she didn't see the smile fall from my face or the guilt that took its place.

Footsteps sounded, and Charlotte scrunched down even further, like a turtle retreating back into the wooden shell of the desk. I glanced up at Sebastian, who had finished his business with Porter and come back into the office. He stepped to one side so he could see what I was looking at.

He sighed. "You're supposed to be in your room for the night, Charlotte. I told you that I was having a guest over."

Charlotte stared up at her big brother, her eyes dark and troubled. She brought her book up to her chest and cradled it tightly, the way some kids might hug a stuffed animal.

Sebastian hesitated, like he wanted to say something else, but he shook his head and held his hand out to me again. "Let's leave Charlotte to her book."

"Of course." I took his hand and let him help me to my feet before staring down at her. "'Bye, Charlotte."

Her only response was to clutch her book even tighter.

"Come on, Gin," Sebastian said.

I let him lead me away, although I glanced back over my shoulder. Charlotte was now standing behind the desk, still holding on to her book. For some reason, the look she gave me seemed even sadder than before, as though she knew some secret that I didn't.

# ❖ 15 ❖

Sebastian escorted me out of the library and shut the doors behind him.

"I'm sorry about that," he said. "Charlotte's been having a . . . hard time dealing with our father's death. More often than not, I find her hiding under his desk, almost like she thinks he's going to come back at any second. I don't think she really understands that he's gone yet."

I frowned. Charlotte was thirteen, hardly a little girl anymore. I'd known all about death, grief, and people not coming back at that age. But Sebastian was talking about her as though she couldn't understand anything that was going on around her.

He didn't say anything else, and I didn't volunteer a response. Instead, he whirled around and hurried away from the closed doors, as though he wanted to get away from the library and all the memories that it raised. I followed him, giving him the space he needed.

Eventually, Sebastian led me through another door, down a set of stairs, and out onto the south lawn. His pace slowed back down to a more normal level, as though he'd left his father's ghost behind inside the mansion.

The estate grounds were just as immaculate as the mansion. Acres of grass rolled out like a thick, lush carpet before giving way to patches of brown woods in the distance. Clusters of trees dotted the lawn, their limbs arching out like canopies and providing shade for the bright summer flowers blooming in the rich beds of black earth below.

Tennis courts, an Olympic-size swimming pool, an outdoor hot tub with its own stone deck. We passed all that and more. And just like inside the house, everything was perfect, from the freshly painted lines on the courts to the crystal-blue surface of the water in the pool to the crisp white towels arranged in deck chairs by the hot tub.

We kept walking, finally reaching a round, domed marble building perched on a small rise above a large pond. I recognized the structure—it had been one of the models that Vaughn had in his office.

Sebastian pointed at the building. "My father's mausoleum," he said. "He built it himself, just like he did the mansion. We put him in there the day of the funeral, right next to my mother. She died in a car accident several years ago."

*I'd* put Vaughn in there—nobody else. But I couldn't tell Sebastian that, so I simply nodded instead, despite the guilt that flared up in me.

Sebastian stared at the structure, his face tight, his shoulders tense, his eyes dark and unreadable. He shook his head, then pulled me forward again. "Come on."

He led me past the mausoleum and over to a stone path that wrapped all the way around to the far side of the pond. Trees had been planted along either side of the walkway, creating a beautiful arch of leaves and limbs above our heads. We stepped past the last of the trees, and I gasped at the sight before me.

"And this," Sebastian said, throwing his hand out wide, "is the greenhouse."

The structure had the same solid gray granite foundation as the mansion, but the sides were made entirely of glass, each panel gleaming in the soft rays of the setting sun. The panes shimmered so brightly that it took me a moment to realize that they were arranged in specific patterns that looked like flowers, vines, and petals, like a garden made out of glass. The sides of the structure rose some fifty feet into the air before veering up to a sharp point, making the whole structure resemble an enormous diamond sticking up out of the ground, just waiting for someone to come along and pluck it out of the earth.

"It's beautiful," I whispered.

Sebastian grinned. "Just wait until you see the inside."

He opened the door, and I stepped through to the other side. The August evening had been muggy enough, but the inside of the greenhouse was almost stifling, and condensation slid down the glass panels in slick, steady drops. Orchids, lilies, and other, more exotic tropical flowers that I didn't recognize bloomed from one side of the greenhouse to the other, their petals as bright and shiny as jewels. I even spotted a few palmetto trees, clustered together here and there, their thick trunks stretching up toward the ceiling.

No matter their shape or size, all of the flowers were set in long, wide white marble planters that perched on waist-high tables. The tables themselves had been arranged into several neat rows running from the front to the back of the building. The clusters of trees stood at the ends of the tables, marking various walkways through the greenhouse.

I listened, but the stone planters only whispered of their pride in housing the gorgeous flowers, along with a few grumbles about all the moisture that constantly dripped off the ceiling and windows and spattered onto them.

Sebastian pointed out several rows of flowers starting in the middle of the greenhouse and going all the way over to one of the walls—roses. The ones closest to the door were a pale, delicate sky blue with forest-green stems, but the farther down the rows you went, the darker the petals and the lighter the stems became. Several rows of flowers close to one of the walls had the same deep, dark, vibrant blue shade and milky stems as the ones that Sebastian had brought me earlier.

"More of my father's work," he said, seeing my curious gaze. "He wanted to see how dark and light he could get the petals and stems on the same plant. It was a hobby of his, along with building models."

Well, I supposed this answered my question about why Vaughn had chosen two thorns for the letter V in his business rune. I made a mental note to tell Fletcher about the greenhouse. Despite all of his digging, he hadn't known that Vaughn was into flowers. I didn't know that it really mattered at this point, but Fletcher always said that the smallest piece of information could be the key to figuring out a job. Maybe knowing about the greenhouse would give him some more insight into Vaughn.

"My father always seemed to be happiest here," Sebastian said, walking over and fingering a petal on one of the sky-blue roses. "Charlotte used to come out here and spend hours with him too."

As soon as Sebastian touched the flower, a murmur rippled through the stone planter that housed it, the same dark murmur that I'd sensed in the mansion earlier. Curious, I reached out with my magic, trying to figure out exactly what the marble was muttering about. But I couldn't understand what the stones were trying to tell me, like a song that you couldn't quite decipher the lyrics to.

"Come on," Sebastian said, dropping his hand from the rose. "There's one more thing I want to show you."

He held out his hand, which I took. Once again, the dark mutters in the marble intensified, but this time, I ignored them. I'd killed Vaughn. There was no danger here now. Perhaps the stones simply realized what I'd done to their master and didn't like my presence. Either way, I was focused on Sebastian now, not them.

He led me out the far side of the greenhouse and down to another, smaller pond that lay at the bottom of a hill. I gasped in surprise again. A romantic table for two was set up at the water's edge. Lit candles the same deep, dark blue as my roses flickered in the summer breeze, while covered silver platters on the table reflected the wavering lights. Fine china sat on top of the white tablecloth, and I could see the letter V with its thorn rune pattern shimmering in gold thread in the fabric.

It was one of the most elegant, elaborate dinners that I'd ever been invited to, and it was definitely the nicest thing that any guy had ever done for me. Finn's idea of a romantic evening had been making out in one of the freezers in the back of the Pork Pit. But this . . . this was *amazing*, like something out of one of the rom-coms I secretly loved to watch with Sophia.

But despite my pleasure, my stomach clenched at all the trouble Sebastian had gone to for me. Or at least had his staff go to for me. Because I definitely didn't deserve it. Not the flowers, not the tour, not the romantic dinner—not one little *shred* of it.

Maybe Finn and Fletcher were right. Maybe this wasn't such a good idea. Because no matter how much I wanted to pretend otherwise, the simple fact was that I had killed Sebastian's father. And if he ever found out, he would hate me for it. How could he not? And I didn't know if I could bear that. Not now. Not after he'd been so wonderful to me.

"Much better than dinner and a movie, don't you think?" Sebastian said.

Somehow I swallowed down my guilt. "Much better," I agreed. "But it's too much. You shouldn't have gone to all of this bother."

He shook his head. "No, it's not too much. You were there for me when I needed someone the other night. I wanted to thank you for that, and this was the best way I knew how."

His eyes met mine, and I found myself drowning, drowning, drowning in his dark, sincere gaze. How did he always know exactly what to do and say to make me melt? We hadn't known each other all that long, but it seemed like Sebastian already knew me better than anyone, even Fletcher.

Once again, my heart squeezed at how I'd hurt him, at this secret that would always stand between us, at the specter of his father that would never leave my mind.

But Sebastian didn't seem to notice my distress. Instead, he stepped even closer and cupped my face with his hand, his skin warm and smooth against my own.

"Gin," he whispered.

He lowered his lips to mine, my eyes fluttered closed, and I forgot about everything else except the way that he made me feel.

At least for tonight.

# * 16 *

The next two weeks were some of the happiest of my life.

Sebastian and I had such a good time at dinner, laughing, talking, and getting to know each other, that he asked me to go out with him again the next night. Since I hadn't had time to look for the file in his father's office, I said yes.

Well, I really said yes because I wanted to see him again, but Fletcher didn't need to know that. No one did but me.

That next night and next date turned into another night and another date, then another . . .

Sebastian and I spent as much time together as we could. Sometimes he managed to sneak away from the office long enough to come have lunch at the Pork Pit, and every evening when my shift was over, he swung by the restaurant and picked me up. Sometimes we drove around Ashland for hours, just talking. Other times, we went to the movies or some of the city's many museums, like Briartop, where we rented a paddleboat and fed the ducks as we floated around the island. We even trekked up to Cypress Mountain one afternoon to explore the shops and sights there. I took Sebastian to my favorite hole-in-the-wall restaurants, like the Cake Walk, while he introduced me to some of Ashland's finer dining establishments, including Underwood's. Some nights, he drove me out to his family's estate, and we explored the grounds hand in hand, before finding a dark, private corner and melting into each other's arms.

Despite all my visits to the estate, I never did get any closer to finding Vaughn's mysterious file. Oh, Sebastian took me to his father's office in the library several times, but he never left me alone long enough for me to search for the file. And after a while, I didn't care about finding it anymore. Vaughn was dead. He couldn't hurt Charlotte anymore. Nothing else mattered.

Except for Sebastian.

With every word, every date, every soft kiss and sweet caress, I fell harder and harder for him. He was just so *good* to me, so kind, thoughtful, and considerate, and so focused on doing whatever he thought would make me happy, whether it was bringing me more roses, buying me a jumbo cookie at a sweets shop, or telling a bad joke to make me laugh after a rotten day at the restaurant. I'd spent so much time creeping around in the shadows that I loved having someone's unwavering focus and undivided attention, like being with me was the highlight of his day. The thing that he looked forward to whenever we were apart.

The *only* thing that mattered.

Of course, Finn didn't approve of my new relationship, but I ignored his snide quips and comments. He was simply being an annoying, egotistical pest, like always. Fletcher wasn't happy about my involvement with Sebastian either, but he didn't give me any more dire warnings to stay away from him. Still, I could see the disapproval in the old man's eyes. That was something else that I ignored, although it was harder than it was with Finn.

But it was worth it, because for the first time in a long time, I was actually . . . *happy*.

Oh, I'd never been *unhappy*, not with Fletcher and especially not learning how to be the Spider. Training with the old man had always made me feel smart and strong and powerful, made me forget the scared little girl I'd been, living on the streets, and especially made me feel like I was in control of my own life, my own fate, my own destiny. Like I could do anything, overcome anything, survive anything.

But being with Sebastian made me feel *alive* in a way that I thought had died the night my family was murdered. I felt like a different person when I was with him, like I really was a simple waitress who was going out with a great guy. When I was with Sebastian, I could forget about all of the bad stuff that had happened to me, and I could just be in the moment with him. Talking, laughing, kissing, canoodling. Things were going so well between us that I even allowed myself to have silly, stupid, romantic daydreams about the future, about *our* future together.

The only thing that ruined my happiness was the fact—the cold, hard, inescapable fact—that I'd killed Cesar Vaughn.

The job hadn't been any different from any other that I'd done. Really, it had been far easier than most. I'd never lost sleep over being an assassin before, but try as I might, I just couldn't shake Vaughn. More than once, I dreamed about stabbing him in his office and his final gasps for breath with Charlotte's name on his lips. I still didn't know what to make of that. But the really bizarre thing was that they weren't even dreams so much as memories of that night that I kept reliving over and over again every time I closed my eyes. Something that I hadn't done since my family had been murdered.

Then, of course, there was Sebastian, who was still looking for his father's killer, despite the fact that the cops had nothing to go on, no witnesses, no evidence, and absolutely no suspects. The Vaughn murder was rapidly becoming a cold case, and everyone knew it, including Sebastian.

Still, after the initial shock wore off, Sebastian didn't seem all that upset by his father's death. Several times, he let it slip that Vaughn wasn't the stand-up guy he'd pretended to be. He never said anything about his father abusing Charlotte, but I was beginning to think that he'd suspected that something was going on. But as soon as he said something to that effect, Sebastian would look away from me, guilt flaring in his eyes, not wanting to speak ill of his beloved papa.

Still, despite the memories, my lingering guilt, and my growing feelings for him, I had no delusions about telling Sebastian what I'd done to his father. That was a stupid way to get a ticket to death row, no matter what kind of relationship we had or how much I thought he cared about me. But more than once, I had to bite my lip to keep from telling Sebastian that he was exactly right about his father and that he and Charlotte were better off without Vaughn in their lives.

"What are you thinking about?" A whispered voice broke into my thoughts.

I focused on Sebastian. The two of us were lying on a thick blanket in the shade of the greenhouse, having enjoyed a picnic of fried chicken, macaroni salad, fresh summer vegetables, and all the other fixings that I'd made at the Pork Pit. "I was thinking how nice it is to be here with you. Just the two of us."

Sebastian smiled. "Just the two of us. I like the sound of that." He hesitated. "Actually, I need to ask you something."

I froze, thinking that he'd somehow figured out my involvement in his father's death. The same paranoid conclusion that I jumped to every single time he asked me a question. And once again, I wasn't sure what I would say if he ever found out the truth.

"I'm going ahead with the event that my father was planning for this weekend," Sebastian said. "The party marking his and Charlotte's birthdays. Only now it will be a celebration of his life too. I was wondering if you'd be my date."

Despite the fact that part of me wanted to say yes, I hesitated. I'd already known that Sebastian was going through with the party, thanks to Fletcher's sources. The problem was that it was going to be a huge event, with people coming in from all over Ashland and beyond. Even Finn had managed to wrangle an invitation, thanks to his internship at the bank. Everyone who was anyone in the city would be at the party, if only out of curiosity about Vaughn's murder, and Sebastian would be the center of attention.

And so would I, if I agreed to this.

"Please," he said, sensing my hesitation. "It'll be fun. I promise. Plus, I figured that it was time for us to be seen out in public together. I've kept you all to myself for too long. Don't you agree?"

His voice took on a light, teasing note, and I finally smiled, giving in to his request. "But I don't have anything to wear." I paused. "Unless you think that showing up in my waiter outfit is okay."

He chuckled, then waved his hand. "Don't worry. I'll take care of everything. All you have to do is get dressed and show up. Please, Gin? This is really important to me. A final way to honor my father."

It was the soft "please" that did me in, despite the guilt that tightened my stomach again. What was it about Sebastian that made it so hard for me to deny him anything? "Okay," I said. "Just tell me when and where, and I'll be there."

"It's a date," he whispered.

Sebastian drew me into the warm circle of his arms, and I forgot about the rest of the world and all the worries that went with it.

For tonight, anyway.

I smoothed down the fabric of the dress I was wearing. "I'm not sure about this. It's a little . . . fancier than I thought it would be."

I stood in front of a full-length mirror in my bedroom, staring at the gown that Sebastian had sent over to the Pork Pit for me to wear. It was the night of his party, and I'd spent the last hour getting dressed. Now I was all ready to go, even if I was freaking out about my dress.

It was a beautiful gown, a Fiona Fine original according to the hand-stitched tag, so I knew that Sebastian had paid a pretty price for it. The dress had wide straps covered with large, milky moonstones that gleamed underneath the lights. The straps led down to a tight, corseted bodice, also covered with jewels, before the gems gave way to soft, muted silver fabric, and the rest of the dress cascaded into a rippling skirt that flowed like a river of silk around my legs. Three-inch stilettos in the same silver covered my feet. He'd even sent over a small silver purse, although the only things I'd put into it were some lip balm, a pack of tissues, and one of my knives.

*I saw this and thought of your beautiful eyes.* That's what a note in the box with the dress said. I didn't know about that, but it was definitely the finest garment I'd ever worn.

"Well, I think it looks wonderful, darling," a firm voice cut in.

A pair of clear, almost colorless eyes met mine in the mirror, and the dwarf smiled at me, her white-blond curls looking even more exquisite than my own.

Jolene "Jo-Jo" Deveraux had come over an hour ago to do my hair and makeup, and her efforts more than matched the gorgeous gown. Jo-Jo had expertly piled my dark brown hair high on top of my head into a simple bun, leaving only a few, softly curled wisps free to brush along my face. She'd rimmed my eyes with silver liner and a smoky black shadow and painted my lips a dark blue, almost the same shade as the dozen roses that Sebastian had sent along with the dress. All put together, I looked like some glittering Goth princess, and I felt that way too.

I sashayed from side to side, watching the dress swish around my body and taking in my reflection in the mirror. No waiter uniform tonight. I wasn't sure how I felt about that, though. Fletcher had taught me how to blend in with the shadows, but this dress would definitely make me stand out in the crowd.

"Jo-Jo's right," a rough voice said behind me. "You look real pretty."

I turned to see Fletcher leaning against the doorway, his arms crossed over his chest, still wearing his blue work clothes from the Pork Pit. He hadn't said much when I'd told him that Sebastian wanted me to attend the party as his date, but the old man had given me a sad, almost disappointed look that I hadn't quite been able to decipher. Tonight, though, his face was carefully neutral. It made me love him even more to see how hard he was trying to let me go have a good time without mentioning his misgivings about Sebastian yet again.

"Thank you," I told Fletcher. "That means a lot, coming from you, especially tonight."

He *harrumph*ed, but his lips twitched up into a small smile.

"Just . . . be careful, darling," Jo-Jo said.

Her eyes took on a cloudy look, like she was staring at something in the distance. Most Air elementals had a bit of precognition, and Jo-Jo was no exception, since the wind whispered to her of all the things that might come to pass.

I waited, wondering if Jo-Jo would say anything else, but her eyes quickly cleared. She smiled at me again before gathering up her makeup supplies, stuffing everything into a bag, and going downstairs, leaving me alone with Fletcher.

I turned away from the mirror to face him. "I know that you think this is a bad idea," I began. "Me seeing Sebastian, spending so much time with him, going to the party tonight, all of it. But I know what I'm doing. If nothing else, this will finally give me a chance to search the library to see if I can find Vaughn's file."

Fletcher nodded. "I appreciate that. But be careful tonight, okay, Gin? I might not have magic like Jo-Jo does, but something about this whole situation still doesn't sit right with me, and the deeper I dig, the less I find. One of my sources is supposed to contact me later on tonight. I'm hoping his information pans out and that we'll finally at least know who hired us to kill Vaughn."

"You're still worried, even though the cops have no leads and the back half of the money for the job cleared?"

The money had shown up in one of Fletcher's anonymous accounts three days after I'd killed Vaughn, right on schedule. Whoever the client was, it seemed like he'd been happy with services rendered, and Fletcher hadn't heard a peep out of him since. No follow-up e-mails, no more ads in the newspaper asking about pork prices, nothing.

He nodded again. "Even though."

I walked over and kissed his wrinkled cheek, careful not to smear the lipstick that Jo-Jo had applied to my lips.

"Don't you worry," I said. "I'm not going to turn into a pumpkin at midnight like Cinderella, and I'll be back home before you know it."

"I hope so." Despite the smile on his face, that strange, troubled light flared in his eyes again. "I really hope so."

## 17

As thoughtful as always, Sebastian had sent a car over to Fletcher's house to pick me up. I stepped out onto the front porch to find that the vehicle had already pulled up the driveway and stopped in front of the house.

Instead of Porter, another giant was driving, one with broad shoulders, a shaved head, and skin that was a shade darker than his ebony eyes. He wore a formal tuxedo, which only added to his air of ultimate cool.

He bowed his head when I approached and gestured at the car. "Your chariot awaits."

I raised my eyebrows, not sure if he was being serious.

The giant flashed me a slightly mischievous grin. "I always wanted to say that."

I grinned back at him. "Me too, Mr. . . ."

"Xavier."

I nodded. "Nice to meet you."

"You too."

I slid into the backseat. Xavier shut the door behind me and walked around the car to get into the front. I glanced over at the house. Fletcher was standing on the porch, his hands stuck in his pants pockets, watching me leave. I waved at him. He hesitated, then waved back at me. And that was the last I saw of him before Xavier threw the car into gear and steered down the driveway.

I hadn't seen Xavier before, so I casually chatted him up as he drove, asking about his background and anything else he was willing to talk about. Fletcher always said that the staff knew all of the best, juiciest gossip about what really went on behind closed doors. Xavier was happy to tell me all about how he was Charlotte's personal driver and took her back and forth to school every day.

"She's a sweet kid," he said. "It's a shame what happened to her father."

I shifted in the seat. "Yeah. A shame."

"But driving Charlotte is only a part-time gig, so I'm getting ready to start working as a patrolman for the police department," Xavier said. "I'm hoping to move up the ranks, but for now, I'm going to be patrolling in Northtown, mostly around this new nightclub that's opening up there."

I kept quiet, letting him talk.

"You should go check out the club sometime," he said. "It's supposed to be something else when it's finished. Besides, I know how much Sebastian loves to party."

I frowned. Sebastian hadn't struck me as the party type. He didn't smoke, and I hadn't seen him have more than one drink at any given time. Plus, he'd seemed perfectly happy with our quiet, low-key dates so far. Maybe Xavier wasn't the best source of information after all.

Either way, I didn't get a chance to question him further, because we'd arrived at the estate. Xavier dropped me off at the front of the mansion, then drove the car around to the back.

Sebastian was waiting for me at the top of the steps outside the mansion. Like Xavier, he wore a classic tuxedo that fit him perfectly. The black jacket and pants showed off the sleek lines of his body, while the white shirt hinted at the hard muscles underneath. His black hair was slicked back in an artful style. His face split into a wide smile when he saw me, one that made his eyes light up like dark, polished gems.

He was the epitome of suave and sexy, but even more than that, the good, kind man underneath the suit made my heart speed up.

He sauntered down the steps and offered me his hand. "You look amazing," he said in a husky voice. "Although seeing you like this makes me want to take you inside and peel that dress off you—slowly."

I couldn't help the blush that blossomed in my cheeks and the heat that thrummed through my body. So far, Sebastian and I hadn't gone beyond kissing and some heavy petting, but I was no virgin, and neither was he. I could tell how much he wanted me whenever we were together, but he'd respected my wishes not to take that next step.

Tonight, though . . . I felt like *anything* could happen.

"Thanks," I murmured back. "I might take you up on that later."

He kept his eyes on mine as he raised my hand to his

lips. The chaste kiss he brushed across my knuckles sent another hot spike of anticipation through me. "It's a date, Gin."

Yes, it was—and a promise of pleasure to come.

His lips lingered on my skin a moment before he straightened up and tucked my arm through his. "Are you ready for tonight?"

"It's your night," I said, smiling up at him. "I'm just your sidekick, remember?"

He let out a low, throaty laugh. "Yes, I suppose tonight *is* my night in many ways. I've worked hard to get here, and now it's finally happening."

I frowned, wondering what he meant, but Sebastian gave me another winning smile.

"Actually, if things go well, I thought that we might sneak out of the party a little early. Have a quiet drink and talk—about us."

"Us?"

My heart hammered in my chest, so loud that I thought he would hear it. I'd been so happy being with Sebastian these last two weeks that I hadn't thought much about the future, other than my stupid daydreams. I hadn't *let* myself think about it, because I knew that as soon as I found Vaughn's file or Fletcher figured out what was bothering him about the job, I wouldn't have an excuse to see Sebastian anymore. Fletcher would insist that I break things off with him, and rightfully so. But Sebastian's serious tone indicated that he'd given a lot of thought to the future and that he wanted me to be a part of his.

"Gin? Are you okay?"

"Of course," I said in a smooth voice, hiding the turbulent emotions racing through me. "But don't you think that it's a little soon to be talking about the future? We've only been seeing each other a couple of weeks."

"I know it's soon, but I also know *exactly* how I feel about you. And I think I know how you feel about me too. So what do you say? Let's slip away from the party later, have a drink, and talk. Okay?"

He smiled again, and I was simply . . . *lost*.

The same way that I'd been lost ever since that first night when I'd talked to him outside the library at Dawson's mansion. And again when he'd kissed me inside the Pork Pit. And yet again when he'd arranged that romantic dinner for us. And all of the sweet, wonderful, thoughtful things that he'd done for me since then.

"Gin?"

I stared into his eyes, letting myself drown in them, in him, yet again. "I'd love that."

*Just like I love you.*

The words rose unbidden in my mind. For a moment, everything just stopped. Then my brain kicked back into gear, and I realized that my heart was hammering even harder than before.

Because the words were true—so very true.

Assassins weren't supposed to fall in love. Oh, it wasn't one of Fletcher's hard-and-fast rules, but it was one of those things that simply went without saying. Because how could someone ever really *know* you, much less ever truly *love* you, when you spent your life in the shadows? When you went from one dirty job and violent confrontation to the next? When being an assassin was what made you, well, *you*, for better or worse?

It was bad enough that I'd been foolish enough to fall for someone, but the unavoidable thing, the really terrible thing, the truly *insurmountable* thing, was the fact that I was in love with the son of the man I'd killed and that Sebastian would hate me if he ever found out the truth.

I'd never thought much about irony before, but I couldn't escape it, not now, when it felt as sharp as one of my own knives buried in my heart and twisting in deeper and deeper. Oh, yes, irony was a capricious bitch, just like luck.

"Gin?"

I gave him another smile, hiding my inner turmoil, then stood on my tiptoes and kissed his cheek. "I would love to talk about our future—later. Right now, though, we've got a party to attend."

Sebastian grinned, tightened his grip on my arm, and led me up the stairs and into the mansion. For a moment, I felt a sinking sense of déjà vu. I'd jokingly told Fletcher that I wasn't some character out of a fairy tale, doomed to heartbreak, that I wasn't Cinderella, but that's exactly who and what I was tonight, because my time with Sebastian was rapidly running out.

And there was nothing that I could do to keep the clock from striking midnight.

Sebastian led me to the grand ballroom on the second floor of the mansion.

It looked like a scene out of one of those old Hollywood movies that Sophia loved to watch. The wooden parquet floor had been waxed until it glinted like gold underfoot, while the crystal chandeliers dripped down from the ceiling like clusters of diamonds, throwing out rainbow sprays of color in every direction. Vases full of those dark blue roses perched in alcoves in the walls, adding more color to the scene. Food tables had been set up around the perimeter of the room, along with several elemental Ice bars, the frosty surfaces steaming slightly underneath the heat from the lights. Members of an orchestra were checking their instruments and warming up in the back corner of the room. Sebastian had had people working around the clock the last few days to get ready for the party, and it had more than paid off. The ballroom had been transformed from a simple open space into a place of lush, opulent elegance.

"What do you think?" Sebastian asked.

"It's beautiful."

"I'm glad you think so, miss," another voice cut in.

A dwarven woman strode into the ballroom behind us. She held a clipboard in her hand, while a black plastic headset was clamped down over her frizzy black hair. I blinked. Meredith Ruiz. The same event planner who'd put together the dinner at Tobias Dawson's mansion.

Meredith's gaze took in my silver dress, shoes, and purse. I waited for her eyes to narrow and sharpen, but all she did was turn up the wattage on her bland, polite smile. She didn't recognize me. Why would she? I wasn't one of the waitresses she could bully around, so I was of no use to her.

She turned to Sebastian. "Now, sir, if you'll step over to the patio doors with me, there's something that I need to discuss with you . . ."

Meredith grabbed his arm and led him away, but I

stayed where I was, looking at first one thing, then another. The glistening chandeliers, the silver platters of gourmet food, the golden champagne that the bartenders were pouring into delicate crystal flutes. I was so focused on the sights that it took me a few moments to realize that the stone walls of the ballroom were whispering. But not with pride at how the room had been transformed.

No, the stones muttered with malice and ill intent.

I frowned, reaching out with my magic, wondering why the stones were so upset. Now that Vaughn was dead, I'd thought that the harsh whispers would slowly start to fade away, but instead, it seemed as if they'd only intensified since I'd last been in the mansion a few days ago—

"Sorry about that," Sebastian said, coming back over to me. "Apparently, there's a last-minute problem with the new fountain that I ordered for the lawn. I wanted the jets hidden inside it to put on a water show to the orchestra music, but the event planner says that Mr. Stills, the blacksmith installing the fountain, tells her that it's not possible on such short notice." He shrugged, as though it were a minor inconvenience. "In the meantime, shall we?"

Sebastian held out his arm to me. I shut the sounds of the muttering stones out of my mind, took it, and let him lead me deeper into the ballroom.

Sebastian's guests started arriving shortly after that. I stood by his side inside the ballroom doors. He shook hands with every single person, thanking them all for coming and offering them all a hearty smile. Sometimes he would engage them in brief conversation. Other times, the guests would wander off in search of food and drink. But more than a few folks lingered around the door, wanting some face time with the man of the hour. In fact, so many people clustered around him that I soon had to stand against the wall so I wouldn't be swept away from him entirely.

Sebastian didn't introduce me to anyone, but I didn't mind. This was his night, and I preferred to stay in the background, anyway. I was thinking about slipping away to get a drink when Mab Monroe walked through the open doors.

The Fire elemental was dressed in a strapless velvet gown in a deep, bloody crimson that somehow set off her creamy skin and coppery hair at the same time. Her makeup was expertly applied, her eyes made even blacker by the heavy liner and shadow that rimmed them. In contrast, her sunburst necklace flashed like a ring of wavy golden fire around her throat, the ruby in the middle sparking like an ember about to ignite.

The crowd around Sebastian quieted and fell away at Mab's slow approach, and suddenly, I was the only one standing next to him. He reached out and gripped my hand, his palm sweaty against mine. Surprised, I looked at him. He hadn't had any problems greeting any of the other power players. But then again, this was Mab, queen of them all, the person most likely to burn you to death on the spot for the smallest perceived slight.

Sebastian bowed his head as Mab stopped in front of him. "Ms. Monroe. What an honor to welcome you to my estate tonight." He held out his hand.

She gave him a slow once-over, then took his hand

in hers. "Being the man of the manor seems to suit you, Sebastian," Mab murmured, her crimson lips curving up into a small smile, as though she'd made some sort of joke.

He nodded at her in return, but Mab didn't notice. Instead, she looked past him at me. Her black gaze flicked over me, far less interested than she'd been in Sebastian, but she did the polite thing and held out her hand.

I had no choice but to take it.

Tiny, invisible needles started stabbing into my body the second her warm fingers closed over my cool ones. I'd thought that Mab's Fire magic had felt intense when I'd been spying on her through the windows at Dawson's mansion, but the sensation was worse now that I was face-to-face with her—so much worse. My skin felt hot enough to spontaneously combust and the bones underneath liquefy just by touching her. No wonder so many people feared her. All it would take would be the merest wave of her hand to reduce all but the strongest elemental to charred ash. More than once, I'd wondered if Mab could be the Fire elemental who'd murdered my family. She certainly had the magic for it, although I couldn't imagine why she would have targeted any of us.

I had to grind my teeth to keep the pleasant, bland smile fixed on my face as I held her hand, but I managed it. Because if there was one thing that I could not afford to do, it was to draw attention to myself from the likes of Mab Monroe or let her know that I could feel her magic.

Mab quickly dropped my hand and moved farther out into the ballroom, trailed by Elliot Slater, who'd apparently come along as her bodyguard tonight. I looked around, wondering if someone else might be with her, since Fletcher had mentioned that there was another Monroe on the guest list, someone with initials instead of a first name. But I didn't see anyone following along behind Mab or Slater, so I focused on Sebastian again.

He grinned at me. "Well, I guess that went about as well as could be expected."

I shrugged. Anything that didn't involve Mab Monroe killing you outright should be considered a victory.

But the next person through the doors surprised me even more than the Fire elemental did: Harry Coolidge.

Like everyone else, he'd dressed up in a black tuxedo, although he kept fiddling with his bow tie, as if he wasn't used to wearing one. Probably not, given that horrible rose-patterned shirt that I'd seen him sporting at the construction compound. Still, the cop cut a handsome figure, and he wasn't alone.

A woman and a young girl stepped into the ballroom behind him. The woman's strawberry-blond hair was swept up into a bun, and her blue eyes were kind in her round face. She wore a modest blue evening gown that clung to what curves she had, and a simple string of small pearls gleamed around her throat. Matching pearl studs adorned her ears.

But it was the girl who captured my attention and made my heart squeeze painfully in my chest—she looked just like Bria.

Long blond hair, rosy cheeks, big blue eyes. The girl couldn't be more than fourteen or fifteen, but she was already stunningly pretty, like a perfect porcelain doll come to life. She wore a simple white dress with a blue ribbon cinched around the waist. A matching blue ribbon circled her throat, although she kept rubbing the blue cameo that dangled off the end between her fingers, as though it annoyed her in the same way that Coolidge's bow tie bothered him.

Coolidge stepped forward. "Sebastian."

"Harry."

They shook hands, but Harry obviously wasn't happy about it. He kept frowning at Sebastian, as if the sight of the younger man greatly upset him for some reason.

I forced myself to focus on Sebastian and put the girl out of my mind. I even went so far as to turn so that I was facing him instead of her. This night was about Sebastian, not me dwelling on ghosts from my past. Besides, this wasn't the first time I'd seen someone who looked like Bria, even if this girl did resemble her a bit more than most.

"Once again, I want to tell you how sorry I am about your father," Harry said, his blue eyes dark and serious. "If the police and your investigators don't come up with something soon, I hope that you'll consider letting me take a crack at things."

Sebastian's mouth puckered. The lack of leads into his father's murder remained a sore spot for him. I tensed too, but for another reason entirely. From what Fletcher had told me, Harry Coolidge was a dedicated cop, the sort who wouldn't stop digging until he found out the truth about Vaughn's murder—and my part in it.

"Where's Charlotte?" the girl asked, interrupting the two men.

I let myself take another quick glance at her. For the

first time, I realized that she was carrying a small white box in her hand, tied with a pale pink ribbon. Tonight was Charlotte's birthday, and a pile of presents had accumulated on a table off to one side of the room. Charlotte had come down to the ballroom when the guests started arriving, but I'd been so focused on Sebastian that I hadn't paid much attention to her. I hadn't seen her in a while, though. I wondered if she was back in the library, hiding under her father's desk again. The thought saddened me, since I was the cause of her grief.

Sebastian waved his hand. "Oh, I'm sure that Charlotte's around here somewhere."

The woman held out her hand to the girl. "Come on, sweetheart. Let's go find Charlotte so you can give her the present you brought her. Sebastian, thank you for inviting us tonight."

He tipped his head at her. "Of course, Henrietta. You know that you guys were like family to my father."

Harry gave Sebastian one more hard stare before moving off into the crowd with his wife and daughter.

"Arrogant ass," Sebastian muttered under his breath.

"Him?" I asked, focusing on Harry again instead of his daughter. "What's wrong with him? He seemed okay."

For a cop who would haul me off to jail if he ever learned what I'd done to his friend.

Sebastian shook his head. "He's an old friend of my father's, and he's been sniffing around ever since Papa's death. I think that Harry blames me because the cops haven't found my father's killer yet. As if it's my fault that the police in this town are so incompetent. As if *he* could do any better."

No doubt Coolidge could do better. He would at least try, which was more than could be said for most of the cops in Ashland.

Still, I wondered at the venom in Sebastian's voice and the seeming bad blood between the two men. From what little I'd seen and heard, Harry Coolidge had appeared to be a loyal friend to Vaughn. He was certainly doting on his wife and daughter. He'd already braved the crowd at one of the bars to fetch his wife a glass of white wine and his daughter some ginger ale. The girl giggled as her father made an exaggerated bow and presented her with the soda, while the mother looked on with a smile on her face. Such a nice, happy family. For a moment, I felt achingly envious of Bria's look-alike.

Sebastian moved in front of me, cutting off my view of the Coolidge family.

"Well, that looks like the last of the guests," he said. "I'm going to go find Charlotte and welcome everyone properly. After the party gets started up again, we'll slip away and have our own private celebration. Okay?"

I smiled, once again feeling that peculiar mix of longing, desire, guilt, and sorrow thrumming through my chest. "It's a date."

He nodded. "Wish me luck."

"Good lu—"

But Sebastian had already turned and was striding away.

# ✲ 18 ✲

Sebastian moved through the ballroom, shaking hands and greeting his guests again. He disappeared from sight but reappeared a few minutes later in the center of the floor, his arm around Charlotte's shoulder, his head bent down as he whispered something in her ear. I wondered where she'd been hiding.

Like her friend, Charlotte wore a simple dress, although hers was black with splashes of deep blue, almost like abstract roses blooming across the pouffy skirt. Her black hair was pulled back into another French braid, the end tied off with a blue ribbon.

Sebastian left Charlotte standing by herself while he went over, grabbed a champagne flute and a fork from one of the bartenders, and gently *ting-ting-ting*ed the tines against his glass. Slowly, the orchestra's classical music faded away, and the crowd quieted down.

Sebastian moved back to the center of the ballroom, putting his arm around Charlotte's shoulder again.

"I want to welcome you all here tonight," he said, looking from one side of the crowd to the other. "Thank you all for coming and helping Charlotte and me honor our father. Tonight is my sister's fourteenth birthday, and it would have been his fifty-first. I can't think of a more fitting tribute to him than being here with all of you, his friends, his family."

Sebastian's gaze flicked over to Mab. An amused smile flitted across her face, as though she were in on some private joke that no one else knew about. Maybe she was simply glad that Vaughn was dead, and some of the problems that he'd caused for her along with him.

"A lot of rumors have been going around about my father's death," Sebastian said. "The police are still investigating this horrible crime, but I wanted to make all of you a promise here tonight. His killer *will* be brought to justice. My father wouldn't accept anything less, and neither will I."

The crowd clapped heartily at his words. This time, Sebastian looked straight at Harry Coolidge, who had his arms crossed over his chest and a sour look on his face. I wondered what the cop knew that I didn't. But like Fletcher had said, I couldn't exactly ask him.

"My father is gone," Sebastian continued. "And although we are here tonight to celebrate his birthday, his memory, his legacy, we all know that we cannot dwell on the past and that we must move forward. That is why I will be assuming control of Vaughn Construction, effective immediately."

Sebastian straightened, and his voice boomed through the ballroom as he outlined how he wanted to continue the work and projects that his father had started. Truth be told, I tuned most of it out, since it was obvious that Sebastian was trying to reassure his business associates that everything with the company would proceed on time and on budget. I wondered if that was why he'd invited Mab. Fletcher had said that she owned a significant stake in Vaughn Construction, and she wasn't the sort of investor you disappointed—not if you wanted to keep breathing.

Charlotte squirmed out from under her brother's arm, although Sebastian caught her hand and kept her close to him. She stared down at the polished floor under her black sandals. I wondered if all the talk about what a great man her father had been upset her, if that was what she wanted to get away from. I wondered if she was thinking about all the times he'd hit her, all the times he'd abused her, all the times he'd hurt her simply because he could.

"And so tonight begins a new era, not only for Charlotte and myself but also for Vaughn Construction . . ." Sebastian went on with his speech.

"What a boring, pompous, long-winded jackass," a snide voice murmured in my ear. "Some people just do *not* know when to shut up. What do you see in him?"

Startled, I looked over to my right at Finn's grinning face. Not many people could sneak up on me, but he was one of them. Finn was lighter on his feet than a cat. Despite my annoyance with him over the past several days, I had to admit that he cut an impressive figure in his tuxedo, and his hair gleamed like polished walnut in the soft glow from the chandeliers. Not that I would ever tell him that, though. His ego was big enough already.

"When did you get here?"

He waved his hand. "Not important. Just like everything your boyfriend is spouting up there on his soapbox."

"He's thanking people for coming and supporting him and Charlotte," I said, rolling my eyes. "There's nothing wrong with that. Give the guy a break. His dad just died a few weeks ago."

"You mean, you just killed his dad a few weeks ago."

Fury flashed through me like lightning striking the earth. My eyes narrowed, and my hands balled into fists. "Is that why you came here? To remind me of that? Because my memory's not that short. I never forget them— *any* of them."

I remembered all the assignments that Fletcher had sent me out on, all the random people who'd foolishly decided to mess with me, all the punks who'd wanted to hurt me when I'd been living on the streets—all the people I'd killed. I remembered the way they looked, talked, laughed, snarled, smelled, and I especially remembered how they'd died and that I'd been the cause of their sudden, violent demises. Maybe that was where my dreams, my memories, were coming from. The fact that I just couldn't forget about all the bad things that I'd done, even if some had been necessary simply to survive.

Finn's face softened at my harsh words. "Look, I'm sorry. I didn't come here to fight. I just don't know what you see in that guy, Gin. Look at him, holding court in the middle of the ballroom, crowing about all the things he plans to do now that his father is gone. He's trying too hard, yet again, like a prince who's finally seized the king's throne and doesn't want anyone to know exactly how ill suited he is for the job."

I glanced at Sebastian. Sometime while I'd been talking to Finn, Sebastian had let go of Charlotte, who'd disappeared into the crowd, and was now waving around his free hand and stabbing his index finger up to the ceiling in order to punctuate his points. Maybe he was being a little overly dramatic, but I knew how important it was for him to make a good impression tonight, now that he was the head of the Vaughn family.

"He's doing the best he can," I said, turning back to Finn. "You can't blame him for that."

"No, I suppose not." Finn sighed. "Just . . . be careful with this guy, okay, Gin? I've seen the way you look at him."

"And how is that?"

For once, Finn's green gaze was dark and serious. "Like you're halfway in love with him."

I kept my face cold, calm, and expressionless, but he must have seen the uneasy agreement in my eyes, because he reached out and gently touched my arm, as if I were a piece of delicate glass. That's exactly how I felt right now—brittle, fragile, and utterly exposed.

"You know that it can never work out, right?" Finn said in a soft voice.

"Of course I know that." I sneered. "I killed his father. I might be an assassin, but I'm not *stupid*."

Finn shook his head. "It's more than just that. It's what we do versus what he does. Our world versus his."

"And here I thought that we all lived in the same world."

"Not people like us. Our world is in the background, in the shadows, in the darkness, where few people dare to tread."

"And his isn't?"

Finn held out his hand, gesturing at the ballroom. "This is about as far from the shadows as you can get, Gin. And I think you know that deep down inside. You can be one thing or the other—you can't be both." He paused. "Except maybe if you're Mab Monroe."

Everything that he was saying was undeniably true. But I had just been so . . . so . . . *happy* with Sebastian, so thrilled with the way he made me feel like I was the most wonderful person he'd ever met. I'd never had that before.

Oh, Fletcher loved me like a daughter, Jo-Jo too, and of course Finn and I had our sibling rivalry going on. I supposed that even Sophia felt some sort of fond, grudging affection for me, although she would never go so far as to say it out loud. But the four of them had been a family long before I'd shown up like a lost puppy on the back step of the Pork Pit, and sometimes I still felt like an outsider looking in. I supposed that was one of the reasons that I'd trained so long and hard to be the assassin Fletcher had wanted me to be—so I could please him in one area that Finn never could.

So *I* could be the insider for a change.

But it wasn't like that with Sebastian. Not at all. He made me feel important, he made me feel . . . *special* in a way that I never had, not even with my own family. Even when my mom and sisters had been alive, I'd always been the one in the middle. Not old enough to hang out with my mom and Annabella and too old for Bria and her dolls, even though I was the one who'd always ended up playing with her anyway, simply because I loved her so much.

I didn't want to give up Sebastian and how he made me feel, but Finn was right. I didn't have a choice. Because sooner or later, the sand would run out in the hourglass of my happiness, the carriage would turn back into a pumpkin, and my glass slipper would splinter into shards. Either I'd slip up and say something that I shouldn't, or Harry Coolidge or some other investigator would get the bright idea to take a hard look at me and when and why I'd appeared in Sebastian's life. I'd rather leave on my own terms, with at least a little bit of my dignity left—and my heart too. More important, I had to go out like that if only not to endanger Finn and Fletcher. I might be willing to risk my own safety but not theirs.

Not even for Sebastian.

"Don't worry," I said. "I'll try one more time to find that file the old man wants tonight, and then I'll get out—for good."

Even if it would break my heart. I didn't want to leave Sebastian behind, but Finn was right. There was no place for me in Sebastian's world, and I didn't want to drag him into mine. Not when he would hate me for it and what I'd done to his father.

Finn studied me, his features eerily similar to Fletcher's in that moment. Then he nodded, apparently satisfied by whatever he saw in my face. He gave my arm another gentle squeeze before snagging a glass of champagne from a passing waiter.

"Now, on to more important matters," he drawled. "Like who I plan on bringing home for the evening. I was thinking about *her*."

He tipped his glass at a woman standing about twenty feet away from us, one of the most breathtaking women I'd ever seen. Her spaghetti-strapped black gown was sleek and stylish and brought just the right amount of attention to her perfect body while also highlighting the rich toffee color of her skin. She had wonderful curves, but her face was even more beautiful, with dark, expressive eyes and glorious cheekbones. A thin diamond headband held her black hair back off her face, showing off her scarlet lips and the gentle slope of her neck. She wasn't wearing any other jewelry, but she didn't need to.

I might have had something of a Goth Cinderella vibe going on tonight, but she was the sort of woman who would look gorgeous long after the ball was over.

"Who's that?"

"Roslyn Phillips," Finn said, never taking his eyes off her as he sipped his champagne. "She's opening up a new nightclub. It's called Northern Aggression."

"Northern Aggression? Clever."

He nodded. "Clever, indeed. She came into the bank a few months ago to get the financing. You should have seen the way she had all of the bigwigs eating out of the palm of her hand. They thought she was just a pretty face to start with, but she really wowed them with her business plan. *That* is a woman to be reckoned with."

And apparently, a woman to be admired, judging from the men standing three deep around her. Still, I had to respect the graceful way she spoke to each of them in turn, never favoring one over another, even though they were all competing for her attention.

"I see two CEOs, a couple of CFOs, and a drug lord gathered around her," I said. "And you really think that she's going to go home with *you* tonight? Keep dreaming, Finn."

"Ah, yes. But I have one thing that all of those other schmucks don't."

"Really? What's that?"

He flashed me a cocky grin. "I'm Finnegan Lane, baby. The best there is at everything—including the boudoir arts."

I couldn't keep myself from laughing or teasing him. "Well, good luck, Mr. Lane. Although I would think that someone like *her* would be more your speed."

I pointed over at the blond girl who had come in with Harry Coolidge, the one who looked so much like Bria. She and Charlotte had finally connected, and the two of them stood next to the table full of birthday presents. The blond girl was talking animatedly, glancing around with excitement at all the people, but Charlotte was focused on the present that her friend had given her. She slowly untied the pink ribbon, lifted the box top, and set it aside. She dug through some tissue paper before pulling out a delicate pink cameo that was a match for the blue one the blond girl was wearing. Charlotte must have liked it, because she immediately hooked the cameo around her neck. The blond girl beamed at her friend.

"Her?" Finn asked, his voice taking on an offended, incredulous note. "She looks like she's fifteen at the most. That's way too young for me, Gin. I do have *some* standards, moral and otherwise." He paused and glanced at the girl again. "Maybe in ten years or so. When she's all grown up."

I laughed at his arrogance, but if there was one man who could make something happen, even ten years into the future, it was definitely Finn.

"You know, one day, you're going to meet a girl who won't automatically fall in love with you or be immediately seduced by your so-called charm," I sniped. "I just hope that I'm around to see it happen, when the ego of the mighty Finnegan Lane gets the bruising and beatdown that it so richly deserves."

Finn threw his arm around my shoulders. "Have I mentioned how much I love it when you talk about me in the third person? Totally makes my ego kick up another notch. Or ten."

I couldn't help but laugh again.

". . . and so I want to raise a toast to my father and to keeping his legacy alive and well for years to come." Sebastian was finally finishing his speech. "Cheers."

He raised his champagne glass high, and so did everyone else in the ballroom. There was a moment of silence. Then the music started up again, and the guests resumed their previous conversations.

Porter separated himself from the crowd and went over to Sebastian, who was shaking hands again with some of his guests. Sebastian whispered something to Porter, who handed him a fresh glass of champagne. Sebastian took that glass and headed in my direction.

"Looks like my cue to leave," Finn said. "Just think about what I said, okay, Gin?"

I nodded, not trusting myself to speak. Despite all of our differences over the years, our childish fights, our failed summer romance, and our continued rivalry, he really was the best brother a girl could have, blood or otherwise.

Finn winked at me, then slipped off into the crowd, heading straight for Roslyn Phillips. One moment, he was standing on the fringes of the men around her. The next, he'd insinuated himself by her side. I didn't know how he managed it. Sometimes I thought Finn was part magician and part cat.

"Ms. Phillips, I don't think you've had the pleasure of my company yet," Finn murmured, his smooth, suave voice drifting over to me. "My name is Finnegan Lane . . ."

And that was all I heard before Sebastian reached my side, a wide grin on his face from his moment of triumph. He passed me the glass of champagne that Porter had given him. I didn't much care for champagne. It was too bubbly, too light and frothy, for my liking, as though I were drinking fizzy air, but I didn't want to be rude. He *tink*ed his glass against my own, and we toasted each other.

"Come on," he said. "Let's get out of here and go have that talk."

"Are you sure you want to leave now? The party is just getting started again."

Sebastian stepped closer to me and pressed a soft kiss against my cheek. I breathed in his scent, sweet and spicy at the same time. Once more, desire stirred in my veins, deeper and more intense than before, because I knew that this night would be the only one that I ever had with him.

Sebastian drew back, his dark eyes searching mine. "I'm sure," he whispered. "Are you?"

All I could do was nod, too overcome with emotion to speak.

He grabbed my hand, and I let him pull me out of the ballroom.

# ✸ 19 ✸

We turned a corner and hurried down the hallway, holding hands like a couple of kids. At the far end, Sebastian risked a quick glance around. Satisfied that we were alone, he put his champagne flute down on a nearby table, then backed me up against the closest wall and kissed me, hot and hard, so hard that I almost dropped my own glass.

He drew back and frowned. "You haven't drunk any of your champagne."

"Later," I whispered. "I'd rather taste you right now."

I pulled his head down to mine and kissed him as deeply as he had kissed me. By the time he finally pulled back, we were both panting for breath.

He grinned. "I know the feeling."

Sebastian scooped me up in his arms, glass and all, and headed for the nearest staircase. I wrapped my hand around his shoulder and nipped at the side of his neck with my teeth.

"You keep doing that, and we won't make it to where I want to go," he rasped.

"Mmm." I nipped his neck again.

I didn't care where we went as long as I was with him. I wanted to make tonight count. I *needed* to make tonight count.

Because I wouldn't have a tomorrow with him.

I kept kissing his neck, while Sebastian carried me up to the third floor, to a room that was at the opposite end of the hall from the library and his father's office. He nudged the door open with his shoulder, stepped through to the other side, then kicked the wood shut again with his foot. Sebastian strode forward and set me down on my feet in the middle of the room.

It wasn't just any room—it was his bedroom. A king-size bed dominated much of the space, the white silk sheets on it standing out in stark contrast to the ebony wooden frame. More ebony tables were scattered throughout the room, along with a matching armoire, while the thick rugs underfoot were a mix of black, white, and gold patterns. Despite all the times I'd been to the estate over the past two weeks, Sebastian hadn't shown me his room before. It was dark and utterly masculine, like him.

I loved it—and I loved him too.

Sebastian plucked the champagne glass from my hand and set it on the nightstand beside the bed. I tossed my purse down onto the settee at the foot of the bed.

Then, with one thought, we came together.

I unknotted his black bow tie, loosened it from around his neck, and tossed it aside, not caring where it landed. Then I carefully undid the top button of his shirt, exposing his luscious tan skin. I kissed his neck again, feeling his pulse against my lips. Racing, racing, racing, just like mine was.

Sebastian captured my chin with his hand, raised my head, and kissed me again, even harder than he had downstairs. There was nothing soft and sweet about his kisses tonight. Good. I didn't want there to be, because this, tonight, now, was about how we could make each other *feel*.

We stood there, rocking back and forth, our tongues dueling, even as our hands began to creep inside each other's clothes. I helped him shrug off his jacket and undid the rest of the buttons on his shirt, exposing his muscled chest and flat stomach. He slid down the straps that held up the bodice of my dress, then unzipped the back of it. I shrugged out of the silk, let it fall to the floor, and then kicked it out of the way, standing there in only a pair of black lace panties. Sebastian's eyes trailed up and down my body, his gaze darkening in appreciation.

"So beautiful," he whispered. "So sexy."

A thrill went through me at his words, and I stepped back into the warm circle of his arms. He bent down and touched his lips to my neck, lightly nibbling at the skin there with his teeth, just as I'd done to him before, then kissing his way down to my right breast. His tongue circled first one of my nipples, then the other, licking, nipping, and sucking in a quick, needy rhythm, even as his hand dipped lower and started sliding under the edge of my panties.

"Condom?" I rasped, even as I arched back to give him better access. I took my little white pills, but extra protection never hurt.

Sebastian scraped his teeth against my right nipple, then my left. It was several seconds before he spoke again. "In my wallet."

I reached around, fumbling in his back pocket. He kept distracting me, kissing me, caressing me, both of his hands now sliding lower and lower, but I eventually pulled his wallet from his pants and found a condom tucked inside. I grabbed it and tossed the wallet away like I had done with his bow tie.

In the meantime, Sebastian had hooked his fingers into my panties and pushed them down. I stepped out of them, kicking the silk away, and Sebastian went down on his knees before me. He slowly smoothed his hands down my thighs, making me shudder with anticipation. His hands trailed back up my legs. I thought he might tease me some more, but he quickly slid a finger inside me, rubbing slow circles and ratcheting up my desire.

My nails dug into his shoulders, and I had trouble holding on to the condom. I had trouble focusing on anything but what he was doing to me and how much I enjoyed it.

"Do you like that, Gin?" he murmured. "How about this?"

He pumped his finger inside me again, and it was all I could do to keep standing.

Sebastian kept talking to me, telling me all the things that he was going to do to me, all the ways that he was going to please me, all the things that he was going to make me feel. Every word he said, every naughty promise and sly stroke, made me ache more for him.

Finally, he kissed his way back up my body to my

mouth. Once again, our tongues stroked back and forth before I pulled back.

I handed Sebastian the condom and gave him a wicked grin. "My turn to play."

I shoved his shirt off his shoulders, exposing his chest. I took my time, kissing his neck again and following the faint trail of dark hair down to his pants. I undid his belt, unzipped his pants, and pushed them down, along with the black silk briefs that he wore. Sebastian stepped out of his shoes and clothes. Then I took his hard length in my hand, stroking, caressing, and teasing, just as he'd done to me.

"That's enough of that," he finally growled.

Sebastian kissed me again, his tongue thrusting against mine as his hips rocked forward. He picked me up and put me down on the bed, before drawing back, ripping the foil packet open with his teeth, and covering himself with the condom. Then he laid his body down on top of mine, wrapped my legs around his waist, and slid into me with one smooth motion. I dug my nails into his back, groaning at how good he felt inside me.

"Oh, sugar," he murmured. "If you think that feels good, how about this?"

Sebastian withdrew a bit, then surged back up inside me, deeper and harder than before. I groaned again, clutching at his shoulders. He grinned and drove himself into me again and again. I met him thrust for thrust, our moans shattering the silence, until I finally screamed from the pleasure of it all and let myself go as I never had before. Sebastian shuddered against me, finding his own release.

And when the world fell away, and the stars flashed

before my eyes, and I finally came back to myself, I almost wanted to weep, knowing that this would be the first—and only—time that we would ever be together.

When we finished, Sebastian collapsed on the sheets beside me. For several minutes, the two of us lay there, panting and coming down from the intense high that we'd reached. Finally, I turned to face him. I wrapped my arms around his neck and started to draw his mouth back down to mine for another kiss, but Sebastian put his finger against my lips, stopping me.

"Let's have a drink."

He got up, grabbed my glass from the nightstand, and handed it to me. Then, still naked, he walked over to a cabinet on the far side of the room, pulled out a bottle, and poured himself a tumbler of Scotch. He came back over to the bed, sat down next to me, and *clink*ed his glass against mine.

"To us."

"To us," I whispered back, my heart clenching, knowing that there wouldn't be an *us*.

Not after tonight.

Sebastian threw back half of his Scotch, but I only took a small sip of champagne, grimacing at the taste. He noticed my sour face.

"You don't like it?"

I shook my head. "Too sweet for me."

"Take another couple of sips," he urged. "You might discover that you like it after all."

He polished off his Scotch. I brought the glass to my lips again, but I didn't take another drink.

"Mmm," I said, not wanting to hurt his feelings. "It does taste better than before."

I quickly set the glass on the nightstand, sliding it behind the lamp so he wouldn't notice how little I'd drunk. Then I reached up and pulled the few remaining pins out of my hair, since most of it had come undone already.

I lay back on the bed, thinking that Sebastian would come back over to my side, but instead, he moved around the room, getting rid of the used condom and cleaning himself up. When that was done, he grabbed his clothes from where they had fallen on the floor and started putting them back on.

One second, Sebastian was as naked as I was. The next, he was fully clothed again. I blinked, wondering where the last two minutes had gone and why I suddenly felt so tired. Sebastian had been an intense lover, but I wasn't ready to conk out on him just yet—not when I'd have to leave him for good in the morning. But try as I might, I couldn't make myself find the energy to get up off the bed. Instead, my elbows slid out from under me, and I hugged a pillow to my chest, even as I stared at Sebastian.

"Where are you going?" I finally asked, my voice sounding weak and far away to my own ears.

"Don't you worry, sugar," Sebastian said, shrugging back into his tuxedo jacket. "I've got a bit of last-minute business to attend to, and I have to make sure that all of the guests leave, but then I'll come back for you, and we'll spend the rest of the night together in bed. Okay?"

"Okay," I mumbled, even though I knew that I needed to get up, put my clothes back on, go to the library, and search for the file while Sebastian was distracted with his other business.

But I couldn't move. Every single part of me felt heavy and languid, as though it would take the greatest effort that I'd ever summoned simply to get off the bed.

Sebastian started to leave, but I made a small noise of protest, and he came back over to the bed. He let out an annoyed sigh, as if I was keeping him from something important, but he leaned down and started kissing my neck, his hands sliding over my breasts again, and I forgot about everything else. But after another minute, I couldn't even concentrate on that, and my body grew slack and still under his.

"That's right, sugar," Sebastian murmured, his voice sounding strangely smug to my ears. "You stay put until I get back."

"Okay," I mumbled again.

And that was all that I remembered before the world went black.

# *20*

A sharp poke in my shoulder woke me sometime later.

At first, I wondered who it was, but then I realized that it was probably Finn messing with me, trying to make me get up before I wanted to.

But wait . . . why would Finn be in my bedroom? We weren't kids anymore, even though he still teased me like it. And he didn't even live at Fletcher's house anymore . . . I started to slide back into the darkness . . .

The poke came again, a little more insistent this time.

"Go away," I mumbled.

All I wanted to do right now was drift back to the quiet, black place where I'd been. It was nice there. Warm, safe, soothing, peaceful.

The poke came a third time, followed by a small hand gripping my shoulder and shaking me. My head snapped to the side, causing an ache to roar to life in the back of my skull and pulling me out of the dream that I'd been in.

Or was I still dreaming now? I couldn't tell, but I finally managed to open my eyes.

Charlotte's face loomed above mine.

I blinked and rose onto my elbows, the room spinning around at that small, simple motion. "Charlotte? What are you doing in here?"

A cool gust of air-conditioning hit my body, and I realized that I was still sprawled across Sebastian's bed, completely naked. I quickly grabbed the sheet and flipped it over my body. More pain spiked through my skull at the movement. I groaned. My head felt so strange, so fuzzy, as if I'd drunk far too much champagne, although I'd only had one sip.

Charlotte stared at me another moment, then bolted into action. She moved around the room, grabbing my silver dress and throwing it at me, along with my panties, purse, and shoes. I watched her, wondering what she was doing, blinking and still trying to clear the fog from my mind.

Charlotte saw that I wasn't doing what she wanted me to. She shook her head, stomped over to the bed, and shoved the gown into my lap.

"You have to get dressed," she said, her voice stronger than I'd ever heard it before. "You have to leave. *Now*."

"Leave? Why? Did something happen? What's wrong?" My words slurred together, and my voice sounded faint and far away, as though I were standing in a cavern and listening to my own echo.

Exasperated, Charlotte reached over and dragged my champagne glass out from where I'd hidden it behind the lamp on the nightstand.

"Because Sebastian drugged you," she whispered. "Because he's planning to hurt you. I heard him talking to Porter about it earlier. That's why you have to leave. Right now."

What . . . ? Sebastian had drugged me? Well, that explained this strange, disconnected feeling and the raging headache I had. But why would he drug me? Why would he be planning to hurt me? He cared about me . . .

Didn't he?

Charlotte grabbed my arm, but I shooed her away. Somehow I managed to slide out of bed and get to my feet. Despite the fact that I was wobbling like a newborn fawn, I turned my back to her and managed to shimmy into my panties and the slinky silver dress.

"Hurry, hurry, hurry," she whispered, helping me slide into my high heels. "His meeting won't last much longer."

"Where?" I croaked. "Where is he?"

"In the library. But you don't want to go that way. You can still sneak out the front with the last of the guests. But you have to hurry. The party's over, and everyone is leaving."

I staggered over to the windows and peered outside. Sure enough, a long line of limos and town cars were coasting down the lighted driveway. I frowned, struggling to make sense of things through the thick fog that just wouldn't leave my mind.

Why wasn't Sebastian here? Whom was he meeting with in the library? And why would Charlotte think that he wanted to hurt me? As far as he knew, I was just a simple waitress, just the girl he'd been seeing the past few weeks. Sebastian couldn't possibly know that I was secretly an assassin . . . he couldn't possibly know about my being the Spider . . . he couldn't possibly know that I'd killed his father . . .

Could he?

The thought chilled me to the bone.

Charlotte kept running around the room, this time grabbing my purse and shoving it into my hands. It took me a couple of tries, since my fingers felt as awkward, clumsy, and detached as the rest of me, but I managed to pop open the top. My silverstone knife lay nestled inside the bag, the one weapon I'd brought with me. I hadn't thought that I'd need the rest of my knives, not here, not tonight, not with Sebastian.

He'd made me feel special . . . he'd made me feel safe . . . he'd made me feel *loved* . . .

I spaced out, and it took me a few seconds to blink away my confusion and focus on my knife again. Still, I hesitated, thinking that maybe Charlotte was jealous, that she was trying to get rid of me for whatever reason, and that was why she was saying all of these terrible things about Sebastian. It would be perfectly understandable, given the fact that she'd lost her father and everything that she'd suffered at his hands. Grief could make people do strange things.

But I couldn't quite quiet the doubts that whispered in my muddled mind—or ignore the mutters that rippled through the stone, even blacker and more ominous than before.

So I reached into the bag and pulled out my knife, feeling the hilt dig into the spider rune scar in my palm, silverstone on silverstone. The solid, familiar weight of the weapon helped ground me and cleared some of the fog from my mind.

Charlotte's eyes widened when she realized that I was holding a knife, but I stepped forward and shoved my purse at her. The knife was the only thing I needed out of it.

"Here," I said, staggering toward the bedroom door. "Hold that for me."

I didn't know what was going on, but I was sure as hell going to find out.

# ❋ 21 ❋

I made it over to the door, opened it a crack, and peered outside, but the hallway was empty.

"Come on! Come on!" Charlotte hissed, pushing past me, sprinting out into the hallway, and gesturing at me with her hand. "This way! This way!"

I looked at the open hallway in front of her, the one that I knew led to a set of stairs that would take me down to the first floor. Charlotte was right. I could still make my escape. But that old, nagging curiosity rose up in me, the one that Fletcher had instilled in me, along with the burning desire to find out what possible reason Sebastian could have had for drugging me.

So I turned and started walking in the opposite direction, toward the library.

"No," Charlotte said, following me and tugging on my hand, trying to get me to stop. "This way. You have to get away before he hurts you."

I looked down at her. "How do you know that he's going to hurt me? Why do you keep saying that?"

Charlotte stared at me, her dark eyes full of pain, pity, and utter misery—too much misery for someone so young. She slowly pushed up the right sleeve of her black dress.

A perfect handprint bruised her bicep in deep blues, as though someone had wrapped his hand around her upper arm as tight as it would go and had then given her a vicious shake.

All the air fled from my lungs, and white stars winked on and off in front of my eyes, as though I'd been sucker-punched in the throat by a giant. If only that were the case. It would have hurt less, so much less.

"Sebastian . . . *Sebastian* did that to you?"

"And more," she whispered.

A sick, sick feeling filled my stomach, making me want to vomit up the drugged champagne. "Not—not your father?"

Charlotte gave me a puzzled look, then shook her head.

That sick, sick feeling intensified, and my knees threatened to buckle, but I forced myself to swallow down the bitter bile rising in my throat and stay on my feet.

"Why? Why did he do that to you?"

"Sebastian likes to hurt people, especially me," Charlotte said in a voice that was far too old, knowing, and matter-of-fact for a teenager. "He always has, ever since I was little. He hides it, though. From everyone but me."

"Did you—did you ever tell your father what Sebastian was doing to you?" I could barely croak out the words.

She hesitated. "No. I wanted to, but Sebastian told me that he would hurt Papa if I ever said a word to him."

All along, I'd thought that Cesar Vaughn was the bad guy, a dirty, rotten, low-down, despicable villain who'd been abusing his own daughter. But it wasn't him. None of this had been his doing or his fault. Charlotte hadn't been suffering because of him. Which meant . . . which meant . . .

*I killed an innocent man.*

The thought slammed into my gut like a sledgehammer, and I almost got sick right then and there. But once again, I forced myself to choke down the bile in my throat, even though it burned me like acid from the inside out.

My head was spinning in a hundred different directions, and not only because of the drugged champagne, but I bent down so that I was at eye level with Charlotte. "You go to your room, and you stay in there. You don't come out until morning, no matter what you hear. Do you understand me?"

"Promise me that you'll leave," she said, pulling on my arm and trying to drag me toward the staircase again. "Don't go talk to him. Just leave. Please. Please, please, *please*, just leave."

I shook my head. "I can't do that, sweetheart. But don't you worry about me. Sebastian might like to hurt people, but I know how to do it too. See?"

I held my knife up where she could see it again. Charlotte gasped. Her face paled, and a spark of understanding began to burn in her dark gaze.

"You're the one who killed Papa, aren't you?" she whispered in a harsh, accusing voice.

I thought that my heart couldn't possibly break any more, but the hurt, miserable, devastated look in her eyes made what was left of my black, brittle, rotten core shatter into a thousand sharp, splintered shards, each one shredding me from the inside out.

"Yes," I said simply. "I did."

I didn't tell her that I was sorry, even though I was. I didn't tell her that it was what I did as an assassin. I didn't tell her that it was simply my own way of surviving and trying to quiet the screams in my own soul. Of trying to protect her the way that I'd so miserably failed to protect Bria all those years ago. In the end, my reasons didn't matter. All that did matter was that I'd killed her father and that she hated me for it.

But she couldn't possibly hate me as much as I loathed myself at this moment for taking an innocent man away from the daughter he'd been trying to protect.

Charlotte slowly backed away from me, as if she thought I was going to lunge forward and stab her with my knife. Then she whirled around and darted down the hallway, running away from me as fast as she could, each soft footfall stabbing into my chest like a red-hot poker. I watched her go, my stomach churning, churning, churning with guilt and my heart aching for how much pain I'd caused her.

My head spun around, as that languid fog threatened to take hold of me again, and I staggered back, bumping into the wall and rattling a photo there. Ironically enough, it was a picture of Sebastian in one of his business suits, smiling at the camera, although now his grin seemed more cruel than kind, his expression more smug than happy.

Sebastian . . . Sebastian knew what was going on. He was the one I needed to find, the one I needed to get answers from.

My hand tightened around the hilt of my knife—one way or another.

I pushed away from the wall and wobbled down the hallway until I reached the library. It wasn't that far, but I didn't pass a single soul. No guards, no housekeepers, no stuffy butlers, no one. Noise drifted up from the floor below, though. Clinking dishes, the scrape of furniture, the snap and rustle of garbage bags. The staff must all have been in the ballroom, cleaning up from Sebastian's soiree.

I passed another set of windows. Through the glass, I could see that most of the cars had vanished, meaning that the party was over and everyone had gone home, like Charlotte had said. That fact only made me more curious about who had stayed behind to meet with Sebastian.

Well, I was going to find out.

It took me longer than it should have, since I was staggering around like a drunken sailor on shore leave, but I eventually reached the library doors. For a moment, I thought about sneaking out one of the windows and trying to cling to the side of the building like I'd done at Dawson's mansion, but that option was foolish at best. I could barely keep my feet under me. There was no way that I had the strength to hang on to the outside of the building for any length of time, much less pull myself across the stone and over to one of the library windows.

But I didn't have to, because the doors were wide open, the murmur of voices drifting outside to me. I recognized the deep timbre of Sebastian's tone, but the voice that responded seemed a bit lighter.

I eased up to the doors and glanced inside, but whoever was in there with Sebastian was deeper in the library. They must be on the right side, gathered around Cesar's desk—Sebastian's desk now.

And I was the one who'd made it his.

I eased through the open doors and tiptoed over to the fireplace. I made sure to stay in the shadows as I peered around the corner of the stone.

Sebastian stood next to the desk, one hip resting on the edge of the antique wood, his legs stretched out in front of him, looking as casual, relaxed, and handsome as ever—if the devil could ever be considered handsome. He held a snifter of brandy in his hand, slowly swirling the amber liquid around and around. He lifted the glass to his nose and drew in a deep, satisfied breath before taking a small sip.

Savoring his victory, in so many ways.

I forced my gaze to move past him to Porter, who was leaning against one of the bookcases in the back of the room, his arms crossed over his chest, standing by like the perfect bodyguard. The giant kept his gaze trained on the person sitting in a chair in front of the desk, his bulky body tense, as though he was on high alert and expecting trouble at any moment.

"Well, I must admit that you've pulled this whole thing off quite brilliantly," a low, throaty voice murmured.

I recognized the voice, and that strange, sinking sense of déjà vu swept over me again.

Mab Monroe stood up and walked over to Sebastian.

# * 22 *

Mab moved over so that she was standing next to Sebastian. But instead of being intimidated by her, as he'd seemed to be in Dawson's library, he gave her a smug grin.

"Well, that's saying a lot, coming from you," he replied. "Cheers to our new partnership. May it be fruitful . . . in *so* many ways."

Sebastian held his glass out, and Mab *clink*ed her brandy snifter against his. Sebastian sidled even closer to her, his smile widening when she tipped her head up instead of taking a step back. I knew that move; I knew that look. He'd given them both to me more than once over the past few weeks. The casual, slightly cocky saunter, the smoldering smile, the deep, dark, liquid stare. I thought I was the only woman Sebastian had ever looked at that way.

I was beginning to realize just how very wrong I was—about a great many things.

Sebastian leaned in even closer, like he was actually going to lower his lips to Mab's, but she held up her finger, and a single red-hot spark shot up into the air between them like a firecracker. It was enough to make Sebastian flinch and step back.

"Don't think that your pretty smile and clumsy attempts at charm will have any effect on me," Mab said. "This is a business arrangement. Nothing more. Unlike some people in this room, I don't sleep with the help."

Sebastian's eyes glittered with anger, but he made an obvious effort to rein in his temper, given whom he was talking to. Smart move, although I was starting to wish that Mab would go ahead and fry him on the spot, given what he'd done to Charlotte and his father.

And what I was beginning to realize he'd done to me too.

But Sebastian wasn't easily daunted, and he leaned in again. "You don't know what you're missing," he murmured. "It's great fun sleeping with the help. You should try it sometime."

Mab's black gaze flicked over his body, cold and dismissive. "Doubtful. But *do* keep trying to persuade me. It seems you enjoy the thrill of the chase as much as I do."

He smirked his agreement.

"But on to the business at hand," Mab said, taking a sip of her brandy. "Your speech at the party seemed to go over quite well. You shouldn't have any problems taking over your father's company now. I'll admit that when you first approached me with your little scheme, I had serious doubts that it would work."

"Really? Why was that?"

"It was far too complicated," Mab said. "Hiring an assassin to murder your father seemed a bit much, especially when you could simply arrange for him to have an accident at one of his job sites."

I sucked in a breath. I'd suspected it as soon as I'd seen the bruise on Charlotte's arm, but it was another thing to have confirmation. Sebastian—Sebastian was the one who'd hired me to kill his own father.

Once again, the thought that I'd murdered an innocent man devastated me, and I had to bend over double and clamp my hand over my mouth to keep from throwing up. It didn't stop the tears from trickling down my face, though, each one as cold and frozen as my heart.

Sebastian shrugged. "Yes, well, I wouldn't have even had to hire that assassin if the old man had agreed to step down following the restaurant incident like I wanted him to."

"Something that you conveniently arranged to push your father out of his own company," Mab shot back. "How *did* you get that terrace to collapse?"

He gave her another smug grin. "That's my little secret."

"Too bad it didn't work out like you'd hoped."

"I thought the public pressure would be too great, that he would get forced out immediately or simply resign out of guilt that one of his precious projects wasn't as strong as he thought. But of course, my father ended up being a bit more . . . stubborn than I anticipated."

"Which is why you went out and hired yourself an assassin. Another needless complication. Why not take care of your father yourself? Afraid of getting your hands dirty?" Her voice took on a mocking note.

"Hardly." Sebastian sneered. "But my father is not without friends. Him having an accident, especially after the terrace collapse, would have raised even more questions. This way, it looks like one of the family members of the victims killed him or hired someone to do it for them. Not me."

Sebastian had wanted to take over his father's company, so he'd arranged the terrace collapse, which meant that he was responsible for the deaths and injuries of those innocent people at the restaurant—not Cesar.

More guilt roiled in my stomach, along with deep, dark, unending shame at what I'd done. I'd been so cocky, so arrogant, so damn *righteous* in my desire to kill Cesar that I hadn't thought things through, like Fletcher had wanted me to. As a result, I'd given Sebastian exactly what he wanted.

I was such a fool.

Mab shook her head, making her coppery hair float around her shoulders before it settled perfectly back into place. "Yes, but the assassin could always trace the payment back to you and use it to blackmail you further down the line."

"Don't worry about the assassin. She's passed out in my bed right now."

I sucked in another breath and straightened up. Sebastian knew that I was an assassin, knew that I'd murdered his father. He'd known the whole damn *time*.

Mab's eyes narrowed with interest. "'She'? The assassin is a woman? Do tell."

"Oh, yes." Sebastian practically purred with triumph. "You're absolutely right about the possibility of blackmail, so ever since I reached out to this assassin, I've been keeping an eye out for anyone new in my father's life. And lo and behold, a few days after I put down the deposit, I see a young woman snooping around."

He went on to tell Mab how he'd found me lurking in the hallway outside the library at Dawson's mansion. I cursed my own carelessness. I should have made sure that everyone was gone from the library before I'd slipped back inside the building, but I hadn't, and it had cost me—even if I wasn't quite sure how high the price was going to be yet.

He finished his story, and Mab arched her eyebrow.

"And you think that some random waitress is really an assassin in disguise? That's a bit thin, darling."

For the first time, a bit of doubt flickered in Sebastian's face. "Well, I don't know for *sure* that she's the assassin, but she was outside the library at Dawson's mansion after your meeting with my father. That can't be a coincidence. And you should see the rest of her family. They've all been giving me the evil eye ever since I cozied up to her."

"I can't imagine why," Mab drawled. "Given your oh-so-honorable intentions toward her."

"Something's going on with them, and I intend to find out what it is."

"And how did you lure this supposed assassin into your bed?"

His face twisted into a sneer. "It was quite easy, actually. Seems she's a bit starved for attention, poor thing. All I had to do was play the part of the doting suitor. She was practically eating out of my hand."

Sebastian told Mab about all our dates, mocking all

the time we'd spent together. I closed my eyes, my stomach turning over, but I couldn't shut out the sound of his voice. He sneered as he told her about all the times he'd looked into my eyes, all the sweet words he'd said, all the lies he'd told me. And then he laughed—he threw back his head and laughed and laughed, as if fooling me so completely was the most amusing thing he'd ever done.

Mab joined in with his self-satisfied chuckles, but her face quickly became thoughtful once more. "And what if you're wrong? What if your little waitress isn't the assassin you think she is? What are you going to do then?"

"Kill her, of course, along with the rest of her family, just so there are no loose ends," Sebastian said in a matter-of-fact voice. "Porter is sending some of his men to take care of her father and her brother after we wrap up here."

My heart seized in my chest. He was going after Fletcher and Finn too. All because of me. All because I'd been too blind to see who and what he really was.

A monster.

"Well, it's good that you're tying up things, just in case," Mab said. "But don't you want to string her along a bit longer? See what else she might tell you? If there's one thing that assassins have, it's access to other people's secrets."

Sebastian shrugged. "I've fucked her all I care to. She's of no further use to me."

My world shattered with every single cruel thing he said. I couldn't breathe, I couldn't move, I couldn't even cry anymore. All I could do was just stand there and feel sicker and sicker at how thoroughly, how totally, how absolutely he'd fooled me. Sebastian Vaughn had been playing me this whole time, this whole damn *time*. Every heated word he'd said, every soft look he'd given me, every tiny tear he'd shed for his supposedly beloved papa.

Lies—all of it damn, dirty, rotten, heartless *lies*.

Even as my heart splintered into smaller and sharper pieces, the rage began to build brick by solid brick in its place, clearing the rest of the drugged fog from my mind. Rage that Sebastian had used me. It wasn't just that he'd hired an assassin to kill his father. That was rather commonplace in Ashland. So was trying to double-cross said assassin somewhere along the way. But to go to such trouble to seduce me after the fact and now to be targeting Finn and Fletcher too . . .

In that instant, everything that I'd ever felt for Sebastian Vaughn burned to ash. Every soft thought, every kind word, every silly, secret hope and hazy, wishful dream. Gone. Incinerated. Obliterated. But in their places rose one thing, stronger than all that I'd felt for him before: a cold, vicious, unending desire to kill him for every lowdown, dirty, rotten thing he'd done.

To me, to his father, and especially to Charlotte.

"Well, if you think that you can manage to take care of this girl and her family, we can move ahead with our plans," Mab said. "How soon can you handle the first shipment?"

"As soon as you give it to me," Sebastian said. "Vaughn Construction has several ongoing projects up and down the East Coast. I'll be happy to include your packages with the building materials that we ship out. That should make it easier to get your drugs into new markets."

"Well, I'm glad that you're so much more amenable to the idea than your father was."

So that's what this was about. Cesar hadn't wanted to help Mab move her drugs, but Sebastian had wanted to be a king instead of a prince, just like Finn had said, and he'd seen his father's reluctance as a golden opportunity. So he'd made a deal to help Mab with her drugs and bump off his father at the same time. I wondered what Sebastian had planned for me—and for Charlotte.

Sebastian hesitated. "Along with the girl, there might be one more loose end, a detective named Harry Coolidge."

"How so?"

"Right before the assassin killed my father, Coolidge gave him a file. I found it in his office safe after I paid off the cops to let me go through his papers instead of bagging them up as evidence. It seems as if my father had Coolidge independently investigating the terrace collapse."

So that was what had been in that file, some sort of proof of Sebastian's involvement. Sebastian must have thought it was his lucky day when he found the file in his father's safe after I killed Cesar.

"What did he find, and how bad is it?"

Sebastian shrugged. "Nothing that I couldn't explain away, but Coolidge is persistent. Worse than a dog with a bone. Plus, he's never liked me. He already thinks that I had something to do with my father's death. He intimated as much at the party tonight."

"Well, then, perhaps you should get your waitress assassin to get rid of him before you kill her," Mab suggested. "Instead of hiring another hit man and making more of a mess of things than you already have."

Sebastian waved his hand. "I'm not worried about Coolidge. He's more hot air than anything else. If he becomes a nuisance, I'll bury him myself. In fact, I'm rather looking forward to it."

"I thought that I made this clear months ago when you first approached me with your grand scheme, but let me repeat myself," Mab said, her voice growing colder and sharper with every word. "Should *you* start becoming a problem, then I'll do the same thing to you that you did to your dearly departed father. Only I won't bother using an assassin. Are we clear?"

The snifter in her hand erupted into flames, punctuating her words, and the harsh scent of brandy filled the library before quickly burning away. Sebastian couldn't stop himself from throwing his hand up and taking several steps back. He was afraid of her. He should be.

But not as afraid as he should be of *me*.

Mab kept her eyes on Sebastian, even as the glass in her hand began to bubble and melt and finally dripped through her fingers like molten lava. And when it was done, when the glass was gone and her point had been made, she brushed the last drops of molten glass off her hands and released her hold on her magic. The flames snuffed out on her fingertips, although the stench of smoke remained behind.

"I trust that's the only demonstration that I'll ever need to give you," Mab said.

Sebastian tried to give her a confident look, as though he weren't about to wet his pants, but the brandy snifter in his own hand trembled, sloshing around the liquid and spoiling his façade. "It won't come to that. I can handle Coolidge and everything else."

"Good. Because you don't want to disappoint me."

Mab patted Sebastian's cheek, her hot hand leaving a faint red welt on his skin. I hoped she would burn off his smug face, but instead, she dropped her hand before turning and gliding away.

Leaving—she was leaving.

I ducked back behind the fireplace, scurrying deeper into this part of the library, and crouched down behind a wingback chair just as Mab stepped into view again. The Fire elemental started toward the door but then paused and glanced over her shoulder, her black eyes flicking over the bookcases and the shadows they cast out.

The lights were turned down low in this part of the library, but I still froze, not even daring to breathe, because if she saw me, I was dead. Mab would realize that every word Sebastian had said about me being an assassin was true, and she'd kill me on the spot—before going after Finn and Fletcher.

But apparently, the Fire elemental had bigger fish to fry, because after a few more heart-stopping seconds, she turned and left the library.

I let out a soft sigh of relief that she hadn't spotted me—

"Where are your men at?" I heard Sebastian snap. "I want everything wrapped up tonight."

I waited a minute to make sure that Mab wasn't coming back, then left my hiding place and eased back over to the fireplace, peering around it once again. Sebastian was still standing in front of his father's desk, talking to Porter now.

"I spoke to them right before Mab arrived," Porter replied. "They're getting ready to leave as we speak. Three of my guys will go over to the son's place. Three more of my men will head over to the house that the girl lives in with the father. Clever of you to send that car to pick her up so you could get the address. Don't worry. We'll take care of them all tonight."

Sebastian nodded. "Good. And Gin?"

"Still passed out on your bed the last time I looked." Porter paused. "You sure you want to get rid of her tonight? She might be fun to have around for a few days."

The way he said "fun" made my skin crawl.

Sebastian snorted. "Not that much fun. Trust me."

I trembled with fury. I wanted nothing more than to run into the room, raise my knife high, and ram it into Sebastian's black, deceitful heart over and over again. But my body still felt weak, wobbly, and slow from whatever drug he'd given me—too weak, too wobbly, and too slow to take on Sebastian, not to mention Porter, who could easily beat me to death with his fists.

Besides, I had Finn and Fletcher to think about. I had to warn them that Sebastian was sending his giants after them. So I whirled around, ready to slip out of the library and make my escape, but I moved too fast, making my head spin. I teetered in my heels and stumbled into one of the tables inside the open doors, knocking off a model of a skyscraper. The stone miniature clattered against the floor. I bit back a curse, but the damage was already done.

"What the hell was that?" Sebastian snapped.

Before I could move, before I could react, he and Porter came rushing into my part of the library. Sebastian and I stared at each other for a heartbeat, then I turned toward the open doors and started to run.

## ☀23☀

*Crack! Crack! Crack!*

Porter managed to yank his gun out from underneath his tuxedo jacket before I made it out of the library. But his aim was lousy, and the bullets *thunk-thunk-thunk*ed into the wall beside me instead of punching into my back.

"Get that bitch!" Sebastian screamed.

So much for my sweet, kind, devoted boyfriend. He'd finally shown his true colors, and I was going to kill him for it.

But first, I had to escape.

I ran through the mansion as fast as I could, which wasn't very fast, given my high heels. But I had no one to blame for this situation but myself. If only I hadn't been so blind, so naive, so fucking *eager* to believe all the lame lines that Sebastian had fed me. Finn had said that Sebastian was trying too hard, and he'd been right.

Finn. My heart twisted at the thought of him and

Fletcher too, both in danger because of me, because I'd been stupid enough to fall for Sebastian and all his smooth, pretty lies. I had to find a way to warn them, save them.

*Crack! Crack! Crack!*

More bullets zipped down the hallway, one shattering a mirror as I ran by it. Yes, I had to get to Finn and Fletcher—but first, I had to save myself.

I kept running until I spotted a set of stairs. I veered in that direction, raced down them to the ground floor, and shoved through the first door I came to. I ended up on the south lawn, well away from the driveway and the front gate. Frustration surged through me. Not the way that I'd wanted to come, but I had no choice now but to go forward.

*Crack! Crack! Crack!*

Porter burst through the door. His first spray of bullets went wild, but the giant paused and took aim at me again.

*Crack! Crack! Crack!*

This time, the bullets kicked up tufts of grass at my feet, much closer to hitting the mark, forcing me to run again.

The tennis courts, the swimming pool, the hot tub. I passed all those and more, keeping away from the outdoor lights as much as I could.

*Crack! Crack! Crack!*

More bullets, so close that I felt the heat of them zing past my legs this time. I wasn't going to be able to outrun Porter, not with the drug in my veins still slowing me down, so I started looking for a place to hide. He might have a gun, but I still had my knife. All I had to do was let him run past me, and then I could come up from behind and stab him in the back. Problem solved. Now I just needed to find a place to make it happen.

As if in answer to my need, a building loomed up out of the darkness, lights burning on the outside of the structure.

Cesar Vaughn's mausoleum.

My steps faltered, my heel caught on a rock, and I almost did a header onto the dewy grass. But there was no going back, only away from Porter, his bullets, and whatever other evil things Sebastian might have in mind for me. Torture, most likely. Charlotte had said that he enjoyed hurting people.

My heart squeezed again at the thought of her, of what she must have suffered at her brother's hands, and especially how I'd taken her father away from her.

But I could have regrets later—if I lived that long.

So I raced through the open doorway and ducked into the mausoleum, stopping inside the entrance. Then I raised the knife that I was still clutching and waited—just waited for him to come inside. No doubt, Porter thought that I would keep right on running through the building and out the opening on the back side, but that wasn't who I was. Besides, maybe if I captured him, I could force him to call off the giants he'd sicced on Finn and Fletcher— before I slit his throat.

*Crack! Crack! Crack!*

More bullets *ping*ed off the doorway as Porter neared the mausoleum. The giant stopped to reload his weapon, so I risked a quick glance around.

A light burned in the center of the ceiling, casting a dim golden glow. The structure was smaller than I thought it would be and shaped like a rotunda. Crystal vases full of those dark blue roses perched on shelves that had been carved into the gray marble walls, and four stone tombs stood in the center of the area. Two of the tombs had words carved into the tops of them, including the one closest to me, which read: *Cesar Vaughn, Beloved Father and Husband.*

I grimaced and turned my attention back to my attacker. Porter finished reloading his weapon and started to run toward the entrance, but Sebastian had finally caught up with us. He held his hand out in front of the giant.

"Stop," Sebastian said. "I didn't see her run out the other side. Unless I'm mistaken, Gin is lying in wait for us in there."

He stepped forward so that he was standing about twenty feet from the mausoleum entrance, bathed in the golden glow from the lights that blazed on the outside of the structure. If I thought that I could hit him with my knife from here, I would have thrown it at him, but my arms felt as wobbly as my legs. Besides, the blade was my only weapon, and I wasn't wasting it like that. No, the only thing I wanted to do with my knife was bury it in Sebastian's black heart.

"Gin, Gin, Gin," Sebastian called out in a mocking voice. "You really should have stayed in bed. You wouldn't have known what hit you. Now I'm afraid that you're going to have to suffer."

"Really?" I called out. "I think that I've suffered enough

already, letting you put your hands on me, you sick, slimy bastard."

He laughed, apparently delighted by my answer. "From what I saw, it seems you were eavesdropping on me and Mab in the library. That seems to be a bad habit of yours. But I take it that you heard what I said to her?"

"Every last word."

"Well, then, there's no need for us to lie to each other any longer, now, is there?" He practically purred. "You know who I am, and I know who you are too."

"I'm not who you think I am. You've got it all wrong. I'm not some assassin. I'm just a waitress."

Yeah, it was a weak denial at best, but if I died here tonight, I at least wanted to give Finn and Fletcher some plausible deniability, even if Sebastian was sending his giants after them.

He laughed again, even more amused than before. "Maybe you can sell that line to someone else but not to me. I'm a much better liar than you are, Gin. Although I can't figure out if you actually killed my father yourself or stood by and watched while your foster father or brother did it. I suppose that any one of you could be the assassin. Care to tell me who it is? Hmm? I'm just *dying* to know." He laughed again at his stupid joke.

"I'm not telling you a damn thing, you black-hearted son of a bitch," I growled back.

"Come on, boss," Porter snapped. "Let me go in there and take care of her."

The giant raised his gun and started forward, but once again, Sebastian held out his arm, stopping him.

"It doesn't have to be like this, Gin," Sebastian called

out. "Come out now, and I promise you that we'll have some fun together before you die."

"No, thanks," I shot back. "I'd rather die where I stand than let you put your hands on me again."

He grinned. "Well, that can certainly be arranged."

I adjusted my knife in my hand, getting it into position. "Well, come on in here, and we'll find out."

Porter tightened his grip on his gun and looked at Sebastian, who shook his head at the giant. Sebastian made a circling motion with his hand, and Porter nodded and disappeared from my line of sight.

"Since you and your family killed my father, I'm sure you did your homework beforehand. I'm sure you know all about his Stone elemental magic, since he used it to shatter all of those stupid models in his office, I assume in a desperate attempt to save his own miserable life."

Sebastian paused, as if he was waiting for me to confirm his suspicions, but I kept quiet.

"Well, I thought you should know that I lied to you before, Gin," Sebastian called out. "Because my father's not the only one in the family with that particular power."

All around me, the marble of the mausoleum began to mutter with deep, dark intent, the same deep, dark mutters that I'd first heard at the construction compound and then again in the mansion. All this time, I'd thought that Cesar had caused the murmurs, a by-product of his abusive actions toward Charlotte. *Wrong again, Gin.*

"Many people sneer at it, but Stone magic is actually quite handy," Sebastian called out. "It has all *sorts* of uses."

A thought occurred to me. "Like crumbling restaurant terraces?"

Surprise flashed across Sebastian's face before he was able to hide it. But he grinned again. "Just like that."

So that's what Vaughn had had Harry Coolidge investigating, and that's what had been in the file: exactly how Sebastian had caused the terrace collapse. Coolidge had said something about getting an elemental to go over the crime scene. It must have been a Stone elemental, one who'd sensed the same disturbance in the balcony rubble that I had at the mansion. The other elemental had just been smart enough to figure out who and what had caused it. Unlike me, the colossal fool.

"Did you even care about those innocent people you hurt at that restaurant?" I called out. "Or were you so eager to get your father out of the way that it just didn't matter to you?"

I already knew the answer, but it kept Sebastian from unleashing his magic for another few precious seconds, which might give me enough time to slip out the back and get away . . .

No such luck.

I hurried over to the far side of the mausoleum, but Porter had already taken up a position there, his gun trained on the entrance, ready to shoot me the second I stepped outside.

Trapped—I was trapped.

If I'd been at full strength, it wouldn't have been a problem. I would have barreled through the opening, used my Stone magic to harden my skin, and then plunged my knife into Porter's chest before racing around the structure and doing the exact same thing to Sebastian.

But whatever drug had been in the champagne had

weakened me, and my frantic run through the mansion and across the grounds had further sapped my strength. My entire body trembled, sweat streamed down my face, and a stitch throbbed in my side. It was all I could do to stand upright and hold on to my knife at the same time.

Everything felt loose and slippery, including my magic. I reached for my Stone power, but it slid out of my grasp like a wet fish. I bit back a curse and tried again, with the exact same result. No, I'd have to find another way to get past Porter and his gun and then disappear into the woods beyond the mansion.

"Don't care who I hurt?" Sebastian mocked. "Oh, Gin. I'm *very* particular about who I hurt. Why waste my time on people who are of no use to me?"

"Oh, really?" I called out, just to keep him crowing.

I stalked from one side of the mausoleum to the other, hoping to find another exit, a trapdoor, or something, anything, that would help me. But there was nothing, and I wound up standing next to Vaughn's tomb, staring down at the words carved into the bottom of it: *Gone Too Soon*.

Because of me. And just like me, in another minute, two tops, if Sebastian had his way.

"Yes, really."

I crept back up to the entrance and peered out. "Is that why you like to slap your sister around? Because teenage girls are so useful to your grand schemes?"

For once, I managed to wipe the smug grin off Sebastian's face.

"Charlotte needs to learn her place," he snarled. "I was

the firstborn. I was the one my parents loved the most—at least, until she came along."

My eyebrows shot up. Looked like Finn and I weren't the only ones who had some sibling rivalry going on—if that's what you could even call Sebastian's twisted jealousy of his baby sister.

"Charlotte's weak, just like our father was," Sebastian continued. "Always whining, always crying, always whimpering about every little thing. She should be grateful that I'm here to look out for her, to teach her how to toughen up and be as strong as I am."

I snorted. The only thing Sebastian wanted to teach anyone about was pain.

"Keep telling yourself that, *sugar*." I mocked him with the same endearment that he'd said to me earlier in bed. "Instead of just the fact that you're a sick, sadistic son of a bitch who gets his kicks beating up kids. A real prince, you are. A real king of industry and empire."

I made my voice as mocking and disdainful as possible, hoping that I would enrage Sebastian enough to get him to rush into the mausoleum to try to kill me himself. For a moment, I thought that it might actually work. Sebastian's cheeks reddened with fury, the hot emotion mottling his tan skin, and his hands clenched into tight fists. He even went so far as to take a few steps forward before he thought better of it and stopped. I had to admire his self-restraint.

Even if it was going to be the death of me.

"You know what, Gin?" Sebastian said. "You're as weak and pitiful as Charlotte is. More so, really. So starved for affection, so hungry for attention, so desperate for someone to love you that you leaped at the opportunity to cozy up to the son of the man you murdered. What kind of sick, sadistic, twisted bitch does that make *you*? Were you ever going to tell me what you did to my father? Or were you under the impression that it wouldn't matter? That we would just live happily ever after? Are you really that delusional?"

This time, the angry blush stained my cheeks, making them burn even in the cool dark of the mausoleum. But like Sebastian, I didn't give in to my anger, and I didn't respond to him. Instead, I glanced over my shoulder at Porter, but the giant stood in the same position as before, ready to shoot me the second I stepped out of the mausoleum.

When he realized that I wasn't going to answer, Sebastian shrugged. "No matter. I don't really care, anyway. I never did care, you know, especially not about *you*."

Despite everything that I'd learned about him in the last hour, his words still hurt me, cutting me to the core and then eating away at everything there like a chain saw slicing through a tough cord of wood. But it was my own fault, for not listening to Finn, for not putting more faith in Fletcher's feeling that something was wrong about the job, but most of all, for being an easy, stupid mark, just like Sebastian had said.

Oh, yes. Arrogance will get you, every single time. I had no one to blame but myself, especially for what was about to happen next.

"Oh, come on, now, Gin," Sebastian said. "Don't be a sore loser. I was always going to win, you know. There was never any doubt about that. You just made it a bit easier than I expected."

Once again, I didn't respond.

"Fine." He pouted. "If you don't want to play any-more, then neither do I. In fact, I think that it's rather fitting that you're cowering in there, right beside my dead father, since you were the one who killed him. It's so ter-ribly, tragically *ironic*. And it will make this all the easier and sweeter."

Sebastian raised his hands, and the amber flecks in his dark eyes, the ones that I'd thought were so beautiful, began to brighten as he reached for his Stone magic. All around me, the marble of the mausoleum took on even sharper, harsher mutters. It knew what Sebastian was going to do with it—and so did I.

He kept gathering and gathering his magic, until his eyes burned like two topaz torches set into his handsome face, and his skin took on a hard sheen, as though it was made of the same marble that he had so much control over. Sebastian was like me in that his magic was com-pletely self-contained. He'd never used it around me, which was why I hadn't sensed it before. But now that he was actively reaching for his magic, I could feel exactly how powerful he was.

He was strong—much, much stronger than his father had been, stronger even than I was. Jo-Jo had always told me that I was a powerful elemental, but Sebastian far surpassed me. No wonder he'd been able to crumble that restaurant balcony. With the amount of magic he was wielding right now, it would have been child's play to him, as easy as knocking over a stack of wooden blocks.

Sebastian grinned, and his eyes locked with mine, de-spite the shadows that lay between us. Then he brought his hands down and unleashed his magic, driving the invisible waves of it into the ground at his feet and then into the mausoleum.

His magic made the ground ripple, like a whip that was rising up and getting ready to crack down—right on top of my head. His Stone power raced through all of the rocks in the ground, leapfrogging from one to another, until it reached the foundation of the mausoleum. And I finally realized what Sebastian was going to do. He didn't dare come in here and fight me himself, so he was going to do the next best thing.

The bastard was going to bury me alive.

Oh, no, the irony didn't escape me. Me, a Stone elemental, about to be smashed to death by the very thing that I felt such kinship with, that I had such control over.

Sebastian's magic raced up through the foundation and then raged outward. The slick floor bucked and heaved under my feet, while chunks of stone broke off the columns that held up the domed roof. Without those supports, it wouldn't be long before the entire structure collapsed in on itself and on me.

Desperate, I looked around, wondering how I could keep from being crushed to death by tons of falling, broken rock. Once again, I reached for my own Stone magic, and once again, it slipped away from me, as though it were water that I was trying to hold in the palms of my hands. Through the thick, choking dust that had sprung up from the shattered marble, I could see Sebastian standing outside the mausoleum, pouring more and more of his magic into destroying every last part of the structure. Through the other opening, Porter waited, ready to put a bullet through my heart should I try to escape that way.

I was trapped, with nothing but cold, hard stone raining down on me.

Still, I looked around, trying to figure some way out of here. Sebastian sent another surge of magic into the mausoleum, and a large chunk of marble broke off from one of the columns, sailed through the air, and hit the top of Cesar's tomb. But the marble shattered instead of the stone slab.

My eyes narrowed as I wondered if I'd really seen what I thought I had. Because that shouldn't have happened, not unless . . . unless . . . the tombs were heavier and stronger than the marble columns.

And a thought finally occurred to me, a crazy way I could save myself from the falling stone. I didn't like it, but it was the only chance I had.

Even as the floor shook under my feet and more and more pieces of stone cracked off the columns, I staggered over to Cesar's tomb. Sure enough, it was made out of a tougher granite, rather than the more delicate marble that made up the mausoleum. Lucky for me, the granite slab was just resting on top of the tomb and hadn't been bolted or welded down. I pushed and pushed against the slab, trying to get it to move, but it was far too heavy for me to lift on my own. I doubted even Porter could have managed it with his giant strength.

I screamed with frustration, even though I couldn't hear the sound over the continual crashes of the plummeting stone. Desperate, I reached for my magic again.

It was difficult, as difficult as catching raindrops in my hands, but I managed to grab hold of a small trickle of power and send it flowing into the top of the tomb, even as I grabbed the edge of it with my hands. I couldn't lift the tomb lid, but maybe I didn't have to.

*Slide*, I commanded the stone with every bit of magic and muscle that I could muster. *Slide, damn you, slide!*

Slowly, very, very slowly, the granite began to obey my frenzied orders. It slid to the right one measly inch. I tightened my grip on the edge and sent another wave of power into the stone, even as I shoved at it with all my might. It moved another inch. Then two more, then five more, then an entire foot.

The stench of death wafted up out of the tomb, and I found myself staring down at Cesar Vaughn's pale, waxen face. His eyes were closed, his arms crossed over his chest and the expensive suit that he wore. He seemed to be at peace, which was not at all how he'd left his life, thanks to me.

*I killed an innocent man.*

The thought slammed into me, as sharp and brutal as before, and I knew that it would *always* feel this way. And that what I was about to do now would only make it worse.

"I'm sorry," I whispered, although the crashes of the crumbling rocks drowned out my voice.

But there was no time for remorse or regrets. Not now. So I sent another wave of magic into the stone, making the slab slide a few more precious inches to the left.

And then I lifted my leg over the side of the tomb and hoisted myself up and inside it.

Another blast of Sebastian's Stone magic erupted through the mausoleum, making me pitch forward onto Cesar, as though he were a lover I was about to kiss. I grimaced at the cold chill of death embracing me, a death that I was responsible for, but I forced myself to wiggle past Cesar, so that his body was the one that was exposed to the falling rocks, while I was partially covered by the tomb lid. Even then, the left side of my body was still out in the open, so I gritted my teeth, reached out, and grabbed Cesar, pulling him close and using the dead man as a shield.

It was one of the cruelest and most horrible things I'd ever done.

"Die, bitch!"

Perhaps it was my imagination, but I could have sworn that I heard Sebastian scream those words even through the cacophony of the falling rock. I pressed myself more tightly against the inside of the tomb and closed my eyes, knowing what was coming next.

Then the rest of the mausoleum collapsed in on itself, burying me in the tomb in the cold, dead embrace of the innocent man I'd murdered.

# ❊24❊

I don't know how long I lay in the tomb, my fingers digging into Cesar's stiff, lifeless shoulders, the marble shrieking and wailing all around me, like banshees calling out for death—my death.

But I lay there, and I endured it. There was nothing else I could do. At some point, I opened my eyes, although all I could see was darkness. Clouds of dust from the broken stones wormed their way down into the tomb, trying to choke me, and I buried my nose and mouth in Cesar's suit jacket to keep from inhaling the dust, even though the stench of death filled my nostrils instead, along with the faint scent of his roses.

But the cracks, crashes, and bangs eventually slowed, then stopped. I felt the marble give out one final, great, heavy shudder, before the foundation settled back into place, the jagged edges scraping together like the tectonic plates of the earth after a violent quake. The stone continued to wail, though, its anguished cries ringing in my ears.

Somehow I managed to shut the sound out of my mind and focus on my own body. The lid of the tomb had shielded me from the worst of the falling rocks, so I was in more or less one piece, although the same couldn't be said for poor Cesar. His body had been buried in the rubble, the mountain of stone blocking my easy escape from the tomb.

Once again, I'd used him, hurt him, *ruined* him. Even in death, Cesar Vaughn couldn't rest in peace. At least, not from me. The thought sickened me, the cold, hard knowledge that I'd killed an innocent man and had then been forced to desecrate his mausoleum, his tomb, and his body in such a horrible manner.

But it had been the only way for me to survive, and I still had a chance to live through this—and to warn Finn and Fletcher. They might not be innocent, not like Cesar had been, but they were my family all the same, and they were in danger because of me.

I'd just started to move when I felt a presence ripple through the shattered stone.

Sebastian.

I froze, my hands curling around Cesar's half-buried shoulders again. The vibration surged through the mausoleum, and the dark mutters started once more. Sebastian must have been using his magic to listen to the marble, to try to figure out whether I was still alive. For a moment, a wild, panicked desperation rose up in me to get as far away from Cesar as fast as I could, to get out of his tomb, out of his mausoleum, and just run, run, run away from all the reminders of how wrong I'd been about everything.

But I couldn't do that. Not if I wanted to live. Not if I wanted to save Finn and Fletcher. I *had* to save them. Otherwise, all of this would have been for nothing.

So I thought of the old man and all the lessons that he'd tried to teach me over the years about being calm, focused, patient. I closed my eyes and made my limbs go absolutely slack and still, and I let the cold chill from Cesar's body sink even deeper into my own, even though I wanted nothing more than to get away from him. Then I listened to the stone, and I let all of its murmurs fill my mind, blotting out everything else—murmurs of death, despair, destruction. I listened to them, and I embraced them, until I almost felt as if I were one with the stone, just another broken piece of rock in agony over the horrors that had been visited upon it.

In a way, I supposed that's *exactly* what I was.

For a long time, that was all I heard, and that was all I felt. But then that dark, evil presence rippled through the shattered marble a third time, and I felt Sebastian's magic brush up against mine, like black vines of kudzu winding through everything, poisoning, strangling everything they touched. I held back a shudder and concentrated harder on the stone, willing it to see me as just another piece of itself—small, broken, and unremarkable.

I don't know how long I lay there, but the black vines of Sebastian's magic slowly slithered away, and I felt his presence withdraw from the stone.

For a long time, there was silence. Then—

"She's dead," Sebastian said, his voice muffled by the

splintered stone that stood between him and me. "You can put your gun down now, Porter."

"Are you sure?"

"I'm sure. There's no sense of life inside the stone."

"I don't know," the giant rumbled back. "She might have found a place to hide in there. From what I've seen so far, she's a tough little bitch."

"Well, she might have been a good assassin, but even if she were still alive, I just dropped a couple of tons of rock on top of her," Sebastian drawled. "Trust me, Porter, there's no way she's crawling out from underneath all of that. But if it makes you feel better, we'll drag her body out of there when we start clearing away the rubble in a few days."

They debated some more, but in the end, they both seemed satisfied that I was as dead as Cesar.

"But what about the mausoleum?" Porter asked. "What are you going to tell people when they ask what happened to it?"

"I'll tell them that I decided to tear it down and build a larger and much more fitting monument to my father," Sebastian said. "I always hated that thing, anyway. Now, come on. Call your men. I want two teams, three men each, sent out, one to deal with the old man and the other to handle Gin's brother, just like you planned."

"Consider it done," Porter said.

"Good," Sebastian replied. "Then let's go have a celebratory drink now that we're almost finished with this whole mess."

The two men started talking again, their voices becoming even more distant before fading away altogether. They must have headed back toward the mansion.

Sebastian thought that I was dead and that he'd finally won. Now he was going to send Porter's men after Finn and Fletcher. Not if I could help it.

The bastard had already played me for a fool. He wasn't taking away my family too—the people who truly cared about me.

So I drew in a breath and started to dig my way out of my tomb.

For once, I'd gotten lucky, and the rocks piled on top of Cesar were small chunks of what had been the ceiling, so I was able to shove them out of my way and wiggle out from underneath the lid of the tomb. But then my luck ran out, and I was stuck. I peered into the gloom, but the moonlight slipping in through the cracks in the stones made everything a dull shade of gray.

The mausoleum had collapsed in on itself, as Sebastian had intended, but the columns had crisscrossed one another, forming a sort of support that had kept the ceiling from completely flattening everything inside, including me. Now the columns resembled spikes lining the inside of a coffin—my coffin, if I didn't find a way to get out of here.

Slowly, very, very slowly, I began to move forward.

The mausoleum hadn't been all that large, maybe fifty feet wide, but it might as well have been a mile. I felt like a worm trying to work my way through a jigsaw puzzle, one with jagged edges that sliced into my body with every move I made. I would slither forward a few feet, only to come up against a piece of marble that was too large for me to crawl around or under. So I'd have to backtrack and try to find another way through the maze of stone.

The good thing about being trapped inside for so long was that it gave my body time to flush the last of the drugged champagne out of my system. I might be buried under a couple of tons of rock, but I finally felt like myself again—especially when it came to my rage.

It burned inside me, as black as Sebastian's magic, keeping perfect time to the slow, steady beat of my heart. *Revenge, revenge, revenge . . .* that was the thing that kept me going, that kept me moving, that kept me crawling through the broken stone, even though all I wanted to do was slump over and stop. But I kept crawling, kept fighting, driven by my need for revenge against Sebastian for everything that he'd done to Cesar, Charlotte, and me and what he had in store for Finn and Fletcher.

Finally, I neared the edge of the mausoleum, only to find my path blocked by a large chunk of stone. It was about the size of a kitchen table, much too big and heavy for me to shove out of the way. It was the only thing standing between me and escape, and I was going to have to use my magic to blast it out of the way if I had any hope of warning Finn and Fletcher in time.

I paused again, listening, but I didn't hear anything other than the still-wailing marble and the soft sounds of the night beyond the ring of stone. Sebastian was nowhere in the area. Even if he was back in the mansion, he might still be able to sense me using my magic, given how strong he was in his own power, but it was a risk that I had to take.

So I held my hand out in front of me, flattening it on the stone. Then I reached for my magic, just a trickle, just enough to let me connect with the marble boulder in front of me. I sent my magic deeper and deeper into the stone, looking for any cracks that I could pour my power into. Then, when I found the stone's weak spots, I exploited them, just as Sebastian had exploited my weaknesses—weaknesses I hadn't even realized that I'd had.

Arrogance. Impatience. Pride.

Thinking about Sebastian made a snarl rise in my throat, and I sent out another wave of magic. Piece by piece, crack by crack, bit by bit, I slowly shattered the stone in front of me, boring a tunnel straight through the center of it like a convict digging her way to freedom. Every few seconds, I stopped to listen, but Sebastian didn't come to investigate.

He thought that I was dead and buried and no longer a threat to him. He should have made sure. Because his mistake was going to cost him his fucking life.

I sent out one final burst of magic, and the last layer of stone crumbled to dust in front of me. I choked on the ashy cloud of marble, but I put my hands on the far edge of the mausoleum and pulled myself through the opening I'd created. I slid forward, then tumbled off the rocks and down onto the dewy grass. I lay there for several minutes, panting and trying to get my breath back. Above my head, the midnight sky twinkled with a thousand stars, while the moon shimmered over the pond a few feet away, as if it was peering down at its own bright, silvery reflection.

When I felt like I could manage it, I rolled over, then slowly got on my hands and knees, before finally staggering up and onto my feet. I wavered back and forth, and the moonlight bounced off a smooth surface, catching my eye. I looked down and realized that it was my silverstone knife. Somehow I'd managed to hang on to the weapon through everything that had happened. My fingers curled around the hilt. Good. I was going to need it to go after the giants hunting Finn and Fletcher.

But the mausoleum hadn't been as lucky as I'd been. The once-beautiful structure had been reduced to little more than a heap of rough, ragged stones, like a cairn for the dead. That's certainly what Sebastian had intended it to be for me.

I dragged my gaze away from the mausoleum and looked toward the mansion itself. Golden light spilled out of the library windows on the third floor. The curtains had been drawn back, and a figure moved back and forth behind the glass: Sebastian.

Even from this distance, I still recognized his sinister shadow. He seemed to be holding court with someone, probably Porter, judging by the way he kept throwing his hands up into the air.

I tightened my grip on my knife and took a step forward, but the motion made pain shoot through my body. I might have escaped being crushed by the rocks, but I'd still taken a beating tonight—physically and emotionally—and I was a torn, tired, tattered mess. Cuts, scrapes, and bruises decorated my body from head to toe, my dress was ripped in at least two dozen places, and most of the moonstones had flaked off the jeweled straps and bodice. I'd even lost my shoes somewhere in the mausoleum, just like the Wicked Witch of the East.

Still, despite my injuries, I wanted nothing more than to march back up to the mansion, storm into the library, bury my knife in Sebastian's heart, and watch him die. For a moment, I seriously considered it. After all, he thought that I was dead, so I'd have the element of surprise on my side.

Then my gaze flicked to the crumbled stone in front of me, and I forced myself to rein in my temper. No matter how much I wanted to kill Sebastian, I wasn't going to give in to my arrogance, impatience, and pride. Not this time. Not when I was bruised and battered, and he wasn't. Even more important, his giants were on their way to kill Finn and Fletcher. I needed to move, not stand out here in the dark and brood about my revenge.

I'd be back for Sebastian, though—soon enough.

# ❖ 25 ❖

I hiked through the trees on the back side of the estate until I reached the main road. Then I started walking. There was nothing else I could do. The Vaughn estate wasn't out in the boonies, but it wasn't exactly close to anything either—except Mab Monroe's mansion.

I stopped and peered through the gates at the enormous compound that served as the Fire elemental's home, but there was no way that anyone inside would help me, and I wasn't going to be dumb enough to try to sneak onto the grounds and steal a vehicle. Mab had dozens of giant guards at her disposal, any one of whom would have been happy to kill a car thief. So I shuffled on past the mansion.

I kept walking down the road, moving as fast as I could. Still, I knew that it would take me hours to get to Finn's apartment and even longer to make it to Fletcher's, which would be far too late to save either one of them—

Headlights appeared behind me.

I was so surprised that I stopped dead in my tracks. It was long after midnight now, and I wondered who would be out so late, especially this close to Mab's mansion. But the lights kept coming and coming, catching me in their hot glare.

I hesitated, then scurried up to the edge of the road and stuck my left thumb out.

Hitchhiking wasn't something that I normally did, not even when I was living on the streets and wanted to get from one side of Ashland to the other. In this city, you never knew whose car you were getting into, and the nicest Northtown smile could hide the cruelest heart, something you wouldn't know until the locks had clicked shut, trapping you with whatever evil was behind the wheel. But I was out of options.

I squinted against the oncoming glare and dropped my right hand down by my side, so that my knife would be out of sight against my body. If worse came to worse, I could always stab my way free. The mood I was in, I was more than willing to do that and pretend that I was killing Sebastian all the while.

The car rolled forward, and I fully expected the driver to ram his foot onto the gas and zoom right on past me, especially since I looked like some haint from a horror movie, but the car slowed, then stopped. The passenger-side window rolled down, and I warily approached the vehicle, still clutching my knife.

A guy who was a few years older than me sat in the driver's seat. His black hair disappeared into the darkness, and the dim blue light from the display cast his face in shadows, although I could still see the crooked tilt of his nose, as though someone had smashed a fist into it once upon a time.

The guy leaned forward so he could get a better look at me through the open window. His eyes flicked over me, taking in my ruined, tattered dress, my dusty bird's nest of hair, and the gray grime that streaked my arms, chest, and face. The only sound was the steady hum of the engine.

"You look like you could use some help," he finally said, popping the door locks. "Get in."

I hesitated again, wondering if this was really a good idea. Nice guys, good guys, didn't pick up girls who looked like me, especially not this late at night. He probably thought that I was some hooker who'd gotten the shit beat out of her by her pimp and that I would give him a freebie for the ride. But I didn't have time to be choosy. Not if I wanted to save Finn and Fletcher. So I made sure that my knife was down by my leg out of sight, opened the door, and slid into the car.

"Where to?" the guy asked.

I eyed him, taking in the thick muscles in his arms and chest. He wasn't a dwarf or a giant, but he obviously did regular, hard, physical labor. You didn't get muscles like that working out in the gym. At best, he was much stronger than I was. At worst, he had magic to augment his physical abilities. I didn't sense any elemental power radiating off him, though. Either way, I'd just have to take my chances.

"Just like that?" I asked. "You pick up some strange chick on a deserted road late at night, and you offer to drive her wherever she wants? What are you, some sort of Prince Charming?"

The guy shrugged, making the muscles in his chest roll with the motion. "Just trying to be nice, ma'am."

I let out a crazy, bitter laugh. He kept staring at me. I couldn't tell what color his eyes were, only that they were light, almost like marbles set into the rough, rugged planes of his face.

"All right, then," I said, rattling off the address of Finn's apartment building. "Take me there."

"You got it."

He threw the car into gear and steered down the street. I studied my would-be rescuer out of the corner of my eye. He was wearing dark blue coveralls, although the front was partially unzipped, letting his pale blue T-shirt underneath peek through. His clothes were wrinkled and rumpled, as though he'd been wearing them all day long, and small black holes marred the sleeves of his coveralls, as though some sort of hot sparks had landed on his arms and burned through the heavy material. Maybe he was a mechanic or welder.

The guy didn't speak for two miles. "You sure you want me to take you to that address?" he asked. "Instead of the police station?"

I tensed. A trip to the po-po was the *last* thing I needed. What the hell would I tell them, anyway? I was an assassin who'd been fucked over—literally—by her client. These last few weeks mooning over Sebastian hadn't exactly been my best. "I'm sure."

"You want to tell me what happened?"

"I had a rough night," I deadpanned.

He let out a low, rumbling laugh. Despite everything, I smiled a little. Well, at least I'd amused someone tonight—someone other than Sebastian.

"It seems like it was a little more than rough."

"What?" I shot back. "You don't like my bed-head look? I spent *hours* on it."

He laughed again, the sound a little deeper and more genuine this time. But his face turned serious, and he stared at me again. "Look, if someone hurt you, or if there's someone after you, I can take you to the cops. It's no problem."

I snorted. "Please. The cops in this town are a joke."

"Maybe so," he agreed. "But you look like you could use someone's help."

"Isn't that what you're doing? Helping me?"

"Well, yeah. But you seem . . . really sad and just . . . hurt."

"It's nothing," I said, biting back a curse at how perceptive he was. "My boyfriend and I had a fight. Apparently, he thought it would be *hilarious* to take me to a party and leave me stranded out in the middle of nowhere Northtown."

"And your ripped clothes?" the guy asked in a quiet voice.

I shrugged. "The party was back in the woods. I didn't know where I was going, and I couldn't see because it was dark. I fell down a hill and landed in a briar patch."

"Funny," he said. "Because you look like you're covered with dust, not dirt."

I glanced down. The interior of the car was dim, but he was right. A pale gray powder covered me from head to toe, as though I'd had a bag of flour upended over my head. No, I didn't look like I'd been out wandering around in the woods.

"Well, aren't you observant," I sniped.

He continued on as though I hadn't spoken. "When I first saw you, I thought you were some haint, some ghost, that had wandered out of the woods."

Oh, I was a ghost all right, one who was going to come back and haunt Sebastian. No, scratch that. I was just going to kill him. More rage burned in my heart, but I plastered a smile on my face. No use scaring my chatty driver. He hadn't done anything to me—Sebastian had.

"You believe in haints?"

He grinned. "Don't you?"

I didn't answer, and he fell silent again. He made a turn that would take us to the downtown loop. The guy drove a few more miles before clearing his throat.

"Your boyfriend is a real dick for leaving you like this," he said.

"You have no idea."

"You just don't do that to a girl, no matter the circumstances," he continued. "I hope you don't plan to see this guy again. He's a total douche bag, if you ask me."

"Oh, I plan to see him again all right. One more time, in fact, to tell him exactly what I think of him." Right before I rammed my knife into his heart, but driver dude didn't need to know that.

He nodded. "Good. I hope you give him a piece of your mind."

Out of sight, below the seat, my thumb rubbed over the hilt of the knife still in my hand. "Oh, you can count on that."

The guy hit the downtown loop, and ten minutes later, he pulled up in front of Finn's apartment building. I glanced up and down the street. Several cars were parked by the curbs, including a black SUV with a bumper sticker that said *Vaughn Construction*, complete with that distinctive V made out of two thorns curving together. Through the windshield, I could see three giants inside, one of whom was talking on his phone, probably waiting for the final go order from Porter. I let out a tense breath. I had managed to get here in time after all.

Driver dude started to stop in front of the building, which would have given the giants a clear view of me in all my marble-dusted glory. Right now, the element of surprise was the only thing I had going for me, and I didn't want to lose it.

"Actually, sweetheart, if you don't mind, pull over into that lot right there," I said, pointing my finger down the street.

"Are you sure?"

"I'm sure."

He shrugged, but he steered the car into the lot. He pulled up to a side door, out of sight of the street and the giants' SUV. He killed the engine, then turned to look at me, his eyes serious once more. "So now that you're not seeing the dickhead anymore, what are you going to do with the rest of your weekend?"

It took me a second to realize what he was really asking.

I gave him a flat look. "Are you kidding me? I've just had the worst date in the history of the world, and you're actually hitting on me?"

An embarrassed flush filled his chiseled cheeks. "Well, when you put it like that, it does sound really bad."

I snorted again. "You could say that. Although you and my foster brother would get along great. He would totally approve of your method of trying to seduce a girl when she's down."

"Hey, now," the guy said, seeming genuinely affronted. "It's not like that at all. You're not the only one who's had a bad . . . breakup. Trust me on that. But you just seem . . . interesting. More interesting than any girl I've met in a long time."

My heart twisted, because those were more or less the same words that Sebastian had so sweetly said to me, the first of many that he'd used to draw me into his sticky web of lies. Anger rose up in me again, along with more than a little hurt.

"Listen, pal," I snapped. "I'm a waitress. Just because you found me wandering around Northtown doesn't mean that I have money. Even if I did, you wouldn't be getting any of it."

He shrugged again. "I don't care what you do. I'm a blacksmith, so I'm not exactly rolling in dough either. Not yet, anyway. I have plans, though—"

"Good for you." I cut him off.

The guy fell silent, still staring at me. I shifted under his scrutiny. For some reason, it seemed like he could see all of my secrets written in the harsh lines of my dust-covered face.

"This guy who left you stranded, he really did a number on you, didn't he?"

I shrugged, trying not to let him see how close he was

to the truth. Sebastian had ripped my heart to shreds, but that wasn't the worst thing. He'd also made me doubt myself, especially my ability to tell the truth from a bald-faced lie. In a few short weeks, he'd undermined all the confidence that I had in myself as an assassin, and I hadn't even realized that I was being taken for a fool until it was too late. If I couldn't tell when a guy was playing me, then how could I ever be good enough to live up to what Fletcher had trained me to be?

How could I ever truly be the Spider?

But I couldn't think about that right now. What mattered was getting to Finn. Time to go. My fingers curled around my knife. Time to kill.

"Thanks for the ride," I said, opening the door and getting out of the car. "But I need to leave now."

"But you didn't even tell me your name," the guy protested.

"It's not like you told me yours."

"Owen," he said with a grin.

"Well, good night, Owen."

He hesitated, obviously waiting for me to tell him my name, but I'd learned my lesson with Sebastian, one that I'd never, ever forget. Finally, when it became clear that I wasn't going to give him any more information about myself, he nodded his head.

"Take care," Owen finally said.

"Yeah. You too."

He waved at me. "Until we meet again."

I wanted to tell him that the odds of that were slim to none, but his crooked grin made me hold my tongue. He'd done me a huge favor, and I'd acted like a total bitch during the entire ride. So I raised my hand and waved back at him, as though he were dropping me off at home after a late-night date. I sort of wished that he was. He seemed nice, this Owen.

The smile slipped off my face. So had Sebastian.

Owen gave me a final wave, then made a U-turn in the parking lot and drove off. As soon as his taillights had disappeared, I crept over to the side of the building and peered around the corner. Apparently, the giant had finished his phone call, because all three men were getting out of their vehicle and heading for the front door. It wouldn't take them long to get inside the building and make their way to Finn's apartment, and I wanted to be in place before they did.

I tightened my grip on my knife and disappeared around the corner.

I hurried over to the side door of the building. Unlike the front door, which was always open, this one was locked. I reached for my magic, and a few seconds later, I was bending over the door, a pair of Ice picks clutched in my fingers. It took me longer than I would have liked to pick the lock, but I managed it, then tossed the thin shards of Ice off into the bushes that lined this side of the building.

I slipped inside and shut the door behind me. I was at the bottom of a stairwell, so I crept up the five steps to the first floor of the building. I peered through the glass set into the top of a door there, which let me see into the lobby. The three giants now stood in front of the elevator, waiting for it to come down so they could ride up to Finn's floor.

I hurried up the steps, determined to beat them, even though I was sucking wind by the time I reached Finn's floor. I stopped in the stairwell and looked out through the glass in that door, but the giants weren't here yet.

I opened the door, stepped into the hallway, and hurried over to the elevator. Behind me, the door to Finn's apartment was closed, but I ignored it. This was a new building, and he was the only tenant on this floor so far, something he crowed about every chance he got. Good. That meant that no one else would hear the screams that were coming. Besides, I didn't need his help with this.

The lights on the elevator slowly lit up as the metal cart climbed from one floor to the next. I stayed where I was, right in front of the opening, and waited—just waited. I didn't mind being patient. Not for this.

*Ding!*

The doors slid back, revealing the three giants. They'd been talking among themselves, and they weren't even looking toward the opening, which gave me time to dart forward, raise my knife high, and slam it into the chest of the man closest to me. He screamed in surprise, and his buddies' heads snapped around as they wondered why some ghostly-looking chick was stabbing their friend to death.

I didn't give them time to wonder long.

I pulled my knife out of the giant's chest and slashed it across his throat. Blood sprayed all over the inside of the elevator, and me too, but I didn't care. I finally had a focus for my rage, and I was going to let it *out*.

The second giant raised his fists and swung at me, but I ducked down, twirled my knife in my hand, and rammed it into his thigh. He collapsed on top of the first giant, and I drove my knife into the side of his neck, feeling the blade scrape against the bones in his spine.

Before I could pull the blade free, the third and last giant dug his fingers into my hair and yanked me up and off his friend. He drew his hand back, as though he was going to drive his fist into my stomach, but I lurched forward, grabbed hold of his arm, and sank my teeth into the soft web of his hand between his thumb and index finger.

The giant screamed and tried to shake me off, like a cat attempting to snap a mouse's neck. I pulled back just long enough to bite him again. This time, he flung me away, sending me flying into the opposite side of the elevator car. But I bounced off like a wrestler on the ropes and went right back at him.

The giant held his hand up, trying to block me from getting close enough to bite him again, but that wasn't my intention. Instead, I darted forward, plucked the gun from the holster on his belt, put it against his chest, and pulled the trigger three times.

*Crack! Crack! Crack!*

The giant's body muffled the blasts, although it still sounded like I'd let off a series of firecrackers inside the elevator. The giant slid to the floor, joining his two dead friends.

*Ding!*

The elevator doors kept trying to close, but they couldn't, given the arms and legs of the dead men that were blocking them. I pulled my knife from the giant's neck and kept the gun in my other hand. Then I stepped over the bodies, went to Finn's door, raised my hand, and rapped politely on the wood with the bloody barrel of the gun.

No answer.

I raised the gun and rapped again, a little more forcefully this time.

"Go away." Finn's voice rumbled through the wood, along with the faint sounds of smooth jazz. "We're busy."

A soft, feminine laugh accompanied his statement.

"Put your pants back on and open the damn door," I growled, loudly enough for him to hear. "Right now, Finn."

Silence. Finn let out a curse, but the door cracked open, and I found myself staring into his green eyes— eyed that widened when he noticed all the blood, dust, and grime on me.

"We have a problem—"

*Ding!*

The elevator cut me off. Finn opened the door wide enough to stick his head outside. His gaze flicked to the dead giants sprawled in the elevator. He sighed and shook his head.

"You just had to come here and make a mess, didn't you?" he sniped. "I've only had this apartment for three months. Now I'm going to have to move."

"I don't care," I said. "We have a situation. The old man's in danger."

# *❋ 26 ❋*

Finn opened the door and let me inside. I left my bloody knife and the giant's gun on a table just inside the door, then followed him through the hallway and into the living room in the back of the apartment. Too bad I'd forgotten that he wasn't alone.

Roslyn Phillips, the vampire he had been ogling at the party earlier, sat on the overstuffed white couch. Up close, she was even more beautiful, and I could see why Finn had been so keen on getting her attention. A couple of glasses of red wine perched on the table in front of her, while jazz music oozed out of the sound system in the corner. But it seemed as though I'd interrupted them before anything had happened, since she still had on her dress and Finn had only shrugged out of his tuxedo jacket.

The vampire's toffee-colored eyes widened as she took in my ruined dress, bare feet, and the blood spattered all over me. Her crimson lips pursed together in thought, but she didn't say anything, and she didn't ask any of the obvious questions. Finn stepped forward and plastered a smooth smile on his face, as if a blood-covered woman showing up at his apartment in the middle of the night was a common occurrence.

"Roslyn Phillips, this is my foster sister, Gin," Finn said. "Gin, Roslyn."

"Pleasure."

"Me too," she murmured.

"Gin's been in a bit of an . . . accident," he said, trying to explain.

Finn hurried over to a phone on one of the tables and picked it up. I knew that he was trying to reach Fletcher, so I decided to distract Roslyn from what he was doing.

"A car accident," I said in a sweet voice. "Just down the street. That's why I came here."

Concern darkened Roslyn's eyes, and she kept staring at all of the blood on me. "Are you all right?"

"Sure," I deadpanned. "You should see the other guys."

Finn winced, but he didn't say anything. A minute later, he shook his head and hung up the phone. Seemed like there was no answer at Fletcher's.

"You need to take me home. I was headed over there to check on the old man when I had my . . . accident."

Finn gave the vampire his most winning smile. "Roslyn, I'm afraid that I'm going to have to cut our evening short. Family comes first. You understand, don't you?"

"Of course," she murmured, getting to her feet. "Just let me get my purse."

I looked at Finn. "But the elevator's broken right now."

He blinked, remembering the dead giants and their blood splashed all over the elevator walls.

"Ah, Roslyn, why don't you make yourself comfortable in here?" Finn said. "Gin and I have something to take care of, but I should be back in an hour—"

I rammed my elbow into his side.

"Or two."

He gave her another bright smile. "Regardless, there's no reason for you to leave."

Roslyn looked at him, then at me, her gaze lingering on the blood that covered me like confetti from a party. But she sat back down on the couch. I couldn't tell if she really wanted to stay until Finn got back or if she just didn't want to get involved in whatever problem I was dragging him into. Smart woman.

"Anyway, Roslyn, help yourself to a drink, watch TV, flip through a magazine, raid the fridge, whatever," Finn said, grabbing his tuxedo jacket and car keys.

He disappeared into the bedroom, then reappeared two minutes later carrying a black duffel bag that I knew contained at least a couple of guns, along with other pertinent items. I had a similar bag hidden behind one of the freezers at the Pork Pit.

I jerked my head toward the kitchen. Finn frowned, but then he realized what I wanted, and he headed in there. I stepped in front of Roslyn, so she wouldn't see him grabbing rags and a bottle of bleach from under the sink and stuffing those into his duffel bag.

An amused smile flitted across Roslyn's face, as if she knew exactly what I was up to, but I didn't care at this point.

Finally, Finn stepped back into the living room. "All set."

I nodded my head politely at Roslyn. "Ms. Phillips, so nice to meet you."

She tipped her head back at me. "And you too, Gin. I'm sure we'll meet again."

Probably, if Finn was as determined to seduce her as he seemed to be, but I decided not to be rude and mention that. Instead, I gave her one final smile before turning and following Finn out of the apartment.

I grabbed my knife and the giant's gun from the table in the foyer and stepped outside.

Finn shut the door behind us, then gave me a sour look. "You do realize that Roslyn will probably never speak to me again?"

"Oh, I don't know," I drawled. "She didn't bat an eye at all of the blood on me. I think she's made of tougher stuff than you think. Then again, she *is* a vampire. She's used to seeing blood."

Finn sniffed, still in a bit of a snit—

*Ding!*

The elevator chimed out its tune. Good thing no one else lived on this floor, or a pissed-off neighbor might have stuck his head out of his apartment, wondering why it wouldn't shut up.

"All right," Finn said. "Tell me what the hell is going on."

I quickly filled him in on everything that had happened tonight, including Sebastian's betrayal of me.

"I knew I didn't like that smarmy bastard," Finn said.

He poured some bleach onto one of the rags and used

it to wipe the giants' blood off the elevator walls. I was already doing the same thing on the other side of the car.

"You were certainly right about him." I couldn't keep the hurt out of my voice.

Finn gave me a sympathetic look. "It's not your fault," he said. "Sebastian played you, but he played me and Dad too. I never suspected that he was the one who hired us, who hired you to kill his own father. I thought it was all about the restaurant incident, just like you did."

Instead of responding, I bent down and started going through the dead giants' pants pockets, pulling out their wallets and IDs and tossing them into Finn's duffel bag, along with the gun I'd used. Finn stopped his cleaning long enough to touch my shoulder, then started wiping down the walls again.

When that was done, we shoved the giants all the way into the elevator and rode it down to the first floor. The doors opened, but no one was waiting for a ride. If someone had been, well, I don't know what we would have done.

We'd cleaned up as much of the blood as we could, and all that was left to do was dispose of the giants' bodies. I hated waiting even a second to go after Fletcher, but we couldn't exactly leave the dead guys in the elevator for some tenant to find when they went out for an early-morning jog.

"Where are we going to put these guys?" I asked.

Finn grinned. "I know just the spot."

Fifteen minutes later, we were carrying the last giant's body out of the elevator, through the lobby, and to the Dumpsters behind the building.

"Remind me never to kill anyone in an apartment building, hotel, or some other place where I have to lug the bodies around myself," I said, huffing and puffing. "Or at least not to kill giants in such places."

Finn was too busy gasping for breath to answer me. After a moment, he managed to suck down enough wind to speak. "Dad totally needs to pay Sophia more."

"Agreed."

We heaved the last giant up and into the Dumpster and closed the lid on him. It was a risk, leaving the giants' bodies here, so close to Finn's apartment, but we didn't have a lot of other options right now.

We hurried away from the Dumpsters and headed to the parking garage attached to the back of the building. We didn't pass anyone, but the stone muttered with sharp notes of worry and the soft, continuous rumble of cars and other vehicles. Garages were a good place for paranoia, especially in Ashland, so I clutched my knife and peered into the shadows, making sure that some thug wasn't lurking behind a concrete pillar, waiting to jump us. But Finn and I were the only ones up to no good here tonight.

Finn whipped out his phone and dialed Fletcher's house. After several seconds, he shook his head. "Busy. He must be talking to someone. I tried him when I went into my bedroom, but it was busy then too, just like it was the first time that I called."

I chewed my lower lip in worry. Sebastian knew where Fletcher's house was, since he'd sent a car there to pick me up for the party, but it wasn't the easiest place to find, especially this late at night. I had to hope that the giants didn't make it there ahead of us or that Fletcher at least saw them coming.

"Where's your car?" I asked, looking around for the old brown van that Fletcher had given him a few years ago.

Finn pointed to a slick silver sports car that was parked all by itself, five spots away from the nearest vehicle.

"An Aston Martin? Really? I thought you were over your James Bond fetish."

"Having impeccable style and taste is not a fetish." Finn sniffed.

I rolled my eyes. "Where did you even get the money for this?"

Finn gave me a smug look. "You didn't think I took that internship at the bank to actually *work*, did you? I took it so I could learn how to grow our money. And some of my investments have already paid off."

My eyes narrowed. "What do you mean, *our money*?"

Finn grinned. "Who do you think helps Dad set up your jobs? Especially when it comes to the e-mail and the bank transfers? I might not have your killer instinct with a knife, but I'm invaluable to the old man as a cutout and money man. You might be content to let your stash molder in tin cans buried in the backyard, but I intend to do things with *my* money."

"Yeah," I sniped. "Like feed your own ego."

Finn opened his mouth, but I held up my hand, cutting him off.

"Well, I hope that thing is as fast as it looks, because we need to get to Fletcher—now."

Finn's face grew somber, and he nodded.

We settled ourselves in the car, and less than a minute later, we were peeling out of the parking garage, racing toward Fletcher's house. I just hoped we made it to him in time. My thumb rubbed against the edge of the bloody knife in my hand. Because if we didn't, Sebastian would pay.

Actually, he was going to pay either way, even if he didn't realize it yet.

# * 27 *

Finn drove fast on the deserted streets, and we made it over to Fletcher's house in record time. Finn pulled into the bottom of the driveway and stopped, although the engine was still running.

"What do you think?" he asked. "Should we do this quiet or loud?"

I held my knife up where he could see it. "Loud—and bloody."

He grinned and slammed his foot down onto the pedal. The car churned up the driveway and crested the top of the ridge. A black SUV sat in front of the house, with the same *Vaughn Construction* bumper sticker as the one that had been outside Finn's apartment.

The giants were already here.

Finn stopped the car, making the tires spit gravel everywhere. He reached into the backseat to get a gun out of his bag, but I was already out of the vehicle. I raced over to the SUV, hoping that the giants had just arrived, but it was empty. They must already be inside—

*Crack!*

*Crack! Crack!*

*Crack!*

Gunshots sounded, and orange blasts of gunfire lit up one of the downstairs windows. I sprinted for the porch. The front door had been kicked in and clung to the frame with one lonely hinge. Finn stepped up onto the porch with me, a gun in his hand. I gestured at myself, then the opening, telling him that I would go in the front. Finn nodded, hurried off the porch, and disappeared around the corner of the house so he could come in from the back.

I eased past the broken door and stepped inside the house. Despite the late hour, several lamps blazed in various rooms, casting pools of light into the hallway. Fletcher must have been waiting up for me again. My heart wrenched at the thought, but I made myself focus. I looked and listened, but I didn't hear any sounds, not even the TV softly murmuring in the den. Fletcher and the giants must be somewhere deeper in the house.

So I crept down the hallway, easing up to all the rooms and peeking inside them. Fletcher's house had always been cluttered, but all of the knickknacks and furnishings seemed to take on a sinister air, given the combination of light and dark inside the house, along with the moonlight streaming in through the cracks in the curtains.

The house itself was also a bit like a maze, given all the additions that had been tacked onto it over the years. Hallways zigzagged here and there, doubled back on each other, and ultimately led to dead ends. Tonight, with the giants lurking inside, it was a maze of death. Still, I wanted to let the old man know that he wasn't alone, not anymore.

"Fletcher!" I yelled. "I'm here!"

Silence.

"Fletcher!" I yelled again.

A floorboard creaked deeper in the house.

I thought for a moment, trying to judge where the sound had come from, then quickly slid through one of the downstairs living rooms and out the other side into a hallway that ran parallel to the one that I'd been in. If I was right, it sounded like someone was in this middle section of the house, close to the den in the back.

I eased up to the doorframe of another living room and peered around the edge—

*Crack!*

*Crack! Crack!*

*Crack!*

I ducked back out into the hallway as bullets slammed into the wood, splintering it. Yep, at least one of the giants was right where I'd guessed he would be. I thought for a moment.

"Fletcher!" I yelled again.

*Crack!*

*Crack! Crack!*

*Crack!*

I stuck my head around the doorframe again and ducked back as more bullets zipped in my direction. Then I turned and hurried away, making sure to thump my bare feet into the wooden floorboards so they'd creak like they had under the giant's weight. I got to the end of the hallway and doubled back the way I'd just come, this time taking care where I stepped so I wouldn't give away the fact that I hadn't run away after all. Ten seconds later, I was right back where I'd started, outside the doorway.

"Jack!" I heard someone hiss inside the room. "It's Frank! Where are you?"

But Jack didn't answer his friend. I wondered if Fletcher had managed to kill that one—and where the third and last man might be.

But my trap worked, and heavy footsteps scurried in my direction. I stayed where I was beside the splintered doorframe and waited, just waited.

But Frank was a little more cautious than I expected him to be. He stuck his gun through the doorway first and swept it from side to side, ready to shoot at anything that moved in the hallway beyond. I stayed where I was, out of his line of sight.

Frank stepped into the corridor. He started to hurry to his right, the direction he'd thought I'd gone, when he saw me out of the corner of his eye. He turned, trying to bring his gun up so he could fire at me, but I was already moving, moving, moving.

I slashed my knife across his stomach, tearing through his muscles and slicing open his guts. Blood spattered onto my hands and sprayed all over the floor and walls. Frank howled with pain, brought his gun up, and pulled the trigger.

*Crack!*

I managed to knock his hand away at the last second, and the bullet blasted by my head instead of going through my skull. But the bright muzzle flash ruined my vision, and the sound seared my ears, disorienting me. I stumbled away, and Frank came after me. He raised his gun to fire again. I staggered back, tripping over the edge of a table. My legs went out from under me, and I fell to the floor on my ass, knowing that I wouldn't be able to keep him from putting a bullet in my chest. I reached for my Stone magic, but I didn't know if I could harden my skin with it before he pulled the trigger—

*Crack! Crack! Crack!*

Frank screamed as three bullets punched into his back, but he raised his gun and focused it on me once more.

*Crack!*

This time, the bullet went into the back of Frank's skull, and he *thump*ed to the floor without another sound.

I blinked the last of the flashing white spots out of my vision and looked up. Fletcher stood farther down the hallway, a large revolver clutched in his hand. The old man shuffled forward and peered down at the giant, making sure that he was dead, before he raised his eyes to mine.

"That was the last of them," Fletcher said. "Arrogant bastards thought they could bust right on in here and take care of me. Well, we showed them, didn't we?"

He smiled and took another step forward. He lowered his gun, and that's when I noticed the blood dripping down his right arm—and how much of it was splashed all over his clothes.

"Fletcher?" I whispered.

He grinned at me again, then collapsed to the floor.

\*    \*    \*

"Fletcher!" I scrambled over to him on my hands and knees.

He smiled up at me, his face crinkled with pain. "Not so loud, Gin. My ears are about the only part of me that doesn't hurt right now."

For the first time, I noticed that Fletcher's face was red, puffy, and bruised, his lower lip was split, and he was holding his right arm across his ribs like they'd been broken. But what worried me most was the bullet hole in the front of his shirt close to his right collarbone. That's where all the blood was coming from, oozing out of the wound in a slow but steady stream.

"Finn!" I yelled. "It's clear! Get in here!"

Footsteps thumped through the back of the house, and Finn burst into the hallway, his gun clutched in his hand. He took one look at his dad and disappeared. He returned a few seconds later with some towels he'd grabbed from the kitchen. He tossed them at me, then vanished again.

"What happened?" I asked, using my knife to cut the towels into long, thin strips that I could use for a bandage.

Fletcher shrugged, then hissed with the pain that flooded his body at the motion. "I heard a car pull up outside about ten minutes ago. I went to the window to look and see who it was, and I realized that it was three giants with guns. They didn't look happy, so I headed toward the kitchen to grab one of my guns from under the sink. I would have made it too, if not for that damn door. Did it stick for them? Oh, hell no. They kicked it in like it was made of matchsticks. That settles it. I'm putting in that black granite door, with extra silverstone."

Finn reappeared, this time carrying a small metal tin. A white cloud outlined in vivid blue was painted on top. Finn popped off the top of the tin with his thumb, then dropped to his knees beside me in the hallway. He dipped his hands into the tin, which contained a clear salve infused with Jo-Jo's healing Air elemental magic. The soft, soothing scent of vanilla wafted over to me as Finn spread a thick layer of the ointment on the bullet hole in Fletcher's shoulder.

Fletcher sighed as the salve started soaking into his skin. The ointment wasn't as good as Jo-Jo healing him herself, but the magic in it would lessen his pain—and, more important, his blood loss—until we could get him to her.

When Finn had smeared salve all over the wound, I handed him the shredded towels, and he wrapped the strips of fabric around Fletcher's entire shoulder, further slowing the blood loss.

Fletcher hissed with pain again. I knew that he was hurting, but the wound had to be bandaged, and he would have been doing the same thing if it had been me lying there instead of him.

It should have been me—I *wished* it had been me.

I took his hand, trying to give him something else to focus on and comfort him however I could. He crushed his fingers against mine, but I didn't utter a sound. He could squeeze as hard as he needed to, and I wouldn't complain.

By the time Finn tied off the towels, sweat had beaded on Fletcher's face, his skin was pale underneath the blood and bruises, and his eyes were fluttering shut.

"We need to get him to Jo-Jo's," I said.

Finn nodded. He knew the signs of shock as well as I did. "On three. One, two, three!"

We each put an arm under the old man's shoulders and lifted him to his feet. Fletcher groaned, but his body went slack, and I knew that he'd passed out. That was probably for the best right now.

Together, Finn and I dragged the old man away from the dead giant and out of the house.

# *28*

Finn and I managed to half carry, half drag Fletcher down the porch steps, across the yard, and over to Finn's Aston Martin. I sat in the backseat with Fletcher while Finn drove.

The bumping and thumping of the car down the rocky driveway roused Fletcher out of his faint. He slumped against the leather seat, his eyes flickering open and shut, almost like the shutter on a camera. I didn't want him to waste his energy trying to talk, so I held his bloody hand in mine as Finn steered the car out into the suburbs. Every streetlight we passed illuminated the old man's bruised, battered face, and the coppery stench of his blood filled the car like an overpowering cologne. He was hurt because of Sebastian, because of *me*.

Once again, I cursed my own stupidity, my own foolishness, my own . . . *sloppiness*. That was the best word I could think of to describe my colossal fuckup. Sebastian had played me like a fiddle, and I'd been so eager to let him that I hadn't given a thought to anything else. I'd been so arrogant, so impatient, so certain that I needed to kill Cesar for what I thought he was doing to Charlotte that I'd tuned out Fletcher, Finn, and my own small whispers of doubt. Now Fletcher was paying the price for my mistakes.

I was an assassin. I was the Spider. I should have known better, I should have been more cautious, I should have realized that something wasn't right the second Sebastian started flirting with me at Dawson's mansion. But I'd believed in my own burgeoning reputation, and I'd let it go to my head. Fletcher had warned me against such things, but I'd done them all the same.

What a sad, stupid, foolish child I was.

Twenty minutes later, Finn turned into a subdivision, then steered the car up the hill to a grand, old, three-story white plantation house, which gleamed like a ghost in the moonlight. Finn stopped the car, and the two of us hauled Fletcher over to the house, up the steps, and onto the front porch.

Finn opened the screen door and used the cloud-shaped rune knocker to rap on the interior door, while I supported Fletcher's weight. The old man never made a sound, although I could hear how strained and raspy his breathing was, as though one of his lungs had partially collapsed. Each slow, shuddered breath was like a knife in my own heart. Because I'd done this to Fletcher. Oh, I wasn't the one who'd broken into his house, beaten him, or put a bullet in his shoulder, but my hands were stained with his blood all the same.

Just like they were stained with Cesar Vaughn's blood.

Familiar footsteps sounded, the front door creaked open, and Jo-Jo stuck her head outside. Since it was creeping up on three in the morning, she had been in bed, judging from the pale pink housecoat she wore and the pink sponge curlers that ringed her head like a plastic helmet. Jo-Jo looked from Finn to Fletcher to me, her clear eyes sharpening as the last dregs of sleep left her.

She opened the door without a word, then turned and headed to the back of the house. Finn put his arm under Fletcher's shoulder again, and the three of us followed her.

Instead of the sitting room that one might expect, the back half of the house doubled as a beauty salon. Cherry-red chairs sat in a row close to the back wall, while tubs of makeup, shampoo, conditioner, and other beauty products could be found on a counter that ran along the far left wall. Glossy magazines with smiling models were stacked on the end tables next to each one of the salon chairs and the hair dryers. The air smelled faintly of all the chemicals that Jo-Jo used to curl and dye her customers' hair, along with the sharp tang of nail polish.

Finn and I helped Fletcher over to one of the salon chairs, and he groaned as he sank down onto the seat. More footsteps sounded, much heavier than Jo-Jo's light tread, and Sophia appeared in the doorway, wearing a fuzzy black terry-cloth robe covered with bright pink skulls.

"What happened?" Jo-Jo asked, moving over to the sink to wash her hands.

"Sebastian Vaughn played me for a lovesick fool." I couldn't keep the bitterness out of my voice. "That's what happened."

Finn had already heard my sob story, but I quickly filled in Jo-Jo, Sophia, and Fletcher on everything that had happened. When I finished, I turned my attention to Sophia.

"Do you think you can take care of the mess that Finn and I left at his apartment building?" I asked. "We got most of it, but the bodies definitely need to be moved to a more permanent location."

Sophia nodded and left the salon without another word. I let out a breath. Well, that was one problem solved. Now to see to Fletcher.

Jo-Jo pulled a chair over to him, along with a freestanding light, which she clicked on. The dwarf leaned over him, peeled away the towel bandages, and peered at the hole close to his collarbone, the one that blood was still trickling out of.

"Sorry, darling," she said. "But the bullet is still in there, and getting it out is going to hurt as much as it did going in."

Fletcher nodded. "Best get on with it, then."

He leaned his head back and closed his eyes, while Jo-Jo held her hand up. The feel of her Air magic gusted through the salon, making me grimace. Even though it wasn't directed at me, I could feel tiny, invisible needles stabbing into my skin as Jo-Jo gathered up her power. Like Mab's Fire, Jo-Jo's Air power was the opposite of my own Ice and Stone magic, and it simply felt wrong to me. Of course, the irony was that Jo-Jo was using her magic to heal instead of to destroy, as Sebastian had destroyed the mausoleum. But the feel of his magic hadn't bothered me at all, since he was gifted in the same element that I was. Not even when he'd been trying to kill me with it.

Jo-Jo's eyes burned a milky white in her lined face, while the same bright glow coated her palm. She leaned forward and began to move her hand over Fletcher's body. Back and forth and up and down. Slowly, the bruises on his skin faded from purple to green, then disappeared completely. The cuts and scrapes that dotted his knuckles closed together, then healed.

Once the minor things were taken care of, Jo-Jo moved on to the bullet still lodged in his shoulder. She reached for more and more of her magic, and the feeling of pins and needles intensified, so much so that I had to dig my fingernails into the spider rune scars in my palms to keep from snarling. But I didn't say a word. I didn't want anything to interrupt her concentration. Not when Fletcher was hurting so much.

Jo-Jo reached forward, and a small piece of metal seemed to float to the surface of Fletcher's skin and then up into her hand. She held it up between her fingers so that Finn and I could see the bullet. It was a large caliber, and I bit back another curse. The giants hadn't been fooling around when they'd come after Fletcher. If that bullet had hit his heart, he would have been dead before he dropped to the floor. I wondered what Sebastian had told his men about why he wanted Fletcher and Finn dead. But I supposed it didn't much matter, since we'd killed all the giants.

And I was going after Sebastian next.

Once Jo-Jo got the bullet out, she finished healing Fletcher a few minutes later. He drew in deep breaths, his lungs free of the rasp that had strained them before, but a sheen of sweat glistened on his forehead. He was worn out from everything that had happened. He wasn't the only one.

But Fletcher still turned his head to stare at me, his green eyes soft and kind, far kinder than I deserved.

Jo-Jo stood up and touched Finn's arm. The two of them left the salon and headed into the kitchen, leaving me alone with Fletcher.

"I know what you're thinking, and it wasn't your fault," he said. "I knew that there was something wrong with the job from the get-go. I should have found out exactly what it was before I let you go anywhere near Cesar Vaughn— or Sebastian."

I shook my head. "There are always doubts about any job. This one just happened to have more than most. Besides, I was the one who pushed and pushed to do the hit. Not only that, I was the one who was sloppy, who let Sebastian see me outside the library in Dawson's mansion. If not for that, he might have never discovered who we are and what we do. At the very least, he wouldn't have found out about you and Finn."

It sickened me that I'd failed both Finn and Fletcher so completely, that I'd failed to protect them from a dangerous enemy, one I'd happily, carelessly invited into our lives. The whole reason I'd become an assassin was to protect the people I cared about, but I hadn't lived up to my own promise to myself. Not at all. The only thing that hurt worse than that was knowing that I'd taken Charlotte's father away from her, the same way my mother and sisters had been taken away from me.

Fletcher reached out and took my bloody hand in his. "It's not your fault, Gin," he repeated. "Don't you think for one second that it is. I know the risks as well as you do. Better than you do, because I've lived with them longer. Besides, I'm the one who dragged you into this life in the first place."

I nodded, although I knew that I'd never forgive myself for the hurt I'd caused him tonight or especially the hurt I'd caused Charlotte, for the rest of her life.

Charlotte. My stomach churned. I hoped that she was okay. I hoped that she had stayed in her room like I'd asked her to.

I hoped that Sebastian wouldn't take his anger at me out on her.

Fletcher cleared his throat, getting my attention. "And now I have to tell you something, Gin. My contact called me earlier tonight, right before the giants attacked. He confirmed a few things for me about the job."

That must have been why his phone was busy when Finn had tried to call him.

"Like what?"

"Like the fact that Sebastian was the one who paid for it."

I thought of all the sad, knowing looks he'd given me over the past few days, especially the one right before I'd left the house tonight to go to the Vaughn estate.

"Did you know that Sebastian was behind all of this?" I whispered.

He hesitated. "I suspected."

"When?"

He cleared his throat again. "The day Sebastian picked you up at the Pork Pit for your first date. He seemed so . . . smug, like he'd just gotten everything he'd ever wanted. It didn't sit right with me, so I started investigating him."

"Why didn't you tell me?" I couldn't keep the hurt and accusation out of my voice.

"Would you have listened?" Fletcher kept his green gaze steady on mine.

"I . . . "

I wanted to say, *Of course I would have*, but that was a lie. Because I'd spent the last two weeks pointedly, repeatedly *not* listening to Fletcher—and Cesar Vaughn had paid the price for it.

"No," I admitted. "I wouldn't have listened. I would have thought that you were being paranoid."

"I was hoping that I was wrong . . ." Fletcher's voice trailed off for a moment. "But I was going to talk to you tonight about everything. When you got home."

So he'd been going to let me have one more night of my fantasy romance with Sebastian before he told me the truth. A small kindness and far more generous than I had been to him lately.

Fletcher kept staring at me, expecting me to say something.

"I understand."

"I hope . . . I hope that you don't blame me for this." His voice cracked on the last few words, making my own guilt rise to the surface again.

I reached over and gave his fingers a gentle squeeze. "Never."

Even though I tried to make myself sound strong and confident, my voice still felt hollow and empty, just like my heart. But I didn't blame Fletcher.

I blamed myself for everything—and I always would.

# * 29 *

After Fletcher and I had said our piece to each other, I went into the kitchen and got the others.

Finn helped Fletcher to his feet, and then the two of them headed upstairs so Fletcher could take a shower and get cleaned up before crashing in one of Jo-Jo's guest beds. I waited until I heard the water start running in one of the upstairs bathrooms, then settled myself in the chair that Fletcher had vacated.

"Think you have enough magic left to use on me?" I asked in a low voice.

Jo-Jo smiled. "Of course, darling. You know that you never have to ask me that. I'm always happy to take care of you."

But I felt like I did have to ask, especially tonight, when all of this was my fault.

Jo-Jo sat back down in her own chair, raised her hand, and reached for her magic.

Pins and needles swept over my entire body, stabbing into my skin and then the muscles and blood vessels underneath, as Jo-Jo grabbed hold of all the oxygen in the air, circulated all those tiny molecules through my body, and used them to put everything back where it was supposed to be. I dug my fingers into the padded arms of the chair to hold myself as still as possible, although I couldn't help but squirm in my seat every once in a while, like a kid trying to wiggle away to keep from having her dirty face wiped clean.

Finally, Jo-Jo released her hold on her magic. The milky-white glow vanished from her eyes, and she lowered her hand to her side. The last of the pinpricks disappeared. I let out a tired sigh. I hadn't been shot, not like Fletcher had, but the long night had still worn me out. Jo-Jo patted my shoulder and moved around the salon, washing her hands again and straightening up.

I left her to her work and headed up the stairs to take a shower and get cleaned up. I was walking down the upstairs hallway toward one of the bathrooms when Finn stepped out of a guest bedroom and closed the door behind him.

"Fletcher asleep already?" I asked.

Finn nodded. I wasn't surprised. Most folks slept for several hours straight after being healed by an Air elemental. That's how long it took your mind to catch up with your body and realize that you were not, in fact, dying anymore. I'd probably do the exact same thing once I got settled for the night. The only thing that was keeping me from collapsing right now was the desire not to dirty up one of Jo-Jo's guest beds with all the filth that covered me.

Finn leaned back against the wall, crossing his arms over his chest and putting one ankle on top of the other. "So," he said, "when are you going after Sebastian? Not tonight, I hope."

The idea had crossed my mind, and if I thought there was any chance that I could have killed him, I would have already been in Finn's car and headed over to the mansion. But that would have been reckless and impatient. So I would let Sebastian savor his victory—for now.

I shook my head. "No. I'm exhausted. I'm in no shape to go after him tonight. Besides, I want to be careful and cautious about things this time, like I should have been all along."

Finn nodded. "Good. But what do you think Sebastian will think when his men don't come home tonight?"

I shrugged. "He'll probably assume that you and Fletcher killed them, not that I'm still alive."

"Either way, he'll be waiting for someone to retaliate."

"I know."

Finn looked at me. "Just promise me one thing: that you and Dad will sit down and plan how to take him out, okay? Me too, if you like. Promise me that you won't go after Sebastian by yourself."

"Of course," I said, lying through my teeth.

Finn had been targeted, and Fletcher had been beaten and shot, all because of me. I wasn't risking them again, not even to help me get Sebastian. Besides, I was the one he'd made such a fool of, I was the one he'd played, I was the one who'd believed his sweet lies. I had to take care of that—of him—myself, or I'd never be as strong as I wanted to be. I'd never be what Fletcher intended me to be.

I'd never truly be the Spider.

Finn's eyes narrowed in suspicion at my easy agreement, but I kept my face blank. Finally, he nodded, satisfied by my false promise.

"All right," he said. "Since Dad's asleep, I'm going to head back to my apartment. I need to do some serious damage control with Roslyn."

"Tell her that Gin says hi," I said, teasing him a little bit.

He winced. "If she's even still there."

I thought of the way Roslyn hadn't batted an eye when I'd shown up covered in blood. Most folks would have freaked out but not her. She'd been completely, utterly cool. Still, I'd seen the sharp interest in her gaze as she'd wondered what Finn and I were really up to.

"She probably is. If nothing else, because she's curious."

He nodded, then flashed me a grin. "Even if she's not, I can always call her and try to smooth things over. I got her to give me her number even before we left the party."

I had to laugh at his utter confidence in his smarmy seduction skills. "Well, if anyone can make a woman forget all about a lot of blood and some big, fat, whopping lies, it's Finnegan Lane, baby."

His chest puffed up with pride. "Damn straight."

But his merriment quickly fled, and his handsome face turned serious again. "I haven't said this yet, but I'm glad you're okay, Gin. I know that we haven't exactly been the best of friends lately, but I don't know what Dad and I would do without you."

I leaned over and lightly punched him in the shoulder. "You're just saying that because you want to get your greedy, grubby hands on more of *our* money. Without me hanging around, you'd be out of a middleman job and all the sweet, sweet cash that comes along with it."

"True," Finn agreed in a happy voice. "But I'd miss you more than the money, Gin. I hope you know that, that you *really* know that, deep down, where it matters."

Hot tears stung my eyes, and my throat closed up with emotion. All I could do was nod. Finn slung his arm around my shoulders and hugged me to his chest. We stood like that for one precious moment. Then we both drew back, not quite looking at each other.

"Duty calls," he quipped. "And so does Roslyn."

"Go get her, tiger."

Finn gave me a saucy wink before striding down the hallway and out of sight. I watched him go, so proud of him, so grateful for him.

My brother—and my friend now too.

I shuffled into one of the guest bathrooms, stripped off my ruined dress, and took a long, hot shower to wash away all the blood, grime, and gore of the night.

Too bad I couldn't slough off Sebastian's betrayal as easily as I scrubbed the blood off my hands.

I got out of the shower, dried off, and slipped into an old T-shirt and a pair of pajama shorts that were among the stash of clothes I kept at Jo-Jo's. Then I got comfortable in one of the spare beds. Despite the long, hard night, my mind kept racing as I lay in the dark and went back over every single moment I'd ever spent with Sebastian. Every word he'd said to me, every smile he'd given me, every lie he'd told me.

I didn't think I'd get much sleep, but I must have been more exhausted than I'd realized, because I quickly fell into the land of dreams, of memories . . .

Even in sleep, though, my mind kept going, churning from one horrible moment of my life to the next. My mother and Annabella disappearing into balls of elemental Fire. The stones of our mansion crashing down all around me. Climbing through the piles of rubble that remained behind, searching for Bria. Finally realizing that she was dead because of me and my magic. My confused, aimless wanderings through the woods that surrounded our house. The moment when I finally stumbled onto a road—a road that would eventually lead me to the Pork Pit and Fletcher, even if I didn't know it yet . . .

My eyes snapped open. For a moment, I couldn't quite remember where I was, but the soft summer sunlight slanting in through the window illuminated the cloud-covered fresco on the ceiling. The splashes of blue and white soothed me, and I realized that I was safe at Jo-Jo's.

I let out a breath and put my hands over my face, as though I could dig my fingers into my skull and pull out all of the memories that haunted me. This was the second time in the last few weeks that I'd flashed back to my past in my dreams. I hoped I wouldn't make a habit out of reliving my life every time I went to sleep. That would be rather tragic—and tiring.

Still, I thought back over my dreams, my memories, trying to find the reason for them, if there was such a thing. I'd thought that nothing could ever be more horrible than witnessing the murder of my family, but in some ways, the pain Sebastian had inflicted on me had been even worse.

I'd been a kid back then, ambushed and tortured in the middle of the night by a stranger who was older and stronger. There was no way I could have known what was coming.

But Sebastian had wormed his way past all of my defenses, which I'd thought were so strong, clever, and impenetrable. But he'd fooled me as easily as he had everyone else. I'd been lucky to escape the mausoleum with my life, and luckier still to have made it to Finn and Fletcher in time to save them both.

Or *was* it luck? The only kind of luck that Fletcher had taught me to believe in was bad luck. He said that we made everything else ourselves. I didn't know about that, though. But I'd survived all the other horrible things that had happened to me, and somehow I had survived Sebastian Vaughn too, despite his best efforts to kill me.

But I wasn't the only one who'd suffered at his hands. Cesar was dead because of his scheming. And Charlotte would continue to suffer, continue to be abused by her brother, unless I did something about it.

She probably wished that she hadn't, now that she knew what I'd done to her father, but Charlotte had saved my life last night. If she hadn't woken me up when she did, Sebastian would have gotten Porter to tie me down to the bed, and the two men would both probably still be torturing me right now. And Finn and Fletcher might be dead too.

I owed Charlotte for that, more than she would ever realize. But I also owed her for being so very wrong about her father, for taking away what was left of her family, just as the Fire elemental had taken my mother and sisters from me all those years ago. That was one of the things I hated the most about this whole situation, how I'd become just like that mysterious killer thanks to Sebastian's machinations and my own impetuousness.

But I couldn't change what I'd done. I couldn't bring Cesar Vaughn back to life. But I could sure as hell make certain that Sebastian died for his sins.

Oh, I knew that killing Sebastian wouldn't make up for taking Charlotte's father away from her. It wouldn't make up for anything I'd done, not one damn thing. Nothing would.

But I still had to try, all the same.

So I threw back the covers and got out of bed.

# *❋30❋*

It was after ten, and everyone else was still asleep. It was Sunday, so the salon was closed, and Fletcher and Sophia didn't have to get up to open the Pork Pit.

It was the perfect time to make brunch for everyone. So I tiptoed downstairs, went into the kitchen, and started rummaging through the cabinets and the refrigerator, pulling out the ingredients for the spread I had in mind.

I whipped flour, sugar, salt, eggs, and milk into a frothy pancake batter, then added some fresh summer blackberries, raspberries, and strawberries that Jo-Jo had left sitting out on the counter. I spooned generous dollops of the creamy berry mixture into a hot skillet that I'd melted a little butter in. While the pancakes cooked, I also crisped up some bacon, put on a pot of chicory coffee, and made fruit smoothies with fresh-squeezed orange juice, vanilla yogurt, and a drizzle of sourwood honey that Jo-Jo had bought at some store called Country Daze, according to the label.

I'd thought that I would keep obsessing about Sebastian, but I quickly, easily lost myself in the rhythms of mixing and stirring, flipping and frying, blending and frappéing. More than that, I enjoyed the motions, knowing that the end result would be a hot, hearty, delicious meal for the people I loved. Who knew that cooking could be so cathartic?

I made more than enough for everyone and left big platters of food on the butcher's-block table in the kitchen. I also grabbed a wooden tray out of one of the cabinets and piled it high with food, dishes, napkins, silverware, and two tall glasses filled with the orange smoothie, along with a cup of steaming chicory coffee for Fletcher. I took the tray up to the bedroom where he was sleeping and knocked on the door.

"Come on in, Gin."

I twisted the knob, opened the door, and stepped into the room. "How did you know it was me?"

He grinned. "Because you're the only one I know who can make pancakes and bacon smell that divine."

I grinned back at him. "And you're a shameless flatterer, just like your son."

Fletcher's grin widened. "Charm has its uses."

I thought of Sebastian, and my smile slipped. "Yeah."

Fletcher sat up in bed, and I put the tray on his lap before pulling a rocking chair from the corner of the room over to his side. We divvied up the food and dug in. I took the time to savor every single bite. The light, fluffy, fruity pancakes; the slightly smoky, salty bacon;

the tart, tangy orange smoothie that washed everything down.

We finished eating. Fletcher put the tray on the night-stand beside his elbow, then leaned back against the headboard and let out a loud, contented sigh.

"That was a mighty fine breakfast."

"I do try."

He grinned again. "That you do."

We fell silent again, although we kept staring at each other.

Finally, I raised my chin and squared my shoulders. "I'm sorry. This is all my fault."

Fletcher shook his head. "I told you last night, and I'll tell you again in the light of day. Don't blame yourself, Gin. I didn't see what Sebastian was really up to either, not until it was too late, and I've been doing this a lot longer than you have."

"True. But you're not the one who fell so easily for his lies. That was all me." I let out a bitter laugh. "You have to hand it to him, though. He definitely has skills. And his magic . . ." My voice trailed off. "He's strong, Fletcher. Very strong."

He reached over and squeezed my hand. "But not as strong as you are, Gin."

I shook my head. "That's where you're wrong. He *is* stronger than I am. He's a powerful elemental. Certainly the most powerful Stone elemental I've ever seen."

"And you're the best damn assassin I've ever seen," Fletcher snapped right back. "Magic is all well and good, but you don't need it to do what you do. That's the difference between you and Sebastian. He does. Not only that, but he needs people to do his dirty work for him. That's why he came to us instead of killing his father himself. He likes manipulating people, getting them to do what he wants without them even realizing that they're playing right into his hands. Just like you, Finn, and I did. Sebastian might like to hurt people, but he likes to think that he's above everything too, including folks like us."

Everything he said was true, but it didn't make me feel any better about things. Still, I knew what I had to do, so I drew in a breath and raised my gaze to his. "I have to do this by myself."

Fletcher nodded. "I know. I know you do, Gin, and it's what I've been training you for all these years. You were strong enough to get away from Sebastian last night. I trust that you're strong enough to end him tonight."

I picked at a loose thread on the blanket. "Even though I completely messed up? I let him get too close to me. I let him figure out who we were and what we do."

*I even let him into my heart*, a sad, tiny voice whispered in the back of my mind.

"Everyone screws up from time to time," Fletcher said. "Including me."

"But even if I kill him, it still might not be over. I don't know who else he might have told about me, about us. I don't think he told Mab my name, but at the very least, Porter knows who I am. We could still be in danger. Even worse, someone could sell us out to our enemies. The Tin Man's and the Spider's. Who knows how many people might come after us then?"

Fletcher shrugged. "Then we'll deal with those people

if and when they decide to target us. There's nothing else we can do."

I wanted to scream in frustration, but he was right. There was nothing we could do but hope that Sebastian had kept his suspicions about our real identities and purposes to himself.

"When are you leaving?" Fletcher asked.

"In a few hours. After I get ready. I don't want to give Sebastian time to think up a new plan or to realize that I'm still alive and coming for him."

He nodded, then tossed back the covers and got to his feet, revealing a pair of worn blue flannel pajamas.

"What are you doing? You need to rest. You're not coming with me, if that's what you're thinking."

"No," Fletcher said. "But you need someone to drive you over there and wait until you come out again, and that someone is going to be me."

I opened my mouth to protest, but he waved a hand, cutting me off.

"Don't worry," he said. "I'm not going to interfere or get in the way of what you need to do. I know better than that. But I want my spot of revenge too, and I'll be more than happy to take it by delivering you to Sebastian's door. Come on, Gin. Let an old man have his fun." His voice took on the same wheedling note that I'd heard in Finn's a hundred times before. Fletcher grinned at me, and I smiled back.

"Okay, okay, you can drive me," I said. "Just let me get my things, and then I'll get on with the business of killing Sebastian Vaughn."

\* \* \*

Several hours later, I crept through the woods at the edge of the Vaughn estate. Fletcher had dropped me off about a mile from the gate that led into the estate, and I'd spent the last thirty minutes hiking through the woods until I reached the back side of the property. It was after four now, and the sun still blazed overhead. Despite the sweltering heat, I was dressed the way I always was for one of my jobs: black cargo pants, long-sleeved black T-shirt, black boots, and a black vest lined with silverstone.

And I had my knives on me, all five of them this time. One up either sleeve, one in the small of my back, and one in either boot. If I didn't kill Sebastian, it wouldn't be for lack of adequate weaponry.

I hunkered down inside the tree line between a large maple with branches that arched up into the sky and a rhododendron with pale pink flowers that drooped in the heat. The humidity was even more oppressive than usual, and dark clouds had started to gather to the west, slowly turning the sky an eerie, brooding black. It would storm soon.

I scanned the grounds, but everything appeared quiet. A few people moved in and around the mansion, housekeepers taking trash outside, movers hauling out rented tables and chairs, a few gardeners doing a bit of pruning. The staff was still cleaning up from the party last night and going about their day as if everything was normal.

The only things I didn't see were a couple of giants patrolling the grounds, as they sometimes did. But of course, they wouldn't be here—Fletcher, Finn, and I had killed them all last night. From what I knew about Sebastian's security force, Porter was the only man he had left now, unless he'd strong-armed some of the construction workers into doing double duty for him. But I doubted he would do that. Sebastian would want to keep up the appearance that everything was fine, despite the fact that he'd sent out six men last night, and none of them had returned.

Still, there seemed to be a bit of tension among the workers. The gardeners kept looking over their shoulders, as though they expected someone to creep up behind them while they were whacking weeds, and one of the cooks shrieked when the lid on one of the garbage cans flew shut because of the wind, banging like a clap of thunder.

Something had the staff on edge, and I was willing to bet that it was Sebastian. He would have realized hours ago that something had happened to the giants he'd sent after Finn and Fletcher. I wondered if he had a creeping sense of dread that things weren't as neatly tied up as he thought they were. I wondered if he'd realized that he'd declared war on Finn and Fletcher by sending his men after them.

I wondered if he'd realized that I was still alive and coming for him.

Part of me hoped so. I wanted him to wonder where I was, what I was up to, and when I was going to kill him. I wanted him to sweat, worry, and wring his hands in helpless frustration, just as I had last night when I realized that he'd sent his thugs after the people I loved. It wasn't smart, and it certainly wasn't logical, but I wanted

Sebastian to know that *I* was going to be the reason for his death, nobody else.

I stayed in my position at the edge of the woods until the sun started to set. The storm was almost here, and the sky had darkened to an eerie blue-black. Lightning crackled in the distance. The kitchen staff scurried back inside the mansion, and the gardeners put away their tools and did the same. Nobody wanted to be out in the elements when the rain came. I didn't mind it, though. The storm matched my rage—strong, wild, electric, unstoppable.

When I was sure that everyone was inside and no one was looking in my direction, I left the woods behind, circled around one of the ponds, and made my way over to the crumbled mausoleum. In the fading light, it looked smaller and more pitiful than I remembered. The elegant, soaring dome had collapsed in on itself, and the entire structure was now no more than a ten-foot-high pile of rocky rubble.

I crept closer to the crushed mausoleum, crouched down, and put my hand on the stone. The dark mutters of Sebastian's magic echoed back to me, the black tendrils of his power infecting each and every one of the rocks. I concentrated on the sounds, sinking even deeper into the stone, and searching for any hint that Sebastian had come back out here to check and see if I was really dead. I would have, if six of my giants had failed to come home last night. But apparently, Sebastian was confident that he'd at least accomplished my murder, because I didn't hear any worried mutters in the stone or anything else to indicate that he'd returned to the scene of his crime. He still thought I was dead. Good.

I eased up to the side of the mausoleum and looked out over the lawn. The coast was clear, so I darted across the grass and over to the mansion, plastering myself against the side of the building. I was close to the kitchen, so I crept up and peeked in through the windows, but the space was empty. All the workers must have finished their chores and gone back to their quarters for the rest of the day, since it was Sunday. I could have made a couple of Ice picks to jimmy one of the kitchen doors and slip inside, but I didn't.

Instead, I reached out, grabbed the side of the mansion, and started to climb.

I could have crept through the first floor and made my way to the upper levels of the mansion, where Sebastian was more likely to be, but there was too much risk of running into a maid and having her scream and sound the alarm that I was here and out for blood. So I decided to climb instead.

Given all the balconies, crenellation, and trellises, it was easy enough for me to scale up to the second floor, but I didn't stop there. I had a feeling that I knew exactly where Sebastian would be, the place he had coveted for so long: his father's office.

To my surprise, the library windows were wide open. I started to pull myself up a few feet higher so I could peer over one of the windowsills, but something made me hesitate. Given the sweltering heat of the day, I would have expected the windows to have been shut tight, in order to keep all of the precious air-conditioning circulating inside the mansion. Sure, someone could have opened the windows in order to let the cool air from the storm blow inside, but the rain was still at least half an hour off, maybe more. There was simply no reason the windows should have been open that wide—unless Sebastian was planning some sort of trap for me.

He'd seen me outside of Dawson's library, and with his Stone magic, he might have even sensed that I had scaled the outside of the mansion so I could look in through the library windows. Maybe he thought that I'd do the exact same thing again here. Either way, it all seemed just a little too *easy*.

So I climbed up past the third floor, going to the fourth. I looked left and right along the wall, but all of the windows were closed on this level, further confirming my suspicions. Sebastian might not know that I was alive, but he'd realized that someone was probably coming after him, and he'd taken the appropriate precautions.

I climbed over to the closest window, hooked my arm over one of the shutters for support, and clung there. I reached for my Ice magic and used it to create a long, thin wand, which I jammed into the top of the window, popping the lock. A few seconds later, I was inside the mansion, with the window closed and locked behind me. No lights burned on this level, and given the dark sky outside, the interior of the mansion was murky with shadows. I moved from one hallway to the next, a knife in my hand, searching for any sign of Sebastian or Porter. They were both going to die, and I wasn't too particular about whom I killed first.

I quickly searched the fourth floor, but neither man was here, and I didn't hear any movement on the levels above my head. They had to be downstairs, most likely somewhere close to the library, waiting to see if I'd be stupid enough to fall into their trap. I crept over to a set of stairs and eased down to the third floor.

Lights blazed on this level, which left me few pools of shadows to hide in. Still, I managed it, moving from one hallway and one room to the next.

I checked Sebastian's bedroom first, but he wasn't relaxing inside the opulent space. I stared with disgust at the ebony bed with its white silk sheets and perfectly fluffed pillows, thinking about how easily I'd let Sebastian seduce me with his pretty words and lies. A wild urge seized me to palm another knife and use the sharp blades to slice through the sheets, the pillows, and even the mattress, until they were all as torn and tattered as my heart. But I forced myself to focus. Ripping up the bed wouldn't change what had happened between Sebastian and me, but killing him *would*.

So I moved on. I went from room to room, searching for him and keeping an eye out for Porter too, but the two men were nowhere to be found. Finally, I came to the last room on this floor, the library.

Just like the windows, the doors were wide open, inviting me to step right on inside and die. If Sebastian had thought to lay a trap with the windows, then he was sure to have left one by the doors too, so I slid up to the wall right beside the opening and stopped. And then I waited—just waited for my enemies to reveal themselves to me.

It didn't take long. I'd only been in position for about

two minutes when a faint *creak* sounded in the library, like someone shifting in a chair.

"Are you sure she's here, boss?" Porter's voice rumbled through the library and out the doors to me. "Because I haven't seen any sign of her yet. Neither have any of the staff, and they've been keeping a watch for her all day long. Plus, she hasn't tripped any of the alarms on the first-floor doors or windows."

I grinned. That was another reason I'd climbed up the side of the mansion. Most folks only thought to arm the first floor or two of their homes and businesses. They figured that no one was strong or crazy enough to try to climb any higher than that. But I was both of those—in spades.

"I mean, I can't believe that she's not dead in the mausoleum," Porter continued. "You buried her in there last night. We both saw it. She went inside, and you collapsed the whole thing right on top of her head."

"True," Sebastian said. "But why didn't any of your men come back? Why haven't we heard anything about them? It's like they just vanished into thin air. Only an assassin could do something like that. Only someone like *her*."

"Maybe it wasn't her," Porter countered. "Maybe it was her brother or the old guy she worked for. If she's an assassin, maybe they are too."

"No," Sebastian snapped. "It was her. She killed them all."

Well, not all of them but a good portion. Enough to restore my confidence that I could do the same to him.

"I know she did it," Sebastian repeated. "Just like I know that she's here somewhere right now. The walls are practically humming with her presence."

Once again, I cursed his Stone magic and my own sloppiness. I'd been so focused on trying to figure out where Sebastian was hiding that I hadn't considered the fact that the granite and all the other stone of the mansion would soak up my own murderous intentions and whisper them back to Sebastian.

Still, I held my position by the doors. I had no doubt that I could outlast him, at least when it came to this. He might have more magic than I did, but he didn't have more patience. For the first time, I realized why Fletcher always kept saying how important that was. I was killing Sebastian, and if I had to stand here all night until he got tired of waiting inside the library, then so be it. I would consider it time well spent.

The seconds ticked by and turned into minutes. One, two, five, ten. Porter and Sebastian remained silent in the library, although the storm had gotten closer, and thunder rumbled in the distance.

Finally, Sebastian let out a long, loud, disappointed sigh, as though he was upset that I hadn't fallen into his trap so easily.

"Well, I guess we'll have to go to Plan B, then."

I frowned, wondering what he was talking about, what contingency he might have put into place that I'd missed—

*Crack.*

The distinctive sound of flesh hitting flesh echoed out of the library, followed by a soft whimper. My heart squeezed tight in my chest, and I remembered something—or, rather, someone—I'd forgotten about.

Charlotte.

"I know you're here somewhere, Gin." Sebastian's voice rang out of the library, as smooth and seductive as ever. "You can either step on into the library, or I can keep hitting Charlotte until you do. Your choice."

# * 31 *

I stayed where I was, still and silent, and thought about my options.

I had none, really. I could let Sebastian beat his sister, or I could step into the library, take my chances with his trap, and try to worm my out of his sticky web—

*Crack.*

Another slap, another soft whimper from Charlotte, made up my mind.

"All right," I called out. "All right. I'm coming into the library."

My knife still in my hand, I eased through the open doors, around the fireplace, and into the right half of the library. Porter stood off to the side, a gun clenched in his beefy hand. As soon as I stepped into range, he aimed the weapon at my heart, his finger curling around the trigger. I tensed, wondering if I could throw my knife at him before he got off a shot.

"Easy, Porter," Sebastian called out. "I want to have a little chat with Gin first. Besides, if you shoot her now, we won't be able to have any fun with her later."

The thought of all that *fun* was enough to make Porter leer at me and slowly lower his gun. I ignored the giant and focused on the real danger, the real threat, my real enemy.

Sebastian stood in front of his father's desk, one hand on Charlotte's shoulder to hold her in place in front of him. The girl's hand was pressed to her cheek and the hot, red welts there. Tears streaked down her face.

"Don't you worry, sweetheart," I said in a soft, soothing voice. "He's never going to hit you again. Not after I get done with him."

Charlotte stared back at me with big, frightened eyes. I could see the doubt in her gaze—and the faint hope too.

Sebastian let out a sinister laugh. "The only one who's dying here tonight is you, Gin."

"Please. You dropped a couple of tons of rock on me, and I still walked away from it," I said. "And that was when I was weak, drugged, and disoriented. You really think that you can go toe-to-toe with me and win? You're fooling yourself."

Sebastian's laughter died down, and he eyed me. "And you look remarkably none the worse for wear. How *did* you manage to survive the mausoleum collapse? And get out after the fact?"

I gave him an evil grin. "You don't really think that I'm going to tell you that, do you?"

He returned my grin with one of his own. "Why not? You told me all of your other stupid, silly, simpering secrets. *Oh, Sebastian, you're so wonderful. Oh, Sebastian, you understand me so well. Oh, Sebastian, you make me feel so* alive."

His mocking words cut me to the core, but I kept my face cold.

"You were so easy to play." He sneered. "So ripe for the taking. So very *desperate* for attention. It wasn't even a challenge. All it took was a few soft words, a few sweet looks, a few teary confessions, and you were eating right out of my hand. Some assassin you are, Gin. Tell me, do you get this emotionally involved with the families of all your victims? Or was I a special case?"

I didn't answer him, but I couldn't help but grind my teeth.

"Oh, ho!" Sebastian crowed. "Just me. Well, I suppose I should be flattered. But really, I think that it's just sad. That *you're* sad—sad and pathetic. Little girl lost, so desperate for someone to love her that she believes any lie she's told."

My hand tightened around my knife. "I'm sad and pathetic? Please. I'm not the one who hired an assassin to kill my own father. I'm not the one who didn't have the balls to do it myself. I'd say that makes *you* sad and pathetic, Sebastian. No, scratch that. It just makes you *weak*."

His eyes glittered, and a muscle twitched in his jaw. I'd struck a nerve, so I decided to press my advantage. Besides, Sebastian had hurt me with his words, and I wanted to do the same to him.

"Totally, utterly *weak*." I sneered. "I'm not the one cowering behind a teenage girl instead of facing my enemy head-on."

Sebastian jerked his hand off Charlotte's shoulder, as if he'd never even thought about how that made him look, using her as a shield.

I stared at Porter. "You really should find yourself another boss. Someone who has a set. Someone who's not afraid to do his own dirty work."

Porter shifted on his feet, and the guilty look on his face told me that he'd thought the same thing more than once. Too bad he hadn't left before now—because he was going to die right alongside his boss.

Sebastian whipped around. He noticed the giant's chagrined look too, and his face tightened with rage.

"See?" I taunted. "Even your own man thinks you're weak. He has no respect for you, and neither do I. Neither will anyone else. You'll never be half the man that your father was, and we all know it. Soon so will everybody else."

Red rage mottled Sebastian's face, his hands clenched into fists, and he took a menacing step forward, as though he wanted to show me how wrong I was by throttling me himself.

That was *exactly* what I wanted. For him to forget the fact that I had a knife in my hand and rush at me so I could stab him to death right here, right now.

But Sebastian controlled his rage. He stopped, his lips curling with disgust.

"You didn't think I was half a man when you were screaming out my name in bed last night." His voice took on a smug, superior tone.

"You weren't the only one who's been faking things," I shot right back. "No wonder you have to drug women to get them into bed, considering what a lousy lay you are. Watching paint dry would have been more titillating— and fulfilling. It would have lasted longer too."

More and more rage flooded Sebastian's face, while his left eye twitched with fury. His lips drew back from his perfect white teeth, making him seem exactly like the sick, rabid animal he was.

"Porter," Sebastian said through his clenched teeth. "I've changed my mind. Put her out of my misery. Shoot that bitch where she stands."

The giant didn't hesitate. He raised his gun and pulled the trigger.

*Crack! Crack! Crack!*

The three bullets *thunk*ed into my chest, and I collapsed in a heap on the floor. The giant's aim was true, and the bullets would have gone straight into my heart if I hadn't been wearing my silverstone vest.

Charlotte screamed and screamed. I opened my eyes a crack just in time to see Sebastian shove her away. She slammed up against one of the side bookcases, bounced off, and fell to her knees. I hated that he had hurt her again, but she was out of the line of fire now, and I wouldn't have to worry about her getting in the way of what I was going to do next.

"Stop your sniveling," Sebastian ordered her, then turned back to Porter. "Empty the rest of your clip into her, and make sure that she's dead this time. I don't want any more mistakes."

My fingers tightened around my knife, but I lay there on the rug and waited for Porter to lean down and take hold of my shoulder. But to my surprise and consternation, the giant stopped a few feet away from me, and I realized that he wasn't going to roll me over onto my back so he could pump some more lead into my chest. He was going to do the smart thing and put a couple of bullets into my head from a distance.

Still, I waited—waited until I heard Porter suck in a breath, and the shadow of his arm on the floor started to move as he raised his gun . . .

Then I lashed out, whipped my knife up and around, and drove the blade into the giant's foot. Porter screamed and tried to readjust his aim, but I ripped my knife out and swiped it at him again, making him jump back out of the way of the sharp blade.

*Crack! Crack! Crack!*

The bullets *thunk*ed into the Persian rugs beside me, but I didn't give him a chance to fire again. I scrambled to my feet and threw myself forward. Porter managed to block my arm, keeping me from driving my knife into his chest, so I lashed out with my heavy boot and stomped it down on his instep, the one I'd skewered with my knife.

The giant howled with pain and hopped away. His foot caught on a table leg, and his head cracked into one of the bookcases, rattling the stone models on the shelves. He dropped his gun and pitched forward, his hands going to the top of the table that he'd tripped over to try to steady himself. That gave me all the time I needed to dart forward and bury my knife in the side of his neck before ripping it out just as brutally. Porter screamed again and arched back, but the wound I'd given him was a fatal one, and a few seconds later, he slumped over the table, then toppled over onto the floor, dead.

I tightened my grip on my knife and headed for Sebastian, who was still standing in front of his father's desk.

Instead of backing away, he gave an airy, almost nonchalant wave of his hand, as though he weren't concerned at all by the fact that Porter was dead. I wondered what he thought he was doing, as if I was going to stop at a simple wave of his hand when I was five seconds away from finally killing him—

The bricks in the fireplace exploded in my face.

One second, I was heading toward Sebastian with every intention of driving my knife through his heart. The next, I was being slammed by bricks from all sides.

*Thump.*

*Thump.*

*Thump-thump-thump.*

The bricks rattled me this way and that, like I was the silver piece in a pinball machine. And it didn't stop after the bricks flew at me from the fireplace, thudded off my body, and fell to the colorful carpets.

No, Sebastian waved his hand, and more bricks erupted out of the fireplace, hitting me and making me scream. I'd always wondered what it would be liked to be Stoned to death, especially in an elemental duel, and now I was finding out. Not to mention the fact that the sharp, broken edges of the bricks sliced through my clothes and into my skin, making blood pour out of a dozen shallow cuts.

Through it all, I could hear Sebastian laughing—laughing at how he was slowly going to kill me. My hand tightened on my knife. Fuck that.

The mass of swirling bricks stopped, although Sebastian waved his hand again, gearing up for another attack. Charlotte pressed herself up against one of the bookcases along the wall, sobs escaping from her lips. She knew that if she moved, Sebastian could easily turn his wrath on her.

I waited until Sebastian's attention flickered from me to the bricks that he was controlling, and then I threw my knife at him.

Being bludgeoned by bricks had wreaked havoc with my balance and equilibrium, so the blade didn't sink into his throat like I wanted it to, but the knife slammed into his shoulder, making him stagger back and hiss with pain. More important, it made him lose his grip on his magic for a few precious seconds. Sebastian stared down in disbelief at the knife sticking out of his shoulder. He hesitated, then lifted his hand and yanked the blade free. He stared at his own blood on the blade, his eyes wide, as if he'd never seen such a sight before.

"You bitch!" he screamed, throwing the knife in my direction. "You're going to pay for that!"

I didn't pay any attention to his tirade. I was already ducking the blade, moving forward, grabbing Charlotte's arm, and pulling her away from the bookcase and away from her murderous psychopath of a brother.

I took hold of Charlotte's hand, and together, we sprinted out of the library.

# * 32 *

Sebastian's screams of rage chased after us, but I shut his loud, thunderous bellows out of my mind and concentrated on getting Charlotte as far away from him as I could. We ran down the hallway, and then I pulled her through a living room and out the other side. When I was sure that Sebastian wouldn't catch up with us for at least a few minutes, I stopped in the middle of the hallway.

Charlotte gasped for breath, and she wasn't the only one. All the bricks flying into my body had hurt, and I had at least one cracked rib, despite the protective silverstone shell of my vest. If not for it, though, my rib might have broken and punctured one of my lungs. Then I would have wheezed to death on the library floor.

Charlotte stood beside me, her trembling body pressed against mine, small sobs escaping her throat, tears streaking down her face like a waterfall of terror. I grabbed her head in my hands and forced her to look at me, trying to snap her out of her fear and panic and get her to focus. After a moment, her empty eyes cleared a bit, and she looked back at me.

"Is there someone here you can trust? A maid, a gardener, somebody, anybody?"

She nodded. "There's . . . a driver," she said in between sobs. "My driver . . . Xavier. I . . . like him."

"Then you go downstairs, find Xavier, tell him to warn the rest of the staff, and get him to take you away from here," I said, letting go of her. "Before Sebastian kills us all. He won't stop now until I'm dead, and I don't want you or anyone else getting hurt."

Charlotte grabbed my hand in a tight, desperate grip, as though she didn't want to leave my side. I gently untangled her fingers from mine and gave her a small push.

"Go," I said. "Go on. Right now. And don't look back no matter what—"

Stone spewed from the wall beside me.

I gave Charlotte another push, this one more forceful. "Go! Run! Now!"

She gave me one final terrified look, her eyes going wide at whatever she saw behind me. Then she turned and ran down the hallway as fast as she could.

Sebastian's laughter floated toward me. "Running won't save her—or you, Gin."

I slowly turned around. Sebastian stood in the middle of the hallway, his hands held down and out by his sides, the amber flecks in his dark eyes glinting as he reached for more of his magic. The granite that comprised the walls slowly began to ripple, as though the entire hallway were made out of water instead of stone. The power Sebastian had—his control over it—took my breath away. He was quite possibly the strongest elemental I'd ever encountered, on par with the Fire elemental who'd murdered my family.

And now he was going to kill me.

I'd never been in an elemental duel before, and I had no desire to engage in one now, not when I knew how much stronger Sebastian was in his magic than I was. But I didn't let Sebastian see my fear and uncertainty. I didn't let him see the wheels of my mind churning and churning as I palmed a second knife and tried to figure out some way to get close enough to ram the blade into his heart.

Sebastian cocked his head to the side and let out another low laugh. "Still hoping to kill me with a knife? Pitiful, Gin. Truly pitiful."

Apparently, my poker face wasn't quite as good as I thought. Something to work on—if I lived through this.

I shrugged. "It's what I do. In fact, killing people seems to be what I do *best*. I didn't have any problems with your father. I don't anticipate too many more with you."

"My father was a fool!" Sebastian shouted. "Always playing the part of the good, upstanding citizen. He deserved exactly what he got."

I shook my head. "No, he didn't deserve it. Because he was trying to protect everyone from *you*. Dollars to doughnuts, he was going to turn you in for killing and hurting all those people. That's why he had Coolidge investigating what happened."

He let out a low, guttural snarl.

"Do you know how crazy you look right now, Sebastian? Better not let Mab see you like this. She might decide to kill you herself. She doesn't like complications, remember? And you are a hot mess if ever I saw one."

He laughed again. "Please." He sneered. "I'll put that Fire elemental bitch in her place soon enough. Just like I'm going to do with you—right now."

Sebastian threw his hands out wide. With one thought, the granite ripped free from the walls and zoomed in my direction.

And all I could do was stand there and let it hit me.

There was no time to move or duck out of the way. Even if I'd managed to crouch down behind a table or some other piece of furniture, it would have only been a temporary respite, since the entire hallway from floor to walls to ceiling was made out of stone. Still, I hunkered down, protecting my head as best I could.

I could have used my own Stone magic to harden my skin, but I decided not to. I'd used my Ice power in front of him a few times, mostly to make cubes for whatever we'd been drinking at the time, but I'd never told Sebastian about my Stone magic. Maybe there was still a chance—however small—that I could surprise him with it and use it to get the upper hand. Besides, I didn't think that he'd kill me right away. No, he wanted to play with me first.

The stone battered me from all sides, spinning me first one way, then the other, as I tried to avoid the projectiles. Wave after wave of rocks splintered from the walls and zoomed in my direction, one after another, faster and faster, as though I were standing in the middle of a tornado that was picking up speed.

And through the whole thing, I could hear Sebastian laughing with delight at my suffering, at the beating my body was taking, at how the stones pummeled me again and again simply because he wanted them to. And I realized that Sebastian wasn't going to give me a chance to get close to him. He wasn't going to make that mistake, and he wasn't going to stop this time until I was dead.

So I retreated.

At least, I tried to. The whirling dervish of rocks made it difficult to tell which way was which. Or maybe that was just all the blows to the head that I was taking. All I really did was spin around and around in a circle, going nowhere fast.

Finally, Sebastian got tired of battering me with the stone. I felt another surge of his magic, and this time, pieces of varying sizes erupted from the walls, and I started ducking and darting through them, almost like I was playing a game of dodgeball. In a way, I was, and if I got hit again, especially in the head, then I was dead.

Still, the bigger pieces of stone gave me a slightly clearer field of vision, and inch by inch, foot by foot, I retreated down the hallway toward a set of stairs that led down to the second floor. But even if I managed to reach them, it wouldn't do me any good. They were made of marble, and Sebastian could easily use his magic to make them crack right out from under me, have me fall in between them, then bring the two halves together to crush me to death. I couldn't help the shudder that rippled through my body at the thought.

And even if by some miracle I did manage to get down the stairs, I still had another level to go before I could get out of the mansion—a mansion made entirely of stone. Sebastian was in his element here, and the entire building was a death trap for me. But I couldn't figure out another way to get out. So I'd just have to try to be quicker than he was, even though I could feel his magic pulsing through the walls, pulsing through this level of the mansion—

*Crack!*

A vivid streak of lightning shot down from the sky, and the window at the end of the hallway gleamed from the white electrical charge, shining like a diamond, even as the rain batted at it from the outside and drowned out the brightness. The storm had finally arrived, and it was a doozy, judging from the roars of thunder that boomed and banged and the lightning that I could see flickering outside through the window—

My head snapped back in that direction, even as I ducked another rock coming my way.

A window.

I needed a quick way out of the mansion, and here was the opening I needed—literally. Sure, I was three stories up, but I could use my own Stone magic to soften the landing. It was the only chance I had.

Now all I had to do was get to the glass.

I stood in the center of a place where two hallways met. One corridor continued toward the stairs, while the window lay at the opposite end of the other hallway, about fifty feet away from my position. I started calculating distances and angles.

Sebastian let the rocks die down long enough to sneer at me again. "Getting tired yet, Gin? Because I can do this all night long."

I ignored his self-congratulatory rant and sprinted toward the window.

Sebastian's mocking laughter once again chased after me. "Oh, Gin. You won't get away that easily. That hallway is nothing but a dead end. You're trapped. Do you hear me? Trapped!"

But apparently, he wasn't quite as confident as he claimed to be, because he sent out another burst of magic, one that rolled through the floor. It began to ripple the same way the walls had. I risked a glance behind me to see the granite rising higher and higher, like an ocean wave about to crash down on top of my head and drown me. Really, that's what it was. Sebastian would drop the granite on top of my skull, cracking it open like an egg, and that would be the end of me.

So I sucked down another breath and forced my legs to move even faster and my arms to pump even harder. Behind me, I could hear the granite muttering with dark delight as it chased me down. The floor shifted under my feet, trying to throw me off balance, but I darted forward, put my hands up over my face, and reached for my Stone magic.

With one final surge, I threw myself out the window.

# ☀33☀

I flew through the glass. My final lurch toward the window pushed me out into the air, several feet away from the side of the mansion, but the night was so dark, gloomy, and rainy that I couldn't tell which way was up, and then I was falling down, down, down. I used my Stone magic to harden my skin, head, hair, and eyes, along with the rest of my body—

*Thud.*

I hit the ground a second later.

The protective shell of my magic kept me from breaking my neck, but the brutal impact still stunned me, and it took me the better part of a minute to realize that I was still alive. I'd managed to throw myself far enough away from the mansion to land in one of the flowerbeds that lined the outside of the building. I'd landed right on top of one of Cesar's prize rosebushes, completely crushing the delicate hedge of flowers. It took me a moment to untangle myself from the thorns that had stabbed into my clothes, roll off the greenery, and stagger to my feet. I took a step, and my left leg started to buckle, but I managed to straighten it and keep on going, even though I was hobbling in the worst sort of way.

A sharp mutter penetrated my daze. On instinct, I threw myself forward as far as I could—

*Crack!*

Part of a granite balcony on the second floor broke away from the side of the mansion and landed in the spot where I'd been standing. It would have squashed me like a grape if I hadn't managed to get out of the way. My head snapped up. Three stories above, Sebastian leaned out of the broken window I'd jumped through.

He glared at me, clearly pissed that I'd escaped his death trap upstairs. He gave a short, sharp, angry wave of his hand. Another balcony, also on the second floor, broke away from the side of the structure and plunged in my direction, but I managed to roll out of range of the falling stone.

I had to get away from the mansion, or Sebastian would keep using his magic to tear it apart piece by piece, even though there could still be other people inside. I hoped that Charlotte had warned the staff and that she'd found Xavier and gotten him to take her away from here, but I had no way of knowing.

I scrambled to my feet and started to run again.

I staggered away from the mansion about twenty feet before I realized that I had nowhere to go. My eyes swept over the rain-drenched landscape, but all I saw was stone,

stone, and more stone. All of the outbuildings were made of either marble or granite, along with the pool, the tennis courts, and the ruined remains of the mausoleum. Even if I could manage to get to the wall that ringed the estate, it too was made of stone, and Sebastian could easily use his magic to throw me off it or collapse the wall on top of me the same way he had done with the mausoleum. I whirled around and around, looking for a way out, but I didn't see one.

I just didn't *see* one—

Another flash of lightning zigzagged through the stormy sky, closer this time, but the light didn't completely disappear when it did. I squinted through the rain and realized that a soft golden glow was coming from farther out on the grounds. The greenhouse. The lights inside were burning steadily the way they always did.

I started to turn away from the structure, since there was nothing there that would help me, but then I whipped around and faced it.

*The greenhouse.*

It was the only building on the estate that was made out of glass, not stone.

Oh, Sebastian would still have his magic, but he wouldn't have as much material to use against me inside the greenhouse as he would if I made a break for the wall. So I lurched in that direction. Even as I moved farther and farther away from the mansion, I could hear the stone start muttering again as Sebastian raced through the corridors.

He was coming after me.

I picked up my pace and made myself move faster, even though the wind howled and rain batted at me from all sides, just like the stone inside the mansion had. It took me longer than I would have liked to reach the greenhouse, but I made it there. The door was locked, but I smashed my elbow through a glass pane on the door and unlocked it. I didn't want to waste any of my magic, not even my pitiful Ice power to make a couple of lock picks. Besides, Sebastian knew that I was here, and there was no use hiding where I'd gone or where I planned to make my last stand against him.

I slid into the greenhouse and shut the door behind me. The lights were turned down for the night, casting the interior in a golden gloom. The scent of Cesar's roses filled the air, almost knocking me down with their sweet, overpowering perfume. I scanned the interior, searching for a good place to hide. I'd only have one shot at Sebastian, and I had to make it count. I might have nicked his shoulder with my knife, but I was still far more beat-up than he was, and he could always strangle me to death with his bare hands. He might not be a giant, but he was strong enough to do that or simply bash my head against one of the planters or tables until my skull cracked open and I bled out.

I moved deeper into the greenhouse, sweat sliding down my skin at the stifling humidity, until it felt like I was still standing in the rain raging outside. Finally, I found a place that I thought would work, behind a cluster of palmetto trees at the end of one of the center aisles in the middle of the greenhouse. If Sebastian came down this aisle, he'd have to move *there*, to that particular spot, to get around the trees, and I could rise up from the shadows over *here* and drive my knife into his back.

That was my hope, anyway, and the last chance I had.

So I hunkered down behind the trees, tightened my grip on my knife, and waited for my enemy to come find me.

# ❊34❊

It took Sebastian longer than I thought it would to reach the greenhouse. Perhaps he'd gone to the front gate first, thinking that I was running away, when I was really waiting on him so we could finish this, one way or the other.

A dozen times, I thought about leaving the building and trying to sneak up on Sebastian somewhere out on the grounds. I wanted to do something, anything, rather than crouch in the dark playing some deadly version of hide-and-seek. But then I thought about how Fletcher had lain in wait for Finn and me at the rock quarry and how he'd managed to mock-kill us both as a result. So this time, I finally decided to follow the old man's example and his advice.

Ten minutes after I entered the greenhouse, the door banged open, causing the rest of the glass panes in it to shatter. Lightning crackled outside again, perfectly illuminating Sebastian standing in the doorway.

"Come out, come out, wherever you are," he sang mockingly.

I didn't bother answering him.

"Oh, come on, now, Gin," he said. "I know that you're in here. I saw your boot prints in the mud outside. Besides, the stones told me you'd come in this direction. Stone is everywhere, you know, even in the earth under our feet. There's nowhere on this estate that you can go where I won't find you. Although I think it's rather fitting that you've retreated in here. Just like my father did so many nights when he didn't want to face the real world. And now here you are, doing the same exact thing, not wanting to face your own death."

He stopped talking, waiting for me to be stupid enough to respond or make some noise that would give away my location. Please. I was through talking. I just wanted to kill him now.

Finally, finally kill him.

Sebastian closed the door behind him and threw the lock, even though the glass had disintegrated, leaving nothing behind but an empty metal frame. Then he leaned over and hit a switch, causing all of the overhead lights to flicker to life. I cursed to myself and slid back as deep into the shadows as I could get and still be in position to implement my plan to ambush him. I should have remembered to disable the lights, but it was too late now.

His dark gaze flicked over the space. I peered around the edge of one of the tree trunks at him, careful not to give away my location by moving any more than necessary.

Sebastian shook his head, as though he was disappointed that I wasn't going to make things easy for him, then wandered over to the far side where the roses were— the deep, dark blue ones that he had brought me at the Pork Pit. The ones that I'd carefully pressed between the pages of a book of fairy tales like the stupid fool that I was.

Sebastian plucked one of the roses, then slowly twirled it around in his hand, studying the dark petals from all angles.

"Soft and silky," he purred. "Just like your skin. You know, it's a shame that we couldn't come to some sort of arrangement, Gin. Given how easily you dispatched my father, I was going to offer you the chance to keep working for me as my own personal assassin."

He paused.

"Well, perhaps it wouldn't have been that much of a choice. People will do almost anything for you when they're hooked on drugs. That bit that I dropped in your champagne was just a taste of things to come for you. But of course, you had to go and ruin things, the way other people always do."

So that had been his plan for me. Shoot me up with drugs until I was completely dependent on them—and him. Just when I thought that he couldn't be any crueler, Sebastian surprised me. But all that mattered now was finishing things—and him—before he hurt anyone else.

Here. Now. Tonight.

Sebastian started tearing the petals off the rose, casually scattering them in his wake, as though he were a flower girl strolling down the aisle at a wedding. He was three aisles over from me but headed toward the center of the greenhouse where I was hiding. So I just waited for him to get close enough for me to strike.

"But I suppose that sort of arrangement would never really have worked," he called out in a light, airy voice, as though we were talking about something of no importance, instead of the complete loss of my own self. "I mean, look how easily I managed to turn you against that old man and his son. I couldn't allow someone to turn you against *me* so easily. I couldn't take that risk. Not with you, Gin. Although I am curious to know how you became an assassin and why."

He paused again, as if he actually expected me to answer him. "I have my own theories, you know. In fact, I've had a lot of fun these past few weeks coming up with one story after another. I'm guessing, of course, that something rather tragic happened to you when you were younger, especially given the fact that you don't seem to have any real family left. Was that it? Your family was murdered, and you became an assassin in hopes of someday getting your revenge and righting the great wrong and terrible injustice that was done to you? Hmm?"

He was closer to the truth than he knew. Those were some of the very reasons I'd become an assassin, although I still wasn't sure who the Fire elemental was who'd murdered my family. But if I ever found out, then that bitch was getting dead.

Provided, of course, that I lived through the next five minutes.

"I've had to speculate, you see, because despite all the times that we were together, you never really talked about yourself," Sebastian said. "Every time I tried to ask you a personal question, you would turn the conversation in another direction. You were quite good at that. In fact, you've been better at keeping your secrets than I expected."

Sebastian reached the end of the aisle and sauntered over to the next one, heading back toward the front of the greenhouse and moving away from me.

I'd previously thought that the longest minutes of my life had been when I was hanging on to the window outside Tobias Dawson's library, waiting for Mab to move away from me and take the horrible feel of her Fire magic along with her. But this was a hundred times worse.

Still, I held my position. All I had to do was wait for him to swing back this way, and then the bastard would be mine for the killing.

I could be patient for that. I could wait *forever*, as long as I knew that Sebastian would die in the end.

"Of course, there's the other possibility," he said, continuing with his musings. "That you don't have any great tragedy in your past. That you enjoy violence. That you simply like killing people, so you decided to make yourself an expert at it. That's certainly what I've done. My father wasn't the first person I ever had murdered. I learned at an early age that it's extremely easy to get people to do exactly what you want. All you have to do is push the right buttons, say the right things, and people will practically fall over themselves to do your bidding. That's the difference between you and me, Gin. You take orders on who to kill, whereas I give them. Another reason I'm afraid that we'd never work out. But you do have to admit that it was fun while it lasted. Don't you think?"

I still didn't respond to his ditherings. I was much more focused on the fact that he had reached the end of the second aisle, had stepped into the third, and was ambling back in my direction.

"But unfortunately, our time together has come to an end," Sebastian said.

He stopped, and I thought that he might stay where he was, about halfway down the aisle, but he slowly headed in my direction. I drew in a breath and got ready. I'd only have one shot at him, and I needed to make it count.

"I know you actually thought that we might have a future together, but I have to admit something," Sebastian crooned, his voice taking on a mischievous note, as though what he was about to say was somehow amusing. "You're just not my type, Gin. Not connected enough, not rich enough, not pretty enough, and certainly not strong enough."

He walked right by my position. I stepped out from the shadows, raised my knife high, and brought it down, aiming for the center of his back—

Sebastian whipped around and caught my hand in his. I tried to break his grip, but he reached for his magic, essentially encasing my arm in his own fist of stone.

He gave me a smug, satisfied smile, then shook his head. "Oh, Gin. Don't you know that you gave yourself away? The greenhouse might be made of glass, but there's still enough stone in here to whisper to me about all of your intentions, all of your hopeless little plans. And there's still enough stone in here for me to kill you with."

One of the stone planters sitting on a table to my left shattered at his words, the bits of resulting shrapnel zipping through the air and straight into my side. I yelped with pain and tried to pull my hand free, but Sebastian tightened his grip. He gave me a bored look, then snapped my wrist all the way back.

I screamed, and this time, he finally let me go. I staggered back, clutching my broken right wrist to my chest, my knife dropping from my suddenly nerveless fingers. Wave after wave of pain shot through my body, and I could feel the pieces of my shattered bones scraping against each other and then my skin on top of them, threatening to break through the surface. Nausea filled me, along with the pulsing waves of pain, and I had to focus on choking down the hot, bitter bile that rose in my throat.

But Sebastian didn't give me a chance to regroup. No, this time, he went on the attack. He stepped forward and backhanded me across the face. He was still holding on to his magic, so his hand was as hard and heavy as a cement block cracking against my cheek.

More pain exploded in my jaw. I fell onto a table. Since it was made of marble, Sebastian used his magic to shatter it, making me stumble forward and slam all the way over into one of the glass walls. I'd thought that by coming in here, we'd be on more equal footing, but he was right. There was still enough stone in here for him to kill me with.

Something he was probably going to do in another minute, two tops. Just as soon as he got done playing with me.

Sebastian stepped forward, dug his fingers into my hair, and pulled me away from the glass. Before I could even think about fighting back, he threw me down onto the ground. I landed on my broken wrist, and black spots flashed on and off in my vision in a dire warning. They tried to come together to blot out the pain, but I ruthlessly pushed them back. If I lost consciousness, then I was dead, and Sebastian could kill me at his leisure.

Or worse, go through with his original plan for me.

Somehow I managed to stagger back up onto my feet. I turned around, but Sebastian was waiting. I raised my left, unbroken arm and attempted to hit him with my fist, but he easily sidestepped the clumsy blow. He wrapped his hand around my throat, lifted me up, and then slammed me down, so that my back and shoulders were on one of the tables. Beside me, a cluster of dark blue roses shook in their stone planter, as if they were shocked by the violence that was taking place right in front of them.

Sebastian kept his tight grip on my throat and held up the index finger of his free hand. "Among all the other little fantasies that I've had about you these past several days, Gin, the one that I've had the most fun with was how I was ultimately going to kill you. I hadn't really decided, but you've given me a grand idea. You seem to be so fond of knives. Let me show you the sort of knife that I like to use."

Sebastian reached out and put his hand on the side of the marble planter. I watched in horror as the stone began to chip and flake and peel away from itself. The planter crumbled, spilling dirt and roses everywhere, and a pleased, maniacal grin lit up Sebastian's face.

A moment later, he held up his weapon so I could see

it. Truth be told, it was a crude knife, sort of like the Ice daggers that I sometimes made. But Sebastian had used his Stone magic to fashion the end into a razor-sharp point, one that was more than capable of slitting my throat.

Sebastian still had one hand wrapped around my neck, holding me down, and he leaned forward and slowly drew the stone blade down my cheek. Not hard enough to draw blood. Not yet.

But I could hear the marble muttering with all of Sebastian's dark, gleeful malice, whispering exactly how he planned to carve me up with the knife he'd created out of his own element—*my* element. Something else that made me sick to my stomach. I could hear all of the stone in the greenhouse muttering now, as it soaked up Sebastian's murderous intentions.

He pulled the knife away from my face and gave it an appraising look. No doubt, he could hear its whispers too, as it murmured with all of his secrets—

*And no matter what, you should never, ever tell someone all of your secrets.* Finn's voice suddenly popped into my mind.

Sebastian had said that I was good at keeping secrets, and I realized that I still had one card left to play, one secret that I hadn't told him, one thing that he hadn't guessed about me like he had everything else. I just hoped that it would be enough to end him, once and for all.

"Tell me, sugar," Sebastian purred, focusing his gaze on me again. "Any last words before I cut open that pretty throat of yours?"

"You fucked with the wrong assassin," I growled. "You fucked with the Spider."

He laughed. "The Spider? Is that the pathetic little moniker you've chosen for yourself?"

"You bet it is."

"And why is that?"

I grinned. "Because you never see spiders coming—until they bite you."

Sebastian snorted. "I never see spiders until I crush them under my boot. Even then, they don't attract any notice."

This time, I laughed. "You know what, Sebastian?" I sneered into his face. "You're all talk and no action. Just like you were in bed. If you're going to kill me, then just do it, already. Because I'm sick and tired of listening to you brag."

He stared at me and raised the knife high, but instead of ramming it into my heart, he slammed it into my right shoulder, adding to the agony on that side of my body. I screamed again. Sebastian chuckled and twisted the knife in even deeper. Oh, yes. He wanted to make me suffer before he killed me, which just might give me a chance to end him instead.

"How does it feels to have a knife in your shoulder, bitch?" he hissed.

I swallowed down another scream. Then I laughed.

He frowned. "What's so funny?"

"You," I said. "Because you're forgetting one small thing."

"Really? What's that?"

"You're not the only elemental here."

He snorted. "You mean that pitiful Ice power that you have? Please. You couldn't make an Ice cube with that right now, much less do any damage to me."

"True. But Ice isn't the only magic that I have."

He frowned, wondering at my words. I sent out a small burst of magic, just enough to get everyone's attention. All of the stone in the greenhouse, including the piece stuck in my shoulder, began to murmur again. But not with Sebastian's ill intentions. No, now the stone whispered with *mine*.

Sebastian cocked his head to the side, surprised by the sudden surge of violence in the stone. His eyes widened, and his mouth dropped open.

"You have Stone magic too," he muttered. "You sly little bitch."

"You're damn right I do," I countered. "And I know exactly what to do with it, you bastard—"

Sebastian tightened his grip on the knife in my shoulder and yanked it out. I didn't even have time to scream before he brought it up, determined to end me this time. I held my hand up at the last second, so that the blade punched through the center of my left palm, inside the circle of my spider rune, instead of into my chest.

We stood there, seesawing back and forth, with Sebastian trying to drive the knife down and into my heart and me trying to keep him from doing that.

"You know, Sebastian, your father wasn't as strong an elemental as you, but he did have one particular trick that I admired," I rasped through the pain.

"Really? What's that?"

"This."

I sent out a small, concentrated pulse of magic, shattering the crude knife in my hand, even though it caused me more agony. Sebastian hissed and jerked back in surprise, trying to duck the flying bits of stone. A long, thin, bloody shard split off from the knife and clattered to the table next to me. I snatched up the wickedly sharp piece of stone, the way I had my silverstone knives so many times before.

Then, before Sebastian could move, before he could react, before he could fight back, I surged forward and drove the point of the shard into his throat.

Sebastian's mouth gaped open, and a soft hiss of air escaped his lips, along with blood that spattered onto my face, stinging my eyes like tears. He staggered back and sent out another burst of magic, shattering the shard, but I'd driven it in too deep, all the way into his jugular, and it was more of a last-gasp reflex than an actual attack. But he'd been holding on to a lot of power, and it rippled out from him in invisible waves, causing more of the stone planters and tables to shatter and sending chunks of rocks everywhere, including through the glass walls of the greenhouse.

Sebastian's hands went to his throat. He pulled them away, once again staring down in disbelief at all the blood on his hands. Then he raised his eyes to mine.

"Good-bye, Sebastian," I said in a quiet voice. "You were right. It was fun while it lasted."

Sebastian made a choking sound in the back of his throat, causing more blood to spew out of his lips, as easily as all of his lies had. Then he crumpled to the ground and was still.

# ❋ 35 ❋

It took Sebastian the better part of two minutes to bleed out. But when the stone planters and tables finally quit shattering, I knew that he was gone. I stared down at the man I thought I had loved. I shouldn't have felt anything but relief that he was dead, that he couldn't hurt me or anyone else anymore.

But all I felt was empty—sad and empty—just like he'd said I was.

I had started to move away from him when I noticed a single blue rose lying on the table where we'd had our last struggle. Somehow it had escaped the destruction of our fight and was as perfect as if it had been cut for a bouquet. I picked up the flower and brought it to my nose. Despite the chaos, the rose smelled as sweet as ever. I hesitated, then tossed it down on top of Sebastian's body.

It was the only bit of sentiment that I had left—and far more regard than he deserved after everything he'd done.

I stared at Sebastian another moment before turning and walking away.

I grabbed my knife from where it had fallen, then left the greenhouse behind and made my way through the grounds, across the lawn, and back up to the library. I picked up the knife that I'd thrown in here earlier at Sebastian, then went over to his father's desk to conduct my long-delayed search for the file that Coolidge had compiled on Sebastian. It didn't take me long to find it, since it was lying on top of a stack of papers on the desk, the folder wide open, as though Sebastian had been admiring his own handiwork over a drink. He probably had.

I took the file too. After that, it was just a matter of hobbling down the stairs, out of the mansion, and onto the driveway toward the front gate. At this point, I didn't care who saw me leaving the scene of the crime. I doubted there was anyone left to look, anyway. If they'd been smart, all of the workers would have fled the mansion the second Sebastian had started to unleash his Stone magic throughout the structure.

So no one was around to see the Spider take her victory lap—such as it was.

No one except Fletcher.

The old man was waiting in his white van down the street from the open gate. I staggered across the sidewalk, opened the door, and crawled into the passenger seat, cradling my broken wrist and the folder against my chest.

Fletcher's sharp green eyes tracked up and down my body, silently assessing my injuries. Broken wrist, stab wound in my shoulder, dozens of cuts and bruises from where Sebastian's rocks had battered me. His shoulders sagged with a tiny bit of relief, although he kept his face calm and composed.

"Looks like we need to get over to Jo-Jo's," he said.

All I could do was nod.

He threw the van into gear and headed in that direction. Fletcher drove slowly and carefully, mindful of my injuries, but every bump and jostle of the van made me wince. So I concentrated on breathing, surfing the waves of pain as best I could.

It was several minutes before he spoke again.

"Seems like you caused quite the commotion in there," Fletcher said in a mild voice. "The staff couldn't drive away fast enough. They all piled in on top of one another, like a bunch of clowns all trying to get into the same cars."

"Good for them."

I hoped no one else had been injured inside the mansion.

"Do you want to talk about it?"

I shook my head. "Not tonight. Maybe . . . later. Okay?"

Fletcher nodded back.

But I didn't have any intention of talking about what had happened tonight. Not to Fletcher, not to anyone, not ever. Part of it was because I was still humiliated by how easily Sebastian had tricked me and how hard I'd fallen for him. And the other part of it, well, I couldn't quite say. All I knew was that all of the things Sebastian had done and said were my burdens to bear now, more secrets to add to the ones I already had.

"Maybe in a few days, when you're feeling better, we can go look at those apartments across from the Pork Pit," Fletcher said. "After all, an assassin should have her own place. Especially one like the Spider, don't you think?"

A quiet note of pride rippled through the old man's voice. He'd called me *the Spider* many times over the years, but this time, I knew he meant it in a way that he never had before. Maybe one day soon, I'd tell him that I finally understood all the lessons he'd been trying to teach me for so long. About when to wait and when to act and how to find that delicate balance between the two. But knowing Fletcher, he realized all of that already. Just like I knew that I wouldn't have survived tonight if not for him.

"Gin?"

I smiled because he expected me to, even though getting my own apartment was the last thing on my mind right now. Still, I knew that he was trying to do something nice, trying to tell me that I'd proven myself in more ways than one tonight.

"Yeah," I said. "That would be great."

He nodded, and we both fell silent.

I leaned my head against the car window, breathed through another surge of pain, and brooded into the night, still thinking of Sebastian and everything that had happened between us. With every mile that passed, I slowly let his betrayal and cruelty ice over the few soft parts of my heart that were left, and I vowed never to let them thaw again.

Not for anyone.

Ever.

# ❊ 36 ❊

## PRESENT DAY

I finished my story and leaned back, feeling tired and drained, as though I'd just relived the whole fight with Sebastian and had once again suffered all the injuries that he'd inflicted on my body and my heart back then. It took me a moment to let go of the memories and realize that I was in the Pork Pit, that what I had described had taken place ten years ago, instead of just ten minutes ago.

"You?" Owen asked. "*You* killed Sebastian Vaughn?"

I grinned. "Who else?"

"I remember that," he said. "It was the talk of Ashland for weeks. It was all over the news. How part of the mansion was destroyed, how the cops found a dead giant inside the house and then Sebastian out in the greenhouse. From what I remember, the police thought that the same person who killed Cesar had killed Sebastian too."

I grimaced. "Well, they were actually right about that. For a change."

Owen took my hand, giving it a gentle squeeze. He didn't ask me to say anything else, and he didn't make any comments about what I'd told him. He simply let me know that he was here for me.

"And to think," he murmured. "We actually met back then."

"I know," I replied. "I'd mostly forgotten about it until now. Did you ever think about that girl you picked up on the side of the road that night?"

"Sometimes," he said. "I hoped that she—you—were okay. And that you'd told that dick boyfriend of yours what was what."

"Well, I guess I did that, after all."

I grimaced again, and Owen tightened his grip on my hand.

We stayed like that for a while before he reached out and picked up one of the roses, twirling it around in his hand.

He frowned. "But I don't understand. Why the roses? Why the note? Why now, ten years later, on the day you killed Sebastian? Who sent them? You killed Sebastian and Porter and even Cesar. There's nobody left."

I reached out and fingered the edge of one of the petals. Soft and smooth, just like Sebastian had said.

"You're forgetting," I said. "I let one person live."

It was a few minutes before midnight when the woman turned on the lights in the library and stepped back into the arms of the man she was with. Both of them were in their twenties, giggling, kissing, and messing around the way young couples do. The guy was a cute blond, with short, spiky hair and a smattering of freckles across his cheeks. The woman was a brunette, with a short bob of black hair and expressive brown eyes.

I stood in the shadows and watched them canoodle. If it went any further, I'd have to excuse myself quietly and come back another night. I wasn't much for being a voyeur. But I hoped they would wrap up their little tête-à-tête soon. I wanted to finish this—tonight.

Finally, reluctantly, the woman pulled back. "Sorry, babe, but I've got some work that I've got to get done tonight. See you in thirty?"

The guy gave her a coy smile. "I'll draw us a bath. But don't wait too long . . . or the water might get cold. Me too."

The two kissed again before the guy left the library. The woman watched him go, a small smile playing across her lips. Then she turned to the desk in the back of the room and headed toward it.

It took her three steps before she noticed the white paper bag bearing the Pork Pit's pig logo that I'd placed in the middle of the desk, along with the chocolate-chip cookie cake. She hurried over to the desk and stared down at the message I'd written in chocolate icing on the cake. *Happy (Late) Birthday*.

Her eyes widened in surprise, and her gaze shot around the library, looking for me. So I stepped out into the light where she could see me.

"Hello, Charlotte," I said.

Charlotte Vaughn drew in a startled breath, and her hand flew to her throat, clutching the pink cameo she wore there, the same one she'd gotten at her birthday party all those years ago.

"Whoa!" she exclaimed. "You scared me to death."

I gave her a thin smile. "We both know that I could do a lot more than that if I wanted to."

Charlotte's dark eyes narrowed. "Is that a threat, Gin?"

"I don't know. Were the roses a threat?"

She stared at me. "Why would you think that?"

"Well, your brother gave me roses like that once upon a time. Things didn't turn out that well for any of us—you, me, him."

Charlotte's gaze flicked to the mantel over the fireplace, where a series of photos in silver frames were propped up. I'd looked at them earlier when I'd first come into the library. Most of the photos showed a teenage Charlotte with her father, but there was one of Sebastian standing by himself, smiling for the camera. His smile was the same as I remembered—smug, confident, cocky. I hadn't forgotten one thing about him, but it had still been like a kick to the gut to see his smiling face, frozen in time.

Charlotte glanced at the photo of Sebastian for a moment before turning away. "No, things didn't turn out so well for Sebastian—or my father."

Her mouth tightened, and pain flashed in her eyes, along with more than a little anger.

"You have every right to hate me for what I did to him. I took him away from you. Not Sebastian, not anyone else, just me."

Charlotte let out a bitter laugh. "Well, you might have killed him, but Sebastian put you up to it. Even as a kid, I knew that. If it hadn't been you, he would have found some other assassin to do the job. I don't blame you for Papa's death. Well, not as much as I blame Sebastian."

"So why the roses? Why the cryptic message? Why now?"

She shrugged. "I suppose I wanted to see if you remembered me after all these years. If you remembered Papa . . . and Sebastian."

"I haven't forgotten any of it, not one thing. No matter how much I might have wanted to." This time, my mouth twisted with bitterness.

Charlotte stared at me, then moved over to a cabinet in the back corner of the library. She opened one of the glass doors, reached inside, and drew out a bottle of gin. She held it up so I could see it.

"How about a drink?" she asked. "For old times' sake?"

I nodded and settled myself in one of the chairs in front of the fireplace. While Charlotte fixed our drinks, I reached out with my magic, listening to the stones around me. According to the news reports, part of the Vaughn mansion had collapsed in on itself the night I killed Sebastian. After his death, it had stood empty for years. But now it looked eerily similar to how it had all those years ago, with one notable difference: the stones no longer murmured with Sebastian's cruelty.

Oh, a current of darkness still rippled through them, but it was the emotion of someone who'd known her share of horrors and would never, ever forget them. Mostly, though, the marble and granite murmured with pride at all the hard work she'd done to restore them to their former glory. Looked like Charlotte had inherited more of her father's Stone magic than Sebastian had realized.

Charlotte walked over and handed me a crystal tumbler full of clear liquid, a few ice cubes, and a thick wedge of line.

"Gin for Gin, right?" she murmured, settling into the chair across from me.

"You've done your homework."

She shrugged. "I had a lot of time to think about things in foster care. That's where I ended up, after everything that happened."

I took a sip of the gin, feeling the cold liquid slide down my throat, then start its slow, familiar burn in my stomach. Charlotte and I sat there sipping our drinks. All around me, the stones kept whispering of secrets—hers and mine.

"The first foster home they sent me to was terrible," she said, staring into her glass. "The sort of place where the adults are only in it for those sweet little checks the government sends them every month. The husband and wife constantly screamed at each other. One day, the husband hit the wife—and me too. So badly that I ended up in the emergency room with a broken arm."

"Something that sadly is not uncommon in the system."

Charlotte shrugged, then raised her eyes to mine. "It's funny, though. The next day—the very next day—they found the husband in an alley behind some Southtown bar. He'd been beaten to a pulp."

"Imagine that," I drawled. "But that's the risk you take when you wander over into Southtown, day or night."

Charlotte snorted. "Well, his beating got the cops involved, and I got shipped to another foster home, a much nicer one, with an older couple. They treated me like their own daughter." She jerked her head at another photo on the mantel, one that showed Charlotte standing between a man and a woman. "The Smithson family."

I'd noticed that photo too. I didn't say anything, although I did take another sip of my gin.

"When people have accidents and walk away from them, lots of them claim that their guardian angels were watching out for them," Charlotte said.

"Mmm."

"My experience has been a little different," she continued. "I was never involved in any accidents, but every time I had a problem, no matter what it was, it was always taken care of. I got a bad foster family, I got a new one. Somebody hassled me at school, he soon stopped. A guy even stole my car once. He brought it back to me three days later, washed, waxed, and with a full tank of gas."

"I guess his conscience caught up with him, and he realized what a bad thing he did."

Charlotte quirked an eyebrow at my sarcasm, but she continued with her story. "Some anonymous donor even paid to have the rubble of my father's mausoleum cleared away and to have him and my mother entombed at Blue Ridge Cemetery, in a new mausoleum that looked just like the one he'd built before."

I didn't respond this time.

"Then, on my eighteenth birthday, just as I'm wondering how I'm going to pay for college, I get a letter from some investment banker saying that my father had set up a trust fund for me and that all of the Vaughn property had been signed over to me. The mansion, the grounds, even the few assets that were left from my father's construction company."

"Good for your father, for thinking ahead like that."

Charlotte leaned forward, her dark brown eyes searching mine. "But you see, I know for a fact that all of the property was in Sebastian's name. He got it as soon as my father died. But Sebastian didn't leave a will, and since I was underage, it was tied up in the courts for years. And there was no trust fund, not when most of my father's money was used to pay off lawsuits from the family members of the victims of the terrace collapse. It came out, you know, that Sebastian used his Stone magic to cause it. A cop my father knew sent his findings to the police. It cleared my father's name, but Vaughn Construction was still liable since Sebastian was part of the company. I didn't mind those folks getting the money, though. I think my father would have paid them himself, if he'd still been alive."

I didn't respond.

"I know it was you, Gin," Charlotte said in a soft voice. "The foster home, the bullies, the guy who boosted my car, the money, the mausoleum . . . everything. It was you—*you* took care of everything. You took care of *me*."

Actually, Finn had done the heavy lifting with the money and all the legal stuff, one of the first jobs he'd ever done at his bank. But she was right. I'd done the rest.

"Why did you do it? Was it because you felt guilty about killing my father?"

I gripped my glass a little tighter, feeling the chill of it sink into the spider rune scar in my palm. "If—and this is a big if—I had anything to do with your good fortune over the years, it wasn't because of the guilt. I'm an assassin. I kill people. Sometimes the wrong ones, but it's still who I am and what I do."

"Then why?"

I looked at her. "Because I know what it's like to be alone and scared and lost and hurt—hurt so deep down in your soul that you know that part of the pain will never, *ever* go away. Once upon a time, someone was kind enough to take me in and teach me how to deal with that hurt the best way that he knew how. He helped me, and I owed it to you to do the same. And then some."

Charlotte kept staring at me. After a moment, she nodded, accepting my explanation.

"Reminiscing is all well and good, but why the roses? Why the note? Why did you really want me to come here tonight, Charlotte?" I asked.

She stared at me for a long time, taking in my black clothes, my cold, determined features, and my wintry gray eyes.

"I wanted to let you know that I was okay," she finally said in a quiet voice. "And I suppose that I wanted to say thank you, since I never did before."

"You don't have to thank me," I said, my voice harsh and raspy with guilt and regret. "I killed your father, Charlotte. Like I said before, you have every right to hate me. Truth be told, I half expected a couple of cops to be waiting in here tonight, ready to finally arrest me for what I did to him."

Actually, part of me had been expecting it for years, but it had never come to pass.

"I suppose that I do hate you for that," she said. "And

I thought about telling the police what you did so many times."

"So why didn't you?"

"Because I am thankful every single day that you killed Sebastian, that you saved me from him."

"But it's not an even trade," I said in a gentle voice. "Your father was a million times the man Sebastian was. Killing Cesar is one of the many regrets that I have, one that still hurts, one that will *always* hurt. If I could have gone back then and changed things, I would have. If I could do it now, I would in a heartbeat."

Charlotte blinked and blinked, but she couldn't quite keep two tears from streaking down her face. "I know," she whispered, her voice hoarse with emotion. "I know."

She wiped the tears off her face and slowly regained her composure. She sat back in her chair and gestured with her drink at the library around us.

"As you can see, now that I have control of my family home again, I'm working to rebuild it, restore it. And I'm starting up Vaughn Construction again. I'm going to continue on with the legacy that my father started."

"Good for you," I said, and meant it.

"So I'm okay now. You don't have to keep looking out for me anymore. I can fight my own battles from here on out."

I reached into my vest and drew out a manila folder. I tossed it onto the table between us. "Then you should take a look at that. Because your new boyfriend is only interested in your money, according to what he's been telling his friends when they go out for drinks at Northern Aggression. And the woman you're thinking about hiring as your CFO plans to start skimming as soon as you give her access to your business accounts."

For a moment, Charlotte looked decidedly unsettled, but she recovered quickly, and a wry grin lifted her lips. "Still watching out for me, Gin?"

I shrugged. "Just keeping my ear to the ground. That's all."

"As an assassin," she said. "As the Spider."

"Yes, as the Spider."

She didn't say anything else. I didn't know what was left to say. It certainly hadn't been the evening I'd expected, and it would take me some time to process it. Still, there was one more thing I wanted to tell her.

"You know, you should give Bria Coolidge a call sometime."

Charlotte blinked. "Bria? I haven't thought about her in years. Not since . . . the night of my birthday party."

"But you were friends with her once, and I'm sure she would love to hear from you again. She's a cop now, just like her dad, Harry, was. She's here in Ashland. Xavier too."

Charlotte gave me a guarded look. "How the hell do you know about Bria and Harry Coolidge?"

"I didn't know Harry, not really." I grinned at her. "But I know all about Bria. She's my baby sister."

She gaped at me.

"I thought that Bria was dead for a long time," I said in a quiet voice. "But I was lucky enough to find her again. I can't give you your father back, but I can maybe return some of your friends to you. So give her a call. I put her card on the desk, next to the cake."

Charlotte kept staring at me, blinking and blinking,

as if she were trying to process everything. Yeah, I knew how that felt.

I gave her a wink and my best, most mysterious smile. "See you around, Charlotte."

Then I raised my glass to her in a toast, drained the rest of my gin, and left the library.

Like her father before her, Charlotte didn't employ any guards. Something that I'd have to speak to her about some other night. I wouldn't want just anyone to waltz in here on her.

I walked out the front door of the mansion, ambled down the long driveway, and headed for the iron gate at the front of the estate. It was closed, but I had no problems scaling the stone wall and dropping down on the far side. After all, it was the same way I'd come in a couple of hours ago.

And just like all those years before, a car was waiting for me on the other side.

A momentary pang of loss shot through me that it wasn't an old, battered white van but instead a flashy silver sports car, the latest Aston Martin. I opened the door and slid into the passenger's seat.

"How did it go?" Finn asked.

I looked at my foster brother, with his green eyes, his walnut-colored hair, and his features that were so much like Fletcher's. Once again, I felt that pang in my heart, but it was softer now, more sweet than bitter.

"Charlotte and I agreed to keep each other's secrets."

He sighed, then rolled his eyes. "Seriously, Gin, could you *be* any more cryptic?"

"'And no matter what, you should never, ever tell someone all of your secrets,'" I said. "Do you remember that?"

Finn gave me a blank look. "Not particularly. Should I?"

"Yeah. You said it to me ten years ago about Sebastian."

His chest puffed up. "Well, then, I was totally right."

I rolled my eyes.

"Seriously, though, what happened?"

I shrugged again. "Charlotte wanted to talk."

"About Sebastian? Or her father?"

"Both. And a lot of other things too." I hesitated. "She figured out that I've been keeping tabs on her all these years. She knows about the money you set up in that trust fund for her."

"Is she going to talk?" Finn asked, a worried look creasing his features.

"No. She's not going to talk. Not about any of it. She actually wanted to thank me."

Finn nodded. "I can understand that."

He stared through the gates at the estate. "All of this . . . it reminds me of that night with Dad, when Sebastian's giants busted into the house."

"Yeah."

Finn looked at me. "He'd be so proud of you, Gin. He was always proud of you, but never more so than after what happened with Sebastian."

"Do you really think so?"

He reached over and squeezed my hand. "I know so."

I stared into the dark of the night, thinking about Fletcher and all the lessons he'd taught me. "Yeah," I said. "I think you're right."

"Are you kidding?" Finn scoffed. "I'm *always* right."

I laughed at his never-ending confidence.

"Now, the night is still fairly young. You want to go get a drink at Northern Aggression?"

"Sure," I said. "I had plans to meet Owen there after . . . this."

"Then allow me to be your chariot," Finn said. "And chauffeur service."

He threw the car into gear and zoomed away from the curb.

I took one last look through the gate toward the Vaughn estate, my gaze settling on the lights that burned in the library. Despite everything, Charlotte had survived—and so had I.

Because that's what the Spider did.

Turn the page for a sneak peek at the
next book in the Elemental Assassin series

# POISON PROMISE

## by Jennifer Estep

Coming soon from Pocket Books

Even from across the parking lot, I could see the two vampires creep a little closer to Catalina, smiling wide and showing off their fangs. Troy's meaning was clear— get with the pill-pushing program or get drained.

Catalina lifted her chin and glared at Troy. She wasn't backing down, no matter what. I admired her for it, really, I did, but it was also stupid of her. She just should have accepted the pills and flushed them later. Oh, I knew Catalina since she worked as a waitress at the Pork Pit, and she seemed like a good kid. She didn't want to get sucked in with Troy and his thugs, but it was too late for that. This was about to get very ugly for someone.

Good thing that ugly was what I specialized in.

I could hear Owen talking through my cell phone. "Gin?"

Realizing that he had asked me a question, probably more than once, I focused on the sound of his voice again. "Sorry, babe. I've gotta go."

"Is something wrong?"

"Nah. I just see a bit of trash that needs picking up. I'll be there soon."

Owen and I hung up, and I slid my phone into my jeans pocket before opening the car door and throwing my bag into the passenger's seat. Then I slammed the door shut.

The sharp *crack* reverberated through the parking lot, and the three guys turned to stare at me. Catalina tried to edge away, but the two vamps spotted her furtive movements and flanked her, keeping her pinned against the fence. I pushed away from my car, stuck my hands into my jeans pockets, and ambled in their direction.

Of course, Catalina recognized me, her boss, at once. She let out a small gasp, her face paled, and she started shaking her head *no-no-no*, although I couldn't tell if she was trying to warn me off or was worried about what I was going to do to the three guys hassling her.

But Troy didn't see her reaction. Instead, his gaze slid past me to my car. When he realized I was driving an Aston Martin, a greedy smirk slashed across his face.

"Hey, hey, foxy lady," he called out. "You lookin' for some action? You lookin' to score a little sumthin' sumthin'?"

I smiled back at him, baring almost as many teeth as the two vampires behind him. "Sumthin' like that, sugar."

Behind Troy, Catalina kept shaking her head *no-no-no*. She opened her lips, but one of the vamps rattled the fence behind her, a clear sign for her to keep her mouth shut. But there was no need for her to waste any more of her breath on these fools, especially not to try to tell them who they were messing with now. Besides, Troy wouldn't have heeded a warning anyway. He was completely focused on me, a potential customer, and I could almost see the dollar signs churning in his head as he calculated how much he could take me for.

His smirk widened. "Well, you are in the right spot, baby. Because I have got just the thing for you."

He held out one of the bags he'd been shoving at Catalina, and I took it from him. A single pill lay inside the plastic, its deep, dark red color making it look like a drop of congealed blood. I flipped the bag over and realized that a rune had been etched into the surface of the drug, but I didn't take the time to squint and make out the details of the symbol.

Still, despite its bloody color and rune, the pill looked more like a kids' vitamin than a dangerous drug, but I knew all too well how deceiving looks could be. Most people didn't think that I seemed anything like a dangerous assassin—until my knife was cutting into their guts.

"What's this?" I asked.

Troy smirked even more. "It's the latest, greatest thing on the market, baby. It will rock your world. Nah, scratch that—it'll burn it down."

The two vamps snickered at his cheesy lines. Catalina rolled her eyes. Yeah, that's what I wanted to do too, but I decided to let things play out.

I tucked the plastic bag with its pill into my jeans pocket. Not because I had any intention of taking the pill, but because my sister Bria would no doubt be interested in it. Detective Bria Coolidge, one of Ashland's few good cops, actually cared about things like trying to keep drugs off the streets. I tried to help her out whenever I could, despite my own life of killing and crime.

"Now that you've seen the goods, let's talk about payment, baby," Troy crooned. "Normally, a hit like that is three hundred a pop."

My eyebrows shot up. "Three hundred for one pill? That must be a hell of a joyride."

"Oh, it is," Troy said. "Believe me, it is. But if you don't have that much cash on you, don't sweat it. I'm sure we can work out some other form of payment."

His brown eyes tracked up and down my body, taking in my black boots, dark blue jeans, and the tight black tank top that peeked out under my black leather jacket. Behind him, the two vampires did the same thing, licking their lips like I was a bottle of booze they were going to pass around.

Oh, everybody was going to get a taste of Gin Blanco, all right. Just not the kind they expected.